"You don't like French food?" Roxanne asked. Did he not *want* the job?

"I don't like French anything," Steve said.

She sat back and crossed her arms over her chest. He was kidding. He had to be. "Not even French fries?"

Steve shook his head. "They're not even French."

"All right then." Roxanne paused and looked toward the ceiling contemplatively. "French poodles."

Steve laughed, and despite herself she felt warmed by it. "Too ridiculous."

"French films?"

"Too pretentious."

Roxanne's lips curved. "How about French bread? Everybody likes French bread."

A short shake of the head. "Too crumbly."

"Hmm. French toast?"

He shrugged. "Too rich."

She raised one brow and sat forward. "French women?"

Steve's eyes grew subtly more attentive and he gave a low chuckle. "Too . . . scary."

"I know . . ." Roxanne paused, studied the challenging look he was giving her and said, "French kisses . . ."

By Elaine Fox

SPECIAL OF THE DAY
HOT STUFF
IF THE SLIPPER FITS
MAN AT WORK
MAYBE BABY

ELAINE FOX

Special of the Day

AVON BOOKS
An Imprint of HarperCollinsPublishers

This is a work of fiction. Names, characters, places, and incidents are products of the author's imagination or are used fictitiously and are not to be construed as real. Any resemblance to actual events, locales, organizations, or persons, living or dead, is entirely coincidental.

AVON BOOKS
An Imprint of HarperCollins*Publishers*
10 East 53rd Street
New York, New York 10022-5299

First Avon Books paperback printing: March 2005

For my mother, Connie Atkins,
who spent my school years
polishing my grammar
and correcting my punctuation,
and without whom
I would never have been able
to embark on this career.

1

Bar Special
Fish House Punch—<u>expect the unexpected...</u>
Light and dark rum, brandy,
    peach brandy, lemon juice, sugar

Roxanne Rayeaux raised her hips and let out a little moan. She tilted her head back, exposing her throat, and arched her back, moving one shoulder to release the tangled locks of her long hair from beneath her.

Enveloped in darkness, surrounded by mystery, she had to admit she was nervous. Yes, very nervous.

She bit her bottom lip and reached out, palms sweating, to find the steely shaft in the dark. Cupping it with uncertain hands, she felt its length. Could she find the right spot? She hoped she wouldn't get wet.

She tried to remember the page in the book that had shown this maneuver. She was not at all sure she was in the right position; it certainly didn't *feel* like the right position. She was . . . uncomfortable.

Though she would have admitted it to no one, she had never done anything like this before.

If only she'd thought to light a candle. She could at least have made sure she wasn't lying down with a rat.

She didn't have a flashlight, not one of her lamps would fit in here, and her body blocked most of the light from the cabinet door.

She was alone under the sink with the pipes. And a more inept plumber she'd be hard pressed to find.

Steve Serrano knocked again on the oak-paneled door, then tilted his head to align an eyeball to the opening. A woman's shoe kept the door from closing completely, leaving a crack through which to see the inside of the apartment.

Nice furnishings. Some boxes. Classical music on the radio. Or no, he leaned further to the right, on the high-end CD system he could see in the corner against the exposed brick wall.

He pushed on the door and it swung wider.

"Hello?" he called.

An orange cat bolted from the couch, lit out across the room and disappeared through a door down a short hallway.

Steve stepped inside the apartment. This one was definitely nicer than his, but maybe that was because there were real oriental rugs on the hardwood floor and actual artwork hanging on the walls.

He moved into the living room and put his hands on his hips. This was one high-class woman. He'd seen the truck from his window when she'd moved in two weeks ago, but he'd never seen her. And he'd expected to. She'd just bought the restaurant downstairs in which he worked as a bartender.

He set the bottle of wine he'd brought as a welcome gift on a sleek glass-topped coffee table and moved toward the kitchen. She had to be home. Why else would her door have been ajar?

He stopped at the entry to the kitchen, his attention caught by the sight of two long jean-clad legs sticking out from beneath the sink. Above the waistband, where her shirt had hiked up, he saw the jut of a hip bone and the curve of a small waist.

He strode across the black and white tiles to look down the drain opening. There, in the dim light, glowed the pale profile of a woman.

"Hey," he greeted mildly.

She gasped, and dropped something loud and metallic beside her.

"Damn it," she hissed.

To herself, he thought, though she could have been swearing at him. Then she started to push herself out from inside the cabinet.

As she wriggled from the space he couldn't help noticing—objectively, of course—that she had a lithe, agile body, if a little on the skinny side. But when her head emerged, complete with a tangled mass of dark hair and black smudges on her forehead and cheek, his breath about left his body.

She was—again, objectively—*gorgeous*. Maybe the most gorgeous woman he'd ever seen in real life.

Even sitting on the floor, covered in dirt, a spiderweb in her hair, she looked like something out of a movie. Her dark eyes flashed above high cheekbones and her mouth was so sensually shaped he couldn't help picturing it sucking strawberries on the big screen.

He almost glanced around to see if someone was playing a joke. As if he might have stumbled into one of those homemaking reality shows, one that pitted beautiful women against average men in some kind of plumbing contest.

She ran one hand across her brow, moving locks of long hair to the side of her face. "You scared me."

"I, uh, I didn't mean to." The words came out like bricks. He'd never been struck so dumb by a pretty face. "I thought you heard me coming."

"What, over the music?" She threw a hand out toward the sound system. She was over her fright now and clearly getting angry.

"Well I was singing along." He couched this with a smile.

Slim, arched brows descended over luscious, inky eyes. "Who *are* you? And what are you doing in here?"

He motioned behind him, unable to pry his gaze from her face. "The door was open."

"And that looked like an invitation to you?" Those lips quirked in a sarcastic—*attractively* sarcastic, God help him—manner.

"Well, I thought, you know, I had this wine . . ." He looked around for it, had forgotten what he'd done with it.

She exhaled. "Listen, I'm not interested, got it? And next time, knock. Though I'd appreciate it if there wasn't a next time."

He looked back at her. She had one hand on her hip,

clutching a wrench. The other hand was slimed from nails to knuckles with trap grease. Still, she managed to look haughty.

He laughed once. Amazing how beauty could dim with the wrong personality attached to it. Words flooded back to him.

He raised his own brows. "No problem, Cinderella. I just thought you should know your door was open."

"Oh my God, the cat—"

"Took off for your bedroom. And I brought the wine as a housewarming, though with the chill in here I probably should have brought a case. I'm your neighbor from upstairs."

She didn't look abashed, exactly. It was more that she looked less combative.

"Oh. All right. Well, thanks—"

"No need to thank me." He held up one hand as if she might get effusive. "But I'll know from here on out to leave you alone. You obviously know what you're doing." He let his gaze sweep her from messy hair to greasy hands to dusty pants, a half smile on his face. "And it's none of my business if you like to leave your door open." He started for the exit. "But, for the record?" He turned before walking out of view. "I'm not interested either. Okay?"

He flashed her a smile and left.

Roxanne's cheeks flamed as she watched the door close to shoe width behind him. She'd forgotten to close the door after bringing the last box up from her car. How could she have done that? Cheeto, her cat, was a master escape artist. He must still be freaked out from the move, she thought, plucking the shoe from the door and closing it firmly.

She had just gotten the last of her things from New York that had been shipped to her rented storage unit before she'd settled on this place. Between that and hauling up the toolbox she'd bought at a yard sale to fix the sink, she'd forgotten to lock the door. Or even close it.

Seems she thought she was back in the Virginia of her youth. When you didn't have to lock your doors to keep strange men from wandering in.

She hadn't even gotten his name. Had just assumed he was some jerk who'd recognized her on the street and followed her home. It had happened before.

Still, this *was* Virginia, and not New York City. She should refrain from jumping to such conclusions. She'd lived in New York for so long she didn't know how to respond to simple Virginia neighborliness.

He probably thought she was a first-class bitch.

And maybe she was. Now.

As she passed the coffee table, her eyes strayed to the bottle of wine. She wiped her hands on her jeans, frowned at how ineffectual that was, then picked up the bottle.

A '94 Bordeaux. The guy knew his wines. She looked again at the door.

He hadn't seemed to know who she was. Evidently he wasn't one of those guys who drooled—or worse— over the *Sports Illustrated* swimsuit edition every year. She'd met some who could rattle off what year each supermodel had appeared and even describe the suit they were wearing. Which surprised her, considering that she'd always thought they were trying hard not to see the suit at all.

So she would apologize to him later if she saw him, she told herself. Not that it mattered. She didn't care what any guy's opinion of her was. She was done trying to figure out what they even thought in the first place. Men were inherently untrustworthy where women were concerned.

Okay, sure, not *all* men. Her dad was a great guy. And her high-school friend Skip. Even Marcel Girmond, her chef due to arrive from New York next week. To all of them she had trusted her heart in some way.

But she was through with romance, at least for a while. Right now she had bigger fish to fry. Or rather, eclairs to bake. She had just finished an intensive course at the Culinary Institute of America and was ready to fulfill her lifelong dream. She'd bought herself a restaurant to convert into a fancy French bistro. And Step One was about to begin.

In approximately twenty-one hours she was to meet with the staff of Charters Fish House, the failing restaurant in the ground floor of the rowhouse she'd just bought in Old Town Alexandria. Her plan was to offer jobs to any of them who cared to stay on and learn the fine art of French restaurateuring. This meant waiting tables with professionalism and aplomb, clearing tables with the subtlety of first-class servants, serving wine with the decorum of a seasoned sommelier, and generally behaving as differently as possible from the pub workers they currently were.

Roxanne was pretty sure she would lose or get rid of three quarters of the staff, but it didn't matter. She had the most important people in place. Her chef, the award-winning Marcel Girmond from New York; his sous-chef, Bertrand Noor; and her maitre d', the ostentatious Sir Nigel from Carruthers' in downtown D.C., where it was rumored the front-room staff trembled in servile awe when he issued an edict. Everyone else could be trained—or hired away from the finest restaurants in town, if need be.

Then she was going to close the place for a few weeks to remodel and re-open it as *Chez Soi*, which was a French idiom she'd always found charming that meant "to have company."

This was going to be the crowning achievement of her life, she'd decided. A life that so far had been spent making money on her looks. For the last ten years she'd worked as a model in major magazines and a few television commercials. But while the living had been good, her looks were something she had done nothing to earn and she knew full well that they would fade before long. When they did, she'd vowed, she would have something real to fall back on. She'd planned to use the money she'd socked away to start her own business.

It was a risk, sure. Nobody with a brain started a restaurant without knowing they could lose their shirt. But the restaurant business was in her blood—and it was one thing she was passionate about. She knew good cooking, she valued excellent service, and she craved a warm atmosphere.

So she would create it. The perfect restaurant. And she would prove to herself that she could make money with her brain instead of her body.

It had been sheer chance she'd been born with looks

that would sell magazines. It was going to be sheer smarts that would make her restaurant a success. Of *that* she would make certain. She would succeed if it killed her.

And it might. She was already as nervous as a wet cat at the prospect of addressing the restaurant staff to-morrow. Though she'd been raised in the restaurant business—she'd been "discovered" while working as a waitress in her parents' homey Italian restaurant in downtown D.C. when she was seventeen—she had never taken on a venture as complicated as this one would be.

She would just have to fake it.

But before that . . . she tossed the wrench in her hand and turned back to the kitchen . . . she had to finish re-placing the trap under the sink. She was pouring nearly every penny she had into the restaurant and saving what was left to deal with restaurant emergencies.

Everything else, like household plumbing, had to be done by herself or not done at all.

Steve plopped his plate of cheese fries onto the bar and pushed them toward the plucky redhead across from him.

"So you say she's a bitch, huh?" the redhead said, never one to mince words.

Steve chuckled. "Now, now, Rita. I said she seemed a little tough. Tougher than she looks. So don't be fooled."

He picked up a fry, stirred it around a mound of yel-low cheese before putting it in his mouth.

"Sounds to me like she's gonna fire us. Hey, Georgie,

think the new owner's gonna fire our asses?" Rita gave George, another waiter showing up for the meeting, one of her trademark devil's grins. "Rumor has it she's a bitch."

"*She?*" George slid onto a barstool and unwound a scarf from his neck. "There's your first clue right there. Hey Steve, gimme a Bloody Mary, would you? My head feels like it's wearing a mashed potato helmet."

"Told you you shouldn't have had that last kamikaze last night. How about a Coke?" Steve bent to fill a glass with ice and pushed the Coke button on the dispenser.

"You are such a sexist," Rita said, pushing a cheese fry into her mouth. "I hope she rips you a new one for dropping that case of Sam Adams last night."

"How's she going to know about that?" George fixed her with a red eye. "Unless some other gossipy female tells her, huh?"

Rita laughed and tipped her spiky red hair back as she popped in another cheese fry. "You just guaranteed it, my brain-dead friend. These fries are gross," she said to Steve.

Steve ate another. "I know. They were left over from last night. I nuked 'em."

"Eww." Rita swiveled on her chair as two more waiters arrived and sat on bar stools.

Before long the whole crew had assembled, four waiters, two waitresses, two bartenders, three busboys and two line cooks. Their numbers were down since the bar had started doing so badly. Mostly, Steve knew, because of the quality of the food. Which would explain why the main cook had yet to show. No doubt he'd already been fired.

Which was great. Because all it would take to save this place was a reliable chef, a plentiful happy hour and a little bit of advertising. He had a bunch of ideas he planned to share with their lovely new boss, once she untwisted her britches over the fact that he'd let himself into her apartment.

Steve looked at his watch. Eleven ten. She was late. That wasn't exactly the right example to set for this crew, he knew. He'd add that to his list of suggestions. Waitstaff were like children, he would tell her. You have to be nice to them, but don't let them get away with a thing.

He glanced at George, who cradled his head in his hands as if it were a delicate scientific instrument trying to get a reading off the bar top. Poor guy had worked a double yesterday and thought he needed the kamikazes to get to sleep last night. He'd obviously forgotten about today's meeting. Steve was about to cave on the Bloody Mary when the door opened and Her Highness swept in on the frigid January breeze.

Her hair was piled onto her head in a casual style with wisps running loose next to her wind-pinkened cheeks. Her dark eyes actually sparkled in the dim light of the bar.

She held a big piece of corrugated cardboard under one arm, a stack of papers in one hand and was unzipping her white ski jacket with the other.

"Hi all. I'm sorry I'm late. I just spent two and a half hours with the decorator." Her voice was slightly husky and she looked no one in the eye as she propped the cardboard against the wall and lay the papers on a table.

Too good for eye contact, Steve surmised. He wondered if she didn't have some henchman she could have sent to fire them all, if that was her intention. Personally, he hoped it wasn't. Looking for a new job did not fit into his current plans at all. He was too busy with his own project for that.

The rest of the crew just looked at her. The busboys seemed to be having trouble closing their gaping mouths. George lifted his head and Pat, one of the rowdier waiters, sat up far straighter and quieter than he probably ever had in his life

"*That,*" George hissed at Steve, canting his body across the bar toward him, "*is one hot chick.*"

Steve just raised his brows. Interestingly, she wasn't as good-looking as she'd been before she'd opened her mouth yesterday. He wondered if anyone else would feel that way after she spoke to them today.

She took off her jacket and the temperature in the room went up another ten degrees. George and Pat were now leaning forward at the sight of her tight jeans and scoop-neck shirt. Though it was not a provocative outfit, technically speaking, the clothes clung to her curves with what could only be described as tenacity.

She lay her coat over the back of a chair and glanced over the assembled crew. "Hi. My name's Roxånne Rayeaux and I'm the new owner of, uh, Charters. I'm sure you all have been wondering what my plans for the place are, since it's my understanding that it's been generally considered an unsuccessful restaurant for some time now."

People shifted in their seats. Steve could tell that comment struck them, as it did him, as an accusation—that she held them responsible for the restaurant's failing.

Steve cleared his throat. "Uh, that's not exactly true."

Her eyes met his and she gave a little start of recognition. "It's not?"

"I mean, it's true we're all curious about you. But it's not true that the place hasn't been successful. It used to be extremely successful, until a few months ago when management pulled the plug on us," Steve continued. "The chef quit, the distributors started cheating us out of the fresh stuff and we couldn't get anyone to sign a check to save our lives. So you see it was all management. With the proper support, this place is a moneymaker."

She studied him. "You're the guy who lives upstairs, aren't you?" she asked. "What's your name?"

"Steve. Steve Serrano. And I can tell you anything you need to know about this place. Including how to get it back up and running at its full potential."

He owed it to her, he thought, because she was his new boss, to tell her that she hadn't just bought a lemon, that they did all believe in the place, though its success had been compromised lately.

A faint smile crossed her lips. "That's all right, Mr. Serrano. I have a pretty good idea of what to do here. Now—"

"Do you?" He smiled. "I don't mean to tell you your business, but I mean it when I say that up until about six months ago this place was hot. The formula we have here, when adequately funded, works. Happy hours were packed, the dinner crowd was consistent, even lunches—"

"Mr. Serrano," she interrupted.

He stopped, irked by her tone. "Yes, Ms. Rayeaux?"

"What this place *was*, once upon a time, no longer matters. If you'll give me a chance, I'll tell you exactly what I'm going to do with it." She smiled tightly at him.

"Well, sure. Go ahead." He gestured with one hand for her to continue. So much for trying to help her out.

"Thank you." She turned the length of cardboard around and leaned it back against a chair. On the face of it were fabric swatches, pictures of furniture, paint samples and various other glued-on pictures that were hard to make out from behind the bar.

Steve noticed all the heads in front of him lean forward in an attempt to make out the clues, and felt the group's perplexity rise like a cloud to hover over the bar.

She lay one hand along the top of the cardboard. "As you can see, my vision is quite different from what this place has been until now. At the end of next week, I'm closing Charters to do a massive redecoration and remodel. I'm having wine caves installed and updating the bathrooms. I'm also replacing all the tables, chairs, carpeting and artwork, so that in the span of about three weeks, this place will be transformed into an upscale French bistro. We will serve only the freshest food, brilliantly prepared by Chef Girmond from La Finesse in New York, and served by a professional staff of well-trained waiters and waitresses. Which brings me to you all."

Steve's heart sank. This was worse than he'd feared.

Her dark eyes made their way down the line of employees sitting on bar stools before her. Her face was an unreadable mask, until she got to Steve, standing behind the rest of them at the bar. To him, she gave a small smile.

Was she gloating? he wondered. Could she possibly know how much he hated French food? Not to mention French chefs, French décor and French women who belittled American men with condescending smiles.

She shifted her look back to the employees. "I'm willing to offer each of you a job if you agree to be trained by the new maitre d', Sir Nigel Wallings. Some of you may know of Sir Nigel, he's been maitre d' at Carruthers, downtown, for many years and we are extremely lucky to have lured him away from that fine restaurant. You'll be paid your regular hourly wage during training, which I recognize is not much compared to what you make in tips, but you will be guaranteed a job at the end of it."

Silence dominated the room before Rita raised her hand. For a moment Steve tried to imagine Rita, who had once escorted an unruly bar patron from the restaurant by gripping him firmly by the balls, brushing bread crumbs from a linen tablecloth with a silver server.

Roxanne's gaze settled on Rita. The two of them were like fire and ice, Steve reflected.

"Yes?"

"I've heard of that Sir Nigel," Rita said, her narrow back ramrod straight. "He's supposed to be a class-A prick. I don't know anybody who's ever worked for him who could say they liked him."

Steve sighed. He was going to miss working with Rita.

For a moment, Roxanne seemed to be weighing something. Then, hands on her hips, she said, "He *is* a prick."

George and Pat tittered and the busboys shared surreptitious smiles. Despite himself, Steve felt a twinge of admiration for her candor.

"But he knows food, he knows service and he knows people. More importantly, people know *him*, and they will follow him to whatever restaurant he chooses to work for. I'm not going to hide what I'm trying to do here. I don't care about keeping whatever patrons Charters happens to have left. If we alienate every last one of them I'll be happy. I want the high rollers. And frankly, so do you. If you spend two hours waiting on a table ordering burgers, you're going to make a helluva lot less money than if you spend two hours on a table ordering sweetbreads."

"Sweet bread?" One of the busboys, Manuel, piped up. "How much you gonna be charging people for sweet *bread*?"

Steve chuckled, but he was the only one.

Roxanne's eyes scanned the group for whoever had spoken.

"Not sweet *bread*, Manuel." Steve directed his words to the wiry young busboy. "*Sweet*breads. It's a fancy way of saying 'brains.' "

"Brains!" The word popped out of Rita's mouth and she turned to Steve. "You're shittin' me."

" 'Fraid not."

Roxanne looked at him in surprise.

"That's right." He grinned back at her. "The savant knows a thing or two about food."

Her lips curved into a smile. "Very good. But it's actually the thymus or pancreas of a young calf. You go to the head of the class anyway, however, for knowing sweetbreads are an organ meat."

George muttered a comment about "organ meat" that made the whole left side of the bar erupt into laughter.

Steve lifted a brow. "I would, ma'am, but I don't want my classmates to think I'm trying to be teacher's pet." To this insolence he added a wink.

She stiffened and her expression went cold. "There'll be no pets in this restaurant, Mr. Serrano, real or figurative." Her gaze dropped his like a dirty dishrag. "Here's how this is going to work. I'm going to be in the restaurant all weekend, seeing how things are currently done before closing down next week. Those of you who would like to be considered for employment at Chez Soi, please fill out one of these forms." She indicated the stack of papers on the table. "Next week, I'll be calling those of you interested in staying on."

"What do you mean you'll be seeing how things are done?" George asked. "I thought you were changing everything anyway."

"She means we'll be auditioning for our jobs, dipstick," Rita said. "Jeez, don't you listen?"

"Is that right?" Steve asked.

The dark gaze was back upon him.

"Will we be auditioning for our jobs?" he persisted.

She seemed to take a deep breath. "My plan is to watch how things are done and make notes on what needs to change. Whether that means personnel or procedure, I can't really say right now. I've never been in here when the place was open."

"It's not much different than it is now," Pat said.

"Except it's crowded now." George snickered.

Roxanne looked from one end of the group to the other. "Anybody have any other questions?"

Everyone was silent. Steve gazed around the room, wondering just what kind of remodeling she planned on doing. If she took out the right wall, he thought, looking at the place where the old staircase used to be, there was a slight chance it could result in a historical gold mine for him.

"Okay, then," she said on an exhale, straightening the papers on the table beside her.

Steve raised his hand. "Yeah, I have a question."

She lifted her chin. "Yes?"

"If you've got this fancy chef coming to run the kitchen, and this Sir Nigel character to run the front, and you're looking at us to possibly keep our jobs, what, exactly, are *you* going to do?"

Rita snorted, then quickly covered her mouth with a hand. She shot a laughing glance back at him.

Roxanne settled those black eyes on Rita, then shifted her gaze back to Steve. "That's a good question. You should know my credentials and why I'm qualified to create and run a successful restaurant. First of all, I've just spent a year at the CIA, and—"

Rita made a noise between a grunt and a scoff, jutting her chin out in disbelief. "You telling us you were *a spy*?"

Steve couldn't help but laugh. "That's the Culinary Institute of America, darlin'."

"Oh." Rita pulled her chin back but looked dubious. "She could have just *said* that."

Roxanne's expression as she looked at Rita was inscrutable but the attention did not bode well for his friend, Steve thought.

"I should have been clearer," she said icily. "In any case, I also have years of waitressing experience as well as firsthand knowledge of the business of running a restaurant, with all of its risks and rewards. I grew up working in a restaurant my parents owned in the Adams Morgan section of D.C."

"Which one?" Steve asked, if only to draw Roxanne's focus from poor Rita, whom he knew needed her job even more than he did his.

"It was a small place—family style—called Mama's." Roxanne's gaze skidded away from the group in a move that looked uncharacteristically vulnerable to him. "My father died and shortly thereafter my mother retired, so it's been gone for several years now."

"I remember Mama's," Steve murmured, trying to call up more than just the sign in his memory.

"In any case," she inhaled and looked steadily back at Rita, "I'm a pastry chef by training. So I'll be in charge of desserts."

Rita turned on her stool and looked at Steve. Just loud enough for him to hear, she said, "*Just desserts*, sounds like. Whether we deserve them or not."

2

Bar Special
Charters Sundowner—in honor of the sun setting on the old Fish House

Brandy, lemon juice, orange juice, van der Hum

Springsteen throbbed over the sound system. *Hard to Be a Saint in the City*—an old song that Steve had long considered his anthem. The driving rhythm and souped-up bass made the blood pound ecstatically in his ears as he poured a line of lime green Jell-O shooters for George's friend Billy and two of his buddies.

It was almost like the old days in Charters, with the place packed and the energy high. The small dining room was nearly full and orders of fish and chips careened out of the kitchen as fast as the line cooks could pull them out of the deep fryer. Girls strutted their stuff and guys laughed too loud over impossible-to-hear jokes while their eyes darted with feral intent from one sexily clad female to the next.

Of course, it was all a fake. The remaining staff of the dying restaurant had called in their friends to fill the place up, begging them to make a showing so they could have a roomful of happy customers to show their new boss. God only knew what they were going to do tomorrow night. These people sure as hell wouldn't be coming back for Round Two.

Steve slid a couple of longneck Budweisers to Manuel's friends at the end of the bar and waved off their surprise.

"On the house," he said over the music.

What the hell, he thought. No sense making the bus-boys' friends go broke so their pals could continue making a couple bucks an hour. What were the chances Ms. Snooty-Pants was going to keep a bunch of Ecua-dorians in her fancy French restaurant anyway?

"Hey, Buttcheeks!"

Steve looked over and grinned at Rita, with her sharp face and porcupine hair. "Hey, darlin'. How's the classiest woman I know doing tonight?"

"I'll be better with two whiskey sours and a scotch, straight up." She pushed a pen behind one ear and re-arranged the checks in her apron pocket.

"Wouldn't we all?" Steve pulled out a couple of tum-blers and set them on the bar.

"So when's Frenchy showing up?" Rita lay her el-bows on the bar and leaned, giving her feet a break. "Don't tell me tomorrow because there's no fucking way my parents are coming two nights in a row."

"Your parents are here?" Steve looked out over the crowd but wouldn't have known Rita's parents if they were throwing back Jell-O shooters with George's friends. And, knowing Rita, they might be.

"Yeah, I finally told them about your passionate desire to marry me and they came to check you out." She rubbed her nose with one hand and scrunched her face. She was allergic to cigarette smoke, Steve knew. "But don't worry, Dad only brought the twelve-gauge."

"Good. For a second I was nervous."

Steve set the drinks on her tray and she disappeared into the crowd with it.

"Steve-arino!" A tall blond man emerged from the horde at the bar and reached a square hand over the teased hair of a woman drinking a margarita in front of him.

"Hey, P.B." Steve reached up and shook his friend's hand, sending the woman with the margarita an apologetic wink. "Glad you could make it."

"Wouldn't miss it, wouldn't miss it." P.B., so tall, blond and good-looking he'd been called P.B.—for Pretty Boy—since high school, looked admiringly around the room. "Hey, looks like old times in here. You guys get a new cook?"

Steve grimaced. "Worse. New owner. This is probably Charters' last gasp, my friend. Say good-bye to the world as we know it."

"What do you mean? The place is doing great, who'd mess with it?" P.B. slid onto the bar stool vacated by Margarita Girl's cohort.

Margarita Girl tapped him on the shoulder. "My friend only went to the bathroom. She's coming back."

P.B. grinned at her, melting her as only P.B. could, and patted his lap with one hand. "I'm saving a place for her."

The girl put one hand into her mass of curls and smiled flirtatiously. "I'm sure she'll appreciate your keeping it warm."

P.B. laughed and turned back to Steve with a conspiratorial look. Having girls come on to him was like a drug to P.B. He had to have a hit of it regularly to keep his high.

"Hey," a customer in front of the beer taps summoned Steve. "This beer's flat." He pushed a pint glass across the bar.

"Which one was it?" Steve asked.

The guy indicated the Bud tap. Steve opened it into a glass and tasted. Sure enough.

"Sorry, pal. What'll you have instead?"

"Bud bottle?"

"No problem."

Steve moved to the cooler and retrieved a bottle.

"Great crowd," P.B. said when Steve returned. "So maybe seeing this, the new owner'll just keep it the way it is. And bring back happy hour. Charters' happy hour was legendary."

"I know. But this, tonight, this is all a show." Steve delivered the Bud bottle, picked up a pint glass, filled it with Bass Ale from the tap and put it on the bar in front of P.B. "Most of the time these days the place is dead. Ever since Mario left to work at the place downtown and we stopped validating parking. We just called in a bunch of people to make it look good tonight for the new owner."

P.B. put a hand to one pocket and frowned. "Shit. You don't validate parking anymore?"

Steve moved down the bar to fix a martini for a young guy wearing what Steve interpreted as a stockbroker suit, then came back to his friend.

P.B. was craning his neck to look toward the kitchen. "So where is he? The new owner? I'll give him an earful about this place. Hey, you should tell him about all that history you dug up here. That stuff's great. You can't close a place with stories like that attached to it."

"Something tells me she won't care about any of that. Besides, she's not closing us. She's *reinventing* us."

"She?" P.B. was instantly intrigued.

"Yeah. 'Rox-Zilla.' The new owner. She wants to turn it into some fancy little French bistro, complete with frog legs and stuffed shirts."

"No." P.B. groaned and lay his head on the bar. Picking it up again he said, "Where's a guy gonna go to get a decent beer around here? This was one of the last great bars in town. I mean, look, you still use real pint glasses. Guess a woman wouldn't appreciate something like that, though. What'd you call her?"

"Rox-Zilla. Her name's Roxanne. Rita's been riffing on it all night. That's one of her better ones."

"Hey." Margarita Girl leaned forward and looked around P.B.'s shoulder to get his attention. "I'm a woman and I appreciate a good bar."

P.B. swiveled to her and gave her another smile. "A woman who likes a good bar?"

She nodded. Her eyes were getting glazed. Steve could tell she was succumbing to the tequila. He scooped a glass of ice, filled it with water, and put it in

front of her. If she ordered another drink he'd make it
weaker.

"Naawww." P.B. leaned back as if to see her more
clearly, turning on the charm. "Women don't like bars.
Chicks do. And you're a chick if I've ever seen one."

The girl, looking as if she wanted to be pleased but
wasn't sure, rolled her eyes and nearly lost her balance.
P.B. steadied her with a hand at the small of her back.

"What're you drinking there? Can I buy you another
one? Steve, another one of those."

"Heads up," Rita called from the waitress station.
" 'Shock-Rox,' coming to a theater near you."

Steve glanced from Rita to the door and saw Roxanne
Rayeaux enter the fray with the aplomb of a seasoned
bullfighter. She was dressed to kill, too, in a form-fitting
white sweater and black jeans with boots. Her hair tum-
bled around her head as if styled by Vidal Sassoon himself just outside the front door and her dark eyes had the
mysterious look of an Egyptian goddess.

"Holy shit," Steve heard P.B. say.

He looked over to see P.B. rise and move reverently
forward, as if to greet the Pope. More power to him,
Steve thought, then smiled to himself. Rox-Zilla might
be the perfect challenge for his pal, who in Steve's opinion did not suffer nearly enough rejection.

"That's an evil smile," Rita said, behind him.

Steve made no effort to conceal it. "Just thinking a little character-building experience might be coming up
for old P.B."

"At the hands of our fearless leader, you mean?"

"None other." Steve crossed his arms over his chest
and leaned against the back counter.

* * *

Roxanne entered the smoky bar with a mixture of surprise and distaste. On the few occasions she'd visited Charters prior to buying it the place had been empty, making it easy for her to see the space and imagine her own cozy restaurant instead.

Now, however, she could barely see across the room for all the smoke, and the loud music and smell of beer made her want to turn tail and run. As she walked toward the kitchen, her shoes stuck to the floor and she was reminded unpleasantly of college frat parties. On the mirror behind the bar, scrawled in what looked like lipstick, were the words BAR SPECIAL: CHARTERS SUNDOWNER, IN HONOR OF THE SUN SETTING ON THE OLD FISH HOUSE.

She turned back to her friend Skip and made a face. This was not going to give him a very accurate idea of what she was planning to do.

Skip had been her pal since high school. A short fireplug of a guy, he didn't look like the type who'd be particularly sensitive. In fact, if anything, he looked like a Mafia thug. But something, perhaps growing up with the name "Skip," had made him unusually sensitive to the world, and he'd always been the most perceptive of all her friends. Even if he did go out of his way to tell her exactly what he thought, and usually in no uncertain terms.

"I thought you said this place was dead." He stepped close to be heard over the din.

"It is. Or it was." She looked around in some confusion, her gaze coming to rest on a drunk young man throwing pretzels at a girl near the front window.

Roxanne leaned back toward Skip. "In any case, it will be. And I'm just the one to put the bullet through its head."

"I don't know if I'd be sneering at a crowd this size." Skip's head swiveled left, then right, to illustrate his point. The place was wall-to-wall people. "Not if I owned the place. Are you sure you want to change it?"

"Skip, take a look at the floor. It's covered with peanut shells. And it smells like Sigma Nu after Fat Tuesday. You think this is the kind of place I had in mind? Come on."

She elbowed her way through the crowd until she met head-on with a tall, blond man wearing a beaming smile.

"You must be the renowned Roxanne." He was good-looking, in a Ken-doll kind of way, and had to bend close to speak over the music. So close that his breath brushed her cheek. He smelled like Binaca.

Roxanne backed up a step, suspicion crawling along her nerves. *Renowned?* He looked like just the type to have the last ten years' worth of *Sports Illustrated* indexed in his closet.

She raised her chin. "Have we met?"

"We're meeting now." He took her hand in both of his and showered her with another smile. "I'm Peter Baron. Here, let me get you a seat."

Roxanne's brows rose and she looked back at her friend Skip skeptically.

But Peter Baron was taking her in the direction she wanted to go, so she let the man lead her by the hand. She was not going to make the same mistake she made with Steve Serrano and assume the worst. She'd wait until he proved himself a snake and then take him down.

They stopped at the far end of the bar, next to the last two bar stools. A girl with big hair was being helped off one of them and into her coat by another girl.

"Do you want to go get sick first?" the helper girl asked. "That's what I did. I feel much better."

The girl with the big hair shook her head. "No, I'll be fine once I get in my car."

Roxanne stopped dead in her tracks. "Let me call you a cab, all right? You're in no shape to drive."

Both girls looked at her as if she'd offered to slap their faces. "We're fine," the first girl said. "As if it's any of your business."

"Actually, it *is* my business. This whole place is my business." Roxanne spread her hands to encompass the stinky bar. "So let me call you both a cab. I'll pay for it."

"I'll do it," the blond man—Peter—said with an indulgent smile. "Don't you worry about a thing."

"That's all right," Roxanne said. Her eyes scanned the bar. "I'll just get Steve to call—"

"It's not a problem." Peter held up a hand. Then, with gallant aplomb, he offered each drunk girl an arm. "Hey, aren't you the girl who said she knew a good bar when she saw one? I couldn't agree with you more. Look, there's a chair by the front door. Let's go sit there and wait for the cab."

Roxanne watched them go. "Who the heck *was* that?" she asked, as Rita marched up with another order.

"Who? The blond guy? That's Steve's friend P.B.," Rita said. "Two more Jaegermeisters," she called to Steve.

Roxanne and Skip sat on the two stools the girls had vacated.

"Well, that was really something," Roxanne mused, looking after the blond. "He just took care of it. Look, they're even sitting down to wait. Smiling."

"Wonder what he said to make them listen." Skip looked over his shoulder at them.

"Probably told them he's a cop," Rita offered. "That usually makes 'em listen."

Roxanne turned back to her. "He's a cop?"

"You bet. Hey, Candyass!" she yelled to Steve. "I said two Jaegermeisters. Did you hear me? Those guys threatened to drop trou if I didn't get back to them within five minutes."

"Drop *trow*?" Roxanne repeated.

"Drop their trousers," Skip supplied. "Where've you been? You're like the parent who wanders into their kids' keg party, Rox."

"Please. I'm not going to feel bad about not knowing what 'drop trou' means. And that is exactly why I have to change this place." Roxanne spun on her seat to look out over a crowd that almost looked dusty with all the smoke in the room. "I have no desire to play mom to a bunch of rowdy kids at a keg party every night."

"I doubt that's the role they'd want you to play either," Steve said, plopping two shots on Rita's tray.

Roxanne turned back to the bar. She had to admit, Steve looked pretty at home in this atmosphere. With his slightly too-long hair, his black shirt and that *play with me* grin, he was just appealing enough to have every big-haired girl in town sucking down drinks at the bar in hopes of getting a flirtatious word from him.

"Steve." Roxanne held a hand out toward her friend,

"This is my friend Skip Williams. Skip, this is Steve Serrano, the bartender."

The two shook hands.

Skip laughed. "Oh, the *bar*tender. I thought maybe he was just a privileged guest, being on that side of the bar and all."

"Very funny. I meant, well, never mind." Roxanne meant that he would probably be the bartender for Chez Soi, too, but she didn't want to give Steve that reassurance just yet. She wasn't sure why. Something about wanting to keep him off balance, she thought, instead of letting him keep *her* that way.

"So, how long you two been together?" Steve asked, picking up a rag and fisting his hand in it to dry the inside of a glass.

Roxanne blushed, grateful to the smoke for at least hiding that. "Oh, we're not—"

Skip laughed. "We're just friends. We've been friends since high school, so we know far too much about each other to ever get involved. Besides, I've got a girlfriend."

Roxanne mentally cursed herself. All Steve had to do was ask one question and he had her flustered. What was *with* that?

Steve's expression was intrigued and he cocked his head toward Roxanne. "So what do you think of your friend's new venture?"

Skip scratched the side of his face and looked dubiously around them. "I think she's nuts."

"Way to make me look good," she said in Skip's ear as Peter—the "Viking," as she had come to think of him—showed up at her elbow again.

"No need to worry." Peter settled himself against the

bar next to Roxanne with a confident smile. "The girls are safely in a cab and out of harm's way." Relieved, Roxanne smiled back at him. "Thank you so much."

"You know, Steve," Peter continued, "bartenders get sued all the time for things their drunken customers do. You ought to be careful."

Steve shot his friend an ironic look. "Thanks, buddy. I'll remember that."

Peter's face was somber. "No really. It's serious business."

"I know that, P.B., and if I could have stopped the last asshole from buying them a drink, I would have." Steve's gaze was pointed, his eyes amused.

"Oh well." Peter shrugged and hunkered himself down, one elbow on the bar. "Those girls were drunk when they got here anyway. So Roxanne, tell me about you. How did such a sweet, beautiful woman, such as yourself, come to be the owner of a place like Charters?"

Roxanne scooted her chair back a tad from the bar to include Skip in their conversation. "It's kind of you to assume that I'm sweet but I can assure you I'm not. And as for ending up the owner of Charters, I have really only bought the building. Charters just happens to be what's in it at the moment."

Steve leaned over at that. "I'm sorry, I missed that last part. Did you say you *bought* the *building*?"

Roxanne's cheeks heated. *Damn.* She had not meant to reveal that she had in fact bought the whole building, instead of just leasing the restaurant space, though she wasn't sure why. Something about keeping her past in the past. She didn't want to be known as the model who was trying to open a restaurant. Having people come to Chez Soi with the idea of seeing her or thinking they were going to a celebrity restaurant was precisely what she *didn't* want.

But then, if nobody had recognized her yet—and it had been a few years since her modeling heyday—chances were they wouldn't. They would just have to guess how she'd gotten her money, if they were so inclined.

"Yes, I did say that." She looked Steve dead in the eye as calmly as she could, almost daring him to ask the crass question.

But he just nodded and went back to drying glasses. His gaze was disturbingly shrewd, though.

"So Steve says you're turning the place into a French restaurant," Peter continued. "I think that's a *great* idea."

Steve's smile turned wry and his eyes rolled briefly up into his head.

Roxanne's mood was restored.

"Do you really?" She turned to Peter. He was the first person she knew to say her venture was a good idea, and she was filled with a ridiculous gratitude. Who was he, after all?

"Yes, really. There aren't nearly enough white-tablecloth restaurants down here. And certainly nobody doing French the way it should be done."

"Which is . . . ?" Skip muttered next to her.

Roxanne tilted her head at Peter. "So you know French food?"

"I love it. It's my favorite." He produced his signature smile again.

"I don't."

All eyes turned to Steve.

"You don't what? Like French food?" Roxanne asked. Did he not *want* the job?

She glanced at Skip, who shot back an I'm-not-saying-anything look. He'd already made it abundantly clear he didn't think she should be doing this.

"I don't like French anything," Steve said. His *play with me* smile was back and Roxanne wasn't sure whether he was joking or not.

She leaned forward on the bar. "Nothing?"

He acted like he was thinking, then said, "Nope. Not a thing."

She sat back and crossed her arms over her chest. He was kidding. He had to be. "Not even French fries?"

Steve shook his head. "They're not French."

"All right then." Roxanne paused and looked toward the ceiling contemplatively. "French poodles."

Steve laughed and despite herself she felt warmed by it. "Too ridiculous."

"French films?"

"Too pretentious."

"I'm with you there," Skip said.

Roxanne's lips curved. "How about French bread? Everybody likes French bread."

A short shake of the head. "Too crumby."

"Hmm. French toast?"

He shrugged. "Too rich."

She raised one brow and sat forward. "French women?"

Steve's eyes grew subtly more attentive and he gave a low chuckle. "Too . . . scary."

"I know . . ." Roxanne paused, studied the challenging look he was giving her and said, "French kisses."

* * *

Peter and Skip laughed. Steve eyed his adversary with fresh respect.

Roxanne continued to look at him, a beguiling half smile on her lips. She knew she had him.

He hesitated a fraction of a second, then returned a smile that was probably a tad less confident than usual. "You might have me there."

Roxanne sat back with a triumphant grin and glanced at Skip. "Well, then."

"I know you've got *me*." Peter put a hand lightly on her back. "Let me buy you a drink."

Roxanne turned to him and smiled. "No, let me buy *you* one. I appreciate your taking care of those girls. Did they give you a hard time?"

So much for P.B. getting a little of what was coming to him, Steve thought.

"Not a bit." P.B. was all graciousness. "And I would never let a lady buy me a drink."

Uh-oh. Maybe there was hope. Steve had been about to check in with the customers down the bar but he decided he had to wait to hear her response.

Roxanne's eyes narrowed. "You wouldn't? Isn't that a bit chauvinistic?"

Oblivious, P.B. laughed. "Absolutely not. I just would never want a woman to think I needed that kind of persuasion to . . . appreciate her."

Steve tried to stop the smile that hit his face but he couldn't do it.

Roxanne laughed. "I hate to disappoint you, Peter, but I only meant to thank you for your help. Not . . . how did you put it?"

Steve leaned in. "I believe he wanted to be persuaded to appreciate you."

P.B. shot him a look. "That's not what I said."

Roxanne put a hand on P.B.'s forearm, which lay on the bar. "Don't worry about it. I'm just teasing you. Steve, whatever he's drinking." She made a motion with her hand that told him to get whatever it was.

Steve executed a short bow—which Roxanne didn't even notice as she smiled at P.B.—and grabbed a glass. This time, Steve thought, P.B. was drinking Bud on tap.

3

Bar Special
Cuban Tango—because it only takes two...
Curacao, pineapple juice, lime juice, white rum,
 with a twist

There was no disguising it this evening, Steve thought, as
he dusted the bottles behind the bar for the third time.
Charters was dead and there was no reviving it. The
only sign that there had been any recent life in the place
was a telltale stickiness on the floor today. Something
the busboys would have mopped last night, if not for
the fact that by the end of the evening, even the staff
was pretty much sloshed.

Except Steve. He had learned long ago that to drink
on the job was to invite trouble. Big trouble. Bartending
was fun, but not when you woke up every morning of
your life with a hangover. At that point, the only thing
scarier than that was *not* waking up with a hangover—

which was when you should know you were well on
your way to alcoholism.

He had the music on low this evening, though he
chose Stevie Ray Vaughan—something with some energy so he didn't risk actually drifting into a coma. There
were two people having drinks in the dining room with
little chance of ordering dinner. In fact, they looked like
a couple discussing the particulars of a breakup.

Perfect for Charters' last night.

P.B. said he might stop by tonight, too, and Steve
knew the only reason was Roxanne. P.B. had been
taken by her, of course. The way he was taken by any
beautiful—or even cute, or even conscious—woman
who'd give him the time of day. What was surprising
was Roxanne's giving him that time.

Steve exhaled slowly and started wiping down the
end of the bar. Again.

He certainly wasn't one to claim he knew what
women really wanted, but if P.B. was attractive to Roxanne, so be it. Best of luck to both of them. So what if
she was high class and P.B. was low brow? What did it
matter that he was love-'em-and-leave-'em and she
was, from all appearances, hang-'em-high?

The door opened and Steve looked up, hoping for a
customer. If he had to spend any more time tonight
with his own thoughts he'd lose his mind.

On his way to work he'd put a letter in the mail to a
publisher asking if they'd consider his book for publication. It wasn't a blockbuster or anything—just the
history of a man who'd lived in this building two hundred years ago—but it had been Steve's passion for

three years. He was almost finished with it, and it was time to make the ultimate move and market it.

Now all he had to do was figure out how to forget he'd sent the query so he wouldn't agonize every time his mailbox was empty.

Sure enough, three thirty-something guys who'd obviously been doing some sort of athletic activity took seats at the end of the bar. Steve took a stack of napkins over and tossed three, one by one, onto the bar in front of them.

"What can I get you guys?"

The three ordered beers, then conversed quietly among themselves, obviously not looking for entertainment from their bartender. Steve got them their drinks and went back to polishing the bar.

He looked at his watch. Five-twenty. It was going to be a long evening.

At eight o'clock—after Steve had eaten a burger, a leftover salad and a cup of ice cream one of the busboys had gotten from Ben & Jerry's, down the street—P.B. showed up. He strolled into the bar with his hair combed perfectly, his shoulders thrown back and his chest puffed out for all the world like an amorous pigeon on a city sidewalk. His bearing was so over-the-top cop that he might as well have been wearing his badge and gun belt.

He greeted Steve with an upraised hand as his eyes scanned the near-empty restaurant. The three athletes had left, to be replaced by two women nursing martinis and a burly-looking bearded man putting away gin and tonics at an alarming rate.

So he was inordinately glad to see P.B., if for no other reason than that P.B. usually revved up the conversation.

Steve smiled as he noted P.B.'s roaming eyes. "You can relax, Romeo. Roxanne's not here yet."

P.B. shook his head and sat on a bar stool. "Who? Oh, no. I was just checking the place out. Looks different empty." He smoothed a hand along one side of his hair, confirming its perfection. "Smells a little like stale beer, too."

"Last night got pretty wild. I don't think any of the busboys got around to mopping the floor, and they weren't too happy this afternoon either. What can I get you?"

P.B. looked at the taps. "Uh, Sam Adams." He paused a fraction of a second then lay his forearms on the bar and leaned forward. "Got a question for you, Steve."

Steve opened the Samuel Adams tap. "Shoot."

"What's this girl really like, huh? This Roxanne." P.B. looked so earnest Steve actually felt a little sorry for him. "And what the hell kind of name is that, anyway? 'Roxanne'? Rocks-Ann. Rock-Sand."

Steve chuckled. "It's French, Pretty Boy. Like the woman in *Cyrano*? You know that story?"

"Cyrano?"

"Yeah. You know, the guy with the big nose who's in love with the beautiful Roxanne, but it's his better-looking friend she really wants?" He slid P.B. the beer.

P.B. looked confused.

"Steve Martin made a movie of it a few years ago. He was the fireman with the big nose?"

P.B.'s brows shot up. "The one with Daryl Hannah?"

"That's the one."

"Oh yeah. And she looked good in that movie, too. She doesn't always, you know."

Steve shrugged. "Blondes aren't my thing. Anyway, that was the Cyrano story, essentially."

P.B. nodded. "Uh-huh. Okay. But do you know if this Roxanne's got a boyfriend? She's not dating that little twerp from last night, I hope."

"I don't think so." Steve took a bar towel from a heap that lay on the cold chest and started folding it. "But I don't know what else to tell you, P.B. She only just popped up on Thursday."

"I know, but . . ." P.B. looked down at his fingers, splayed on the bar top. "You *have* talked to her. You have, you know, been around her a little."

Steve nodded, wondering what to tell him.

P.B. sighed. "She *is* a hottie, though, isn't she?"

"Yeah. I suppose." Steve bit the inside of his lip thoughtfully. *If you didn't know that inside, she's as prickly as barbed wire.*

"Did she say anything about me? You know, after last night?"

"P.B., I told you, I haven't seen her. She hasn't gotten here yet." Steve took a moment to study his friend. "Look, what's going on here? Are you really that worked up about this girl? She doesn't seem all that different from the rest, if you ask me."

"Are you kidding? She's like the ultimate babe." P.B. ran a hand through his hair again, this time actually messing it up, which tweaked Steve's concern. "But I know. It's crazy to get worked up about her. It's just, she's just . . . there's something about her. She's hot, but it's like . . . she's really cool, you know?"

"A riddle wrapped in a mystery inside an enigma?"

P.B. considered this. "Yeah. Like that. She's kind of irresistible."

Steve heaved a sigh of his own. "God help the man blinded by a challenge."

This wasn't going to be nearly as fun as he'd thought. If his friend's heart was involved, then Roxanne's rejection would be hard to watch, as opposed to mildly enjoyable, just seeing P.B.'s colossal ego taken down a notch or two.

"Look, P.B., I gotta tell you. I think she's something of a hard-ass. And a woman like that, who looks like that, she can be . . ." He shrugged one shoulder. "She can be hard to get."

"Hard to get?" P.B. straightened on the stool. "Are you saying you don't think I have a chance with her? Is that what you're saying?" He looked genuinely surprised.

Steve laughed. "Hell, I don't know. Why? You think it's not possible for you to be turned down?"

P.B. took a swig of his beer, his expression suddenly shrewd. "I know what it is. You've got a thing for her too, don't you." It wasn't a question. P.B. was far too smug for that.

Steve scoffed. "Believe me, no."

P.B. slapped one palm on the bar in delight, laughing. "I love it! Hah! No need to deny it, old buddy. How could you not? It's just a natural fact." He took another swig of his beer, looking happier than he had since he'd walked through the door.

Misery not only loved company, Steve thought, it

looked for it in the most unlikely places. There was no way he was or ever would be interested in Roxanne Rayeaux.

"Tell you what," P.B. continued. "Let's make this fun. I've got a hundred bucks says I'll get her before you do. You ready to match that? Put your money where your mouth is?"

Steve rolled his eyes and put up both hands. "No way. I don't make bets like that. Especially when we both know it's not my mouth we're talking about."

"Damn right it's not. You chicken?" P.B.'s grin regained its usual cockiness. "A month ago you told me you could get any woman you wanted, you just didn't want anyone right now. So what is it really? Not so sure of your way with the ladies these days?"

Steve already missed his lovesick friend of sixty seconds ago.

"That's not exactly what I said." Wasn't anywhere close, actually, but he didn't mind P.B. thinking he'd said it.

"Come on, *wuss*. A hundred bucks to whoever gets her first." P.B. pulled out his wallet, took out some bills and placed them on the counter. "Here."

"P.B., forget it. Put your money away. I'm not playing that game."

P.B. stopped and gave him an indulgent smile. "Okay, here's what I'll do. Make it fair. I'll spot you some good words. Work on making you look good to her."

Steve's ire blossomed. He dropped the towel he was folding and crossed his arms over his chest. "And why would you do that?"

"Because . . ." P.B. held a hand out and moved it up

and down to encompass Steve's person. "Well, you know. The girls think you're a nice guy and all, but I got the whole cop thing working for me. A real, upstanding profession. You know, stability. A future. Stuff like that. Chicks love that shit." He smoothed a hand along his hair, straightening it back out.

Not only did Steve know P.B.'s hair was one of his biggest vanities, it now appeared to be an emotional barometer of sorts as well.

Steve swept the money up with one hand, folded it tight and tucked it into one of the many chinks in the brick wall behind the bar. Out of some of the other chinks around the mirror stuck such things as a Redskins pennant, a lace garter and a stack of unused bar checks.

"Great." Steve pushed the bills far enough in that they weren't visible without looking hard. "We'll just put this up here as a reminder of what a stable, upstanding professional you are."

"Don't forget about yours." P.B. directed a finger from Steve to the wall.

Steve laughed.

Rita pulled up to the waitress station. "Two Fosters, drafts." She plucked a swizzle stick from the glassful and stuck it in her mouth, chewing.

"Besides," P.B. added, settling back on his bar stool, "Roxanne seems to listen to me. I think she respects my air of authority."

Steve sputtered as he grabbed two pint glasses. "Yeah, right. That's why she refused your offer to buy her a drink. I've never seen anybody step on so many land mines when talking to a woman without getting blown to smithereens." He tipped a glass under the Fosters tap.

"You see what I'm saying?" P.B. grinned. "She liked me."

Steve shook his head. "Listen, I don't know why she didn't blow you out of the water last night. Maybe she appreciated you taking care of those girls—"

"Authority," P.B. sang.

"But in every other way I can guarantee you alienated her." Steve stopped the tap and leaned forward. "Listen to me, whatever else Roxanne Rayeaux might be, she's definitely an intelligent woman. And an intelligent woman likes to be treated as if she can tell sincerity from a load of crap. Tell you what, you want to bet so bad, I'll bet you a million bucks right now she saw half of what you said last night as the thinly disguised chauvinism it was."

"You're on."

"Good luck figuring out how to prove that," Rita said.

Steve finished filling the pints. "If you really want to date her, Pretty Boy, I suggest you start treating her as an equal, not some little lady who needs you to take care of things."

"See? That's where you're wrong." P.B. sipped his beer, unperturbed by Steve's diatribe. "That's where you get into trouble with the women you date. Women *like* to be taken care of. Even the strong ones. Maybe the strong ones most of all, because nobody thinks to do it. So when a guy comes along and treats her like her problems are his problems they love it. Too much equality makes them feel insecure. And I'll bet on that, too, my friend."

Steve glanced over at Rita, who was looking at P.B. with a penetrating, but surprisingly not hostile, gaze.

"You don't have anything to say to that, Rita?" Steve threw a hand out toward P.B. "You think women want guys like him to carry them over mud puddles and bring them flowers to solve their problems? Or do they want a real man who treats them like an equal? Like they're strong and smart enough to handle their own problems?"

Rita looked from Steve to P.B. and back again. "We want both."

Steve gaped at her.

P.B. beamed.

And Roxanne walked through the front door.

"Speak of the devil." Rita scooped up her tray of beers and moved back to the lone table in the dining room.

The first thing Roxanne did was check out the kitchen, noting the mess left from the night before and resolving to fire both line cooks. Same with the busboy who was supposed to mop the floors last night. The place stank.

She would keep whichever waiters wanted to stay, especially hoping that Rita would want to. Rita was rough around the edges but she kept up with the craziness last night and every single one of her tables was happy. Whereas George got a little too tangled up in the bar crowd to keep his from complaining.

Not that any of last night's tables were going to complain much. It was obvious from the first few minutes of observation that the staff had stocked the room with friends.

In any case, George did a serviceable job and could probably be counted on to improve with training, though Steve might have better insight on that. She wondered if the bartender would be inclined to share his opinions on the staff with her, despite their rocky introduction and apparent disagreement. His experience with the others was a lot more valuable than her two-day evaluation.

First, though, she had to see if Steve was interested in staying on.

After tonight, Charters would be closed and on Monday the decorators would begin the transformation. Over the next two weeks the waitstaff she chose would be trained.

"So Steve," Roxanne said, moving through the swinging doors from the kitchen to the bar. "Are you interested in working for Chez Soi?"

Steve turned to her and cocked his head. "Why, Ms. Rayeaux, are you offering me a job? Even despite my professed hatred for all things French?"

Roxanne slid onto the empty bar stool next to P.B. "Are you turning the job down?"

She was pretty sure he wasn't. She didn't know him well but she could already spot the look in his eye when he was teasing. Kind of a cross between devilment and laughter, even when he wasn't smiling.

"Well now . . ." Steve scratched his chin. "What are the terms? Are you giving me a raise?"

"Why would I do that?"

"So I'll stay?"

She smiled. "You'll stay. We both know you'll stay, Steve, so let's not waste time taunting each other. Terms are the same as you have now. But you'll be making more money, nonetheless. Which you probably already know."

"*If* the restaurant succeeds."

She inclined her head. "It will."

"You're pretty confident."

She crossed her legs. "I have to be." She glanced to her right and smiled. "How are you tonight, P.B.?"

"I'm just great." He leaned one arm across the back of her bar seat and gave her a significant look. "*Now*."

Roxanne looked back at Steve, laughter welling in the back of her throat. "See? If I can make P.B. happy by just sitting down, surely I can make my restaurant a success."

One side of Steve's mouth kicked up wryly. "Yeah. P.B.'s a pretty tough sell."

Roxanne glanced at P.B. to see how he took that. He just grinned.

Steve studied her a moment. "I knew you were going to offer me the job."

She leaned back, determined to humor Steve. They were a little like oil and water, but it was important to get along, so she wouldn't let him get to her. Besides, most of the time he was just playing with her. She *thought*. "And how did you know that?"

He smiled. "Because you own the building. You fire me and I can't pay my rent. You could kick me out but that would mean more expenses. Easier to keep me on, I figure, than upset the whole equilibrium. Plus, I'm good at my job."

She smiled and tipped her head. "You are good at your job. Though you could be better. And, besides, I knew you would take me up on it."

"You did, huh? How?"

Because you're a career bartender, she thought. *And career bartenders get stuck in their jobs just like every other kind of lifer.*

She knew his type all right. Handsome, charming and going nowhere.

Right now it was fun, like playing. He could socialize, get dates, make good money, without having to challenge himself at all. But before long he'd start looking a little haggard. He'd cease being able to handle the long hours, or the after-work drinking, the way he could when he was younger, and he would feel fed up with the routine. But by then he'd have nowhere else to go. He'd have squandered his most productive years in a dead-end job and he'd be stuck in it for the rest of his life. Because who would hire a guy, who should be twenty years into a career, who'd done nothing but bartend?

Yes, she'd seen it before and she knew all the signs.

She couldn't even count the number of bartenders, waiters and waitresses she'd known who still considered the job temporary—just a stepping stone to their *real* career, whatever that might be—despite being on the job for a decade.

"I knew you'd want to stay, because you're a creature of habit, Steve Serrano." She kept her tone light and her lips smiling. "And creatures of habit hate to move. At any rate, I know you'll be good at the job I'm offering, even though your experience here is somewhat . . ." she let her eyes scan the bar . . . "unrelated."

Steve scoffed and looked at P.B. "What'd I tell you? Hard-ass."

"Did you just call me a hard-ass?" This pleased Roxanne inordinately.

"I did. And what makes you think I'll work out at Shaaay Swahhh?" He exaggerated the French accent and extended his arms with a short bow.

"First, because of that bottle of wine you left me the other day. It's good wine. And it's *French*."

Steve straightened, chuckling. "In vino veritas."

Latin. Roxanne raised her brows. "And second, because I suspect you are a chameleon who will fit into any atmosphere. All the best bartenders are."

"So Steve-arino brought you some wine, huh?" P.B. said, obviously tired of being left out of the conversation.

Something about P.B. appealed to Roxanne. Not his looks, despite being classic and clean-cut, or his personality, which was like a TV car salesman's. It was more because he was such a caricature. At some point in his life he'd adopted the role of playboy, clearly from some seventies role model, perhaps appearing on *Love, American Style*, and he'd mastered every stereotype of the character. It was impossible not to be entertained by him.

"Yes." She turned to him. "As a housewarming gift."

P.B. snaked a smile to Steve. "Well, isn't that neighborly? You're just a stand-up guy, aren't you, Stevie?"

"That I am, my friend. That I am." He grinned and looked down the bar, checking the other customers. Nobody flagged him so he looked back at Roxanne. "I hope you liked the wine."

"I haven't opened it yet."

P.B. swooped in. "Looking for someone to share it with? I love a good French wine, myself."

"You wouldn't know a good French wine if it slapped you across the face," Steve said. "And it might."

"Sure I would."

"Name one vineyard. Hell, name one *varietal*."

P.B. turned to Roxanne. "Did you know that in addition to being a pompous ass about wine, Steve here is also a pompous ass about history? He's bored the pants off more women than I can count with that stuff."

Roxanne looked at Steve. "Seems like a handy skill for a single guy."

Steve laughed. "Unfortunately, P.B. didn't mean that literally."

"But you are a history buff?" she persisted. Roxanne considered it important to find out details about people that surprised her. Especially people who worked for her. And anything scholarly about Steve Serrano would definitely surprise her.

Steve shrugged. "A little."

"Oh come on." P.B. needled. "He's got his head in a book more often than anybody I've ever seen. It's about all he does, other than work here."

"That's me. Mr. Excitement." Steve moved off toward the other end of the bar, where the ladies finally looked ready for another round.

P.B. sat forward on his stool, closer to Roxanne. "I'll tell you, though, Roxanne. That's a beautiful name, *Roxanne*, you know that?"

He looked as if he wanted to take her by the hand, so she picked up her water glass. "Thank you."

"Were you named after the character from *Cyrano*?" he asked. "That's always been one of my favorite stories."

This surprised her. P.B., a reader? "As a matter of fact, I was, in a way. My mother never liked that story, but she did like the name." She grinned. "Personally, I liked the Steve Martin movie best."

P.B. put his chin on his hand. "There was a movie?"

"Don't tell me you read the play? By Rostand?"

"It was years ago." P.B. waved a hand nonchalantly. "Hey, I'm glad you decided to keep Steve on." He glanced toward the other end of the bar where Steve was pouring a scotch and chatting with a white-haired man. "He's a really good guy. And he needs this job."

She too glanced at Steve. "You think so? There are a lot of other bars in town and he's a *very* good bartender." It was true. If last night was any indication, he was one of the better ones she'd seen.

"Well, sure. But you know, you had it right about the creature-of-habit thing. Old Steve's been here for years. It'd take a lot out of him to start over doing something different."

Roxanne looked at P.B. Was he trying criticize his friend or did the truth just come out that way?

Steve returned to the conversation and P.B. changed the subject.

"As I was saying," P.B. sat up straighter. "Stevie does find some interesting historical stuff every once in a while in all that reading. He started out by researching this house we're in right now. And you'll never guess who used to live here."

He looked expectantly at Roxanne. She raised her brows and looked from him to Steve. "I can't imagine."

But she was pretty sure if it was somebody famous the previous owners would have used it to get more money out of her.

"None other than Thomas Jefferson!" P.B. crowed. "It was after he was president, but—"

"Hang on a minute." Steve shook his head and gave his friend a look of exasperation. "I can see the years since high school haven't honed your skills as a student any."

Roxanne had to admit, she loved the interplay between these two. They were so antagonistic it was hard to believe they were really friends. And yet they had been for years. One of those kinds of friendships only men seemed to have.

Steve fixed P.B. with the eye of an unhappy schoolteacher. "Thomas Jefferson did *not* live here. If he had, you can bet we wouldn't be sitting in a restaurant in this building. Or if we were, it would be run by the Park Service and we'd all be eating hot dogs."

P.B. looked scandalized. "But you told me—"

"I told you a *cousin* of Thomas Jefferson's lived here. Portner Jefferson Curtis. A little-known and rather morally impoverished cousin, as a matter of fact."

"And I told all those guys down at the station . . ." P.B. muttered.

"'Little-known'?" Roxanne looked to Steve, concerned. It would be just her luck for this guy to dig up something the Historical Society would be interested in. Something that could get in the way of her business plan. "I would think anyone related to Jefferson would have been somewhat known. Especially one who was doing well enough to have lived in a house this size. Surely this was considered an expensive house, even back then."

"That's actually a really good point."

She could swear he looked impressed and she wasn't sure whether that gratified or annoyed her.

"It's something of a mystery," Steve said, leaning against the bar and warming to his topic, "who actually bought this place. Some say Jefferson did, for Portner to live in. But Jefferson himself wrote shortly after Portner moved into the house to ask how he was faring and whether he might divulge the nature of the business he was engaged in. That makes some historians question whether Portner bought the place with some kind of ill-gotten gains."

"And did he?" Roxanne asked. "Surely by now everything there is to be known about this guy is known."

Steve shrugged. "Actually, no. We're not sure. Not only did Portner not divulge what business he was in when he wrote back, but he essentially told Jefferson to mind his own damn business."

Roxanne laughed. If the exchange was public enough for this bartender to know about it, it certainly wouldn't take the Historical Society by surprise. "How rude."

Steve smiled with her. "You bet. So rude it marked the end of their correspondence, as far as we can tell. And especially rude considering that in his earlier days, just after Jefferson moved back home from Washington in 1809, Portner was unemployed and pretty bad off, so Jefferson let him stay at Monticello. It was Jefferson who got him back on his feet and enabled him, one way or another, to move here, in 1810."

"That kind of makes you wonder . . ." Roxanne began, then stopped. She was never very good at history, truth be told, and she had no desire to reveal her ignorance to these two overconfident guys. Especially not when she was trying so hard to exude competence. Not that P.B. would care one way or the other. Roxanne was sure that as long as she "smiled pretty," he'd say she was just as smart as could be.

"It does make you wonder," P.B. said. "Makes me wonder, too. Mostly about having another beer, eh, Steve?" He laughed.

"Makes you wonder what?" Steve directed this to Roxanne, ignoring P.B.

Roxanne was about to answer when two big guys—construction workers?—came in and sat down on the other side of P.B., who instantly straightened on the bar stool to his full height and stretched in such a way that his chest expanded impressively.

If he up and peed on the bar he couldn't have looked any more territorial, Roxanne thought.

Steve held up his index finger to Roxanne. "Hold that thought."

She watched him go, appreciating his professionalism. Yes, he'd be a good hire. She just needed to know a little bit more about him, a little bit more about Steve Serrano, career bartender, who seemed to have hidden depths.

"Pretty interesting stuff, huh?" P.B. asked. "Maybe you can use some of that history in marketing this place. Spread a rumor that it's haunted." P.B. made a low, spooky noise and fluttered his hands out by his sides.

Roxanne considered this. "You might be right. Though it would have been better if it had been a cousin of Lafayette's who lived here."

P.B. gave her a blank look.

"Because he was French?" she prompted.

Steve was back before P.B. could reply.

"Now, what were you saying?" Steve asked.

Roxanne regretted saying anything, her thought had been such a silly one. "Well, it just made me wonder. The fact that . . . uh . . . Portner . . . ?"

Steve nodded.

"The fact that Portner was living at Monticello when Jefferson might have gone out of his way to get this place for him makes me think Portner was rude early on and Jefferson just wanted him out of his house. I mean, first of all, we're *miles* from Monticello, and second, since Portner was so disrespectful later it would make sense that he had been pretty ungrateful all along."

Steve looked at her with a contemplative smile.

"What?" she said, laughing uncomfortably. "Was that stupid? I guess I like to make things into soap operas."

"No." Steve rubbed the side of his face with a palm. "No, not at all. I'd had the very same thought. The fact is . . ." He looked from Roxanne to P.B. and back again.

"The fact is . . . ?" P.B. prompted.

Steve chuckled lightly. "Well, it makes perfect sense when coupled with something else I read recently. I had this idea that . . ." He stopped himself and took a step back from the bar. "But you're probably not interested in my boring theories."

Roxanne couldn't help being apprehensive. If he really was some kind of amateur historian bent on making this house famous—or at least historically interesting, even if just to others of his ilk—she needed to know. The Alexandria Historical Society took things like this very seriously—so seriously they could hold up entire building projects for archeological purposes. Postponing a little remodeling in a place where a famous person had resided would be far from out of the question.

"I'm definitely not bored," she said. "Come on, you can't leave us hanging here."

"Yeah, come on," P.B. said, with a look of utter insincerity.

"Okay." He leaned forward, his arms on the bar. "There was something in Jefferson's letter to the land agent who arranged for Portner to move into this house. Something about Portner being 'prone to mischief,' he believed. And for years, in historical circles, there've been rumors that Portner stole something from Jefferson that caused the rift between them."

Roxanne was filled with dread. "What was it?"

Steve grinned like he held the punch line to a scary story. "A draft of the Declaration of Independence."

"No way," P.B. said. "Are you shitting me?" Then, remembering Roxanne, he leaned toward her abjectly. "I'm so sorry."

She gave him a blank look. What was he sorry for? Could he be thinking what she was? That this would interest more than just the *amateur* historians? She couldn't afford to hold up the opening to her restaurant so a team of archeologists could climb all over it.

But P.B. merely turned back to Steve with an amended version of his question. "Are you kidding me?"

Steve shook his head, smiling like the cat that swallowed the canary. "Furthermore, speculation is that the draft was hidden here in this very house for his heirs. But he never had any children and no one else was very intent on searching the place for something that might or might not exist. It was pretty well established that Portner could be less than honest, at times."

"Shut *up!*" P.B. shouted, catching the attention of everyone at the bar. "You mean to tell me there could be an original copy of the Declaration of Frickin' Independence hidden in this building right here right now as we speak?"

Silence throughout the room greeted this outburst.

The construction workers looked at them with great interest, and even Rita and George stared in from the dining room.

Roxanne frowned, dread growing within her. "Surely not, after more than two hundred years."

Steve let his eyes scan the room. "I doubt it, too. For one thing, this place has to have been remodeled dozens of times over nearly two centuries. And for another, historians have been talking about this for decades and in the few documented searches that were made, nobody found anything. So, I'm sure there's something somewhere that refutes the possibility. But I spent most of the last month looking for evidence that the draft turned up and haven't found anything yet."

She heaved a sigh of relief. *Historians have been talking about this for decades.* So it wasn't news.

"Where do you look for this stuff?" she asked. "I've always wondered how people still discover things now that happened hundreds of years ago."

"Mostly I go to the Library of Congress. Have you ever been there?"

Roxanne shook her head.

P.B., coming out of a reverie, said, "What? Where?"

"The Library of Congress," Steve said with a conspiratorial smile at Roxanne. It was obvious to both of them P.B. was losing interest. "It's just across the river and one of the most incredible places I've ever been. You can actually look at old letters and documents and books, sometimes things that haven't been touched in years. Once you've been there, it's easy to see how not everything has been discovered yet. And maybe never will be."

"I should go," Roxanne mused.

"I'll take you sometime." Steve's eyes met hers and she caught her breath.

"Oh you don't need to do that," she said quickly, to cover a sudden and inexplicable blush.

"So," P.B. said, "how much you think a draft of the Declaration of Independence would be worth now? I mean, if it were found."

Steve blew air out of his cheeks and thought a moment. "Hell, I don't know. It would probably be sold at auction and those things can either skyrocket or tank. But I would think maybe millions, at any rate."

"*Millions,*" P.B. marveled, looking as if he might just go out and buy himself one of those Declaration of Independence lottery tickets.

4

Bar Special

Tom and Jerry— _for those who like to play cat and mouse_

White rum, brandy, maple sugar, allspice, nutmeg, 1 egg, boiling water

Roxanne wrestled with taking the wine, then decided she was making too big a deal of it. She'd just take the bottle with her to Steve's apartment to ask him about the staff. It would serve as a kind of olive branch after she'd been so obnoxious the first time they met.

Her one other concern was that he would think she was asking his opinion because she didn't know what she was doing. But all she wanted was some confirmation, or denial, of the reliability of some of the servers. Like George, for example. And getting the opinion of someone who'd worked with them for years was just good business. Getting that opinion with honey—or in this case wine—instead of vinegar was also good business.

So, in the name of competent management, Roxanne closed her door firmly behind her and, with the neck of the wine bottle grasped in one sweaty hand, she proceeded up the stairs to Steve's apartment.

The moment she reached the top step his door opened. With a mental curse she stopped in her tracks. She thought she'd have a moment to compose herself outside the door and figure out what to say. Now he was leaving and she was stuck on the stairs, directly in the path of rejection.

Without noticing her, he pulled the door shut and turned his key in the deadbolt lock. A duffle bag was looped over his shoulder, out of which the handle of some sort of tool protruded.

For a split second, she contemplated fleeing. If she could have turned around and disappeared without his noticing she would have. But there was no way he wouldn't at least hear her clomping down the wooden steps and then she'd look an even bigger fool than she already did, standing silently on the top step with a bottle of wine in her hands.

Instead, she took the initiative.

"Going out?" she asked.

Startled, he turned swiftly. "Jesus. You scared the crap out of me."

He took a step forward and his eyes raked her from head to hands, landing squarely on the bottle of wine.

"Sorry." She raised the bottle with a wan smile. "Guess you don't want any of this, then."

He quirked a brow, his expression going from wary to surprised. "You bringing it back?"

She opened her mouth to reply.

"Wait, don't tell me," he said with a cock of his head. "As my boss, you can't accept gifts. Favoritism and all that."

"No, of course not." She forced a smile. "Feel free to give me as many gifts as you want. This isn't the army."

He grinned. "Oh, right. It was the boot camp that threw me."

Maybe it was being a couple steps below him but she felt at a disadvantage in more ways than she was comfortable with. She stepped up to the landing.

"It's called training, Mr. Serrano. But you can think of it as gourmet boot camp, if that'll make your martyrdom any more satisfying."

"Actually yeah, that'll help." He looked from the bottle to her face again and frowned. "So . . . what's up with the wine?"

She took a deep breath. In for a penny, in for a pound. "I just had a couple questions. Not about the wine. I was hoping you'd have time to talk about the restaurant with me." She looked down at her own hands and gave a light laugh. "And I was bringing the wine as a bribe."

He hefted the duffle bag higher on his shoulder. His expression was almost one of confusion, though what he had to be confused about was, well, confusing.

"This is a change of heart, isn't it? I gathered from the meeting last week that you didn't need or want my input." He gestured toward the wine. "Let alone that you might decide to bribe me for it."

Roxanne's cheeks warmed and she looked down at the bottle. He was being somewhat contrary, she thought. "I know what I'm doing with the restaurant. There's really no question of reverting to Charters' old, uh, strategies, so I wasn't looking for input on that. I just thought, because you know the staff so well, I'd ask your opinion about some of them."

There was a window right next to him on the landing and he leaned one hip against the sill, one thumb looped through the duffle bag's shoulder strap. Light from an outdoor streetlamp shone through his gray eyes, making his assessing gaze even more penetrating.

"You want me to rat on my coworkers?"

She lifted her chin. What was *with* him?

"Absolutely not! I would never put you or anybody else in that position." She put a hand on one hip. "You know, I don't know where you get off thinking I'm such a bad person just because I happened to buy the place where you work. Is it just because you don't like anything French? Or is it me? Because all I wanted was to know . . . was . . . you, you're . . ."

In the middle of this speech her brain finally registered his teasing look. Unfortunately it was a few seconds before she could get her mouth to stop running.

Steve chuckled and straightened from his leaning stance. He moved a couple steps toward her on the landing, his expression amused and, she thought, exasperated. "That's right. I was kidding."

"Well." She nodded once, then took a deep breath. "Well. I hope so."

Her voice sounded petulant. She wished she'd never left her apartment. Why couldn't she have deliberated another five minutes about this stupid course of action?

Another *two* minutes? He would have already been gone and this whole conversation would never have taken place.

"I was."

"Okay." She swallowed. *Keep it light*, she told herself. He was; why couldn't she? "I was just looking for a little psychology, which you bartenders are supposed to be so adept at."

Tone, Roxanne, tone. She could have smacked her own forehead. She could tell by his face that though her words had said one thing, her manner had said something else. Something derogatory.

"Yeah, we're pretty savvy at judging people," he drawled. His gaze judged her where she stood.

"Well, if it makes you at all uncomfortable to talk about your coworkers, then never mind." She paused, unsure how to end this debacle. "So where are you going?" she asked—though it sounded like she demanded—and waved a hand toward his duffle bag.

He glanced over his shoulder at it.

"Me? I'm going to a friend's house." Steve gestured for Roxanne to precede him, so she turned and headed down the stairs ahead of him. "She's got something she needs help with. Well, not help really. Just, something she wants me to look at."

Roxanne glanced back at him as they both clopped down the wooden stairs.

"In the garden?" she asked as they reached the landing.

"Garden?" They paused in front of the door to her apartment. "Why do you say that?"

She inclined her head toward the handle sticking out of his bag. "It looks like a hoe. Or something."

He laid a hand on it. "This? No. Too short to be a hoe, for one thing." They stood looking at each other a moment. "Well, gotta go. See ya."

He turned down the hall toward the last flight of stairs, then stopped. "We can talk another time, if you want, about the restaurant. And you don't need to bribe me with wine. Just let me know."

"Sure. Yeah, see you." She watched him go.

He had long legs, she noted as he walked away from her. And an easy way of carrying that bag that looked awfully heavy.

Had it just been her imagination or had he been uncomfortable when she'd asked him what he was doing? Maybe it was because he was seeing a woman, and he'd thought she might be bothered by that. Because she'd brought the wine.

Damn. She clenched one hand into a fist so that her nails bit into her palm. She should have been clearer that she was just trying to be friendly. Business friendly. The last thing she'd wanted was for him to think she was coming on to him.

She opened her apartment door and went straight to the kitchen. She set the bottle firmly on the counter, pulled open the utility drawer and dug through utensils until she found the corkscrew. Then she opened the bottle and poured herself a glass of wine.

She'd drink the whole thing, if necessary. She didn't ever want to be tempted to share it with him again. He was obviously the type who'd misunderstand. He probably thought every woman was coming on to him. Hell, maybe every woman *was* coming on to him. He was pretty cute.

But the last thing she, Roxanne Rayeaux, needed was an employee thinking she was making a pass. Because she was *not* making a pass. Or if she was, it was just a friend pass. A pass at making a friend. Instead all she'd gotten was a cocky, suspicious employee. Not to mention a neighbor who thought he'd just had to reject her.

She took a sip of the wine and let it roll around her tongue a second.

Damn again, she thought. It was excellent.

Steve hopped in his pickup truck and sat for a moment in the dark.

That was weird. Roxanne Rayeaux wanted to share a bottle of wine with him. Ostensibly to talk about the restaurant, but come on. They could talk about the restaurant any day of the week, during daylight hours, at one of the staff meetings—or rather, training sessions—she had set up. Or over lunch.

But at night? With a bottle of wine? Wheels turned in his head.

Surely she wasn't coming on to him. That just wouldn't make any sense. She thought he was an unsophisticated beer jockey. Someone beneath her social notice. He'd seen that on her face the night he'd impulsively offered to take her to the Library of Congress and she'd nearly recoiled.

He took a deep breath, fished his keys out of his

jacket pocket and started the truck. Despite the cold, the old Toyota purred quietly to life.

What would have happened if he hadn't been going out? he wondered. Suppose he'd said yes to sharing the wine with her? They'd have talked about the restaurant, maybe gotten a little loose—what with the wine and no food—and . . . what? Was she lonely? Would she have expected him to make a move of some sort? Would she have *wanted* him to make a move?

Of course, there was the fact that he didn't *want* to make a move on her. She was hot, sure. And smart, he'd give her that. But she was the type to eat men like him for breakfast. High maintenance, all the way. He'd sensed it the moment he laid eyes on her.

He didn't know her well, but he knew as surely as if she'd told him so that she required her men to live up to an unrealistic standard. And he was really not into living up to other people's standards, unrealistic or not. Not when he was just figuring out his own.

Which was why he dated women like Lia, who was expecting him. He put the car in reverse and backed out of his parking space.

Technically, he and Lia had broken up a few weeks ago, but they'd both known they'd slide back into something. Such was the nature of their relationship. Break up, take a breather, get back in touch, sleep together, stay together a few months, break up.

Only this time Steve wasn't sure he wanted to slide back. The only reason he was seeing her tonight was because she was offering him an opportunity that would be otherwise unattainable.

Lia did a lot of housesitting in the historic district

and sometimes she let him come snoop around if a place was particularly interesting. Tonight she'd called and told him to bring his metal detector, she was in a house near where a Civil War armory had stood and there would probably be, as she'd put it, *bullets galore*.

He figured it could be interesting. He'd never used the metal detector, which his mother had gotten him for Christmas and which he and Lia had joked about incessantly afterwards, but there were stories of people making some interesting finds with them. Not to mention that it would please his mother to know he'd finally unboxed it. She was always buying things to keep him interested in history, as she was sure it would eventually lead to a "real career."

His only hesitation about doing this was that Lia was not above having ulterior motives. She was lonely, he would bet. It was part of the pattern.

But he wasn't. In fact, before the last time they'd broken up, he'd spent weeks canceling dates and not calling and generally acting like the worst kind of boyfriend ever, to get her to end things.

He wasn't proud of it, but then he'd never been very good at telling women he wasn't interested.

With the exception of Roxanne Rayeaux. For some reason that had been easy.

He pulled up in front of the house where Lia was staying and cut the engine. Gathering up his bag from the backseat, he glanced up and down the street to be sure no neighbors were out walking their dog or anything to see him enter the house with a metal detector and bag of tools.

It had taken him a while to convince Lia he was responsible when it came to poking around people's historic homes. She always questioned what he got out of it. So he wanted to come *look*, what good would that do him? It wasn't as if he ever discovered anything. Even if he did, he wouldn't be able to tell anyone. How would he explain poking around someone else's house?

It was a good point. One he couldn't satisfactorily answer, not without revealing goals he'd rather keep to himself until he was sure he could achieve them.

For now, he told Lia, he just liked seeing if he was right about things. He liked to theorize about historical sites and personages, and if he could find things that confirmed his theories, it would tell him his instincts were right, his research was valid.

That was something he did a lot. Tested himself, to see if he was right. He'd make bets on people at the bar, who they were, what they did for a living, where they were from, and kept a mental tally of how often he was right (most of the time, he was pleased to note).

He rang the bell, but he was not thinking about Lia, or even the possibilities of the metal detector.

No, he was thinking about Roxanne Rayeaux and her bottle of wine. And he was wondering if he was right about her.

Roxanne didn't get through the whole bottle of wine. She didn't even get through half before falling asleep on the couch, dreaming that she and Steve were in the restaurant waiting for her ex-boyfriend, Martin. In the dream she was tense, then hysterical when one of the brick walls slumped in front of them, stray bricks tumbling across the floor and dropping from the ceiling to tear the fabric on the new chairs.

Dimly, as she drifted in and out of sleep, she knew she was focused on these subjects because of the remodeling that had just started. That, and the ongoing fear that Martin actually would show up, promising that *this* time he really *would* leave his wife for her. The wife she didn't know he had until they'd been dating close to six months.

She woke up fully after dreaming that George dropped an entire tray full of stemware—wineglasses stacked dozen upon dozen—onto the hard brick floor of a wine cave, the pyramid crashing to the ground in a symphony of shattering glass.

She jerked up on the couch and one hand went reflexively to her neck, which had crimped from her odd resting angle on the pillow. Her eyes swept the room, deducing at a painfully slow rate that it was late at night and she was here, in her apartment in Virginia, and not in her New York high rise.

As she eased herself up off the couch her eyes landed on the box she'd been unpacking before a nap seemed like a good idea. There was the reason she'd dreamed of Martin. In the box she'd found a package of condoms. Martin's condoms. He had never been without them, always so afraid of a "mistake." He'd practically begged her to go on the pill—which she couldn't do because, for her, the pill changed her body too much for modeling—and finally had bought what looked like a case of Trojans, which he left everywhere they might end up getting intimate.

He'd never understood how much that hurt her, his

mortal fear of a mistake. And after a while she'd stopped trying to explain it.

She picked up the package and moved purposefully toward the bedroom. Opening up the bedside table drawer, she thought defiantly, *Just in case*, and tossed them in.

She went back out to the living room, determined to get rid of the last couple of boxes, when she heard footsteps on the wooden stairs outside her door. An automatic hit of panic shot through her and she tiptoed to the front door to look through the peephole. The downstairs door was not open to the public, so if this was anyone but Steve, she should be ready to call the police.

Cheeto trotted up behind her, no doubt hoping to bolt out the door if she opened it. Skip said she should have named the cat Magellan, since he was such an explorer.

For a minute she hovered between standing at the door and going to retrieve the phone, finally opting to stay by the door and see who it was.

The footsteps topped the first flight, then started down the hall toward the second. For a mere moment in the warped lens of the peephole she saw Steve Serrano's profile as he walked by her door in the light of the hall's overhead bulb.

It was only a fleeting view, but she thought he looked tired and kind of mussed, as if he'd been doing something physical.

Yeah, physical, she thought, remembering that he was going to a woman's house that night. Then, unexpectedly, she was assailed by an image of him shirtless and sweaty, bending above her with that dark grin on his face. The image was so sexy and so powerful that heat rushed to her core and she put a hand to her stomach, where a whole flock of birds simultaneously took flight.

For God's sake, she told herself. *Get a grip*. It had obviously been far too long since she'd had sex.

She brushed the hair from her forehead and crept away from the door, then turned out the living-room lamp and closed herself in her bedroom. There she lay awake for precisely five minutes before falling into a hot, steamy sleep, filled with images of a lean, naked man with hair just a tad too long, doing all manner of devilish and delightful things to her.

The next morning she awoke with the cat on her head and the sheets tangled around her legs. Rarely had she spent such a restless night.

It was nine before she made it downstairs to start coffee for the trainees. Sir Nigel was coming today to teach them all about French table service and the different glasses and silverware it required.

Also, workmen were coming to install the wine caves and she wanted to be sure they had a clear path through the kitchen to bring them in.

She pushed through the swinging doors from the bar to the kitchen and headed for the coffee service. She had just scooped out some coffee and was filling the pot with water when she noticed a cold breeze on her back.

She turned, expecting to see someone coming in the back door, and froze. A second later the water overflowed the pot onto her arm and she turned back to fumble with the faucet.

After laying the carafe in the sink with a shaking

hand she turned back to the rear door, her eyes riveted on the pile of broken glass on the floor.

Slowly, she moved her gaze around the room, her brain putting the pieces together.

Someone had broken in.

Someone must have taken something.

Something must be missing.

Someone could still be here now.

Adrenaline shot through her veins, making her shake.

Last night, she'd awoken because she'd dreamed about breaking glass. But maybe it was this she had heard. Could she have heard this door breaking from her living room?

Her eyes scanned the room. Things were disturbed, little things overturned along the counters. A refrigerator had been pulled away from the wall about six inches. The freezer was not closed tightly. A trash can lay on its side, its contents strewn about the floor. Workstations had obviously been messed with—knives and whisks, side towels and clipboards were scattered helter-skelter.

She looked at the floor. Near the door to the office a floorboard had been pried up. One end was split and gnawed-looking.

What in God's name was going on? What had the intruders been doing in here?

Her mind flew immediately to the theoretical draft of the Declaration of Independence. She almost had to laugh at herself for thinking anyone would take that conversation seriously enough to break in, but it was too odd for this to happen right after that discussion.

Plus, there'd been plenty of people around when P.B. had blurted out the possibility that it existed right here in this very building.

She frowned. But to come in and scatter tools on the workstations . . . to be rooting through the trash . . . No, this had to be something else.

The mayhem didn't quite look as if whoever had broken in had been looking for something. More that they'd been trying to do damage. Could the cook have been that angry at being fired? What about the busboys she'd let go?

Her mind flew to the moment she'd woken up last night. Moments afterward she'd watched Steve go past her apartment door on the way to his. Maybe he'd noticed something when he got home. Maybe he'd seen a car pull away, or a person in the back alley. Something he might not have registered as odd last night, but that would fit with what had obviously happened here.

She strode to the office, taking care not to touch anything or trip over the displaced floorboard, and looked at the phone list. Then she grabbed the receiver and dialed his number.

He answered on the fifth ring. A low, gruff hello that sent her reeling back to the dream she'd had last night of him bare-chested and hot with arousal. She blushed as she spoke, angry with herself for being so sexually deprived that she couldn't keep her mind on a break-in, for God's sake.

"Steve, it's Roxanne."

There was a muffled sound. Then, "Huh? Oh."

"I'm sorry to wake you."

His voice became clearer. "No, it's okay. Don't worry

about it." He cleared his throat and she relaxed a tense breath. Not being irritated when awakened by a ringing phone said a lot about a person. "What's up?"

"Could you, uh, could you come down to the restaurant? Soon, I mean?" She suddenly wasn't sure calling him first was the right thing to do. She should call the police. What was wrong with her?

She could hear what sounded like him rolling over in bed and a cool mist of perspiration broke onto her forehead.

"Sure." He cleared his throat again. "Yeah, sure. Is something wrong?"

Yes, yes, *yes*! Something was wrong, *that's* why she was calling. Not to give fertilizer to her already unmanageable sexual urges.

She mentally took hold of herself. "It seems we've had a break-in. The window on the back door is broken and things in the kitchen look . . . disturbed."

"What?" His voice was crystal clear now. She imagined him sitting up straight in bed. "Somebody broke in?"

"Yes, I—"

"Stay right there. I'll be right down." The phone on the other end clattered and went dead.

She exhaled. He was awake now, she thought, as she pressed the OFF button on the phone and looked at it a moment. She should call the police. She'd need a police report for the insurance. Not to mention that she didn't want whoever did this to come back.

Had they found what they were looking for? There hadn't been any money in the place. That had been deposited yesterday morning. They hadn't even been open for business yesterday, so there was no reason to think there would be any money.

It had to have been the cook. Or the busboys. It had to have just been someone wanting to scare her, or make a point. There wasn't anything here worth stealing. Nothing that would get you any money, that you could get out the door in the dead of night, anyway. She'd like to see the thief who could steal a steam table or a walk-in freezer. If they'd been thieves who knew anything about kitchen equipment they would have stolen some of those knives, not just scattered them around the workstations.

She pulled the phone book from the desk drawer and looked up the non-emergency number for the police. After all, it wasn't as if there was a theft in progress or anything. She didn't need to call 911.

Her finger landed on the number and she'd just picked up the portable again when a noise in the kitchen caught her ear. She had just enough time to think she'd been a fool not to call 911, because the thieves could still be in the building, when Steve appeared in the office doorway.

She heaved a sigh of relief.

"Are you okay?" His face was sober, but it was his sleep-rumpled hair and disheveled clothes that caught her attention. Never had a mere bartender looked so good.

Roxanne shook her head against the thought. Lord, one sex dream and she had completely lost control. This was just Steve, she reminded herself, her inherited employee.

She looked down at the phone book. "I'm fine. A little

surprised, maybe, but fine. I was just calling the police." She held up the phone in illustration.

He came toward her and gently took it from her. "Your hands are shaking. Here, let me call P.B."

Her hands *were* shaking, she realized, just as her knees were. She sat down in the desk chair and watched him dial the phone.

"Yeah, Peter Baron," Steve said into the receiver. He gave her a grim smile.

He'd obviously come straight from bed the instant she'd called. She couldn't even tell him how grateful she was. Not that she couldn't have managed this on her own. She *could* have, and *would* have, if she hadn't thought he might know something that would help. Still, she had to admit she was glad she didn't have to do it alone. Starting this restaurant by herself was scary enough. To think someone might want to sabotage it made everything seem that much harder.

"Hey, P.B. It's Steve." He ran a hand back through his hair, making a vague, halfhearted effort to straighten it. "Listen, we've got a situation here at Charters. Someone broke in last night . . ." His eyes slid over to Roxanne and his lips turned up wryly. "She's sitting right here and she *looks* fine. Are you all right, Roxanne?"

She gave a strained laugh. She could just imagine the he-man way P.B. had put the question. "I'm fine."

"Yeah, she's fine. Hmm. I don't know." He shifted the receiver down away from his mouth and addressed her again. "Anything missing?"

She shrugged. "I'm not sure. But things have definitely been disturbed." She pointed to the floor behind him. "Look, someone even pried up one of the floorboards."

He turned to look, taking a step closer to try to peer inside. "P.B.? Yeah, things are definitely messed up, but we're not sure if anything's missing yet. What?" He looked back at Roxanne. "Was there any money taken?"

She shook her head. "It was all deposited yesterday morning. There was nothing here."

"No," he said into the phone. "Yeah, okay, good." He hung up. "He's coming right over."

She sighed. "Thank you, Steve."

He leaned one hip against the desk and looked down at her. "No problem. Hey, I know these things can be unnerving. Me? Snakes are what get to me. I can handle anything but snakes."

She shifted her eyes to his. "Snakes, huh?"

"Yeah. I don't know what it is, but they make my skin crawl." He shivered once, apparently just thinking about it, then wandered over to the pried up floorboard and squatted beside it, adding, "You got a snake problem next time, call somebody else to deal with it."

"Sure. But . . ." She raised her chin and looked at him. "I could have handled this on my own. I wasn't hoping you would 'deal with it' for me. That's not why I called you."

He issued a short laugh and gave her a look that seemed to say, *Sure you could, little lady*. "I didn't say you couldn't."

He poked a couple fingers into the age-old, lintlike insulation filling the space below the floor and stirred it around a little.

"Can't imagine they found anything in here," he murmured, wiping his hand on his jeans.

She studied him. Was he being condescending or did it just seem like it? "Listen, the reason I called is because you came home last night right about the time I think this happened."

He turned to her, his eyes widened. "What? How do you know when I came home last night?"

"Because I heard you coming up the stairs."

He stood up. "Really? How do you know it was me?"

She threw a hand out. "Well who else would it be?"

"I don't know." He looked around with exaggerated wonder. "An *intruder*, maybe?"

She shook her head. "No, smart guy, it was you. I saw you through the peephole."

At that he seemed to color. "You saw me through the peephole. Great, now I've got a spy living below me."

"I wasn't spying. How paranoid are you? You think I've got nothing better to do than wait for you to get home from your girlfriend's house? I was looking to be *sure* it was you. If it wasn't, I would have called the police, because you're the only one other than me who should be on those stairs."

"So you sit up nights guarding the stairwell by looking through the peephole?"

"Oh please. I just happened to wake up and hear you—"

"At *three o'clock in the morning*?" He looked incredulous.

"That's right." She glared at him. "What are you insinuating?"

He moved back into the office. "I've said what I was

insinuating. What are *you* insinuating? You think *I* had something to do with this?" He spread his arms wide, his face indignant.

She stood up, angry at being deliberately misunderstood. "No! I'm not accusing you of anything, Steve. I just thought you might have seen something."

"Like a broken window? You think I'd just go on to bed if I did? What kind of idiot do you think I am?"

She put her hands on her hips. "Why are you being so defensive?"

"I'm not being defensive." He crossed his arms over his chest. "I just want to know what the hell you think I did."

She rolled her eyes. "Oh, that's much better."

He just looked at her. "Look." She steeled her voice and gave him a hard look. "I woke up last night about three because I thought I heard glass breaking." There was no way on earth she was going to tell him about her dreams. "Then I heard you coming up the stairs. This morning, when I found this," she indicated the mess around them, "I thought maybe you might have seen someone in the alley, maybe a suspicious car or something. That's *all* I thought, okay?"

His expression went from belligerent to wary.

"So? *Did* you see anything?" she asked.

"No."

He didn't even think about it.

She was so mad she could spit. He was so damned secretive he couldn't even take the time to think whether or not he might have seen something suspicious last night. Either that or he thought she was so desperate for company she had stayed up late to spy on him. Either way, he wasn't very concerned about getting at the truth.

So, all right then, fine. He'd be the police's problem. She'd tell them what she just told Steve and let them take care of it.

"Forget it." She shook her head and moved past him toward the office door. When he didn't move she turned back. "Are you coming? We should probably wait in the dining room. Make sure we don't touch anything in here."

Slowly, Steve turned and followed her out the door, through the kitchen and into the dining room. When they reached the bar, the front door opened and a tall, distinguished gentleman with thinning dark hair and an ebony cane entered.

Roxanne took a deep breath and forced a smile. "Sir Nigel." She moved toward him, looking at her watch. "You're early."

"Good morning. I wanted a chance to examine the dining area before beginning," he said in his precise British accent.

He was perfectly turned out, in a three-piece suit complete with watch chain and French cuffs. She'd forgotten how tall he was, nearly six foot three, and she wondered if his cane, which he did not appear to need except as an accessory, was extra long.

Roxanne suddenly became acutely aware of her untamed hair and jeans.

He took her hand in his and bent over it with great formality. He smelled just faintly of cologne. "Lovely to see you, madamoiselle. I trust everything is in readiness for today's training."

"Well, actually . . ." She glanced over her shoulder at Steve. He lounged idly on one of the bar stools, looking like he'd just done the very thing he had: rolled out of bed. "We have a little problem this morning. Someone broke into the kitchen last night."

"Good Lord," Sir Nigel exclaimed, if saying the words in the same even tones of his clipped Oxford accent could be called exclaiming. "Was anyone hurt?"

"No, it was nothing like that. Just a little breaking and entering."

Sir Nigel's hawklike eye moved past her to spear Steve with a haughty glare. "I see you've caught the culprit. Good show. Have the authorities been called?"

Roxanne strangled half a laugh. "No. That is, yes, the police are on their way. But this is not the culprit. This . . ." She turned and held a hand out toward Steve. "Is our bartender. Steve Serrano. Steve was the bartender at Charters but he really knows what he's doing. Steve, this is Sir Nigel Wallings."

"Our bartender?" Sir Nigel said incredulously. "The bartender for our elegant little French restaurant with renowned chef Marcel Girmond—this . . . person?"

Steve didn't rise. Instead he fixed Sir Nigel with a look of thinly veiled hostility and said, "Nice to meet you, too."

Roxanne clasped her hands together in front of her and slowly exhaled. With a tight smile at no one she said, "Well, this is getting off to a great start."

5

Bar Special
Sidecar—<u>have one when three's a crowd</u>
Brandy, Cointreau, lemon juice, with a twist

P.B. sidled up to Steve near the bar. "So, how's she doing?" He jutted his chin in Roxanne's direction and donned a concerned expression.

Steve, still slumped on a bar stool and wishing he'd gotten more sleep, looked up and said, "She's fine. Look at her. She's her own pit bull. You don't need to worry about her."

They could see Roxanne through the kitchen doors, which were propped open, looking over the shoulder of the fingerprint guy. Steve would bet she was pointing out places he missed.

P.B. turned to him. For some reason, P.B., in his blues, always looked about twice his normal size. Maybe it was the gun.

"You seem a little pissed, big guy. What's up with that?" P.B. leaned a square hand on the bar. "The burglars didn't make off with anything of yours, did they?"

Steve shook his head, gazing at Roxanne. She thought he had something to do with this, he was sure of it. She and her pompous pal *Sir Nigel*. They were the purebreds and he was the mongrel, so it had to be him to blame for the mess on the floor.

"Let's just say I've been robbed of my dignity." Steve turned on the bar stool and reached across the bar for the bag of pretzels he knew was on top of the cold chest.

He unfolded the plastic bag, relishing the loud crunchy sound as it went a small way toward drowning out the pompous Sir Nigel's voice in the dining room, droning on about show plates and fingerbowls, *guéridons* and *réchauds*. He was accompanied by Rita, George, Pat and some French chick whose sole purpose seemed to be demonstrating the proper way to open a wine bottle.

Tomorrow, Sir Nigel had threatened, Steve was to get a lesson in Armagnacs. As if Steve needed anyone to tell him about brandies. He *lived* brandies. Hell, he *bathed* in brandies. Brandies were his *life*. He didn't need to spend an afternoon with Sir Nigel's ebony cane up his butt to serve Armagnacs to a bunch of French-restaurant-bar patrons who were probably too old to tell the difference between brandy and Listerine.

P.B. laughed and slapped him on the back. "Get over it, buddy. You never had much dignity to speak of anyway. Besides, that's what women are all about. They bust your balls just to see if you're strong enough to stand up to them."

Steve stuffed a pretzel in his mouth and looked at P.B.

"And if you are? What does that mean? You argue with them, walk away or just keep taking their shit?"

"You let their shit roll right off your back, my friend. Don't even listen to it. They don't mean it anyway. They're just exercising their control muscles. Let them spit it all out, pay them a little lip service, then forget about it."

"I can't believe you actually think that's good advice. Is that what you do, P.B.?" Steve raised a skeptical brow. "Because if you keep talking like that, you might have to turn in your male chauvinist membership card. Sounds like you let women walk all over you."

P.B. wagged a finger at him. "I let them *think* they're walking all over me. Then I do whatever I want." He dug into the pretzel bag and pulled out a handful.

Steve settled back in the stool. "I guess I have to say that's probably the right tack to take with Roxanne. She likes giving people an earful, if my experience with her is any indication."

"What do you mean?" P.B.'s eyes were suddenly alert. He almost looked like the detective he was supposed to be right now. "What's your experience with her?"

Steve chewed his pretzels and smirked. "Ooh, down boy. I didn't mean *that* kind of experience. I just meant having to try and work with her. She's tough as nails, even when she doesn't have to be."

"Hm." P.B.'s eyes trailed back to Roxanne and his mouth took on a little smile. "Fiery. I like that."

Steve grunted. "Positively searing."

"Listen, I'm going to ask her out. How do you think I should do it?"

Steve shook his head. "Very, very carefully."

"No, I mean, what should I ask her to do? You know her a little better than I do. I was thinking I'd take her out to eat or something. What do you think?"

"I think that's a great idea. Because she probably doesn't spend enough time in restaurants."

P.B. put a hand to his chin. "Good point. Hmm. Then again, maybe she'd like to check out the competition. I was thinking that new pizza place on King. You know the one?" Steve looked up at him with his first truly delighted smile of the day. "Are you serious?"

P.B. scratched the back of his neck. "Yeah. Why?"

"Pizza," Steve confirmed.

P.B. drew his chin back, defensive. "Yeah."

Steve shrugged. "Okay. I guess she might like pizza. I mean, really, who doesn't?"

"Exactly." P.B. looked at him warily. "What?"

Steve pulled another pretzel out of the bag, but hesitated before eating it. He turned his eyes from the snack to P.B. "Well, considering she's putting everything she's got into opening a top-drawer, chi-chi, you-better-own-a-tie type place, I'm thinking she might like a restaurant that doesn't rely too much on plastic knives and forks."

P.B. looked into the dining room, where Sir Nigel was demonstrating the proper way to align a white linen tablecloth.

Steve ate the pretzel.

"Yeah, maybe . . ." P.B. brooded.

"Not to mention," Steve continued, "she's not striving for the pizza market, so that wouldn't exactly be her competition."

P.B.'s tongue found the side of his mouth as he deliberated. "So, you're thinking . . . French?"

"I'm thinking *expensive*."

P.B. narrowed his eyes, thinking hard. "What's that little place on Washington Street? You know the one I mean? Isn't it French?"

"Yep. And way out of your budget, Pretty Boy."

He dropped his hands to his hips. "Hey, I make a good living."

"Oh yeah. I forgot you're the consummate, up-standing professional. The guy with a future." Steve let his eyes linger sardonically on P.B. a minute. "Then sure, that's the kind of place I'm talking about. Go for it."

P.B. tilted his head. "I know why you're being such a jerk about this."

"I'm not being a jerk."

"Sure you are." P.B.'s expression was smug. "And you're probably giving me bad advice too, just so I'll blow it with her. Well, I'm onto you, buddy. I'm taking her to the pizza place. She's probably sick to death of French."

Steve snorted. "She better not be. We haven't even opened yet."

He glanced back toward the kitchen and wondered if, after this morning, Roxanne might be hoping he'd quit. She couldn't think he was behind a break-in and still want him working for her. Hell, maybe she'd even fire him.

Roxanne strode out of the kitchen and P.B. swiftly straightened.

Steve stifled an urge to do the same. Manners be damned, they were adversaries now.

She drilled Steve with a challenging look. "Steve, I've

told Officer Stuart that you got home last night about the time I thought I heard breaking glass."

Slowly Steve pushed himself up on the stool and glanced at P.B., wondering if he noticed her accusatory tone.

"He wants to ask you some questions," she added.

Officer Stuart stepped forward. A short, stocky guy, he was obviously new and looked at P.B. as if one bad question would make P.B. fire him on the spot.

He cleared his throat and poised his pen on his tiny, spiral-topped pad. "Mr. Serrano, approximately what time did you arrive home last night?"

Steve gazed coolly at Roxanne and answered, "About three. This morning. As I'm sure my *employer* informed you."

The cop nodded and wrote on his pad.

With a last lift of her brows, Roxanne excused herself and went back to the kitchen. P.B. immediately followed.

The little cop breathed an audible sigh. "And when you arrived home, where did you park?" He studiously made notes on the pad.

Steve wondered if he was writing down the questions as well as the answers.

He sighed. "In the alley, at the back of the building. Where I always park."

"And did you see anything suspicious?" *Scratch, scratch, scratch.*

"You mean other than the guy with a grappling hook, dressed in black, wearing a ski mask and crawling up the side of the building?" He shook his head pensively. "No. No, I don't think so."

Officer Stuart stopped writing and looked eagerly

from his pad to Steve's face. "A man in a ski mask? Is that what you saw?"

Steve sat back and studied the guy until the cop actually blushed. "What do you think?"

In classic P.B.-style, Officer Stuart puffed his chest out and looked stern. "Mr. Serrano, I need you to take my questions seriously."

Steve's gaze moved into the kitchen, where P.B. was standing too close to Roxanne, speaking to her with an overly charming look on his face.

Great, that would be all he needed. Roxanne for a boss with P.B for her boyfriend. The two of them would be insufferable. And P.B. would think he owned the place.

Steve turned back to the officer just as Roxanne reemerged from the kitchen. She looked flushed and slightly flustered. Had P.B. done that to her? He tried to imagine her being girlish and flirty, really interested in P.B., and couldn't do it.

He had to admit, though, every time she came into a room he was reminded of how beautiful she was, as if his memory changed when she was absent, because he couldn't quite believe it unless she was right there in front of him. It wasn't that he desired her, he was just taken aback time and again by her presence. Perfect lips, ivory skin, ink-dark eyes and that abundance of thick shiny hair. Not to mention the way she moved. Graceful. Catlike.

He'd have been in real trouble if she'd turned out to be nice.

Right behind her, however, came P.B. and in his hands was something to startle both Steve and Officer Stuart.

With a big grin, P.B. held aloft a dead squirrel. At least Steve thought it was dead. It wasn't moving.

"Found the perp!" he announced. Two fingers gripped the squirrel's tail. He swung it from side to side.

Everyone in the dining room stopped and turned at his voice.

"Is that a squirrel?" Rita called.

P.B. turned his grin on her. "Sure is. Nothing like wildlife trapped indoors to make a helluva mess."

"I'm thinking Brunswick stew tonight, chef." George guffawed. "A Virginia classic!"

"Good Lord, Officer." Sir Nigel sniffed and turned his head partly away, keeping one wary eye on the thing. "Please remove it from the dining area expeditiously."

P.B. turned back toward the bar.

Steve looked from the squirrel to Roxanne's face. So that's what had made her flush. Good, he thought. His faith in her was restored. She hadn't seemed the type to make a fool of herself over P.B.

"We're going to have to sterilize the entire kitchen." She grimaced and threw herself on a bar stool. "Fill the entire place with boiling water."

"Is it dead?" Steve asked.

P.B. swung the animal so close to Steve's face he had to pull back to avoid being hit.

"Of course it's dead," P.B. said. "You think it'd let me do this if it wasn't?"

Steve moved sideways away from the swinging animal. "For God's sake, P.B. What are you, in fourth grade?"

"What? It's cute." P.B. backed off but swung it a little more, watching it with a boyish grin.

Steve glanced at Roxanne, who watched P.B. with a look of concern.

"So how did it die?" Steve asked. "There's not a drop of blood on it."

"Huh?" P.B. stopped the animal and dropped his arm to his side. "I don't know. Scared itself to death, I guess."

Steve laughed. "You're saying it gave itself a heart attack?"

P.B. looked at him with heavy-lidded eyes. "You want me to ask the department to autopsy it?"

"Can we just," Roxanne motioned the squirrel away, "put it in a bag or something? I don't want its fleas or whatever other parasites it might have flung all over the restaurant. We're going to have to sandblast the place as it is."

"Oh sure." P.B. was instantly contrite. "Sorry about that." He went back to the kitchen.

"So . . ." Steve looked cautiously at Roxanne. "A nocturnal squirrel."

"Hm." She nodded, not looking at him. "So it would seem."

"A nocturnal squirrel that threw itself through the back window."

She turned her eyes to his face. "I had the same thought."

He held her gaze. "Curious."

"Yes." She looked away again, nodding. "Yes."

Then, after a second, she turned a sly look on him and said, "Good thing it wasn't a snake."

"You agreed to go *out* with that guy?" Skip sounded appalled. "That big blond guy with all the teeth?"

Roxanne turned from the seafood case and laughed at him. "All the teeth?"

They were standing in the Whole Foods Market, trying to figure out what to buy. Roxanne had invited Skip and his girlfriend, Kelly, to dinner and had promised to cook. Besides, she wanted to try out a couple of desserts on them, see which they thought were the best. But Kelly couldn't make it so it was just the two of them.

Skip shook his head with dismissive disgust. "He bares his teeth a lot. He's the kind of guy who makes people think he's smiling, but he's not. He's showing dominance."

Roxanne snickered and bent over again to look more closely at the scallops.

"I like the look of these scallops. I can do them with asparagus and black truffles. Or I can do the sole. What do you think?" she asked.

Skip leaned over next to her. "I don't know. How about a burger?"

"Funny." She waved the clerk over and inquired about the sole, then ordered the scallops.

They waited while he wrapped the order.

"I don't get it, Rox, why that guy? He gave me the creeps." Skip looked at an older woman who was carefully examining four different types of cocktail sauce. "Get the *organic* kind," he leaned over and confided. "They'll think less of you here if you don't."

The woman glanced up, saw he was talking to her and her expression turned haughty.

"Really." Skip nodded. "People talk."

"Skip," Roxanne admonished, with an embarrassed smile at the woman.

The woman grabbed the organic one, turned on her heel and left.

Skip laughed. "I'm sorry. It's just that everyone here is so pretentious. Look at them, with their tiny carts and their designer vegetables."

"This place is great. You're just jealous because all you have in your neighborhood is a Safeway."

"I like hormones in my meat. Keeps me manly." Skip flexed.

"That explains *that*."

"I'm serious, Rox. I mean, it's one thing for you to lose your mind and give up the big bucks of modeling for the hardscrabble life of a restaurant owner. But to go completely nuts and start dating G.I. Joe?"

"You really think P.B.'s that bad?" She tried to remember her thought process this morning when P.B. had caught her off guard with his offer. "He's actually nice. And he's helped me twice now with difficult situations."

"Oh please. Putting a couple of girls in a cab? I could have done that."

Roxanne snorted. "But you didn't."

She grabbed a pound of organic butter and they moved toward the cheese section. This was by far Roxanne's favorite area. Huge wax-coated wheels of cheddars and Jarlesburgs and Romanos stood amidst wedges of jack, Swiss, gouda and edam. Piles of bries and camemberts vied with goat cheese of every description and fresh balls of mozzarella in plastic tubs.

It looked like a Disney-inspired Cheese World.

"And his help with the burglary was his job." Skip picked up a paper-wrapped round of Cowgirl Creamery. "He was *paid* to help you out with that, sister." He put the cheese down and studied a jar of dried fig spread. "If you ask me, the only one who's really helped you out so far is the bartender. He's the one who got up first thing in the morning to help without getting paid for it. If you give anybody a gratitude date it should be him."

"Steve? He's not even looking for a gratitude date." Roxanne scoffed, but couldn't help remembering that steamy dream, albeit with nothing but consternation now. "He's got a girlfriend, for one thing. And for another, he is *so* not my type."

"Oh, I forgot. Your type is—what, now? Married?"

Roxanne stopped dead in her tracks and glared at him.

Skip threw his hands up in immediate surrender. "Sorry. Sorry. That was below the belt. I'm sorry." He lowered his hands and picked up a bag of grated parmesan. "I just don't see this P.B. guy being any better for you than Marty What's-his-face. P.B.'s got arrogant written all over him. Is that what you want? Someone to push you around?"

"He has not once pushed me around, Skip. And besides, I'm just going out to eat with the guy. I'll probably save moving in with him for the second date."

Skip inhaled and exhaled heavily. "All right."

"Oh good God. Now you sound like my mother."

"How is your mother?"

They moved to the wine section and Roxanne picked up a bottle to read the label.

"Fine. And every bit as optimistic about my success as you are. Thank God she lives in Florida now and can't visit me with her dire predictions."

Skip raised his brows but didn't look at her. He picked up a bottle, too, then placed it in the cart. "Well, she *did* own a restaurant most of her life. She must know what she's talking about."

Roxanne turned around, one hand on the cart handle. "You know as well as I do that she *loved* owning that restaurant. You were a waiter there; you saw her. She loved the customers, the food, the day-to-day planning and delivery. She loved being in control of everyone and everything. *And* she loved complaining about it."

"That's true." Skip nodded.

"Trust me. It's not that she doesn't think it's a good thing to do. She just doesn't think *I* can do it."

She put the wine she'd chosen in the cart and started to turn around to move back down the aisle. Skip stopped her. "That's not what *I* mean, Rox. I know you *can* do it. I just don't understand why you want to. You've worked your tail off and made a boatload of money. Why not relax for a little while?"

"Because I haven't *accomplished* anything, Skip."

"What do you mean? Your face was all over everything for a while. You were in *Sports Illustrated*, for crying out loud. I *still* get more respect from the kids because I know you, by the way."

She smiled. "I'm glad it helped you. But it didn't do much for me. Beyond making money, that is. Which was nice. But still. It was just my face."

"And your body."

She rolled her eyes toward him. "Right. But I didn't *do* anything. I wasn't respected. I've told you all this before. It's important for me to succeed on my own, using my head."

"I know." He picked up a loaf of bread, sighing. "I just can't help thinking I'd like to fly all over the world having my picture taken and getting paid tons of money instead of coaching a bunch of spoiled high schoolers to throw each other around."

"Skip, you are molding young minds. Shaping people's futures. Being a role model for the leaders of tomorrow." She shot him a smirk. "And you only work nine months out of the year."

"You've got me on the last point. The other three are highly debatable."

They got in line to check out. Roxanne, in front of the cart, pulled down a *Yoga Journal* and started flipping through it. Behind the cart, Skip pushed into her gently.

She looked over.

Look, Skip mouthed, pointing in front of her.

Roxanne glanced ahead and saw the back of a tousled male head. Her stomach lurched. *Steve.*

Skip pushed on the cart again.

Roxanne looked over.

Skip mouthed something she didn't get. She shook her head, squinting at him. He mouthed it again, as incomprehensibly as the first time.

She leaned across the cart and whispered, "*Vitamins?* What are you talking about?"

Skip rolled his eyes. "No. I said *invite* him."

She pulled back and whispered indignantly, "Where?"

"To dinner," he whispered back. "Tonight. With us."

She shook her head. "No way. You're crazy." She looked away.

Skip pushed on the cart again.

"*What?*"

"You said you wanted to talk to him and you blew it the other day. Now's the perfect opportunity."

"No!"

"Come on. I'll be there to keep it from looking like a date. Besides, I want to know a little more about his toothy friend."

She gave him an admonishing look. "Then definitely no."

"If he knows you're going out with his friend, he's not going to think you're coming on to him. Besides, I'm just kidding."

She turned back to the magazine. "Good."

"No, I mean asking about G.I. Joe." He pushed on the cart again and jerked his head in Steve's direction. "Look. All he's got there is a wrap. He's having a friggin' *sandwich* for dinner. As a chef, that should offend all your sensibilities."

"I'm a pastry chef. Besides, their wraps are very good here."

"Just invite him," Skip said. "It's neighborly."

Roxanne, visions of that evening on the stairwell still vivid in her memory, shook her head. "Absolutely not." She looked back at her magazine.

Skip was silent a minute. Then Roxanne noticed the cart pressing harder and harder into her hip. She braced a foot outward and pushed back.

Skip pushed harder.

She dropped the magazine, turned and put both hands on the cart and glared at him. "What are you *doing*?" she hissed.

Skip grinned and looked just beyond her. "Oh hey. How you doing?"

Roxanne closed her eyes, then turned to look behind her. Steve had glanced back, no doubt to see what all the stage whispering was about, and Skip had caught his eye.

Roxanne put on a smile. "Hello, Steve. Fancy meeting you here."

He looked genuinely surprised—as she knew she did not—and glanced from one to the other of them. "Hey, hello." He extended a hand toward Skip, avoiding any contact with Roxanne by leaning pointedly away from her. "Skip, right?"

Skip smiled and looked smugly at Roxanne. "That's right. Good memory."

Steve straightened back up. "Trick of the trade." He shot Roxanne a small, albeit fiendish, smile. "How're you doing, boss?"

She answered with a slight nod. "Fine. You don't have to call me boss."

His smile grew. "I know."

"Whatcha got there, Steve? A wrap?" Skip asked, gazing over the basket toward his small wrapped parcel on the conveyor belt.

Steve glanced back at it a second. "Yeah. Chicken Caesar."

"Those are good," Roxanne said.

"And it looks good, but you should join us," Skip said. "We're having scallops and truffles. Roxanne's one helluva cook."

"Is she? I thought she just did desserts." Steve inched forward as the food on the conveyor belt in front of him was tallied.

"That too. In fact," Skip turned a pleasant face to Roxanne, "didn't you say you had some desserts to sample tonight? Steve's opinion would be a good one to get, too, don't you think? Especially since Kelly couldn't make it."

"Of course." Roxanne shot daggers at Skip with her eyes before turning back to Steve. "You're welcome to join us if you've got nothing better to do."

Steve glanced from Roxanne to Skip.

"Really." Skip nodded confidently, gesturing toward Roxanne. "Excellent cook. And you guys can talk about the restaurant. I won't mind."

"Ah, a working dinner." Steve sent a lazy glance to Roxanne.

"Six eighty-nine," the cashier told Steve. "Do you want plastic or paper?"

"Neither." Steve pulled out his wallet and glanced back at Roxanne. "I don't want to interrupt your—"

"Don't think twice. Roxanne and I are sick to death of each other." Skip grinned at her, while she *did* try to look pretty sick of him. "Just come on by in about half an hour."

Steve picked up his wrap and, with a wry smile, said, "All right then. Thanks."

6

Bar Special
Angel's kiss——<u>devilishly delightful</u>
Crème de cacao, heavy cream

"I can't believe you did that." Roxanne pressed the button on her car key and the automatic door locks beeped as they opened. "You shanghaied him into coming."

"Come on. I did you a favor. You said yourself you need to get on better terms with this guy and you were right." Skip ducked into the passenger side and pulled the door shut.

Roxanne got in her side. "What do you mean, I was right?"

"Well from the expression on his face when I invited him, he looked as if he thought you might be planning to serve him arsenic." Skip fastened his seat belt.

She stuck the key in the ignition, then, sighing, lay her head on the steering wheel. "Great."

She'd seen it too, that look on Steve's face. They kept

butting heads, misunderstanding each other, and she didn't know how to fix it. She hoped it was just a matter of earning his respect, but she feared it might be some prejudice he had against women owning restaurants. Young women, in particular. *Her.* Maybe he felt defensive, being her employee. Embarrassed about being older and without a career other than bartending.

Maybe he just didn't like her.

In any of those cases, Skip was probably right to have invited him, or rather, bulldozed him into coming.

"Look," Skip continued, rubbing a hand on her back comfortingly, "for all your mother's idiosyncrasies, she didn't tolerate friction among the staff, right?"

Roxanne raised her head with a laugh. "That's right. Everyone came together to curse her."

She started the car.

"So, you could do that, or you could make nice. Right now, most of your staff know Steve and are loyal to him. Not you. You need him on your side, Roxanne."

Roxanne grumbled, "Or I could fire him."

Skip patted her back one last time. "Easier to just make friends. He seems like a nice guy."

"Sure. To you. Me, he took an instant dislike to." She remembered how snotty she was to him that day he came to give her the housewarming wine. A simple misunderstanding, but he hadn't known where her attitude had come from.

"All right," she capitulated. "You're probably right. But Skip, promise me one thing."

"Anything."

"Don't tell him what I used to do for a living." She turned pleading eyes to him. "I really want to get away from that, from being looked at like that. Right now he sees me as a kind of bitchy newbie owner, and that's okay. He can still think I know what I'm doing. But if he found out I used to be a model I just know he'd lose all respect for me."

Skip studied her for a second. "All right. Laying aside that I think it's unhealthy to be ashamed of something you spent ten years making a success of, I'll honor your request. In the name of baby steps."

She quirked a smile. "Baby steps?"

"Yeah, you know. Forward movement, progress. Sometimes it can only be accomplished by taking one baby step at a time. Whatever you can handle."

She put the car in reverse and looked at him sideways. "Laying aside how condescending that sounds, I appreciate your agreement to keep mum."

Steve hadn't been sure what to expect, but it wasn't the smiling, self-deprecating woman who was in the kitchen sautéing scallops and drinking wine when he arrived.

"Can I pour you a glass of wine, Steve?" she asked when Skip ushered him into the kitchen. "I have to warn you, though, it's French."

He laughed. "I think French wine was a positive on the list of French things."

He looked around the room. She'd fixed the place up since he'd last seen it—and apparently had been successful in fixing the sink drain—because the kitchen was warm and inviting and bubbling over with delicious scents. A basket hanging from the beamed ceiling held fruits, vegetables and herbs. The counters were clean, with minimal clutter, but were lined with sophisticated-looking salt and pepper shakers, an espresso machine and what might have been a pasta maker. A long loaf of French bread lay on a cutting board near the sink and a rack with copper pots hung near the stove.

An island in the center of the kitchen held an open bottle of white Bordeaux, a wedge of brie, and plates of asparagus, mushrooms, butter and several spices, presumably to be added to the dinner dish.

Steve slid onto one of the island's bar stools. "The place is looking great."

She poured a generous dram of white wine into a large goblet and handed it to him. When he took it, he met her eyes and she smiled. A genuine smile, he thought. Less guarded than usual.

"Thanks. It's been a lot of work, but as of today the last of the boxes is gone. Not only that, the painters have finished downstairs. Now I can relax."

She held up her wineglass and he touched it with his.

"Cheers," he said. "To your new home."

She smiled, her dark eyes seeming to look all the way through him, and sipped from her glass.

He wondered what was going on. In the grocery store, he could tell that inviting him to this dinner had been Skip's idea, and Roxanne had been none too pleased about it. But now she seemed different.

Maybe she'd thought he would refuse to come. (And he would have, if Skip hadn't been so damned insistent.) Or maybe she felt awkward after practically accusing him of being behind the squirrel break-in.

Who knew? She was a riddle (wrapped in a mystery

inside an enigma, etc. etc.). Maybe it was time to sit down and talk right up front about how they could work together amicably. Or *whether* they should work together, amicably or not.

Roxanne threw a glob of butter into a hot sauté pan and directed a question over her shoulder at him. "So Steve, where are you from, originally?"

He put his wineglass down carefully on the butcher block surface. "D.C. Out Sixteenth Street."

"Really? An actual D.C. native? That's rare."

"Where are you from?" He directed the question to her but looked at Skip too. If they went to high school together they must have come from the same place.

"Right here in Alexandria." She reached behind her for the plate of mushrooms. She lifted the plate slightly in his direction. "Do you like truffles?"

"Is that what those are?"

She narrowed her eyes as she smiled, as if he was trying to pull one over on her. Fact of the matter was, he may know his alcohol but he had no idea about fancy French cooking. He'd heard of truffles and foie gras and all that, but he hadn't spent much time eating any of it.

He was about to pick up his wineglass when a huge orange cat, the same one he'd seen that first day, leaped onto his lap.

"Whoa," Steve said reflexively, moving his hand from his glass lest he knock it over. "Who's this big guy?"

Roxanne looked back over her shoulder. She laughed. "Oh, that's Cheeto. You're lucky he likes you. People he doesn't like tend to leave with shredded pant legs."

Steve scratched behind one of the cat's ears, but the

animal ducked his head, giving him a look that said he was an imbecile and doing it wrong. He lifted his hand and looked into the cat's face.

"Cheeto, huh? That's kind of an uncultured name for a French restaurant's mascot. I would think something like Paté or Fromage would have been better."

"Not for him." Roxanne slid the truffles into a bath of boiling water, then moved the scallops around a little in the sauté pan. "He's definitely a junk-food cat. Besides, Cheetos are my downfall. Horrible for your health, just deadly to any diet, but oh so irresistible."

Aha, Steve thought, a chink in her armor. She *did* have weaknesses. "So will we be seeing Cheeto Almondine on the new menu? Vichyssoise with ground-Cheeto garnish? No wait, you're desserts. Cheeto à la mode?"

Skip laughed.

Roxanne said, "Believe it or not, those all sound pretty good to me."

This drew a laugh from all of them.

He tried petting the cat again, this time stroking him from head to tail. As he did, the cat rose up, arched his back and dug his needlelike claws into Steve's legs through his jeans.

He removed his hand again. Cheeto looked back at him, eyes narrowed. They regarded each other a moment.

"So what are your plans for the bar," Steve asked, "if you don't mind my asking?"

Cheeto leaped from his lap and thudded to the floor. After a pointed yawn, he proceeded to saunter off, obviously disappointed in Steve's petting abilities.

"My plans?" Roxanne said. "You mean the decorating?"

Steve picked up his wineglass. "No. I mean the pop-ulating. Charters had a great happy hour. Brought in tons of people. People who then got hungry and stayed for dinner."

She made a light scoffing sound. "If only to sober up before getting in their cars and driving home, no doubt."

She flipped the scallops over in the pan, shook the whole thing in a circular motion, then slid them onto a plate. He had to admit, he liked the way she moved. Graceful. Practiced. Like a ballerina in the kitchen.

"Happy hours are great," Skip volunteered, pouring himself more wine. "They give people a chance to taste your food, too. It's like advertising."

"Exactly." Steve shared a companionable look with Skip. He was starting to like the guy. Maybe Roxanne wasn't all bad, if she had normal friends. And if he could get her friends on his side, then maybe he wouldn't end up yawning through nothing but pre-dinner *kirs* night after night once the place became a haunt for people following the latest haute cuisine.

If they were that lucky.

"I'm not interested in catering to the happy-hour crowd." Roxanne threw the asparagus rather vehe-mently into some boiling water. "Happy-hour drinkers are people after a cheap drunk and they're not particularly discerning. Furthermore, generally speaking, people who show up for free food are not going to fork over twenty-eight bucks for *cuisses de grenouilles*."

Steve raised his brows. "What the hell is that?"

She smirked at him through her lashes. "Frog legs."

"No. Please. Tell me you're kidding."

She just laughed and continued slicing asparagus.

Steve looked at her face—so much easier to do with her eyes downcast—and realized again how stunning her features were, especially when she was smiling. She looked like someone off a magazine page. Advertising mascara or face makeup with those lush lashes set against smooth skin.

"Okay, well, frog legs aside. You don't have to serve dollar beers and hot wings for happy hour," he offered. "You could put out some showy, frou-frou stuff and lure them in with, I don't know, change-back-from-your-ten brandy night or something."

Roxanne looked up and laughed again. Perfect teeth, Steve noted. And he liked the way her lips curved into a flawless bow. Was she wearing lipstick? Or were her lips just naturally that color?

"Change-back-from-your-ten," she repeated. "I like it."

He couldn't believe this woman had agreed to go out with P.B. Steve tried to remember the face of the last girl P.B. had dated, but could only recall big hair and giant breasts.

Roxanne, on the other hand, was sleek. Both her hair and her body. She was tall, thin, and knew how to dress to accentuate her curves, as opposed to putting them up on display like a tray of hors d'oeuvres.

"I'll think about it," Roxanne said, her voice low and husky. For a second Steve had to work to remember what it was he'd last said. For another second he wished he'd said something more provocative and gotten the same response.

Skip cleared his throat. "Speaking of happy-hour crashers, what about this friend of yours: P.B.?"

Steve's eyes shot to Skip's as if the latter had been reading his thoughts. "What about him?"

"Oh Skip, please." Roxanne's expression was stern. "Don't bother Steve with that."

Skip looked at her and shrugged. "What? I'm just wondering what kind of guy he is."

Steve took another sip of wine. "He's all right. Why?"

Skip filled Steve's glass again, then his own. "Did you know he asked Roxanne out?"

Roxanne checked the asparagus.

Her back was ramrod straight and her hands moved with confidence. She took the truffles off the stove and drained them. Then did the same with the asparagus. Steam rose in the air over the sink like a ghost.

"I heard he might." Steve looked at Skip, keeping his face bland. Skip obviously didn't like the idea of Roxanne going out with P.B. He didn't need to know that Steve was disappointed in her for accepting the date, too.

"Well? Is he a good guy?" Skip asked.

Steve made a noncommittal gesture. "I think he is. But then I've never been on a date with him. He could be a total cad. Talk with his mouth full, split the check, that kind of thing."

Roxanne turned back to the island with a chuckle. She picked up her glass. "That, I can handle."

"I'm sure you could." Steve tilted his head. "What couldn't you handle?"

"Is that a rhetorical question?" She sipped her wine.

"I'll tell you," Skip said, reaching across to cut a piece

off the wedge of brie. "She doesn't handle liars very well. He doesn't have a wife tucked away somewhere, does he?" He popped the cheese in his mouth.

At that, the look Roxanne shot her friend was enough to burn holes in his face. If her friend wasn't already immune, that was, as he seemed to be. There was a story there, Steve could tell.

He shook his head slowly. "No, he doesn't have a wife. Not unless he's keeping it secret from me, too. Though it wouldn't be like him not to ask for a wedding gift."

Roxanne moved to a cabinet and pulled out a trivet. She looked as if she wanted to hurl it at Skip but she merely placed it in front of him.

"Make yourself useful and put this on the table," she said to Skip. Then, turning, she said, "Look, Steve, no offense, but I'm just going out with P.B. as a friend. He . . . well, he doesn't really seem like my type. Though he certainly seems to be a nice guy."

Steve chuckled. "How would that offend me?"

Skip got up, took the trivet and went into the dining room.

"He's your friend." She paused. "Isn't he?" She looked genuinely curious.

"Sure." Steve nodded.

"I just don't want you to think I don't like him. Or that I'm—using him or anything."

Steve lifted his brows. "*Using* P.B.?" he mused. "That would be novel."

She frowned and looked down at the cutting board. She pushed a few truffles around on it.

"Roxanne"—he leaned slightly toward her until she

lifted her eyes to his—"what goes on between you and P.B. is your business. He doesn't need me to protect him and I'm sure you don't want me chiming in about your decisions." He let that stand a minute before adding, "Me, I'm just the friendly barkeep."

"Ah yes." Skip re-entered the kitchen, his glass raised. "To the friendly bartender. You probably see romances come and go all the time."

"This is *not* a romance." Roxanne began cutting the truffles in circles.

Steve raised his glass to Skip's and smiled. "I do, that's true."

They drank, emptying their glasses.

"You any good at telling which ones will stick?" Skip poured the last drop of wine into his own glass, made a face at its demise, then got up and grabbed the second bottle.

"Sometimes. Here, let me." He took the corkscrew from Skip and opened the bottle swiftly with a soft pop. He first poured more into Roxanne's, then Skip's goblet.

Roxanne turned from the conversation to combine the scallops, truffles and asparagus on a plate. "I'm sorry, Steve, it was not my idea to put you in the middle of this. I'm sure you have no interest in what I do."

He rubbed one side of his face thoughtfully. "I wouldn't say that."

She turned to look at him, her face aglow either from the heat of the stove or from a blush.

"I'm very interested in what you do with the restaurant." He swirled the new wine in his glass, sniffed it, then took a sip. "Pretty good," he admitted. "I could get used to this part of the French atmosphere."

"What is it you want to know?" Her eyes seemed to glow, paralyzing him where he sat. "I'll tell you anything."

A shiver ran up his spine and he was again transported to some completely different situation in which she might say the exact same words.

A married man, he pondered. *How long had that gone on?*

He patted his breast pocket halfheartedly and smiled. "And here I've gone and forgotten my list of questions. Can I get back to you?"

She inclined her head. "Any time." Then she turned, took up the platter now filled with scallops, truffles and asparagus and added, "But first, dinner. Come on, into the dining room."

The dining room was really a dining area between the kitchen and living room, just as in Steve's apartment. But through the miracle of fabric and screens and lighting, not to mention a generous wooden country dining table, the place was transformed. It felt cozy and intimate.

Skip lit a series of candles on the table and a couple more on tall pedestals near the sideboard as Roxanne set out the food.

"So what did you do before buying this place?" Steve asked as they sat down around the table, arranging wineglasses, moving water glasses and picking up napkins.

Roxanne shot a quick glance at Skip, then said, "I was at the CIA for a year. I told you that, didn't I?"

"Yes, but, what did you do for a living? Acquiring this place was a pretty brave thing to do and couldn't have been cheap." He sent his eyes around the room as if to encompass the whole building.

She was silent a long minute and he looked back over at her. It might have been his imagination but her cheeks looked pink as she dished scallops onto Skip's plate.

"I, uh . . ."

"Do you mean does she have restaurant experience?" Skip interjected, picking up his knife and fork. "Because that's what I'd want to know if I were you. Who *is* this person taking over my place of employment?"

Skip looked at Roxanne and prompted her with a nod.

"Well, yes, of course you'd want to know that," she said with a light laugh. "And I have *years* of restaurant experience, trust me. My parents owned a restaurant in downtown D.C. I practically grew up in."

She held out a hand for Steve's plate.

"You mentioned that." He handed it to her. "At that first meeting. Mama's, right?"

She gave him a brilliant smile. "That's right. Did you know it?"

He watched her hands as she put his plate down on her empty one. "The name sounds familiar, but I can't really say I remember it."

She nodded, her smile fading slowly as she filled his plate. She handed it back to him. "So, have you, ah, been a bartender . . . long?"

He chuckled wryly and speared a scallop. "Too long, yes. Since college."

"So you went to college?"

His eyes shot quickly up to hers. Was that surprise in her voice? Did she think a lowly bartender wouldn't have gone to college? "Yes, in fact. UVA. History major."

Her brows rose, impressed. *Score one for Steve*, he

thought, and popped the scallop into his mouth. Perhaps he was rising in her estimation, if only a little.

As the first bite sank onto his palate, he had to stop and look down at his plate. The flavor was amazing—a rich, creamy burst of it in his mouth that was totally unexpected because of the simple look of the dish.

"This is incredible." He poked the fork at another scallop, as if making sure it was real. "What did you do to this?"

"Isn't it?" Skip said. He was focused on his plate as well.

"I wish I had gone to college," Roxanne said, almost wistfully.

Steve stopped eating. She hadn't gone to college? Now *he* felt like the snob. There was nothing wrong with her not going, of course, but he had her pegged as such a princess he was surprised she hadn't been personally escorted through Vassar or someplace.

"Never too late," was all he could think to say.

She laughed and her beauty hit him again. "I guess I've done all right without it so far. And I think I'll be a little too busy for a while now."

He gazed at her a long moment, longer than he'd intended. When she glanced back at him he dropped his gaze to his plate.

She had done all right, he thought, realizing that she hadn't answered his question about what she'd done before this. He hadn't been kidding when he'd said this building couldn't have been cheap. Throw in a business on top of that and she had to have some serious assets.

Family money? he wondered. His eyes swept her

face again, marveling at the smooth skin, the way her dark eyebrows gave the perfect tilt to her eyes.

She caught him looking at her again and his eyes darted away.

"Sorry," he said, "I don't mean to stare. I was just thinking how you could have been a model. You've got that look."

She gaped at him, clearly startled. She turned her head to Skip.

He looked back down at his plate, ashamed that he'd been reduced to saying something that sounded so much like a pickup line. "But I'm sure you've been told that before."

"Well, yes." She cleared her throat. "But I don't want to make money off my appearance. Ever. I did nothing to earn my looks."

She was so firm he felt stupid for having said anything. He wasn't even sure why he had, except that without the spoiled-rich-girl mantle he'd given her she had suddenly seemed even more stunning. *And she could be a model*, he thought, *let's face it*.

"Well, not so for me." He laughed a little too heartily. "I've worked hard for my craggy face and I use it. I think it makes the customers open up to me more."

She smiled, her voice emerging gently. "You don't have a craggy face."

He laughed again, stupidly, and ate one of the truffles. "This really is the most amazing food."

The entire meal was amazing, Steve thought. The best food he'd ever eaten, in fact. He didn't know why she was hiring a chef when she had this kind of talent herself, and he told her so.

She smiled self-deprecatingly. "If you think this is good, wait until you taste Monsieur Girmond's food. He's . . . he's a magician. He does things with food that you just have to see and taste to believe. He's an absolute artist."

She held her hands together at her heart as she said this and Steve could see the passion she had for her work. Considering it was food, it was a wonder she was so thin.

The conversation loosened up nicely throughout the meal and laughter began to flow almost as freely as the wine.

Steve found himself enjoying not just Skip's irreverent company, but Roxanne's wit as well. She seemed to have figured out the waitstaff pretty astutely, making it easy for him to offer what tidbits of information he had about each one. And he admitted to her that up till now he thought she'd made pretty prudent hiring and firing decisions.

She was surprisingly gratified by that.

"Thank you," she said warmly, "that makes me feel good. Especially when everyone's been saying how crazy I am to attempt this."

"Really?" Steve glanced at Skip.

"He's the worst one," Roxanne said sourly, sipping her wine.

"Well, don't you agree?" Skip said to Steve. "I mean, you've worked in restaurants since college, haven't you? Would *you* want to own one?"

Steve tilted his head, looking from Skip to Roxanne. "I don't know. It's not something I've ever considered."

Skip threw out a hand. "There you go."

"I don't mean it that way. I just was thinking about other stuff. Other goals."

"Like what?" Roxanne looked at him with interest.

It was his turn to be firm. If there was one thing he was sure of, it was that he didn't want to talk about his aspiration before he achieved his goal. He didn't want to be seen as some pathetic wannabe. Not by anybody, but especially not by Roxanne Rayeaux.

"Nothing I've accomplished yet," he said with a tempering smile. "But I'll let you know when I do."

His tone was obviously effective, because Roxanne didn't press. Instead she excused herself to get the desserts.

If Steve thought dinner was fantastic, dessert was a whole other story. She'd prepared several things to try out for the restaurant, so it was something of an orgy of sweets after the meal. A crème brûlée, something called a *bombe Andalouse*, a chocolate Napoleon and fresh fruit in a sabayon sauce.

"I think I've died and gone to heaven," Steve moaned, leaning back in the chair.

Roxanne brought out espressos for the three of them. "Did I kill you?" she asked with a wicked grin.

His eyes warmed on her. "You did. And what a way to go. This was the most incredible meal I've ever had. I know I keep saying that, but it's true."

Roxanne laughed and cast her eyes down to her coffee as she sat. "I'm glad you liked it. Maybe now you won't be so resistant to French food."

"I think a lot of things on that list are getting more palatable." He held up a hand to Skip. "But don't go out of your way to track down a French film."

"How about a French poodle?" Roxanne asked.

Skip put a hand to his chin and drummed his fingers along his cheek. "Hmm, I'm trying to remember what else was on that list."

"Skip." Roxanne's voice held a warning. She knew just what he was referring to; she could tell by the fiendish look he gave her.

"French toast, I think." He grinned at Roxanne and she lifted a brow. "But it's not quite time for breakfast. Yet." He glanced at his watch, then sat bolt upright in his chair. "Holy shit, is this right? Is it really midnight?"

Roxanne smirked and looked into the kitchen at the clock. Nothing like instant payback for his evil intentions. "So it is. And on a school night." She tsked.

"Oh my God, I've got to go. I have an eight a.m. P.E. class to teach." He shot out of his chair and looked around for his coat. "Rox, I'm so sorry to leave you with all these dishes."

"Don't worry." She waved a hand. She was feeling so relaxed at the moment she was even thinking she might leave them until morning, something she almost never did. "Go, get some sleep. Thank you for coming."

"Thank *you*, doll." He kissed her cheek while dragging on his jacket. "Spectacular meal, as usual." He turned to Steve, hand outstretched. "Steve, good to spend time with you. Hope to see you again."

They shook.

"Might be hard to avoid me," Steve said.

Roxanne looked at him in surprise, her cheeks heating. What did he mean by that? Had she been too nice to him? Had he seen through her to that tiny piece of her that tonight had found him attractive?

Oh God, she thought. Did he think now that maybe . . . maybe he would be having, uh, dinner here more often?

But he must have caught her expression.

"I live right upstairs," he added quickly. "And work right downstairs. Hell, I never leave the building except for special occasions."

Roxanne sighed.

Skip laughed and slapped him on the back. "Oh. For a second there I thought you meant—"

"Good night, Skip," Roxanne said firmly.

"Good night, Roxie." With a grin and a wave, he dashed through the door.

Steve looked after him, his face a study in contrasts in the candlelight. He was really quite handsome, she thought, noting the shadows at his cheekbones, the light shining through his gray eyes. She even liked the way he slumped in his chair, all casual and angled.

But Steve, here for, uh, dinner, more often?

No, she shook her head. *No.* He was an *employee*, for God's sake. Not to mention just totally inappropriate for her anyway.

She tried to picture him at the Met and knew he'd sooner hunt rattlesnakes than go to an opera. Tried to imagine him strolling through an art gallery, sipping a glass of chardonnay, and could only imagine him scoffing at the idea. *Real men do Jell-O shooters.*

No, he was not her type. She wanted a guy like Martin. Handsome, cultured, urbane.

Steve might be handsome, but he was as cultured as a dime-store pearl.

Martin, on the other hand, had had connections all over New York City, knew everyone who was anyone, had his own limo and never failed to get into the most exclusive openings.

Yes, call her shallow, but she knew what she wanted, because she'd almost had it. It was another Martin she was after.

Well, a Martin minus the wife.

"Is he going to be okay to drive?" Steve asked, looking back at her.

She forced herself back to the present and started picking up plates. She was *not* going to start thinking about Martin. "He takes the metro."

Steve rose too, and picked up glasses. "You're kidding. That's like a mile away. I should give him a ride."

That got her attention. He was completely sincere. It would never have occurred to Martin to give Skip a ride. "What a nice thought. But don't bother. He runs. You'd never catch him now."

"He *runs*?"

"Yeah. He's a fitness instructor and a coach. He prides himself on being in shape. I know it's crazy, believe me, I tell him all the time, but he regularly runs to the metro after a night out. Says it works off the night's excesses faster."

"Okay . . ."

Roxanne laughed and shook her head. "I know." She headed into the kitchen.

Steve followed. When she turned on the hot water, he took her by the shoulders and gently moved her aside.

The instant he touched her, her skin warmed and she felt like melting back into him. How long had it been since she'd been held, or even touched? A year?

Longer? Sometimes she felt starved for it, and now was one of those times.

"Let me do this," Steve said, adjusting the water temperature. Water flowed over his hands and through his fingers, making them look both graceful and hard. "You just cooked the best meal I've ever had. You are *not* doing the dishes, too."

She stepped back carefully and attempted to get a grip on her libido.

One kiss, she thought, *would be so nice. Just one hot kiss, hard arms around me. Passion. Heat. God, it would feel so nice.*

She sighed. Steve looked over at her and smiled.

But not with Steve, she told herself, moving away to one of the island bar stools. *Definitely not with Steve. The last thing you need is a one-night stand with a bartender. Or worse, a relationship with someone so different from what you want. If you want to be touched by someone, wait for your date.*

But the idea of P.B. was as appealing as trying to eat another piece of cheese. She was stuffed and tired and pleasantly hazy from the wine. And Steve was right here . . .

She pushed the leftover brie away and picked up a wineglass. She was fairly certain it was hers. She tipped the contents into her mouth and watched Steve's back.

"You're doing a pretty efficient job there, Steve. Somebody raised you right."

She could see him laugh even as she heard it, his head dipping slightly and his back moving under his shirt, but he didn't turn around. She smiled.

"I'll take that as a compliment," he said. "You see, I have hidden assets as an employee."

There, she pointed out to herself. *Right there, even he's saying he's an employee. And boss-employee relationships don't work. Especially when it happens only because the boss is horny and the employee handy.*

"So in a pinch I can use you as a dishwasher," she said, thinking, *It's a pinch now, can I use you for something else?* This thought actually made her giggle.

Steve turned around, a half smile on his face. "What's going on back there?"

She sighed and put a hand over her mouth. "I'm sorry. I seem to have had a bit too much to drink."

"Join the club." He turned back to the dishes. "Good thing I don't have to get up in the morning."

She sat in silence and watched him work for a while, alternately marshalling her fantasies and letting them run free. She felt so relaxed and happy at the moment she almost couldn't hang on to the idea that anything she did now would be wrong.

She'd gotten through a vigorous year of schooling. Made the move from New York. Broken off completely with Martin. Bought this house and started a restaurant. Or rather, almost started it. But here she was, back home with friends. She'd had a lovely evening with people who wanted nothing from her. Everything so far had worked out. She should celebrate that.

She smiled to herself and folded her arms in front of her. She was happy, she thought. What a lovely feeling that was.

Steve finished the dishes, just as she was coming to this conclusion, and he turned from the sink, wiping his hands on a dish towel.

She even had a handsome man in her kitchen. What could be better?

"I think that's it." He looked at her warmly. "I better go, too. Let you get some sleep."

"Hmm, yes." She rose from the stool as he moved into the living room.

At the door, he stopped. She stopped too, maybe a little closer than she might have a bottle of wine or two ago. Just slightly inside his personal space.

"Thanks for dinner. It was . . ." He looked down at her and she could tell he was aware of how close they were. "Amazing."

"Thanks for coming." She smiled slightly, let her eyes drift to his lips. "And for cleaning up. There's nothing like a man who cleans."

She was close enough to smell the soap he used. To hear his breathing. To feel the slight breeze of it on her cheek.

Slowly, she moved her gaze from his lips back to his eyes and saw the heat in them. Her lips curved a bit more. She would see if he did something, if he made a move. If he did . . . well, maybe just one kiss . . . a kiss didn't have to mean anything . . .

"Okay," he said softly.

She watched the pulsing of the artery in his neck, thought about how it would feel to put her lips on it.

She was incorrigible, she thought. But God, she was *hungry*.

She looked back up into his face and saw an answering hunger there. So when he bent down to kiss her cheek, she shifted her face, ever so slightly, at the last minute so he caught the corner of her mouth.

He drew slightly back, just enough for them to focus on each other's eyes, and stayed there an eternal moment. Roxanne held her breath under his assessing gaze. Then, when she couldn't take it another second, she moved forward that bare inch and touched her lips to his again.

She almost felt the *whoosh* of the genie leaving the bottle.

Steve stepped closer and put an arm around her waist, cinching her in tight to his body. She raised her hands to his shoulders and her mouth opened under his. Their tongues found each other and mated, their lips moving in synch, a dance, an age-old interplay of heat and sex and desire.

And restraint.

Steve pulled back first, his expression intense, his eyes searching.

Roxanne couldn't hold his gaze. She put a hand to her lips and tried to slow her breathing. "Thank you," she said, apropos of nothing, in a near whisper.

He hesitated a fraction of a second, then answered, "Good night."

7

Bar Special
Scotch Sling ~~for that unexpected injury~~
Scotch, soda, lemon peel

"How come you sound so muffled?" Steve's sister, Dana, asked.

"Because I have a pillow over my head." Steve pushed the pillow off and readjusted the phone receiver at his ear.

"What are you doing still in bed? It's almost noon."

He could hear Dana doing something in the background. No doubt cleaning or cooking or doing something for one of the kids. She had a husband and three children and never seemed to stop moving.

"I'm getting over one of the stupidest nights of my life," he said, with probably too much honesty. But what the heck, Dana almost always got his secrets out of him anyway, and he usually felt better after the swift shot upside the head she gave him for them.

"Oh no. What have you done now?" She was stern, but he could hear the grim smile in her voice.

"Hell, I don't know. I was stupid, that's all. There's something wrong with me. If there's something I shouldn't do, I do it."

"Oh good God, you didn't get back with Lia, did you? If you ask me, that girl is the reason you've never had a decent relationship."

Steve turned over onto his side and looked at the digital clock—11:57. "Well, I didn't ask you, but now that it's out there, why do you say that?"

Dana sighed. "Because she's there for you. You need sex, she's there. You need some kind of female companionship, she's there. She's not perfect, but she's *there*. And that satisfies you enough that you never look for anything different."

He scoffed. "That shows how much *you* know. If that were true I wouldn't have done the stupid thing last night."

"Which was . . . ?" She sounded intrigued.

It was his turn to sigh. He almost didn't know how to describe what had happened. On the one hand, it was simple. He'd *kissed* her. But on the other, it made absolutely no sense at all. For no earthly reason, without any anticipation of doing it beforehand, he'd kissed her.

What the hell had he been thinking?

From the headboard, the pillow dropped back onto his head and he let it stay. "I think I hit on my new boss."

Dana let out a burst of air. "*What?* The one P.B.'s going out with?"

Steve frowned and put his hand over his eyes. "He just has a date with her, that's all. It's not like she's his girlfriend or anything."

Still, the feeling burning his skin was shame. As unintentional as it was, he'd undercut his buddy. P.B. may be a lot of things, but he'd been a friend of Steve's for a lot of years.

Dana was still sputtering on the phone. "Oh yeah, he just has a date with her. Nothing to keep you from hitting on her. So, what—how—what did you do? How in the world did it happen?"

Steve chuckled wryly. "Well, she looked good, better than usual."

Dana inhaled sharply, in preparation for, he could tell, giving him hell.

"Just kidding," he said quickly, laughing. "She always looks fabulous, it's one of her biggest flaws. But last night she looked . . . accessible. Or something. Smiling. She has this great smile. Real first rate, when she decides to trot it out. And last night for the first time it seemed really, I don't know, easy. Uncalculated."

"So, you, what? Asked her out? Pinched her ass? What?"

"I kissed her."

"You kissed her," Dana repeated, dry as dust.

"And her friend was there," Steve continued, needing to explain, if only to make himself understand, "not when I kissed her. Before. This guy Skip. And he was funny and kind of laid back. Made us all laugh. Got rid of some of Roxanne's usual edginess."

"So, you kissed her."

"I guess I was lulled into a sense of security. Yeah, that's what it was. She made this incredible meal, we had a lot of wine."

"So . . ."

"I kissed her."

Dana laughed. "How'd she take it?"

Steve thought, remembering the moment at the door, when Roxanne had stood so close to him that he could smell her perfume, or maybe it was just her shampoo. In any case, she was *close*, with that little knowing smile. She had done it on purpose. Hadn't she?

He simply could not fathom why she would.

But, she had turned her head for his kiss, hadn't she? Turned her head at the last minute to capture his lips as he went for her cheek.

It just didn't make sense. She wouldn't do that. She was control personified. Coolness incarnate. She had the world by the balls. Didn't she?

Who knew? He sure couldn't figure her out when he was having a hard time understanding himself.

"She didn't slap me or anything, so I guess she took it okay. Hard to say. I was so surprised by it myself, I can't imagine what she was thinking." He scratched the side of his face and pushed the pillow back again. "Honestly Dana, for the life of me I can't figure out why I did it. I was leaning in to kiss her cheek as I was leaving, which was weird in itself, and then it just . . . happened."

"But, you were there for dinner? She invited you to dinner? That must have meant she was interested." She paused. "Except she's your boss. That's not good."

He grimaced. "Her friend invited me, really."

"The guy? Is he gay?"

"No. He's just one of those guys. We ran into each other at the grocery store. They were buying stuff for dinner and he said I should come. It was obviously a whim. And she didn't look too into it. I tried to get out of it but this guy Skip was pretty relentless. But then, we . . . I guess we had a good time."

Good enough that she would need—or expect—a kiss good night? No. *What had he been thinking?* But there it was. He'd accidentally kissed her, and he wasn't even a kiss-on-the-cheek kind of guy.

It was a damn fine kiss, though. Damn fine.

"I have to say, Steve,"—Dana's voice was matter-of-fact—"I think you might have taken something the wrong way. From what you've said about this woman, it doesn't sound like she'd want to carry on with someone she works with."

"We're not *carrying on*, Dana. It was a *moment*. A really strange moment." He pushed himself up in bed and leaned back on the headboard.

"You sure it wasn't just a forbidden moment? You know how you are, Steve. You always want what you think you can't have."

"Thanks for the pop psychology, Sis. Really clarifying."

"Glad you liked it."

"I'm serious. Something weird happened right at the door, as I was leaving. She was standing really close and, I don't know, I think she went for the kiss. I can't imagine why, but she did. It was like there was some kind of weird, gravitational pull or . . . or . . ."

"Destiny," Dana said dramatically.

"Yeah right. That's the word I was looking for," Steve said dryly. "And now I'm destined to get fired."

The Call Waiting beeped.

"Steve—"

"Wait. That's my other line. Hang on a sec, can you, Dana?"

"Actually no. As riveted as I am by this turn of events, I have to go get Jamie. Call me later, though, okay? I'm going to mull this over and come up with the answer."

"You do that." He pushed the flash button on the phone, finally awake and realizing it was nearly noon. He had work to do. He couldn't lie in bed all day lamenting the most stupid thing he'd done in years.

"Yeah," he said into the receiver.

"Where the hell are you?" P.B., too loud and sounding annoyed, spoke from what sounded like an echo chamber.

"Where the hell are *you*?" Steve rubbed a hand through his hair, massaging his scalp.

"I'm at the gym, where *you're* supposed to be. Remember you said you'd fill in for Larry?"

Steve closed his eyes, remembering some vague conversation about a handball game.

"Today?" Steve rubbed his eyes. He couldn't see P.B. today. P.B., who would want to talk about his date this week, with Roxanne Rayeaux.

"Yes, today, genius. Right now. Jesus, what the hell have you been doing?" The sound of tennis shoes on a wooden gym floor squeaked through the receiver.

"I, uh, overslept. Sorry, Peeb. Can't we just do it another—?"

"Oh come on, you're five minutes away. Drag your ass outa bed and get over here. It'll do you good. What'd you do last night, see Lia again?"

Steve sighed. "No, nothing like that. I'm just tired. All right, let me get my stuff together. I'll be there in ten minutes."

"Great, I'll reserve the court for another hour, if I can."

Steve hung up the phone, trying several times to set it straight in the cradle.

So now he had to go face P.B.

He wasn't a fool. He wasn't going to tell him what happened with Roxanne—especially since he was absolutely certain it wouldn't happen again. In fact, he wouldn't be surprised if Roxanne didn't want him to work there now.

Not that she'd fire him, he thought. No, she'd just pull him aside and talk to him in that low, sultry voice, making him understand that it would be better for both of them if he didn't take the job after all. Surely he could see that, couldn't he?

For some reason, he could picture the scene perfectly.

He got out of bed, his bare feet hitting the cold wood floor. He wondered if the wood floor in Roxanne's bedroom was as cold and doubted it. She probably had rugs. And comforters on the bed. Pillows, lots of pillows. Maybe a canopy. He pictured her hair spread long and lacy on a white pillowcase, those dark eyes half closed and catlike . . .

Steve swore. This was nuts. He opened a dresser

drawer, pulled out gym shorts and slammed the drawer shut. Opened another, pulled out socks and slammed it. Opened a third, grabbed a T-shirt and slammed it, just as the phone rang again.

It was Dana, from her cell phone. "I just thought of an important question."

"What's that?" He sat on the side of the bed, pushed the receiver between his cheek and shoulder, and un-balled the socks with both hands.

"When you kissed her, your *boss*, you randy dog, did she kiss you back?"

Steve stopped, one sock in each hand, and let his arms drop to his sides. "Yeah," he said slowly. He took the receiver in his left hand and straightened his neck, remembering the way her lips had opened under his, the way her hands had taken the front of his shirt in a tight, unequivocal grip. "Yeah, actually, she did."

He frowned. His body had responded so powerfully, so instantly, he'd been shocked at himself. Which is when—and why—he'd stopped, as if awakened from some truly bizarre dream. One you had no idea where it came from.

And at the end—it was coming back to him now—had she really said "Thank you"? Or had he just dreamed that too? At that point his mind was so blown he couldn't trust himself to remember any of it right.

"Huh," Dana said, road noise washing white in the background.

"Yeah," Steve said, "huh."

Roxanne was thrilled Monsieur Girmond was finally arriving. Ever since she'd met him—eight years ago in his restaurant in New York—he'd been like a father to her. She had been fairly close to her own father when he was alive—the whole family, she, her sister, brother and father, had united to deal with her mother, their feared and fearless leader—but her father had never been as protective and nurturing as M. Girmond.

When she met him, she'd been lunching at La Finesse with her agent, a fast-talking, know-it-all dealmaker named Derek Gold, picking through a dressing-less salad when the chef had come to their table. Apparently he knew Derek—as all of New York City seemed to—and wanted to know why he was lunching with a beautiful girl and only buying her a salad. Roxanne explained that she was a model and had to watch what she ate, though she eyed the food around her covetously.

M. Girmond immediately declared this a crime, and vowed that the next time she came in he would prepare for her a feast fit for a queen but that would add not an ounce of weight to her peerless frame.

She'd laughed, embarrassed, and had not taken him seriously. But the next time she'd gone in, as it happened about two weeks later, again with Derek, M. Girmond prepared a salad with a light vinegar dressing, followed by sole on watercress, followed by a tiny scoop of fresh homemade sorbet. When she'd gone back to the kitchen to thank him, he'd insisted she come in at least once a week so he could keep her healthy. It was one thing to be skinny, he said, but another to be sick. He would keep her thin and glowing, he promised, if she promised to come "take his light offerings off his hands."

They had become fast friends. Roxanne had often

thought it lucky that she'd met M. Girmond when she had, before she'd been in New York too long. Before her modeling career had taken off and she'd stopped trusting anyone. If she had met him after five years instead of two, for example, she would never have gone back to the restaurant, figuring he wanted something from her she would not want to give.

Then, years later, when she told him she was giving up modeling to go to the CIA for a year, he confided that he was thinking of retiring. La Finesse was too big, New York too busy, and he missed his daughters, who now lived in D.C. Roxanne said she was thinking of going back to D.C., too, and would love to open a pastry shop. After much discussion they realized that together they could start a French restaurant that would accommodate both of their desires while remaining small enough to keep them both sane.

If she had gotten nothing else from her years in New York—and she had, of course—she was glad to have met M. Girmond.

He was coming to the restaurant at noon and they were to discuss the kitchen, the menu and the staff. She had been consulting him all along on the renovations and equipment purchasing via email and fax, and now it was time for him to put his stamp on things.

Roxanne was relieved. So much of running a restaurant lay on the chef's shoulders, and M. Girmond was experienced enough to handle this with ease. Shifting some of the burden onto him would be a welcome relief now.

She unlocked the restaurant door from the street and entered the small front foyer. It smelled like fresh paint and new varnish. She inhaled it deeply, thinking, *I've still done this right, whatever else I might have screwed up.*

She pushed the image of Steve behind the now-empty bar from her head. She had to focus. She didn't have time for adolescent hormonal reactions to men. Particularly not men on her staff.

The decorators had done a wonderful job on the small space, successfully transforming it from a gritty college-style pub to a quaint, warm restaurant. The bar gleamed in the unlit room, ambient light from the windows glancing off its surface and making the copper on the lamps hanging from the ceiling glow.

The exposed brick walls gave the place a close feeling that was warmed by the rich wood of the bar and tables and the light French country fabrics on the chairs and window treatments. Individual lamps hung over each table, and plants, low screens and a few carefully chosen metal sculptures broke the room up into separate areas where diners could eat and converse in relative privacy.

Roxanne was extremely pleased with the look.

She moved into the dining room and sat in a chair near the fireplace. It was cold, of course, but she imagined the roaring fire she would ensure was tended nightly in the winter months. She stared into its imaginary depths and thought about what she'd done last night.

Her impulse was to believe she'd made a fool of herself. For a stupid, stupid reason. But she fought that. No, she understood why she'd done what she'd done, and it certainly wasn't a crime. She was a woman nearing thirty, no longer a green girl with illusions of romance, and she had, well, needs. Physical hungers. She'd been without a man for over a year—though

Martin had shown up at the CIA one night and very
nearly convinced her he was ready to commit to her—
and she wanted one. It was as simple as that.

Her stupidity lay in choosing Steve. He was her employee, and getting involved with him, even just sexually, would be a distraction on the job she could not
afford.

She needed to be careful. If she wanted a convenient
relationship, she needed it to be separate from her job,
separate from the place she'd created here. Restaurants
were a small, small world when it came to relationships.
Not to mention that she didn't want a relationship with
Steve. She wanted someone with class and stability,
someone who'd be interested in the symphony, plays at
the Kennedy Center, dinner at the Willard. Someone
who knew what he wanted from life and how to get it.

The bottom line was, she wanted someone who liked
the same things she did, wanted to do what she liked to
do. She had no idea what she and Steve would find to
do together.

Other than the obvious.

A hot flash of hunger seared her as she remembered
last night's kiss. They both had enjoyed doing *that*, she
thought wryly.

The question was, what did she do now that she'd
cracked open that can of worms? Talk to him about it?
He wasn't exactly the easiest person to talk to. Most of
the time he seemed to deliberately misunderstand her.
But then, subtlety wasn't likely to work either.

"Bonjour, mon ange!" M. Girmond's voice rolled into
the room like a warm breeze on a cool day.

Roxanne turned to the door and smiled, rising to her feet. "Monsieur Girmond."

He was a tall man but he gave more an impression of roundness, with a round balding head, round glasses, a wide girth and thick, sausage-fingered hands. The next most noticeable thing about him was that he was always smiling. When he ran La Finesse, people were constantly calling looking for work with him because not only was he one of the best chefs in town, he was also one of the most liked.

She walked toward him, her hands outstretched. He took them in his callused ones and they kissed both cheeks, European style.

"I'm so glad you're finally here," she said, unable to dim the smile on her face. "How is the move going? Are you all here?"

"Ah, *oui*. It goes very well, very well, *mon trésor*. And you, how are you living here back home? You feel good, *oui*? You look *magnifique*." He held one of her hands out and stepped back, as if they'd just performed a dance move, to survey her from head to foot.

"*Merci beaucoup*." She inclined her head. "The move has gone fine. I'm still adjusting, I think, to being here, but I'm all unpacked. And I'm glad I did it. It's been good to see old friends again."

She thought about last night's dinner, how relaxed she'd felt, but the memory was ruined by its ending. Would she feel so bad, she wondered, if she'd impulsively kissed someone who did not work for her?

"And this place," M. Girmond said, walking into the center of the small dining room and turning in a slow circle, "*c'est parfait! Bien joue!* I feel that I am back in Provence, in the house of my *grande-mère*. Lovely, lovely."

Roxanne clutched her hands together in front of her and scanned the room again. "Do you really like it? There were so many decisions to make, I second-guessed myself every step of the way."

"It is perfect." M. Girmond faced her again with a smile. He took her clasped hands together in his and separated her tensely entwined fingers. "No more worries, *oui*? You and I, we do this to escape such things. This is *un petit restaurant*. Simple! We will enjoy ourselves. Have fun."

Roxanne felt as if a huge weight were being lifted from her chest and she inhaled what felt like the first truly unencumbered breath she'd taken in weeks.

"I know," she said on a long exhale. "Yes, you're right. Everything is fine now that you're here."

As she looked up into his face, her eyes were caught by a shape in the front window. She shifted her gaze only to have it land on Steve's as he peeked inside.

He looked as startled as she did and she raised her hand in an awkward wave. Steve did the same, then turned quickly away. He jogged across the street and down the sidewalk, out of sight.

"Who was that?" M. Girmond asked, turning his eyes back to her face, which was much hotter than it had been before seeing Steve.

"That was our bartender. Steve Serrano." She brushed the hair from her forehead and ran her fingers through it over the top of her head, looking toward the bar. "You'll meet him soon. He also lives upstairs, on the top floor."

At M. Girmond's silence, she looked at him and saw

his brows had risen. A small, very French smile curved his lips and he stroked his chin with one thick but gentle hand.

"I see," he said slowly.

She wasn't sure if it was just her guilty conscience, but she was afraid he really did see.

"Okay—*oof*." P.B. slapped the handball with a gloved palm and crab-jumped back to the center of the court. "I've made reservations at Le Gaulois, think she'll like that?"

Steve returned the ball, forcing P.B. to the back corner and took his place in the middle. "Sure."

P.B. lumbered to the corner, hit the ball and then grunted as his shoulder hit the wall. "What do you think we should talk about? I mean . . ."

He returned Steve's volley.

". . . what's she interested in?"

Steve slammed the ball to the crease where front wall met floor and it rolled off, impossible to return. He turned a triumphant grin on P.B. "Game!"

P.B. put his hands on his hips and panted. "Damn, Serrano. For a guy who doesn't exercise, you seem mighty cool."

Steve rolled his shoulders back a couple times and dipped his head from side to side, loosening up. "I exercise. Every day, practically."

"Bullshit." P.B. leaned over, hands on his knees.

Steve jogged in place. "No shit. I run and have free weights in my apartment. Come on, one more game, Blue Boy. How you gonna catch the bad guys if you can't play three straight handball games?"

"Give me a minute." P.B. straightened. "I want to know about Roxanne."

Steve made an annoyed face. "What makes you think I know anything?"

"Well for one thing, you had dinner at her place last night." P.B. wiped his forehead with a sweatbanded wrist, his eyes tight on Steve. "I still don't understand how you finagled that."

"Gimme a break. I didn't finagle anything. I was forced into it."

P.B. wagged a finger at him. "Trying to upstage me to win that bet? It ain't gonna work, compadre."

Steve laughed cynically. "You and your bet. Okay, I'll tell you what I observed last night. She's got class. She has posters from the New York City Ballet on her walls. She plays classical music. Bach, I think, last night. She speaks some French, though it might just be menu French for all I know. She reads, has tons of books on her shelves. Ah . . ." He stretched one arm overhead and did a side bend to stay warm, thinking about Roxanne Rayeaux's apartment. He was surprised how much he could recall about it. "She's got a knack for making a room comfortable. Good design sense, I guess. Likes rich colors. Is good with plants. And, most important to you, she loosens up nicely with a bottle of wine."

He tried not to imagine Roxanne leaning into P.B. the way she had leaned into him. Tried not to picture her lips parting and P.B. taking advantage of it. Tried not to see her lithe body being swallowed up by P.B.'s big muscular one.

He jogged in place again. "Come on, let's play."

P.B. stood with one hand on his hip, watching him. "That's a lot to remember."

Steve waved a hand in his direction. "Take notes."

"No, I mean for you. You seem to have been paying pretty close attention."

Steve shrugged. "I'm an observant guy. Now come on. Your serve." He trotted to center court and bounced on the balls of his feet.

"Tell me one more thing."

Steve sighed and dropped his hands, turning. "What?"

"What did you guys talk about last night?"

"I don't know. Regular stuff. Where're you from? Where'd you go to school? What did you do before? That kind of thing. The kind of thing *you* should ask her. Be interested."

"Hey, you don't have to tell me how to *date*, big guy. I *know* how to date. I just want to know what she's interested in so I can be prepared."

"Oh, so, what, you gonna go home and listen to some Bach?"

P.B. grinned. "Got any I can borrow?"

"Yeah, right. And I'll lend you my tape of *Swan Lake*, too. Come to think of it, I do have one of those NFL tapes set to ballet music."

P.B. snorted. "I've got that one, too. That's pretty funny. Maybe she'd like that."

Steve just turned and gave him a deadpan look over his shoulder. "Come on, let's play."

"One more thing."

He turned back. "You said that a minute ago."

"I mean it this time." P.B. tossed him the ball. "You get a look at her bedroom?"

Steve crossed his arms over his chest and tried to look stern, but he couldn't help wondering if he might have been *able* to see her bedroom last night, if he'd reacted differently to the kiss. If he hadn't stopped it, if he'd said something other than "Good night."

His gut clenched.

He scowled. "No, I didn't see her bedroom. Why?"

P.B. gave him a shit-eating grin and said, "Just want to know what color flowers to bring, 'cause I'll be carrying 'em in there at the end of the night."

Steve dropped the ball and slammed it, hard, into the front wall. It went untouched by P.B. An unreturnable serve.

8

Bar Special
Rum/Brandy Flip—first one, then the other
Rum or cognac, bar syrup, nutmeg, 1 egg

Roxanne must have been crazy to have agreed to a date two days before the opening of Chez Soi. Especially a date with someone like P.B. From the first moments of the evening it was obvious he had no desire to talk about the restaurant, or indeed anything but himself. Not that Roxanne blamed him for this; she was sure the restaurant wasn't all that interesting if you weren't involved. And since it had been about all she'd had on her mind for months, she found she was something of a one-note conversationalist.

During dinner a lovely French country meal at Le Gaulois, she'd had a hard time not examining the food and pointing out how they'd cooked it, what was in it, and how Chez Soi would be either the same or different, just as good or better.

P.B. listened with patience at first, making the effort to look interested and nodding along, asking the occasional question. But after a while he'd begun to interrupt her and soon was talking pretty much nonstop about himself.

Surprisingly, Roxanne found this something of a relief. She didn't want to have to think up other things to say about her life when all she could think about was her current project—and by *project* she meant the entire move from New York and the subsequent shift in her way of thinking.

She was busy breaking old habits—like thinking about how she looked all the time and watching every little thing she ate. She was relieved to be out of the pressure cooker of the high-fashion scene, and had given up the destructive pattern of alternately fitting in and kicking Martin out of her life. Now she was concentrating hard on making new habits, healthy ones.

So letting P.B. ramble on about "life on the job" and "collaring perps" was fine with her. And he was interesting. She'd never known a cop personally before. It sounded like a world unto itself.

The only problem was, he wouldn't let the evening end. She had unfortunately started out the date tired from a long day in the kitchen with M. Girmond and overindulging at dinner had only left her sleepier. But after dinner, P.B. had insisted on taking her to Murphy's Pub, his favorite bar now that Charters was gone.

Murphy's was a lively place with lots of people and good music, and because P.B. knew almost everyone who worked there they were still able to score a seat at the bar. Though it was freezing outside, the crowd was so tight and the thermostat had been cranked up so high to compensate that after about ten minutes Roxanne had to take off her sweater.

She pulled it over her head, trying hard not to elbow anyone next to her, and shook her hair loose, glancing at P.B. just in time to see his eyes jerk up from her breasts. It startled her, the suggestiveness of his gaze.

He leaned close, his breath fanning her cheek, and grinned. "Can I help you with that?"

She brought the sweater down between them, forcing him back a few inches, and pulled her hands from the sleeves. With an impersonal smile she said, "No thanks."

He backed off. "Hey, I heard you had dinner with Steve the other night." He raised a pint glass of Guinness to his lips, his eyes steady on her.

Roxanne folded the sweater in her lap and rested her fingers against her glass of wine but did not pick it up. "I did, yes. Skip and I ran into him at Whole Foods. We saved him from a night of carry-out."

"Hah! Good old Steve and his carry-out. That's what he said." P.B.'s light eyes were on her with a small smile that made her wonder just what else Steve had told him about the evening. "He's a pretty good guy, Steve is. But we're all still waiting on him to grow up, if you know what I mean."

"We are?"

He shrugged one shoulder. "Sure. I'm pretty close to his family and I know his sister wishes he'd get a real job and settle down. For a long time now he's been, you know, pretty stuck."

Roxanne stifled a yawn. "You mean stuck in his job?"

"Yeah and, you know, in his life. He doesn't have much drive. No ambition. I tried to get him on the force once." P.B. boomed a laugh. "Said he didn't even want to attempt it. He was happy doing what he was doing."

Roxanne tried to picture Steve's lanky frame and general air of insouciance contained in a police uniform. "No, I can't really see him as a cop."

"Me neither, tell you the truth. He doesn't have the right attitude. But he needed some direction and I thought he could cut it, make it through training. Maybe make something of himself, you know?"

"You don't think he's made anything of himself?"

P.B. tilted his head and gave her a benevolent smile. "Don't get me wrong. I think Steve's a great guy. But let's face it, he could be doing something a helluva lot better than bartending. I mean, where's that gonna get him?"

Roxanne nodded, not really liking the fact that she agreed with this. Or maybe she just didn't like talking about Steve with P.B. She still hadn't talked to him about the kiss they'd shared and was feeling strange about what he must be thinking. It had only been a couple days, but she felt more and more strongly that she needed to define it for both of them as something that could not be repeated. But the two times she'd gone upstairs to knock on his door he hadn't been home.

Or he hadn't been answering.

"What about all that history he studies?" Roxanne asked. "Does he do anything with that?"

P.B. grinned. "Hell, yeah. He impresses the hell out of women at the bar. Makes him sound smart, I think."

"Surely that's not the only reason he does it. He even

goes down to the Library of Congress. He must be doing something with it."

P.B. shrugged, careless. "It's just a hobby. I mean, what's he gonna do with history, huh? It's not like he's gonna become a professor or anything."

"He could go to law school," Roxanne mused. Would that make him seem more eligible, she wondered. Was she really just all about careers?

No, she knew it was more than that. It was a guy with direction. Purpose. Somebody looking for some meaning in life.

"Yeah, right," P.B. scoffed. "Steve, a lawyer. He'd be about as cutthroat as Santa Claus."

"Santa decides who's naughty and who's nice," she pointed out.

P.B.'s eyes gleamed. "And are you naughty, Roxanne?"

Roxanne resisted the urge to roll her eyes. Instead she shifted her eyes away from him and said, "Well, all I know is Steve's making good money and he seems happy enough. Isn't that all any of us can ask? To be happy in our work?"

"Sure." He smiled at her, his eyelids half lowered. "I like the way you think, Roxanne. You're generous, you know that?" He let that statement hang a moment, while Roxanne took a sip of her wine. "And who could blame Steve for being happy? The way things were at Charters, back when it was popular, he was like a rock star. You know how the bartenders at hot spots are. He got the girls, made the bucks, partied after work and slept all day. Great life for a twenty-five-year-old. But Steve's thirty now. How's he gonna feel in five years?

Or ten? Permanently hungover, that's how. Hungover by *life*."

"Hmm." Roxanne let her eyes scan P.B.'s solid frame as he looked off down the bar. He waved to another friend—he had many here—and laughed at something they said or did. Roxanne was too tired to turn around and look.

But P.B. was right. Steve was the kind of guy with a lot of charisma, the kind that made him a social success early in life. But it took drive in addition to charisma to really get somewhere. And it took a lot of hard work.

"So what's your goal, P.B.?" she asked him, forcing herself to remember with whom she was on a date. And as dates went, she could do worse than P.B. He'd taken her out for a nice dinner.

"Me?" He looked delighted at the question. "I'm working toward detective. Then, what the hell, maybe chief. I tell you, I got a helluva lot more ideas for running that place than the current chief. He's all right, but he doesn't think, you know? I'm always thinking." He tapped a finger to his head and looked at her intently, as if she might not have understood just what he meant.

"Sure," she said, holding back another yawn as if her life depended on it. "I can tell that about you."

And she could. But she would have used the word *calculating* instead of *thinking*. Something about him struck her as very shrewd.

"So, Roxanne." He said her name in a half growl and grinned at her. "I like saying your name. Rrrrrroxanne. Roxie."

She smiled, wishing she were home in bed. Alone.

He leaned one hand on the bar beside her and let his

hip touch her legs. "I was looking in the paper and saw the National Symphony's playing some Bach in a couple weeks. Wanna go? Bach's one of my favorites."

"Really?" Roxanne couldn't hide her surprise.

"Yeah, I like all that classical stuff." He waved a hand nonchalantly but kept his eyes expectantly on her face. "Whaddya say?"

The last thing she would have guessed was that P.B. was a classical music fan. But then, ever since Martin, she'd had to doubt all her perceptions about men. And this was just more evidence of how off her instincts could be.

She straightened on the bar stool and took a deep breath in an attempt to wake up. "Well, it sounds great, but I'll have to let you know. I'm not sure how the restaurant will be doing, but it's going to keep me really busy, especially at first. These things take up a lot of time. And I mean *a lot*."

P.B. sank down on an elbow, bringing himself even closer to her, and fingered the ends of one lock of her hair. His hand lingered close to her breast. "Aw, come on." He gave her a boyish smile. "It's just a couple hours, one evening. I'll make sure it's a night you're closed."

She was sorry now she'd told him they were only going to be open Wednesday through Saturday at first. But then she wondered why she was sorry—an evening at the symphony sounded fabulous. Just the kind of thing she'd been missing without Martin. But . . . with P.B.?

"Okay," she said, regretting it instantly.

He beamed and clutched her upper arm in one big square hand. "Great. That's great."

"But, can I let you know when it would be best?" She was desperate to backpedal. From the look on P.B.'s face it seemed he thought she'd just agreed to far more than a night at the symphony. "I just know these first few weeks are going to be hell. Exhausting hell. And speaking of that"—she looked pointedly at her watch—"I really should be going. I have so much to do tomorrow."

P.B. stroked a hand down her upper arm familiarly. "Sure, Babe. Whatever you say. I'm ready to blow this joint, too."

Roxanne felt simultaneously drawn to and repelled by the contact. Her body ached for a soft touch—she'd always been very physical in her relationships—but her desire was different from what she'd experienced the other night with Steve. Then she had felt overwhelmed with need, and blind to the consequences. With P.B., all of her senses rebelled against the idea of him touching her.

They drove the short blocks back to Roxanne's building. P.B. pulled his Chevy Suburban into the back alley and left it in the spot where Steve usually parked his truck, as well as part of the space next to it. Getting out, he looked displeased as she opened her own door and let herself out her side, just as he had earlier in the evening. And just as he had earlier in the evening, he said, "I was going to get that for you."

"That's all right." She moved toward the back door, rummaging through her purse for her keys, and turned when she reached the threshold. "Thanks so much, P.B. I had a really nice evening." She smiled and held out her hand.

P.B. looked taken aback, then covered it quickly with

a smile and took her hand, cradling it in both of his. "I was going to walk you to your door."

"This *is* my door." She laughed lightly, hoping to sound less off-putting than she knew she was being.

He paused, his expression skeptical. "So it is." He lifted her fingers to his lips and kissed them.

Involuntarily, her fingers clenched, more out of a desire to make a fist and pull away than anything else. But P.B. misunderstood and tightened his grip. He tried to draw her closer.

She resisted.

"You are . . ." He growled low in his throat and smiled as if they were playing a game. "Irresistible. *Rrroxanne*. Now come on, all I want's a hug." He pulled on her hand again companionably. "I had a nice night, too."

She was being a jerk, she thought, and let him pull her into his bearlike embrace. There was actually something somewhat comforting about it. He was big and solidly built, and he smelled clean, like laundry detergent. She patted his back with one hand, her face squished against his chest. But the hug went on just a tad too long.

And then a car's headlights lit up the alley. Roxanne pulled her head back enough to see Steve's truck round the corner from the street.

P.B. didn't let her go immediately, but leaned down and gave her a solid, closed-lip kiss on the mouth before stepping slowly back.

More than enough time, Roxanne was sure, for Steve—who was vainly looking for his parking spot— to see them and suspect that they'd been doing more than sharing one reluctant kiss.

Roxanne's face burned with humiliation. Nothing

like being caught kissing one man by the man you'd kissed just days earlier.

What in the world would Steve think of her? And what would he tell the rest of the staff? They'd been bought by a slut, that's what.

Steve pulled his truck into the half spot next to P.B.'s Suburban. The SUV dwarfed the pickup like a territorial Rottweiler standing over a friendly spaniel.

The door opened and Roxanne caught a glimpse of Steve's tousled hair in the cab light before turning to unlock the door to the building.

"I forgot, was this date night?" Steve's voice sent a shiver up her spine and she was finally glad P.B. was there, if only because he could talk to Steve and she could beat it upstairs.

She called good night to the two of them as P.B. was shaking Steve's hand and, ignoring what sounded like a protest from P.B., she trotted up the steps to her apartment.

She realized as she was sighing and closing the door behind her that she'd left her sweater in P.B.'s car, but that would just have to wait. She could get it from him when they went to the symphony. *If* they went to the symphony. Heck, she didn't really need that sweater back.

She took off her coat and hung it in the closet. The symphony. Why had she said yes? It didn't matter if her instincts were all off about men. That didn't mean she had to go out with guys she wasn't attracted to. It just meant she had to be careful of the ones she *was* attracted to.

And she had no business thinking about *men* right now anyway. She had a restaurant to open. This was it, the culmination of months of work, her lifelong ambition coming true before her very eyes. And she was putzing around with a couple of unsuitable guys who were nothing but an unwanted distraction.

She needed to focus. They were opening in two days. No doubt there'd be some kinks to work out in both the menu and the service, too, so it wouldn't run smoothly at first.

It was exciting and stressful and scary. All the things dating was, so she certainly didn't need *both*.

She started down the hall toward the bathroom, anxious to get all her makeup off and crawl into bed, into oblivion. But she couldn't stop thinking about all she needed to do. Her mind spun with excuses to get out of going out with P.B. again—too busy, too tired, menu problems, dough preparation, she couldn't get involved right now.

And when she tried to turn her mind from that it reeled over to what she should say to Steve. I was crazy? Temporary insanity? I kiss everyone like that after dinner? (Except P.B.)

She was halfway to the bathroom when someone knocked on the door.

Roxanne's stomach flipped with dread. P.B., she'd bet. Steve probably let him in and he was here for a better good-night kiss, at her *real* door.

She walked back across the living room and opened the door to see Steve, holding her sweater.

"Delivery," he said dryly, holding it out in front of him.

"Oh. Thanks." She took it from him, concentrating on smoothing the wrinkles and folding it neatly. She couldn't meet his eyes, she was so embarrassed.

"You guys have a good time?"

She glanced up, his face was bland. She had no idea what he was thinking, but she knew it couldn't be good.

"It was fine. We . . . just ate." She waved a hand to encompass everything else.

They stood in awkward silence a long minute. Was he waiting for an explanation? She knew he deserved one, but she couldn't think how to begin. It was crazy to even find herself in this situation. It was like middle school all over again—the awkwardness, the uncertainty, the boys.

"Look, about the other night," he began.

"I know. I'm so sorry about that," the words rushed out on an exhale. "It's just—"

"*You're* sorry?"

Her eyes flicked to his. He was genuinely surprised.

"Well, yes, I, uh," she said haltingly. "I shouldn't have . . . well, you know . . ."

She *had* kissed him. She remembered that. She'd turned her head when he'd obviously been going for her cheek. Then she'd leaned forward and put her lips on his again. She had done it and she had gotten what she'd asked for. Boy, had she ever.

He laughed once, then sobered. "I thought *I* shouldn't have. But then, I wasn't even sure—"

"I know. I wasn't either—"

She stopped herself. *Sure of what? Let the man finish!*

But he stopped, too, and they stood looking at each other.

"Look, do you want to come in for a minute? I, uh . . ." She leaned on the doorknob. "Maybe we should clear the air, you know? And I have part of a bottle of wine, if you'd like a glass."

He paused and she wondered if she should have just left it at whatever point it was they'd gotten to.

He glanced at his watch. "Okay, sure. I guess it's not too late."

It was close to eleven, late enough for Roxanne to be exhausted when she'd been with P.B., but she was wide awake now and ready to "clear the air," as she'd said. She tried to remember all the little speeches she'd made up in her head the day after their dinner, but recalled only "it was a mistake" and "it should never happen again." At this moment, though, those only sounded condemning, and somewhat accusatory, and she didn't want to stir the waters up any more than they already were.

She stepped back and ushered Steve in. He dropped what looked like a bookbag by the door, took off his coat and she led him into the kitchen.

"Wine? Or would you rather have tea or hot chocolate?" She glanced around the kitchen nervously, then moved to the refrigerator and opened it. "I also have some soda, I think. Ginger ale?" She peered back over her shoulder at him.

He seated himself at the kitchen island. "Tea would be great, actually."

She straightened, pushing the door shut. "Okay. I think I have herbal, if you don't want the caffeine. Or do you like regular?" She opened the cabinet next to the stove and poked around. "I don't know about you, but I can't sleep at all if I have caffeine at night."

She heard him chuckle. "Either way. I just got cold out there, talking to P.B."

At the mention of his friend, Roxanne felt humiliation return and with it her unmistakable blush. She kept her back to Steve, turned to the stove, picked up the kettle and moved to the sink. She filled it with enough water for probably ten mugs of tea, then placed it back on the stove, adjusting the flame to high.

The box of tea she'd pulled from the cabinet lay next to the stove. She picked it up and brandished it in his direction. "How about Red Zinger?"

"Fine."

She opened the box, pulled out a bag and placed it in a mug, making all moves deliberately while she tried to come up with something to say. Finally, she turned around, box of tea in hand. She leaned against the counter, her fingers fidgeting with the flap of the box.

"I don't know what you must think of me," she said breathlessly. "I was just—out there—" She extended a hand to indicate the back alley. "With P.B. But I—"

"Roxanne. That's none of my business." Steve shook his head, his eyes on the island in front of him.

"I know, I know." She pushed her hair back from her face and felt it fall in disarray. "But actually it is, in a way. I mean, a few nights ago I was kissing you and tonight . . . well, I just want you to know that I'm not playing games with you guys, no matter how it might look. I'm not even interested in P.B., not that way."

Steve looked up at her, his brows raised as if to say, *And me?* But he just murmured, "Is that right?"

"And as for, well, you, the other night, I don't even

know what happened, why that happened. But it's obvious, isn't it? I mean it's clear we can't be, uh, doing that. We *work* together. We, I, I *own* the place. I can't be . . ." She flipped a hand out in front of her and searched for words. But there weren't any. All she could think was, *I can't be screwing around with the flippin' employees*, and she knew *that* wouldn't sound right.

Steve took the words right out of her head. "You can't be fraternizing with the employees." His voice was low and rich with sarcasm.

Beside her, the water in the kettle started to stir.

Her hands gripped the counter behind him. "Well, yes. Don't you think that's true?"

His gaze was steady on her, his eyes slightly narrowed. She wished to God she knew what he was thinking. "I understand why you do."

On the burner, the kettle began to hiss.

"What does that mean? You don't think so?" She stared at him, trying to fathom what he was saying. "I mean, you don't think I should? Or rather, you do?"

He looked confused. "You should what?"

She threw a hand out. "Fraternize!"

"With me?" He put a hand to his chest. His eyes seemed to be laughing at her now, *dammit*.

The action in the kettle increased. A trickle of steam floated upward in the air next to her.

"With anyone." She swallowed. "Look, if you thought you started things the other night, then you obviously—you must have, well, *thought* of starting things. So maybe we need to agree . . ."

She turned and slapped the box back down on the counter. She was making a mess of this.

"Roxanne," he said. His voice was so calm she was sure she sounded like a neurotic idiot in comparison.

She turned around.

"I think we've gotten off to a strange start." He pushed himself around on his seat so that he was facing her more fully. "But it's obvious we've both been caught off guard by events that . . . well, maybe we consider missteps."

Her heart thrummed in her chest as she looked at him, and she willed herself for once to keep quiet to hear what he had to say.

But she couldn't help herself.

"What did you consider a misstep?" she blurted. It was one thing for her not to want to "fraternize," as he'd put it, quite another for him.

The kettle beside her was about to whistle, but she didn't want to relinquish his gaze. What, *exactly*, had he regretted? It was suddenly very important for her to know.

Steve rose and made the two strides it took to reach the stove. He stood close and with one arm reached around her to move the kettle and turn off the burner.

She glanced at the floor in an effort not to look too closely at his face, which was now practically beside hers. That's what had resulted in the kiss the other night. He'd been so close, his lips *right there*. His body, his warmth, his seductive appeal . . .

What *was* it about him?

His words low, he said, "Why don't we just stop analyzing this?"

She glanced quickly up at him, then away. "I can't. I don't know what to do."

He paused a long moment, during which time she expected him to move away again. But he didn't.

Finally, he said, "I think you can do whatever the hell you want."

She looked up, into his eyes, blue-gray and sharp. His face was calm, his cheeks brushed with the barest stubble, just enough to make him look sinful. His hair, too long, lay about his head in casual disorder, and his white Oxford shirt was unironed. He looked like every mother's nightmare. And every young girl's bad boy.

"Whatever I want," she repeated, thinking, *How the hell should I know what I want?*

But she *did* know what she wanted, she told herself. Someone like Martin, but not Martin. A non-lying Martin. Someone with whom she had something in common.

Steve's eyebrows twitched and he smiled in such a way that sent her thoughts careening wickedly, away from logic, past common sense, and straight into desire. Heat blasted through her body and she felt like the tea kettle, steam wafting out her pores.

Whatever I want.

Her body knew what that was. Even Steve seemed to know what that was. Wasn't that why he was standing here, so close to her? Giving her that look that said, *Take what you want, you idiot, or stop bothering me.*

She inhaled quickly and exhaled, realizing as she did that she was breathing as if she'd just run up the stairs. Her nerves pulsed, electrified.

Her eyes dropped from Steve's face to the open collar of his shirt. She wanted to put her lips there, on that sweet space of skin, just below the stubble. She licked her lips.

"Roxanne," Steve said, this time in a near whisper.

His hand reached out and skimmed her waist to lie warmly on her hip. With a gentle grip he pulled her toward him.

She swallowed hard and moved forward with his hand, coming up against his chest, her palms flat against his ribcage. She looked up at him, saw again that hunger in his eyes and felt her insides go molten.

She parted her lips. He lowered his head. And they kissed.

9

Bar Special
Between the Sheets—happy tonight,
   hungover tomorrow
White rum, brandy, Cointreau, lemon juice

Okay, so he was attracted to her. And okay, so it wasn't smart.

But hell, she was a beautiful woman and her body was pressed up against his like she wanted to crawl right inside his skin.

He had stopped the kiss the other night. Out of consideration, confusion, uncertainty over whether he'd crossed the line or she had.

Well, tonight, they both had. And if she wanted it stopped, then she was going to have to do it.

The kiss started out frenzied. Her mouth was hungry on his, he answered with equal energy. Their hands groped, clutched and traveled over each other's bodies, exploring, grasping, needing closer contact.

Steve felt as if he were going to explode right out of his body. His blood sang, his senses spun, his desire was out of control.

With great effort he slowed the kiss, running his hands up her back and into the dark softness of her hair, then to the sides of her face.

She sighed against his mouth, and he teased her lips with his teeth and tongue. His hands held her head gently as he tasted her, sending her the message that he wanted to appreciate every slow sip of her.

Roxanne's mouth was rich and sweet under his, the skin of her face so soft he felt as if she were a delicacy exotic enough to have come from another world.

Her hands moved down his back and rounded over his hips. With surprising strength, she pulled him into her, his desire, hard and obvious beneath his jeans, straining toward this oblique touch.

His hands ran down her sides, found the spot at her hips where the shirt tucked into her jeans and pulled upward. His fingers found flesh and she gave a little moan. Her body melted against his.

She was smooth and hot, her torso toned and strong, taut like a bow flexed against his frame.

His hands touched her bra and moved around to cup her breasts. He groaned as he found the nipples peaked against his fingers.

Tilting his head, he trailed his lips to her neck. Just below her ear he took a soft bite and sucked as his fingers softly pinched.

She gasped and pulled him tighter, her hips moving into his.

"The bedroom?" he murmured against her ear.

He felt her nod. Slowly, he peeled himself away from her, letting his hands slide down her belly to her hips.

Her face was flushed, her dark eyes nearly black with dilated pupils. Her lips were slightly swollen from his kisses. And her expression was pure desire.

He could hardly believe she was real. The most exquisite woman he'd ever seen, hot, disheveled and glowing with passion *for him*.

Freeing his hands from her shirt, he cupped her face, then took another long sip from her mouth. She responded like a magnet, leaning into him again, her hands grabbing the belt loops on his jeans and yanking him against her.

"You know where it is." Her voice was low, husky, and she gave him a heavy-lidded smile that was so seductive it kicked him in the gut.

Taking her hand he led her down the hallway that was identical to his, turning left into the bedroom.

She followed him into the room and he closed the door behind them. They fumbled for each other in the dark, clasped hands and drew close.

Steve's hands took her shirt and pulled it up over her head. Her fingers went for his shirt buttons, but got tangled as he ducked to kiss the mound of one breast. He moved the lace of her bra downward and captured her nipple.

She made a soft sound deep in her throat and gave up on his buttons, throwing her head back as his lips pulled her nipple and his tongue played with its peak.

Her hands held his shoulders and she pulled them

both backward until he felt her lower herself on the bed. As his eyes adjusted to the dark, the light from the window illuminated the room. He could see her, a dark fluid mass on the bed, her hair spread out around her and her tender skin glowing pale in the moonlight.

He pulled his own shirt over his head and let it drop behind him. Then he leaned over and kissed her again, his hands plunging onto the mattress to snake behind her. He undid her bra with a practiced snap and pulled the straps down her arms.

Dropping the bra behind him onto the floor, he felt her hand find his crotch and cup him. Her thumb stroked his erection and he groaned. Her other hand unbuttoned his jeans and slid the zipper down.

He slid down the length of her body until he crouched at the side of the bed, his lips and hands trailing from her breasts to her belly to her thighs. He pushed his jeans off with one hand and rose again, kissing her belly button as he undid the top of her jeans.

She raised her hips and he drew her jeans down her legs and off. Beneath them, she wore a thong.

"Oh sweet Jesus." Steve's voice was hoarse, a guttural plea for control.

In the dim light of the room he could see Roxanne Rayeaux's incredible figure, naked but for the dark strings of a lacy thong. From bountiful breasts, over a taut belly to the luscious curve of her hips. He wanted those long, long legs around him now.

He rose up above her and pushed his erection against the thong's slip of fabric. His lips found her breast, first one, then the other, and she arched into him, her hands holding his head. Then he rose and took her mouth again.

She opened to him hungrily, her legs loosely circling his hips. His hardened penis in her hands, she stroked it so that he thought he'd lose his mind. Her touch was perfect, magic. He dropped his hand to the thong and slipped a finger easily around it to find the center of her heat.

She was more than ready for him. He plunged two fingers inside her and she pushed her hips up with a soft, high-pitched sound of pleasure. She was slick and soft as silk. His thumb found the spot and moved a slow circle around it.

"Oh," she said on a hot, heavy breath. "Ah." She slid her hand to the top of his penis and moved it in short rhythmic strokes.

He exhaled hard, throbbing in her hands and nearly desperate for relief. He circled his thumb faster. She writhed beneath him.

"Steve," she breathed. "I—I . . . *ahhh*. In the drawer . . ."

He paused.

"A . . . you know . . . for protection," she added in a near whisper.

"Of course." He rose, looked blankly around. "Where?"

She turned over onto her hands and knees. Steve's body tensed and throbbed at the sight of her. She leaned across the bed and opened a drawer to a small night stand. Then she sat back and handed him a condom.

"Wait a minute," he said, when she started to turn around.

Slipping the condom on, he took her hips in his hands and turned her onto her stomach, nearly coming undone again as he saw the perfect rounds of her buttocks, neatly defined by the strip of thong.

She rose onto her hands and knees and he pulled the piece of fabric away from her center, moving himself toward it.

He touched the head to her and strangled a moan. She pushed her hips back but he pulled away, teasing. She groaned. He pushed the head against her again, up and back, along her slickest spot, tormenting her silken heat as she moved her hips again. He leaned over her, bit softly at her shoulder and ran one arm around her stomach. With his other hand he kept the thong aside and positioned himself. Then, body trembling with need, he thrust deeply inside her.

She inhaled sharply and he pushed again. She arched back into him and cried, "*Yes.*"

He thrust again, holding the string of the thong as if barely restraining a wild horse.

The sensation was exquisite. She was tight and hot and wet. He slid effortlessly, deeply, pleasure cascading up his spine as his eyes drank in the lithe form of her back, her tangled hair. Her tight round buttocks moved smoothly, soft and firm, toward him and away, his penis disappeared again and again into her core.

Curving around her once more, he moved his arm across her belly and his fingers again found her spot, this time swollen and primed for his touch. She made a soft sound as he touched her, his hips still thrusting against her. Then she grabbed him, her body did, down deep, and she uttered an ecstatic cry as she shuddered in his arms.

Steve exploded inside her, pulsing as if every ounce of his soul was being pumped into her body. He gasped, then moaned and, as she lay her body slowly onto the mattress, he came down on top of her, their bodies still joined.

Roxanne opened her eyes. She was in bed, facing the windows, and the clock on the bedside table read 6:57. Her body was molten relaxation on the mattress, and she'd slept as soundly as if she'd run a marathon the day before.

Lying perfectly still, she listened for the sound of Steve's breathing. Was he still here? Did she *want* him to still be here?

If he was, how did she act now? What did she *say*? She guessed it was too late to talk about what a mistake the kiss had been.

He stirred, the mattress dipped slightly, and she exhaled in surprising but undiluted relief. He hadn't left. He hadn't snuck out like a forbidden suitor who had gotten everything, the *only* thing, he'd wanted.

She closed her eyes again.

She had to talk to P.B. That was her first problem. She couldn't do this balancing act of having one guy she allowed herself to go out with and another she couldn't stop herself from touching.

Nerves tingled across her body as she remembered last night, the way Steve had touched her, the rough desperate need each of them had had for the other.

Then the complete and utter fulfillment of that need.

She was quenched to her core. If it weren't for the obvious lack of wisdom in her choice of bedmate, she would be completely, blissfully satisfied.

Steve stirred again and she turned slowly onto her back. He was pushing himself up to a sitting position on the edge of the bed. His back was long and tapered to a trim waist, one hand rubbed the back of his neck. As she moved, he looked over his shoulder at her.

His hair was a tousled mess and his cheeks bore the swath of overnight stubble. His eyes were piercing gray in the daylight, and they were smiling.

He was, quite literally, as handsome as sin.

Her lips curved cautiously as their eyes met. Heat suffused her.

"Menu run-through today, right?" His voice was warm and low. Intimate.

She liked that he'd said something mundane about their day, as if this were not a colossal mistake that needed a dramatic conversation to conclude it.

"Yes." She pushed herself up against the pillows, holding the sheets to her chest, and ran a hand through her hair to push it off her face. "Monsieur Girmond will be cooking for the staff at noon. He's probably already in the kitchen. Four apps, six entrees, four sides. I'll have three desserts."

They'd go over how each was made, the ingredients, the flavors, the sauces, the portions, so the waitstaff would be familiar with what the customers were ordering. They would also go over wine accompaniments and pronunciation of each dish—something she hoped Rita could master, as it would go a long way toward making her the best server they had. Right now she was still saying *blanquette de veau* as "blanket of view." Confusing, to say the least. And hardly appetizing.

"I'll come hungry."

For some reason Steve's words made her blush as he reached down to pick up his clothes.

"Not too hungry," she said. "We'll all be sharing."

She tucked the covers in tighter around her, wondering what to do. She watched Steve's back as he rose, admiring his body in the cold light of day. He was sinewy and strong, defined muscles covered that lanky frame and his legs were lean and powerful, runner's legs.

She wondered if in fact he was a runner. She wondered what he did with all his time when he wasn't working. She wondered who on earth he was, this man she'd just uninhibitedly made love with.

At the same time she felt as if a wall was constructed inside her chest. A wall that would not let her through to ask these questions, nor to get any more intimate than they'd been physically.

He was different from anyone she'd ever been with. More intense, less predictable. He challenged her, and though it made her feel stupid to admit it, she didn't want to be challenged. She had too much challenging stuff on her plate already.

What she needed was somebody simple and undemanding. Somebody to support her when she needed it and disappear when she didn't. Selfish, sure, but that was all she felt she could handle right now.

Steve donned his pants and picked up his shirt, now

even more wrinkled than when he'd arrived last night. He put it on without noticing and didn't tuck it in. She loved the way it looked, white against the tawny skin of his throat and chest, loose across the expanse of his shoulders and over his flat belly.

He turned to look at her, his eyes raking her from head to blanket-covered toe as he stood next to the bed.

"Damn," he said softly, with a short shake of his head. "It's hard to leave you looking like that."

She didn't know what to say. She pressed her lips together, a small smile, and looked at the covers. She should get up, too, but she didn't feel comfortable enough to be naked in front of him in the morning light. Which, considering what they'd done last night, was ridiculous.

"I'll see you at noon." She kept her voice even. She didn't know what tone to take, how to be, *who* to be. She glanced back up at him.

"You bet." His grin was cocky and before she knew it he'd knelt on the bed and planted a solid kiss on her lips.

Without thinking, her mouth opened under his and her body ignited like a gas burner to a match.

One of Steve's hands cupped her cheek, but as their tongues found each other and mated as easily as if they'd been doing it for years, it slid down her neck and over her shoulder to her breast. His fingers found the nipple under the covers and she inhaled, her body instantly turning to liquid for him.

Steve groaned and pulled back, his face intent, his eyes hot. "You are . . ." he said with a devouring look, but he didn't finish. He just smiled one last time and concluded, "See you at noon." He strode out of the room.

Roxanne's head dropped back onto the pillows as he left and she exhaled a huge, pent-up breath. Her body hummed as if she were a guitar string he'd just plucked. One note of desire singing through her, reverberating to infinity like a soprano in a cathedral.

She'd never felt so on fire with a man. She didn't know what it was he did to her, but whatever it was, it should be classified and controlled by the FDA. He was damned dangerous. And, she feared, addictive.

The *fervor*, she thought again, closing her eyes. The *vehemence* of their lovemaking had been astonishing.

She pushed the covers aside and got out of bed. Her clothes were scattered about the room, fabric shrapnel testifying to the explosion of desire that had taken place.

This was the strangest thing about modern relationships, she thought, in an effort to be objective. Not that she'd call what she and Steve had a *relationship*. But you could sleep with someone, share the most personal parts of your body, open yourself in the most physically vulnerable way to a man, and not have the foggiest idea what to say to him the next day.

It was sick, really. And sad. This kind of passion was supposed to come with love.

Wasn't it?

She snapped her jeans off the floor. If only she had fallen head over heels in love with someone when she was twenty-two. Then she could have avoided all these years of false starts and missteps, failed relationships and disappointing mistakes.

If only Martin had been all that he'd seemed. Cultured, clever, sentimental and romantic. He had made a life of passion and friendship seem possible.

Too bad he had been a liar. And too bad the lies had colored all that was good a dirty hue.

She tried to picture his face and couldn't do it. She'd spent so long blocking out his image, she could no longer make him real. All that lingered was a melancholy impression of a sandy-haired man in a tuxedo, his elegant fingers holding a wineglass.

And yet she had felt so close to him, once upon a time.

She wondered what Steve would look like in a tuxedo, and the mental picture made her stop and take a deep breath.

After a second she picked up her shirt and bra, and walked into the bathroom, dumping the clothes into the hamper. Then she turned on the water in the shower.

She had éclairs to bake, sauces to make and custards to prep. She couldn't sit around thinking about her latest male mistake. Or, okay, not mistake. At this point he was a compulsion. A physical obsession. A dangerously beguiling substance, like chocolate.

The worst part, though, was that she knew he was just a Band-Aid, a temporary substitute to sate her hunger for the real thing. Steve Serrano was a gift from the gods in bed, there was no doubt about that, but ultimately he wasn't right for her. Nor was she right for him. What she needed was someone she could fall in love with. Someone easy and uncomplicated. The guy from *Father Knows Best*, she thought. Or *Leave It to Beaver*. One of those kindly TV husbands who went through life just trying to do the right thing.

Someone fictional, she told herself with a laugh.

Someone—and this was important—who didn't need her to be June Cleaver to his Ward.

Just before she stepped into the shower, wondering if maybe it should be a cold one after Steve's scorching good-bye kiss, she pictured Steve's eyes. The sharp, intense look he sometimes gave her, the one that made her think he was seeing right through her. And her stomach did a little flip.

A flip, she thought vaguely, that had nothing to do with sex.

Steve's shower was cold, and long. He stood under it, letting the water beat down on his upturned face, until he could stand it no longer and he shut the whole thing off.

He was possessed. That was it. He'd been possessed by the devil. The devil in the dark eyes of Roxanne Rayeaux.

He couldn't stop himself last night. Could barely stop himself this morning, then wondered why he had. She had certainly been willing, he could see it in her eyes. In her devil eyes.

He dried himself roughly and got dressed. This was ridiculous. He could control himself. He wasn't going to lose it over a pretty face; he never had before.

But it was more than her face, more than her beauty, that drew him. There was something downright electric about her, something sultry and fierce and uncompromising. She had let go of her inhibitions as if she'd never had any. For weeks now he'd thought of her as the queen of control, restraint personified, but last night she had broken those bonds as if they'd been web-thin silk. At the same time she'd drawn him in as inextricably as a spider does a moth.

And God help him, he did not trust himself to resist her again.

Would he have to? he wondered. Would he have to at least pretend to try?

What did this mean?

Steve dressed, packed up his books and went to the library until eleven thirty, but it was no use. His research could not compete with the buzzing of his skin as he grappled with uncontrollable memories of the night before.

It wasn't until he remembered P.B. that he could get his physical reactions under control again. Like a bucket of cold water, Steve knew he had to tell his buddy that Roxanne was . . . what? Not available? He had no illusions that last night meant they were in some kind of relationship. They barely knew each other, for one thing. Ironically.

But he wouldn't—couldn't—let P.B. think he had some kind of chance with Roxanne while she was sleeping, or had slept, with him. Maybe it was altruistic—he truly didn't want his friend's heart broken, or even bruised—but mostly he knew it was selfish. He couldn't stand the thought of P.B. even trying to hold her hand when he, Steve, wanted to see and touch and hold so much more.

Steve packed up his notebooks and papers at quarter to twelve and headed for the restaurant. He'd be late, but he doubted everyone would get there on time anyway. And he didn't want Roxanne thinking he was too eager to see her again, a panting puppy who didn't know when to stop begging for play.

But when he arrived, the dining room had nearly the full complement of servers and cooks the restaurant now employed. George was the only one later than he was, but he was routinely late. When the restaurant was Charters, they would tell George his shift started half an hour before it really did, and he had never caught on.

The cooks, he'd never seen before—certainly not the tall rotund man with the moustache and round glasses. He assumed that this was the Monsieur Girmond Roxanne had talked so rhapsodically about.

Assisting him were two men wearing chefs' whites and black-and-white checkered pants. The three of them wore black clogs on their feet.

Sir Nigel was there as well, in his trademark three-piece suit with French cuffs and watch chain. His hair was slicked back over his balding English pate and he looked over the crew with a haughty eye. Most particularly, his gaze seemed caught on Rita.

In white shirt, black pants and long white apron, she was dressed like the other three waiters, but her spiky red hair made its trademark impertinent statement.

As Steve entered the room not wearing his white shirt and black pants all eyes turned to him.

Sir Nigel's colorless gaze swept him and his lips twitched just enough to convey displeasure.

"Sorry." Steve shrugged with a grin, his peripheral vision searching for Roxanne. "I didn't know this was a dress rehearsal."

"No matter, no matter," M. Girmond boomed, waving him in with a substantial hand. "You are the bartender, no? I saw you, through the window the other day." He indicated the front window with his head.

"Did you?" Steve strode across the room and shook the man's hand. "Steve Serrano. Good to meet you."

"Marcel Girmond, at your service." He spread his arms to encompass a table full of plates containing appetizers and laughed. "We are just now beginning. Roxanne said we are not to wait for stragglers, but now we are down to just one missing. *Oui*?"

"Yeah." Rita turned to send Steve a wink. "Just George now. Then our motley crew will be complete."

Steve took off his coat and laid it over a chair back, ignoring Sir Nigel's glare. He went to stand next to Rita.

"Lookin' good, darlin'," he said out of the corner of his mouth.

"I *know*." She looked down at herself with a pleased grin. "I'm a real professional now."

Steve smiled at her. He wasn't often surprised by people—last night notwithstanding—but he wouldn't have expected this from Rita. He thought she'd fight the fussy nature of this restaurant every step of the way, just as he had planned to. But now . . . well, now he had bigger fish to fry.

He was just settling comfortably in to the instructional nature of the program, listening to Monsieur Girmond's lilting accent, when Roxanne emerged from the kitchen. She too wore chef's whites with the black-and-white checkered pants, but with her hair in a bun and the memory of last night so fresh, Steve felt sucker-punched.

She was gorgeous no matter what she put on, and knowing what was under that primly buttoned jacket raised his blood to an instant boil. Their eyes met and as stupid as it sounded even to himself, he felt a bolt of electricity pass between them. The sensation was so strong, he colored as if the rest of the group might have perceived it.

"Steve," she said coolly. The control queen was back. "So glad you could make it."

She held a towel on which she was wiping her hands, and her eyes, after branding him with their heat, moved to the table of food Monsieur Girmond presided over.

Rita glanced up at him, a long look through her pale lashes.

Had she seen it?

To Steve's surprise, the presentation of the food was actually interesting. Girmond was so enthralled by his topic, so enthusiastic about his productions, that it was impossible not to be drawn in. Indeed, most of the staff seemed taken with the food—even George, who had shown up in time for the last bite of the appetizers.

Roxanne's desserts were likewise a big hit and she looked gratified by the effusiveness of the reactions.

As the group broke up, and Steve's eyes kept track of Roxanne as she answered questions from Rita and Pat, Sir Nigel glided over to him.

"I trust you will be appropriately attired for tomorrow's opening," he said in a voice coated with British pomposity.

"Why Nigel, I didn't know you cared," Steve said. He was thinking he should make his way over to Roxanne, figure out a way to ask her when they could see each other. Without, of course, seeming like he was worried about it. He hadn't quite worked that part out yet.

"Mr. Serrano, you don't seem to have grasped that I am your boss."

That got Steve's attention. He turned a deceptively lazy expression on the man. "Congratulations. You must be very proud."

Sir Nigel regarded him a long moment, his eyes flat, like a shark's. "You might want to think harder about the situation. I make decisions regarding your future employment here. No matter what edge you think you can gain by . . ." He stopped, cleared his throat delicately, and let his eyes drift pointedly to Roxanne. ". . . pursuing alternate means of job security. Whatever else our new owner may be, she is not one to be deeply affected by a fleeting bit of charm."

10

Bar Special
Third Rail—<u>Danger! Touch it</u>
 <u>and it might just kill you</u>
Dry vermouth, sweet vermouth, rum, orange juice

"Roxanne, baby. Glad you called." P.B.'s voice seemed too loud on the line and she pulled the phone receiver a couple inches away from her ear. "Listen, just got some news about a possible match on some fingerprints from your break-in."

"Oh. But I thought it was just the squirrel." She tapped a pencil eraser on the counter in front of her. Her kitchen was bright from the morning sun. *The hard light of a new day,* she thought. She rocked the sole of a clog on one of the bottom rungs of a stool by her kitchen island.

She'd come up from the kitchen downstairs to make this call, the obligation weighing too heavily to put it off any longer. She was already nervous about tonight's opening of the restaurant. She didn't need the prospect of this conversation taking up any more mental space too. So while her dough rested, she made a temporary escape to lower the boom on P.B.

"Sure, it probably was." P.B.'s voice was unconcerned. "But we ran the prints anyway. For all you know, you've got someone working for you with a record."

"I really doubt that."

"I know you do, honey. But it's my job to protect you, isn't it?"

Something about P.B.'s tone irked her. Was it in the nature of cops to think everyone else around them was a criminal? And did he mean he was supposed to protect *her*, in particular, as in the "little woman"?

She gritted her teeth. "A possible match. What does that mean? Do you know whose fingerprints they are?"

Her palms were sweating and she dropped the pencil.

"Not yet. Maybe later today. I thought I'd drop by your place tonight. Let you know the details."

"P.B., I'm opening the restaurant tonight. This is our first night."

Didn't he *know* this? It was all she'd talked about for weeks with anyone.

"It'll probably be slow," she added. "But I'll be busy at least until midnight anyway."

Papers shuffled in the background. "Oh yeah. The opening. That's tonight?"

She sighed. "Yes."

"Well, I'll just stop by the restaurant then."

Roxanne pictured P.B. coming into Chez Soi with his

"Roxanne-baby's" and his "honeys" in front of Steve and knew she could not handle the juxtaposition. She was torn enough as it was over the strange turn her dealings with Steve had taken. She didn't need to add to what was already an awkward threesome by having them all together in one spot.

"By the way"—P.B. covered the mouthpiece and said something to someone nearby, she could only hear muffled murmurings—"yeah, sorry. Uh, by the way, I got the symphony tickets you wanted. Hope you don't mind balcony seats."

She wanted?

She took a deep breath. First things first. "Listen, P.B., I really don't think tonight's going to be a good time to come by. Opening night, as I said. We could be busy working out kinks in the service. I know I won't have time to talk."

"Oh, well." He paused. She hoped he was digesting this as a possible rejection. "No problem. I can talk to you later. But you can always use another customer, right? I'll just shoot the shit with Steve. Maybe grab a bite to eat at the bar."

Roxanne closed her eyes, picturing the scene perfectly. P.B.'s blustering candor bumping right into Steve's quiet perception. No doubt—*no* doubt—P.B. would mention the symphony date. No doubt Steve would put together his own theory on how that had come about. No doubt she would end up looking even worse than she already did.

"P.B., I just don't think—"

"Babe, listen, sorry, I gotta go." She could hear someone talking in the background and P.B.'s answering "uh-huhs." He came back on. "Really, sorry. I'll come by tonight, let you know what's going on."

She gave it one last shot. "Not tonight, please, Peter. Let's have lunch sometime this week, okay?"

"Uh-huh. Right. Gotcha."

She breathed a sigh of relief until she realized he was talking to whoever was with him.

"Okay, Rox, see ya later," he said to her.

"Bye," she said dispiritedly, but he was already gone. She took the phone from her ear and slowly pressed the OFF button.

She just wouldn't come out of the kitchen, that was all. He could talk to Steve all he wanted and she wouldn't show. Come to think of that, though, he and Steve probably had already talked, on the phone or whatever. They were friends. Maybe Steve had told him what had happened the other night. But no, P.B. wouldn't have been so casually proprietary with her as he was just now. He probably wouldn't have been so easy about "babe"-ing her either. And he certainly wouldn't have been interested in "shooting the shit" with Steve. Not after being upstaged by him.

She got up off the stool and headed back downstairs. Realistically, it would probably be slow tonight. They had done very little advertising, just enough to let the neighborhood know they were opening up, so they'd be lucky to turn tables even once. Which meant that there would be plenty of time for her to be expected to socialize with P.B.

Well, so what, she told herself. She was the boss and P.B. was someone she'd been out with *once*. She didn't owe him anything. For that matter she didn't owe Steve anything either.

Let 'em talk, she thought cavalierly. That's what a man would think and do.

Not any man she'd want to be with, however.

They were slammed.

From the moment Sir Nigel opened the doors that night, people streamed in. Apparently word had gotten out that the three-star chef from New York's La Finesse had come to Alexandria and all the Washingtonian foodies pounced on it, exclaiming to each other how lucky and/or prescient they were to have gotten a jump on the culinary scene by being there the first night.

They were standing two deep at the bar as Steve's gaze raked the crowd, searching for the tiny blonde woman who had ordered the Amaretto sour.

"Amaretto?" a dark-suited, power-tied man of about fifty called.

Steve caught his eye and held up the drink. The man nodded, indicating the top of a blonde head at his side, hidden by the crowd.

"Seven twenty," Steve said, over the head of the white-haired gentleman on a barstool in front of him.

Without batting an eye, the suited man handed him a fifty.

Considering nobody was supposed to know the restaurant even existed yet, Steve was amazed by the sheer numbers of people here, not to mention amused by their ease with the high prices of the drinks. At Charters it had taken several hours of drinking for people to get so free with their credit cards. Here they didn't bat an eye at paying nine bucks for a martini.

And still they kept coming through the door. Even the unflappable Sir Nigel looked a little hot under the collar. Steve caught him glancing out the door to the street at one point as if there might be a bus unloading somewhere nearby.

Rita, George and Pat, expecting an easy opening night, were flying wild-eyed through the double doors from the kitchen with plates of exquisitely presented food, looking as if they were having to negotiate an obstacle course with their mother's best china on their heads.

Steve himself was kept hopping by such orders as Pink Ladies and Green Turtles, drinks he'd almost never gotten orders for at Charters that now he had to wrack his brain to remember how to make. He'd even had to look surreptitiously at the dusty bartender's manual under the register at one point to figure out what the hell a Queen's Park Swizzle was.

Catering to an older crowd was definitely different from the burger-and-beer stuff he'd been doing for Charters. Back then, the most complicated drinks he'd had to produce were six different kinds of margaritas and the latest craze in shooters, neither of which required much presentation.

Mixed in with all the crazy drink drinkers were also a host of fine-wine fanciers. Each wanted to know the years and varietals of every offering they had by the glass, not to mention "how it was." Full-bodied? Fruity? Lots of tannins?

Steve started out saying things like "robust" and "oak-y," and eventually branched out into "a little floral" for the cheaper labels to a "hint of blackberry"—or lingonberry or chocolate or whatever—for the more expensive ones.

It seemed to be working. Everyone liked what they were drinking and nobody had looked at him yet and repeated, "*Lingonberry!*"

About half past nine, P.B. pushed his way through the crowd. As usual, he was visible from the moment he walked in the door and audible shortly thereafter.

"Steve!" he called, raising a hand high. His grin was expansive and all-encompassing, benevolent to the masses around him. That, and the casual way he brushed by Sir Nigel at the door, spoke volumes about how close he thought he was to being lord of the manner.

"Hey, Peeb." Steve glanced at him as he filled a pint glass with Stella Artois, a Belgian beer they now carried. "What's up?"

P.B. shouldered between two men in suits who had their backs to each other to secure a standing spot at the bar. "I promised Rox I'd stop by. She here?"

Rox?

Steve couldn't help it, he scowled. "Of course she's here, Peeb, she's the owner, for Chrissake."

He moved down the bar to deliver the Stella, irritation crawling along his nerves like bugs. It wasn't P.B.'s fault. In fact, if there was fault involved it was all Steve's. Not P.B.'s, not Roxanne's. Steve's. He was the one who'd initiated things with Roxanne and pushed them beyond what either of them had expected.

And he was the one who had not yet spoken to his friend about it. P.B., in this instance, was just an innocent bystander to his, Steve's, lack of control.

He moved back toward P.B., taking a deep breath and marshalling his annoyance.

"What can I get for you?" he asked his friend.

P.B. grinned. "Roxanne, straight up, slightly warmed."

Steve almost laughed—cynically—at how ironic that was. She'd been warmed all right.

"Man, you shoulda seen the looks I got at Murphy's the other night," P.B. continued, laughing. "Walking in with her. Christ, I couldn't have done better if I'd brought in all the MTV Spring Break girls together. Don Flannery about pissed his pants when he saw she was with me."

"That's great," Steve said. He could just imagine P.B.'s cronies talking about her.

"You know it. My stock went *up*, brother, let me tell you." He laughed again, pounding his palm on the bar with glee. "She's by far the hottest chick I've ever brought in there—they all said so—and you know I've brought some hot ones in. She takes the cake, though."

"So? You get to see her bedroom like you predicted?" Maybe it was mean, since he knew full well the answer to the question, but P.B.'s cockiness set him off.

P.B. chuckled. "It's just a matter of time, buddy. Just a matter of time."

Steve looked at him, wishing, hopelessly, that P.B. would hear how he sounded and shut the hell up. He'd always treated his women like trophies and it seemed Roxanne was to be no exception.

"So where is she, huh?" P.B. looked around, apparently oblivious to what a crowd this size would mean to a chef. "I gotta tell her she's a star at the pub."

"She's in the back. *Cooking*," he said pointedly.

P.B. shrugged. "Tell her it's break time."

Steve scoffed. "I don't think so. Look around you, P.B., she's probably up to her eyeballs in orders right now." He glanced over the heads of the people at the bar into the bustling dining room. "We turned section one over an hour ago, so there're probably a bunch of desserts on order right now."

In fact Steve himself had seen her only a couple of times that evening, once when she'd run out of rum for something she was doing, and once when she'd come to refill the pitcher of ice water she kept back there. Both times she'd looked both elated and shell-shocked. All she could do was stare wide-eyed at Steve and shake her head in wonder.

Steve had laughed and said, "Looks like you're on your way."

To which she'd shaken her head again and said, "We all are."

But it wasn't just the amazing crowd that stuck in his mind at the moment. Like an adolescent schoolboy, what he kept running over and over in his thoughts was the moment when he'd handed her the pitcher and their hands had touched on the handle. For a second they had both frozen, prolonging the contact and looking at each other with such heat that Steve could feel it deep in his gut.

Or had it been just him?

He exhaled and wiped down the counter.

"I'll just hang out here for a while then," P.B. said. "I told her I'd be coming by, so she'll probably be out before too long looking for me."

Steve figured they'd just see about that. He threw the

bar towel down on the cold chest and took an order from the woman next to P.B. for a Cosmopolitan.

P.B. looked down the bar, then back at the shelf of liquors. "Think I'll have one of those," he added, pointing to the Queen's Park Swizzle as Steve mixed the Cosmopolitan. "What's in that?"

"Roxanne knew you were coming by?" Steve asked, unable to help himself as he slid the Cosmo to the woman.

Had Roxanne made a date with P.B.? Maybe an after-work thing? He himself had done that plenty of times, with plenty of women, but it galled him to think of Roxanne being so casual about seeing both him and P.B. Not to mention seeing them both in the same place at the same time.

"Yeah." P.B. shed his jacket and hung it over the seat back behind him. They had tall bar stools now, with cushioned seats and backs, and Steve had to admit the whole place felt more comfortable. "I was going to tell her about the fingerprint results, from the break-in."

Steve raised a skeptical brow. "Squirrels have finger-prints?"

"No, smart-ass, people do. Thought we'd gotten a live one—maybe someone working here, one of those Ecuadorans or something—but we didn't. Close, but no cigar."

"So you came by to tell her you have nothing on the break-in." Several people at the bar were looking restless but Steve couldn't let this go. "That's full-service police work."

P.B. frowned at him. "What bee got up your butt? No, I came by to see her, talk about our next date. We're go-

ing to the symphony and I just got tickets. Bach, thanks
to you."

Steve felt his blood go cold. He shouldn't be surprised. She'd gone out with P.B. first. The thing between himself and her had been a spontaneous
moment that had gotten out of hand, and that was all.
Clearly, that was all. Still, he felt a little sick.

What had all those protestations of hers meant about
only liking P.B. as a friend? About how P.B. wasn't her
type? Had she felt guilty about Steve and been giving
him lip service? Come to think of it, her assertions on
that score could conceivably be construed as coming on
to him, couldn't they?

This was stupid. Maybe he should just tell P.B. about
him and Roxanne. Didn't P.B. have a right to know that
his best friend was making tracks with the woman he
was dating?

Then again, wasn't it Roxanne's place to tell P.B.
what she was doing, seeing as how she had a date lined
up with him and all?

Confused, Steve shook his head and moved down
the bar to a man waving a twenty at him.

"Hey, get me a beer, will you?" P.B. said as he
moved off.

Steve nodded.

This was about as uncomfortable as Steve had ever
been with his friend, or anybody, come to think of it.
He felt like a liar and a cheat, and he wasn't even sure it
was worth it.

What was he doing this for? Why had he gone after
Roxanne when he wasn't even certain that he liked her?

Well, that wasn't true. It was more that he didn't

know what she thought of him. Roxanne's feelings were a mystery, but he was not naïve enough to believe she'd fallen for him. They had some amazing physical chemistry, but whether it could be more than that remained to be seen.

He just hoped he wasn't the only one looking . . .

Roxanne wiped her brow and breathed a sigh of relief. No more tickets. Dinner service was over and the last dessert had been plated and taken to its table.

The night had been incredible, a rush to her system she had never experienced before. Chefs, cooks, waiters, busboys, dishwashers all working excellently in concert for the first time was like piecing together a motor with nothing but an instruction manual and hearing the gratifying roar when you first turn the key.

Knowing that this all boded extremely well for the future of her venture was no small part of the equation either.

The only thing marring the evening was the knowledge that P.B. was sitting at the bar and had been for the last hour, waiting for her. Rita had told her during a hurried pass through for food that he was making "a bunch of dog-in-heat noises" about seeing her and if she wanted her bartender to stay sane she ought to get out there and say hi, "or whatever."

Roxanne had thanked her as if she couldn't have cared less, then wished she could park her head in the sand and leave it there.

Now, though, she guessed she had to go out there and face the music. She wished she had someone to talk to about it. Rita, of everyone present, would probably give her the most unvarnished assessment of the situation, but she was too tight with Steve to be trusted. Not to mention that Roxanne wasn't eager to hear Rita's honest opinion of her and the awkward problem of having varying degrees of entanglement with two guys.

In the past, she'd spoken some to M. Girmond about Martin, but she didn't want him thinking she expected him to be her psychologist as well as her chef, so she wouldn't talk to him about this. Besides, he was out back with his sous-chef, both of them smoking well-deserved cigars she'd provided for them.

Roxanne pulled off her toque and pushed her hair back from her temples. She probably looked a mess, what with sweating it out in a hot kitchen at full throttle for six hours, but maybe that was best. She didn't want either one of these guys thinking she looked good. Except—

She stopped herself. She wasn't going to spend one more minute thinking about that look in Steve's eyes, or the moment when their hands had touched on the water pitcher and she'd felt as if her insides had melted all over again.

She brushed her palms down the sides of her chef's jacket, took a fortifying breath and pushed through the swinging doors to the bar.

P.B. spotted her immediately and beamed, turning on his stool with arms outstretched as if she might walk into them for a hug.

Her eyes shot immediately to Steve, who, thankfully, was serving a white-haired gentleman farther down the bar and didn't see her.

Instead of going toward P.B. she moved toward the

service bar and ducked under it to put the main bar between him and herself. To cover for this move, she grabbed a glass and filled it with ice, then water from the soda gun.

"Hey, babe. I thought you were never gonna come out of there." P.B. smiled but she sensed an edge. "Didn't anyone tell you I was here?"

She leaned back against the liquor shelf and sipped her water. "Rita told me, but I've been in the weeds for the last hour and a half. I'm *exhausted*."

"Yeah, I had a tough day, too. Not too tough to want to see you, though." He laughed jovially as if this wasn't the accusation she knew it was. "I'll always have *that* energy, believe me."

He winked at her and leaned forward on his elbows, as if trying to get closer.

She stayed back, leaning against the cabinets, her stomach contracting at the carnal appetite in his expression.

"We had an amazing night," she said, clinging to the wonderful part of the evening. "It took all of us completely by surprise, but wow. It worked! Everything worked. It was so great."

"Yeah, hey, I wasn't expecting to see a crowd here either, that's for sure." P.B. laughed again and Roxanne struggled with feeling insulted. Had he meant that the way it sounded? Because it sounded as if he was blown away that the restaurant wasn't an immediate failure.

Steve approached from the other end of the bar and Roxanne turned her eyes toward him.

His expression was cool and he was shaking his head. "I don't get this guy. All night he's drinking scotch, one after the other, the good stuff, you know. And now suddenly he's got a hankering for Chambord, if you can believe it."

"Old coot's drunk as a skunk, that's why." P.B. didn't bother to lower his voice. "Probably couldn't taste the difference at this point anyway."

Steve ignored P.B. and turned to Roxanne, standing before her a second as if awaiting her opinion on the subject.

She looked up into his face, felt that fire start low in her body and stopped breathing. His expression was grave. What had P.B. said to him?

"Excuse me, darlin'," he said in a tone similar to the one he used with Rita—though not as friendly—and stepped closer. Putting his hands lightly on her hips, he pressed her to the left.

It took her a moment—during which desire sprang onto her skin like raindrops in a thunderstorm—to realize that he was moving her aside to get to the Chambord.

She flushed hot and laughed. "Oh! Sorry." She stepped left.

But Steve's left hand lingered on her hip as he grabbed the bottle with his right, leaning so close to her she could smell his clean masculine scent. Stepping back, he let his hand slide slowly off her torso but his eyes met hers with undisguised, and clearly sensual, hunger.

He turned, took a cordial glass from the shelf and poured the Chambord.

"Another beer, P.B.?" he asked, not looking at his friend.

But Roxanne did, and what she saw was a look of calculating displeasure. Whether that was because he didn't like Steve's touching her at all, or because he saw something more in the exchange, she couldn't tell. All she knew was that she had to set P.B. straight. She had to tell him that they—she and P.B.—were *not* in a relationship and they never would be.

"Yeah." P.B. drained his glass in one gulp and pushed the empty toward Steve. Then he reached into his breast pocket and pulled out an envelope. "Hey, Rox, look what I've got here." He smiled at Roxanne and held the paper out to her.

"Be right back," Steve said and went to deliver the cordial to the white-haired man.

Roxanne pushed off the back counter and took the envelope from P.B., setting her water glass on the bar. "What is it?" she asked, not opening it.

"Tickets. To the symphony. Remember I told you?" He had on his most sincere eager-puppy-dog look.

Remember I told you not to come tonight? she wanted to retort. *Remember I said I'd be too busy to talk? Remember I told you I wanted to pick the night for the symphony?*

She sighed and flipped open the envelope, glancing inside. Sure enough, two tickets.

"It's a Wednesday but you can get someone to cover for you, right?" P.B. added.

Steve returned with P.B.'s beer and snorted at this last comment.

"What?" P.B. gave him a belligerent look.

Roxanne gave P.B. an appalled one.

"No. I can't get someone to 'cover for me.'" She shook her head.

P.B. turned back to her, his expression caught between quarrelsome and confused.

"Peter . . ." She noticed she used his real name only when she was annoyed with him, like a mother trotting out first and middle names to warn her child that he was in trouble. "I told you I needed to pick the night. I also told you I couldn't go unless it was a night I had off. Don't you see? I *own* this place. I'm the pastry chef. I have a responsibility to be here."

"Don't *you* see?" he countered, leaning forward and taking her hand before she could jerk it away. She hoped to God Steve was doing something that prevented him from seeing it. "You *do* own this place. Which means you can decide when to come in and when to take a night off. What're they gonna do, fire you?"

Ire burned in her breast and she tried to pull her hand away gently. But P.B.'s grip was tight, his expression oblivious.

"P.B., it's not a lark, what I'm doing here," she said. "I *work* here. I've put everything I have into this place. And I'm the only pastry chef I've got, so I *have* to be here if there are going to be any desserts."

P.B. looked at the bar, his fingers toying with hers, sulking. "It's only one night."

She pulled her hand forcefully from his. "No it's not. It's my life. This is *my life*."

P.B. looked at her. "Isn't that a little dramatic?"

Steve turned from ringing up the old man's cordial at

the register and directed a slightly smug look at Roxanne, as if to say, *See what a moron you've attached yourself to?*

"You know I'd cover you, *Rox*," he said with a lazy grin, "if I could."

Roxanne shot him a quick mind-your-own-business look, then glared at P.B.

"We need to talk," she said firmly.

Steve raised his brows and turned back to the register, flipping through the bar checks on its deck.

"Let's go out front a minute." Roxanne ducked back under the service bar and approached P.B. "Bring your coat."

With an exaggerated look of fear directed at Steve, P.B. complied and followed her out the front door.

The frigid air hit her face, delivering equal parts of relief and shock. Her sweat-salted skin contracted in the icy breeze. Mostly it felt good after her hot night in the kitchen, and it cooled her desperation to set P.B. straight just enough so that she could approach it calmly.

She took a deep breath. "Listen, P.B., I am truly sorry if I led you to believe—"

"Oh, *no*!" he exclaimed, shutting her up with the vehemence of the words.

She looked at him in surprise as he lay one hand on his face and tipped his head back. He laughed contemptuously, presumably at himself, and turned once in a circle.

Lowering his hand, he faced her again. "Don't tell me. Are you *blowing me off*?"

He didn't appear angry so much as appalled.

"No, not 'blowing you off,'" she countered, "just, telling you how I feel. I am in no position to start a relationship right now and I should have told you that right up front. It seems we've been operating under two different assumptions. I looked at our getting together as developing a friendship. And you . . ." She trailed off. "Well, I'm not sure you were looking at it the same way."

"Huh." It wasn't quite a laugh but his lips were quirked. "I was thinking you liked me." He paused a moment, his mouth working as if to control a sneer. Finally he said, "It's Steve, isn't it?"

She was taken aback by this—wondered again what Steve might have told him—and could come up with nothing to say other than, "What?"

He laughed harshly. "*Dammit*. I knew it. I've seen how you look at him."

She was glad for the dark and the cold. It made it easier to keep her expression composed. "Steve and I have nothing to do with this."

"Shit." P.B. ran a hand through his hair and looked at the stars. "You and *Steve*. *Shit*. I knew it. I knew it." He shook his head. "That *dog*. I mean it, he knew how I felt about you."

"It's not Steve," she said, but her voice lacked conviction. It felt like a lie, even if it wasn't. And she suddenly felt worse than ever for coming between these two friends.

"Oh please." His laugh was so derisive she felt stupid. As if he really did know all about what had happened.

"That bastard." P.B. shook his head some more. "Well, I'll tell you." He pointed a finger at her. "You tell Steve he wins, he can go ahead and keep that hundred bucks, but I don't like the way he competes."

"He wins? What do you mean?" She frowned. Was this some kind of masculine game talk? Or was he talking about something completely different now?

"The bet." He laughed again and smacked his forehead mockingly. "But no, of course he wouldn't tell *you* about the bet. You, of all people."

Roxanne's stomach clenched. "What bet?"

"About you, babe." He chucked her softly under the chin with a light fist. "Whoever got you first."

Roxanne felt as if he'd punched her hard in the stomach.

"That's a terrible thing to say." She squeezed the words out of a suddenly airless chest.

"Oh, you don't believe me." He nodded knowingly. "That bad, huh? Well you just go in and look in that little cubbyhole by the register. The one in the brick wall there. There's a hundred dollars in there that's got Steve's name on it now. And good luck to you, doll."

With that, he put his hands in his pockets, turned and sauntered off.

She watched him go, barely breathing, hating the indolent air of his stride. Any ounce of sympathy she had for him before was gone as surely as if it had never existed.

A bet. The two had made a juvenile, disgusting, humiliating bet. About *her*.

What had been the crowning blow? What line had she crossed that had cemented the win for Steve? When she'd kissed him? Or when she'd let him into her bed, into her body?

She turned on her heel and strode back into the restaurant. George and Rita sat at the bar, sipping beers, while Steve stood behind it drying a glass with a white bar towel.

She stalked the length of the room, ducked under the service bar and went straight for the chink in the brick wall next to the register.

"You guys get everything worked out?" Steve asked. His tone was still mocking, still superior.

She looked straight at him as she put her fingers in the hole, then closed her eyes briefly as they found something.

She pulled the folded sheets of paper out, their edges catching on the rough brick, and looked down at a roll of twenties.

Fearing she might throw up—or worse, *cry*—she tossed the twenties on the counter in front of Steve and said, "You're fired."

Then she walked, on wooden legs, straight through the kitchen and out the back door.

11

Bar Special
Gin & Bitters on the Rox——for the day after
Gin, angostura bitters, with a twist

Steve drummed his fingers on his desk and looked at his notes. He'd gone to the library and hadn't been able to concentrate. He'd come home, turned on the computer, and still wasn't able to concentrate.

Last week's notes lay inert on the desk beside the keyboard, waiting for some brain other than his to piece them together and turn them into something coherent.

He tried going through them again. Notes from Portner's will. He'd found the will a couple of weeks ago, and it was interesting but hadn't contained anything new. There was one intriguing line just after the part where he left everything to his sister, in which he said, "includes the contents under the first step as described to my Executor." But that had been well known by historians for years.

What had been described to the Executor would probably forever remain a mystery, but the "under the first step" part had at one time led to an examination of all the staircases in the house. The search had turned up nothing, furthering the case made by most historians that if the "contents" Portner was talking about had in fact been what Jefferson termed the "fair copy" of the Declaration of Independence that Portner had been suspected of stealing—the one that included edits made by John Adams and Benjamin Franklin—then he'd unloaded it sometime before his death.

The fact that that's the one draft that did not survive to this day was the only thing keeping alive the idea that it might still be hidden in the house.

The weakness of the evidence was brought home to him last week when even the supremely indifferent P.B. had said, after hearing this story, "And that's *it*? That's all you've got to back up that stupid story you tell everyone who happens to walk into the bar? Jeez, Steve, you might as well be telling ghost stories."

Beyond the will, however, Steve could find no other clues to the document or Portner's role in it's having gone missing.

He put his notes down. He couldn't do this now. He would just get more discouraged about his book. And besides, his brain was fried. It had been fried last night.

Last night, when it had become obvious that anything between him and Roxanne was most definitely not going to work. Last night, when P.B. had blown up all three of them with one traitorous bomb.

He'd considered wringing P.B.'s neck.

Then he thought about how, if he were P.B., he'd be pretty eager to wring Steve's.

It was only when he considered how much it must have hurt Roxanne to hear P.B.'s version of the bet that he actually rose from his desk to get the portable phone to call up and lambaste P.B.

Then he thought about Roxanne and wondered if he should be calling her first. How, from her point of view, he, Steve, looked bad. Really bad.

On the other hand, it could be argued that *he* was the one wronged. After all, she hadn't *asked* him about the bet. Hadn't even asked him if it were true. And even if she was sure it was true, she hadn't given him the opportunity to explain. She'd just believed the worst, right off the bat.

On the other hand, he had to concede, a hundred dollars in a hole in the wall looked bad. Really bad.

Still, it could have been anything. She didn't know, and she didn't ask. She just didn't trust him. That was the bottom line.

On the other hand, something like that would hurt first, then seem suspicious later. Maybe.

But he'd never done anything to hurt her. She was the one who'd had an attitude about him from the start. To just walk in and fire him—in front of the staff—was emotional and unprofessional. She'd leaped to a conclusion, then stood on it like a pillar of righteousness.

On the other hand, she didn't know P.B. like he did. Maybe she believed he was sincere, an injured suitor setting her straight.

But then, if P.B. was in on the bet, that made him as guilty as Steve.

On the other hand . . .

He groaned and lay his head down on the desk. Too many hands. He couldn't figure this out. It was an ugly, messy situation that should never have come up. If he'd kept his hands to himself, he wouldn't have this problem. She'd still just be the prickly new boss.

And then there was P.B. Why had he done it? Roxanne must have been canceling the symphony date and he got bent out of shape and screwed them both. Or he got cocky and told her she was just a bet between himself and Steve. It would be just like P.B. to confront rejection with some nasty jab of his own.

Had he known how far down he was taking Steve? Had Roxanne maybe even said something about what had happened between them?

He needed to talk to her.

But he knew she wouldn't talk. Not to him. She'd made up her mind about him the moment she'd first laid eyes on him. The first day she'd said she wasn't interested.

Well, maybe *she* wasn't, but her body was. They'd proven that much.

A knock sounded at the door.

Steve's head whipped up and he spun on his desk chair, pulling a Post-it note from his forehead.

Roxanne? he thought. Here with his final paycheck or some other confirmation of his termination? The last nail for his coffin perhaps?

Or maybe—just maybe—she'd come to discuss this in a calm, rational manner.

He strode across the living room and opened the door.

Rita stood in the hall holding a bouquet of flowers.

"Rita," he said in surprise. "I didn't know you cared."

She scowled. "I don't, you idiot, these are for *her*. You owe me fourteen dollars."

"Her?" He stepped back as she pushed through the door. "Her who?"

She turned to him with a look of exasperation. "Roxanne, of course. You take them to her, you explain, and you beg for your job back."

Steve crossed his arms over his chest and gaped at her, not bothering to move from, nor close, the front door. "Explain and beg? This is your advice? Without knowing any of the particulars, you want me to *explain and beg*?"

She put the bouquet down on the coffee table and shrugged out of her coat. "Yep."

She looked even smaller out of her puffy down coat, but she put her hands on her hips and stared him down anyway.

"We both know you can be a dog with women, Steve. I'm guessing you did something stupid—like nailing the boss and then not calling her—and now you've got to suck it up to keep your job."

"And this concerns you how?" Steve reached one hand out and slammed the door closed.

"Do you know how much money I made last night?" Rita glared at him as if it were somehow his fault.

"I don't know. It couldn't have been that bad, we were swamped."

"*Bad!*" She laughed, a ruthless sound. "Bad? It was *fantastic*. The best night waitressing of my entire life. And I don't want you or anybody else fucking this up for me. If Roxanne gets ditzy or we go without a decent

bartender and screw up the damn good start we made
last night, that's going to affect my income. My *new* income. Which is only one night old but already I'm
pretty attached to it. So you go and explain and beg to
Ms. High-and-Mighty and make sure that this damn
restaurant is a success so I can finally get out of that
hellhole I'm living in."

Steve looked at her red face and fierce eyes and
couldn't help smiling. "What makes you think she
didn't nail *me*?"

Rita threw her head back and sighed. "Because
you're the one who's got no sense when it comes to
women."

She moved into the kitchen.

"That's not true." He followed to where she opened
the refrigerator door and peered inside. "When have I
ever been stupid about women?"

Rita scoffed and craned her neck sideways. "You got
any soda?"

"No. And answer the question."

She rolled her eyes toward him. "What about Lia?
On-again, off-again, come-when-you're-called Lia? I
wouldn't call that a good example of being smart about
women."

He shrugged. "It's easy."

She pulled out a piece of pumpkin pie on a paper
plate wrapped in plastic. "Can I eat this?"

"I wish you would. It's been in there since Christmas."

She made a face and slid it back onto the refrigerator
shelf.

"Besides," she continued, opening up the vegetable

bin, "Roxanne's totally out of your league. I mean, look at her. She's a beauty queen with a shitload of money. You're just a guy with a nice smile."

"Gee, thanks."

She made a compromising movement with her head and added grudgingly, "I also hear you're pretty good in bed."

"What?"

She shrugged. "Girls talk."

She bent forward and disappeared behind the refrigerator door.

Despite himself, Steve's heart rate accelerated. "*Roxanne* told you that?"

Rita's head popped back up, an orange in her hand and her expression gleeful. She pushed the door shut. "Would Roxanne *know*?"

Damn.

"No—"

She raised her brows skeptically.

"—comment."

"Hah!" She leaned against the counter. "Okay, don't tell me. But whether she went slumming or not, you have to admit you are now in the position of having to apologize for whatever it is she thinks you did."

"I don't have to admit that. And what do you mean by 'slumming'?"

She grinned. "No comment."

"Look, I'll admit she's pretty. And she does seem to have some money. But what does that mean? That she can walk all over people? That she can be excused for thinking the worst of everyone? Even after lowering herself to—to *fraternize* with one of us?"

Rita, with her fingernails in the skin of the orange, raised her eyes to his, their green depths alight. "Holy shit, Serrano. You have no boundaries at all. You *did* nail her, didn't you?"

Her smile was straight from the devil.

Steve exhaled and ran a hand through his hair. "I didn't say that."

She widened her eyes innocently. "Oh yeah, right. Officially, sure. Gotcha." She pulled back the skin of the orange and the scent filled the kitchen air. "So what'd she fire you for, exactly?"

He studied her a second. Then he moved to the counter by the sink and pushed himself up onto it, resting his feet on a partly opened drawer beneath. "Okay, listen to this. You know how P.B. is."

Rita snorted and rolled her eyes, nodding.

"One night he was talking all kinds of trash about Roxanne and . . ." He filled her in on the genesis of the bet. "So I took the money just to shut him up," he finished. "Not to mention that it was fun to deprive him of a hundred bucks for a while. But I was *not* taking him up on the damn bet. Anybody who knows me knows I wouldn't make a bet like that. Hell, I'd forgotten all about it."

Rita narrowed her eyes and put another section of orange into her mouth.

Steve looked at her incredulously. Didn't Rita know that? How bad of a reputation did he have?

"I do know that about you," she said finally.

Steve exhaled.

"But *she* doesn't," she added. "Roxanne. Probably, I mean."

Another knock came from the front door.

Steve and Rita looked at each other.

"Think it's her?" Rita stage-whispered.

"Couldn't say." But his pulse quickened as he pushed off the counter and jogged to the foyer.

Opening the door, Steve couldn't have been more surprised to see the rotund figure of Monsieur Girmond. Even Roxanne would have been less startling.

"Steve. Ah, good. You are home," he said in a curiously hushed voice. His smile, however, was broad. "May I come in?"

Steve stepped back and extended a hand into the apartment. "Sure. Why are you whispering?" He peered out into the hall as the large man stepped past him.

Girmond shook his head, answering in a normal tone as soon as he entered the living room. "No reasons. Just a little frog in my throat."

Steve gestured for Girmond to follow him. "Come on into the kitchen. Rita's here, too."

"Rita?" Girmond stroked his moustache quizzically. "Waitress? Red hair?"

"Ah, yes. *Mon petit chou.*" He grinned and looked around the living room. "This is just exactly like Roxanne's apartment, no?"

Steve glanced around his barely decorated space, remembering the cozy atmosphere of Roxanne's.

"Not just exactly. But similar," he said, leading the way into the kitchen.

Rita was throwing the orange peel into the trash when they walked in. "Oh. Hi." She looked from Girmond to Steve with obvious curiosity.

"*Mademoiselle.*" Girmond gave a short bow and

turned back to Steve. "You are wondering why I am here."

"I have to say I am." Steve stepped toward the refrigerator. "Can I get you something to drink?"

Girmond looked around the kitchen with the critical eye of a chef, no doubt seeing the derelict, half-clean space of a non-cook. "Always the bartender, eh, Steve? No, thank you. I am here to speak with you about your job at the restaurant. May I speak freely?" He inclined his head toward Rita. "Pardon me, *mademoiselle*."

She shrugged. "You're pardoned."

Steve leaned back against the counter. "Go ahead. Rita knows most of my problems anyway."

He wondered how much say Girmond had about the running of the restaurant and guessed he had quite a bit, considering that without him there would *be* no restaurant.

Girmond nodded curtly. "Excellent. I have come to ask you to reconsider leaving your job. We need you, obviously, as we have no other bartender. And I believe you would maybe rather not look for new employment?"

Steve frowned. "I don't think it's me who needs to reconsider. I didn't quit, I was fired."

The older man held his hands behind his back and made a small, deferential bow. "Of course. I know that. Still, I ask you to come back."

Steve looked at him, perplexed. "What do you propose? That I tell Roxanne I don't accept her offer to be fired?"

Girmond's face was confident and he laughed. "Do not fear. She will want you back, as well."

"She will?"

"She is a passionate woman, our Roxanne. Sometimes led more by her emotions than is, ah, prudent." He gave a Gallic shrug. "But such is the nature of women, eh? They bring spirit to this world of ours."

Steve glanced at Rita, who was looking torn between insult and flattery.

He turned back to Girmond. "You seem to be forgetting something. She's also the owner of the restaurant. If she fires me, I gotta believe I'm gone."

Girmond inclined his head. "I intend to talk with her."

Steve looked at the floor. "Look, Mr. Girmond, I'm sure you have her best interests at heart, but generally speaking she seems to know what she wants. And what she doesn't."

Girmond chuckled. "Does she?"

Steve looked up. What did he mean by that?

"She is upset with you," Girmond said. "For what reason, I know not. She was not forthcoming with me."

"Hah! Join the club." Steve smiled to soften the edge on his words.

Girmond held up a meaty hand. "But to me it was a heated moment. She was inflamed, not thinking clearly. All I would like to know from you is, if she were to agree, would you take your job back?"

The man acted as if he knew he had some influence on her, Steve thought. Not only that, Steve could sense in the way he talked, the quiet sureness and humor of his expression, that Girmond knew Roxanne better than any of them had realized. Even if that weren't true, however, as the chef, the premier draw of the restaurant, chances were he could demand Steve be rehired and Roxanne would cave.

Besides, God knew they'd need a bartender tonight, if last night was any indication.

"I don't know . . ." The devil in him didn't want to capitulate so easily. "If she's going to be this hotheaded I'm not sure she's the ideal employer."

Steve could feel Rita gaping beside him.

"For God's sake, Steve," she said. "Just tell him you'll take the job back. You know you will anyway."

He looked at her. "Do I? I was rather unfairly terminated, I think." He turned back to Girmond. "No offense, but your friend is a distrustful, suspicious woman with a heart of stone."

Girmond frowned and stroked his moustache. "She has some trouble trusting, for good reason. She should not be punished for this. She is a very beautiful woman, *monsieur*, and she deserves a second chance."

Steve folded his arms over his chest. "Beauty's only skin deep. Coldness goes all the way through."

Rita sighed. "Oh brother."

"She needs to stop jumping to conclusions about me," Steve added. "She's done that since the first time we met."

Girmond gave him a look that cut right through his bullshit. "Roxanne is perhaps reserved, and fearful of getting hurt. The unperceptive man," he enunciated this pointedly, "might see this as cold." The Gallic shrug again. *Nothing he could do about stupid people*, it seemed to say.

Steve's eyes narrowed. So the old guy had some manipulation in him. He'd have to remember that.

"All right," Steve said. "I'll come back. If she asks. But tell her she needs to stop thinking the worst of me."

Girmond smiled, eyes twinkling. "I will tell her to strive to look beyond the obvious."

Roxanne gritted her teeth and punched down her dough, dumping it out on the table into a mound of flour. She coughed as the cloud that ensued enveloped her.

She didn't want to see him. Didn't want to talk to him. Didn't want to have anything to do with his ugly little world. He belonged in a bar like Charters—smoky, dirty, scented with stale beer and filled with other juvenile minds—not in her radiant temple of gastronomic pleasure.

Steve was beneath her, she told herself, devoid of common human decency and sentiment. Anybody who could place a bet on emotion, on passion, was a degenerate of the worst sort. He did not deserve her notice.

At least Martin, for all his flaws, respected the passion that was between them. He hadn't belittled it by turning it into a . . . a *conquest*.

Or had he? Maybe hooking up with a young woman who graced the covers of magazines was a kind of triumph for him over what he'd always termed "the stagnation" of his marriage.

She shook her head. She didn't need to impugn anyone else with Steve's falseness. And she certainly didn't need to be thinking about Martin in any context. Though she had to wonder how in the *world* she'd managed to learn nothing from Martin's treachery. She'd trusted Steve when she should have been at her most vigilant. After learning how selfish men could be, she had turned around and trusted another liar, all the while believing her only problem with him was their lack of common interests. What a fool she was.

She punched her dough again and began rolling it out.

She would just stay here in the kitchen. She didn't need to see Steve. If she needed more water, she could send a busboy.

No.

No, it wasn't incumbent upon *her* to hide from *him*. Let him be the one worried about seeing her. Let him be anxious about what to say now that she'd discovered his true character.

He was just lucky M. Girmond was able to convince her that having a lying, philandering bartender was better than having no bartender at all. Business first, he'd said. And that would be her motto from here on out.

Business first.

"No, no, no!" she heard M. Girmond say to one of the assistants—the garde-manger—behind her. "You treat asparagus like a *flower*, do you understand me? You do not lay it in a tub full of water to soak like a baby. You stand it *up*, like a flower!"

"But before I always—"

"I do not care about before. Before means nothing to me. *Rien!* Before you did not work for a place that respected the food, or they would have stood the asparagus up."

"Like a flower . . ."

"*Exactement.* Now, about the fish. It should be stored in the same position in which it swims, *oui?*"

Roxanne smiled to herself. She couldn't help but feel confident with M. Girmond in the kitchen. He was a master, a perfectionist, with an attention to detail unrivalled in culinary circles. And she knew, even if tonight was as busy as last night, and tomorrow night as busy as tonight, that that attention to detail wouldn't waver in the slightest.

She turned from her dough and began working on the custard filling.

Roxanne's strategy for dealing with Steve worked and didn't work. She succeeded in not seeing him all night, but she also succeeded in not leaving the kitchen. The crowd was in fact the same as the previous night's, and while that elated her, it also ran her ragged.

Sir Nigel came back at one point early in the evening to report, with what constituted a smile on his face, that reservations for Friday night had been filled.

Booked! she thought, her stomach sailing with excitement. Open two days and she was already booked solid one weekend night.

She wished she had a moment to call Skip. Even though he'd been negative about her plan to open this restaurant she knew he'd be pleased for her. As he had said, he didn't *want* her to fail; he was just afraid she would.

It didn't look like that would happen now, she thought with a deep, quiet joy. Everything was coming together perfectly. And with that thought she pulled a perfect raspberry soufflé out of the oven.

The kitchen was quiet, she was wiping down her counter, and M. Girmond was packing up for the evening. Out front, most of the waitstaff was gone, but she could still hear the vacuum being run in the dining room. George, probably. It was his night to close.

"Well, my dear. It is another night of adventure, *n'est pas*?" M. Girmond stopped behind her and gave her shoulders a squeeze with his big warm hands. "You should be so proud of yourself, *mon ange*."

She smiled and dropped her head as he kneaded her aching muscles. "I'm proud of *you*, mostly. It's because of you that everyone came. But I am proud of the way the employees all came together and worked so well. Who would have thought there would be so few glitches?"

He patted her back. "There is time for glitches. But here we are getting our feet in the door. Problems later . . ." He put his hands up, nonchalantly. "We will deal with them."

She smiled, tired down to her very bones. "No, no. No problems. I won't allow it."

M. Girmond laughed, his hearty, comforting laugh. "We cannot hope that there will never be problems, *ma puce*. We can only aspire to dealing with them well."

"Spoken like a true Zen master."

M. Girmond laughed again, patted her once more on the back, then wished her good night. "Go to sleep soon!" he called as he went out the back door.

Roxanne locked the door behind him, then turned out the lights. She pushed through the swinging doors to the dining room, which was dark. Everyone had finished, cleaned up and gone home. The only light was from the bar, where soft spotlights on the bottles gave them a jewel-like glow.

She sighed and sat in one of the bar chairs, looking out over the dining room. Street lamps from the sidewalk outside lit the tables by the front window, gleaming off the glasses and silverware laid out for tomorrow's service. Some of the tables were bare, waiting for clean dishes to be set out, but for now the place looked quiet and ready for another day. Everything was under control.

Her restaurant was a success.

She let the thought wash over her. A calm such as she had never known settled within her. Even the fiasco with Steve seemed small compared to all that was right. Besides, Steve was still here.

Not that it mattered that he was still here. Mostly it just meant that she hadn't screwed up so badly that she was without a bartender. That was all.

She should go to bed, she thought. She was too tired to be thinking these thoughts. But she was too tired to get up off the chair, too. She thought briefly about laying her head down right here, but knew she'd only wake up in an hour with a stiff neck wondering where she was.

She hoisted herself out of the chair and stopped abruptly.

Had she heard something?

She stopped breathing. It sounded again. Someone working at the lock on the front door.

Her heart immediately started hammering in her chest. What if last time there really *had* been an intruder and it was not just the squirrel? What if he had come back to finish the job? At a million thoughts a minute, she had already constructed the scene of her demise when whoever was at the door succeeded in getting it open.

She gasped. The door swung wide. She stood frozen as a hand hit the switch for the light over the maitre d' station.

She squinted in the light. It was Steve. And he was apparently as startled to see her as she was to see him.

"Jesus," he breathed, after visibly jumping when he saw her. "You scared the shit out of me."

She took a deep, wavering breath. "What are you doing here?"

Her tone was imperious. She knew because she made it that way. And Steve obviously picked up on it.

"I forgot my backpack." He gave her a cool look as he walked around the bar. "Don't worry. I'll be out of your hair in a minute."

She didn't say anything, just watched him lift the hinged door of the service bar and root around in the lower cabinets for his bag.

"So what are you waiting for?" He pulled the bag out and looped it over his shoulder. "Got a hot date?"

Roxanne brushed her palms down her sides, her posture impeccable. "I could ask the same of you."

"You could. But *I* would answer. There's the difference." He closed the service bar quietly behind him.

"What does that mean?"

"It means . . ." He stopped before her and tilted his head. "That if I'd heard a story about you, I would ask you about it before flying off the handle."

"Would you?" she said, her tone reflecting that she didn't believe it for an instant.

"I would."

"I did something different." She crossed her arms over her chest and forced herself to hold his gaze, though it did all kinds of syrupy things to her insides. "I consulted the evidence, and in doing so found confirmation of the whole sordid story."

"And by evidence you're referring to . . . ?"

"The money, of course."

"Ah, of course." He nodded his head. "For women, money always talks, that's for sure."

"And men are so impervious to money."

"Some men."

"I wouldn't bet on that," she replied with a chuckle.

He stood quiet for a moment, studying her. She fought the urge to squirm under his regard.

"Roxanne, listen, I'm only going to say this once—"

"Is that a threat? Because I don't feel very afraid."

His brows lowered. "I had nothing to do with that bet, other than taking P.B.'s money to shut him up."

"Which apparently didn't work." She gave him a mock-sympathetic look.

He took a frustrated breath. "I just want you to understand that I did not bet on you. On us. On—you know. I didn't bet that I could *get* you."

"And yet, you did."

"No I didn't! Oh, you mean . . . I didn't plan on that. I didn't plan on anything that evening. Surely you know that."

"And now we both regret it. But look on the bright side. *You* won a hundred dollars."

He shook his head. "I'm not keeping that. I told you, it was never a bet."

"So P.B.'s getting his money back?" She laughed cynically, spreading her arms wide. "All this and change back?"

"Roxanne . . ."

She shook her head, nerves shaking from her head to her feet. "I think I should get it."

"You—what?"

She held out a hand. "The money. You should at least split it with me."

Steve gave an incredulous laugh. "You want the money?"

"Half of it. I want to get a new lock for my door."

The smile was still half on his face. "That only works if you don't open it yourself."

Her eyes were steady on his. "I don't think that'll be a problem anymore."

He laughed again, shaking his head, and plopped his backpack on the bar. Unzipping an outer pocket he said, "I'd rather you have this than P.B. anyway."

He held out the roll of bills to her.

She stepped toward him, took the roll and counted the twenties, five of them.

"Thank you." She pushed them into her pocket. "Now we're even. So from now on if you'll keep your mind on the job and your pants zipped, we won't have any problems."

She turned away.

Steve's hand took her upper arm and turned her back to face him. "Excuse me?" he said. "If *I'll* keep *my* pants zipped? Can we just jump back in time a little bit and remember who kissed whom first that night at your apartment?"

He dropped his hand.

"*You* apologized for that." Heat rose in her cheeks but she didn't care. He was off balance now.

"As did *you*." He glared at her. "And if you're honest with yourself you'll remember that I did not exactly have to force myself on you the other night. You were right there with me. Right there," he repeated, stepping closer, "*with me.*"

She stared back at him, her chin lifted and her heart beating wildly. He was close to her, his eyes fiery, and God help her, she felt a wave of desire wash over her.

Something flickered in his eyes, and after a second a slight smile curved his lips. "Don't pretend you didn't feel anything. Don't pretend you don't feel anything right now, Roxanne."

She inhaled slowly to brace herself and said, cool as she could, "How much do you have on *this* encounter? Huh, Steve? Another hundred?"

"Consider this a gentleman's bet," he said. "With you."

She laughed. "Control yourself, Serrano. I don't like betting on the same horse twice. Besides, your charm has a limited life span."

His eyes were soft now, enticing, and somehow they compelled her to stay where she stood.

"I know that," he said, his voice low.

He stood close, too close for her to draw an even breath, and he reached a hand up to touch her cheek.

The contact zinged through her and she felt that now-familiar melting at her core that signaled her body's unequivocal desire.

"But something tells me it hasn't worn off yet." With that, he took her chin in his hand and laid a kiss on her lips.

Despite herself, her mouth opened under his. Their tongues met. Heat flared within her and the kiss deepened.

He wanted her too, she could feel it in his mouth, his tongue, his lips. Could feel it in the heat coming off of his body, in the way he stood rigid, unwilling to touch her beyond his fingers on her chin.

Just as she was willing to throw the whole damn fight out the window, just as she raised her hand to touch his body, he pulled back.

She stood before him, on fire, but unable to move.

Dead serious, pulse beating hard in his neck, he let his fingers trail her cheek as he dropped his hand.

"I'm not the only one who can't control himself," he said and stepped back. With one shake of his head, he added, "Don't kid yourself, Roxanne."

12

Dessert Special of the Day
Bombe Chez Soi—<u>what you least expect</u>
Strawberry ice mold filled with vanilla mousse,
    surrounded by sliced fresh strawberries

Steve hunched over his notebook, open books spread
on the table around him in the hush of the Library of
Congress. He scratched out one sentence on the pad in
front of him, then another, then sat back.

Portner Jefferson Curtis was proving to be an inade-
quate distraction from Roxanne Rayeaux.

He should call Lia, he thought. That was the kind of
distraction he needed. Flesh and blood. Not musty old
papers and unprovable theories.

Of course, with Lia he'd also get guilt and remorse,
additional proof that she and Steve had absolutely
nothing in common.

He scratched his forehead, then rubbed his palm
against it.

He didn't want Lia, couldn't even quite remember what was appealing about Lia, with Roxanne taking over his mind. All he could think about was Roxanne's thick, glossy hair cascading through his fingers. Her hot, soft skin, pale in the moonlight next to his. Her lithe body as eager and hungry as his, pressing, shifting, winding around him like a cloud of erotic energy— or an impossibly seductive serpent.

His body began to tighten and he leaned forward again, staring at the portrait of Portner in the dusty book in front of him.

Thin, pointed face. Slick black hair. Beady, unscrupulous eyes. The man's face screamed *thief*.

Steve was as certain he'd stolen the "fair copy" of the Declaration of Independence as if he'd known him personally. And he probably did know him better than he knew most modern-day people. He'd read the man's letters, examined his will, studied his history, lived in his house.

Steve sighed.

The worst part was, it wasn't just Roxanne's body that made her so irresistible to his thoughts. She was completely unpredictable. He never knew what she was going to say or do.

Lia, he could predict like the sequence of the old *Mousetrap* game. Say this and that falls, do this thing and you end up in that trap, make her mad and the whole thing comes tumbling down.

Roxanne was just the opposite. Do something you think will earn you a slap across the face and you end up having the night of your life. Challenge her in a way that would make other women explode and she throws it right back at you.

He couldn't have been more stunned, or more impressed, when she said she deserved P.B.'s bet money. He chuckled even now just thinking about it.

"Mr. Serrano?" A rumpled man of about fifty with glasses on the end of his nose stood next to him with a cardboard box.

"Yes?" Steve sat up, feeling as if he'd been caught talking to himself. He used the opportunity to stretch elaborately, and his back muscles screamed in protest.

"We came across another box of letters you might be interested in." The man smelled heavily of body odor as he leaned over to put it on Steve's table. "There are at least a couple letters that other people wrote to Jefferson, but there might be one in here from the cousin you're looking for."

Steve's eyes shifted to the box. It looked like something that might come out of his mother's attic. Fatigue washed over him. How many boxes like this had he prowled through? How many times had he thought *here* was going to be the evidence he was looking for?

"Thanks," he said, mustering a smile. "Thanks very much."

The man nodded and went back to his desk.

Steve stood up and ran a finger along one edge of the box to remove a spiderweb. He tried to remind himself that this *could* be the very box that would contain what he most needed, despite his being tired and discouraged. He even tried to tell himself he could find something else, just as good, to give merit to all his time spent studying this degenerate Jefferson cousin.

But he didn't believe it.

Still, he reached a hand in and gently pulled forth a sheaf of folded parchment. Slowly, he laid the letters out on the table, one by one, searching for the hand-writing he'd come to know so well . . .

"And it'll be delivered this afternoon?" she asked, hold-ing the phone between her ear and shoulder as she put her wallet with her credit cards in it back into her purse. "Yes, just put them in a box. That's great, thank you."

She hung up the phone and smiled. Roxanne: 1, Steve: 0.

After locking the apartment door behind her, Rox-anne trotted down the stairs to the restaurant, her kitchen clogs galloping on the wooden treads like a herd of horses.

She felt good. No, more than good. She felt like the world was her oyster. Something about that kiss had set her free. Or maybe it was the moments leading up to it. When she'd realized this was not something to ag-onize about, but maybe something she could have a lit-tle fun with.

The bottom line was, she was in control.

Strange, she knew, considering she was most defi-nitely *out* of control when Steve kissed her—at least physically. But there it was.

It helped that she believed him about the bet. She'd seen enough of both Steve and P.B. to know who was probably telling the truth and which scenario was more likely. So she was able to shed the ugly fear that she'd been the object of some sick joke between them.

Not that that meant she was eager to be involved with either one. Quite the contrary. It just meant she and Steve could probably get back to some semblance of a decent working relationship.

The best thing—the thing that really kept her spirits buoyed—was that the restaurant was doing well, far better than expected. Her life in New York was becoming a distant memory and—most of all—she was barely thinking about Martin, at least not with any sort of longing. When she left him over a year ago to go to culinary school, she thought he'd be in her thoughts forever. A constant ache of failure, of love lost.

Now the only reason he was even a blip on her radar was as a cautionary tale. A lesson.

Instead she was excited by her work. By her whole new life. And even by the way she was dealing with her mistakes.

She let herself into the restaurant, taking a good long minute in the dining room to appreciate the warm colors, the welcoming French country prints, the coziness of the brick walls. Winter sun poured through the front window, making the whole place feel like a little oasis of spring, even though it was twenty degrees and as windy as a Chicago city street outside.

Maybe someday she'd have to open for lunches. The place was just too charming in daylight to be empty.

With a smile she moseyed back to the kitchen, where she was greeted by gleaming chrome and the fresh smell of a meticulously clean room.

She was going to make *le délice de Montecito* for dessert tonight. A special cake made with chocolate and meringue and Amaretto. Her favorite part, however, was the French butter cream.

As she got out the ingredients, she noticed a cold draft on her feet. Trepidation oozed up her spine as she remembered the last time she felt an indoor breeze— when the back door had been broken into—and she looked toward that exit now.

Shut and locked tight, the windows intact. She glanced around the room. Nothing seemed amiss.

She kept working. But every now and then another draft would eddy around her ankles and creep up her pants legs. Was it just because she wore clogs that she felt it more on her heels? Or was the breeze coming from someplace low, some vent gone awry?

She squatted and put her hands near the mats covering the floor. There was definitely a draft. She tried to follow it toward the back door, but it was coming from across the room.

From, she discovered as she hobbled low across the floor, the basement door.

She put her hand by the crack at the base of the door and felt the frigid air wafting through it.

She stood up. This wasn't normal, was it? Surely it wasn't *that* cold out, that the basement would let fly a frosty breeze.

The office was the next door over and she entered it to get her keys. Normally the keys to the basement, the freezer (which they never locked, but *could*, if they wanted to), and the middle drawer of the desk hung on a nail protruding from the door trim.

That nail was empty.

She narrowed her eyes and stepped back out of the office. Turning to the basement door, she put a hand on the knob and paused. Should she call someone before going downstairs?

No. She didn't want to call Steve. She'd done that last time and regretted it. And she certainly didn't want to call P.B. She could call Skip, but he was at school and wouldn't be able to come over until later. She could call the police and ask for someone other than P.B., but it wasn't as if she knew something was wrong. Right now it was just a case of missing keys, and you didn't call the cops for that.

She turned the knob. The door opened.

Maybe she'd gone down here earlier and just forgotten to lock up again. Or maybe M. Girmond had put something down here and accidentally pocketed the keys. They had talked about using the basement for additional dry goods storage.

She flipped the light switch and was glad to see the bare bulb come on. It wasn't particularly bright, but it was better than nothing.

She trod carefully down the stairs, taking each step as if it might collapse under her weight, her eyes slowly adjusting to the dim light. The breeze grew and the temperature dropped the farther she descended.

When she neared the bottom she saw a huge hole dug in the hard dirt floor of the cellar, just at the base of the stairs. She stepped around it and looked inside. It was empty. Nothing but chopped up dirt and clay.

She turned in a circle. It took her eyes a moment to fully adjust to the contrast of outside light and cellar darkness, mixed with the dim glow of the bare light-bulb, but when they did, what she saw was destruction.

At the opposite end of the cellar, daylight shone through the split boards of the trapdoor to the alley, illuminating a space strewn with broken wood, scattered bricks and cracked mortar.

This was not the work of any squirrel. She doubted even a bear could do this.

One side of the brick foundation had been picked at here and there, as if someone had taken several large pieces out of the jigsaw puzzle that made up the wall. The bricks that had occupied those spaces lay scattered on the dirt floor.

At the far end, broken boards lay in haphazard piles and the cotton-candy trailings of fiberglass insulation blew in the breeze.

Roxanne put a hand to her throat, felt her heart pounding in the arteries there. For a moment she thought she might throw up.

The abandoned cellar entrance from the alley had been boarded up and nailed shut, she happened to know. Not only that, but the space beneath the trapdoor had been stuffed with that pink fiberglass insulation.

She would bet anything most of that insulation was now swirling around the back alley in the wind.

And at the bottom of the trapdoor stairs, too, was a hole. Not quite as large or as deep as the other, but still a hole.

But . . . if someone had broken in through the outside entrance, why were the keys missing?

The answer came to her immediately.

To break in again.

She heard a slight sound behind her and jumped, whirling toward the dark end of the room. She saw nothing, then spotted a piece of the paper that had covered the insulation listing in the breeze.

She had to call the police.

She jumped over the hole at the bottom of the kitchen steps and took the stairs two at a time, started to slam the door at the top but realized she shouldn't touch anything. She wondered what they would get fingerprints off of in the basement, what with all the broken wood and brick. Would brick hold a fingerprint? The back cellar entrance looked like someone had taken an axe to it. Who would do such a thing?

And why hadn't she heard it?

Because she'd been exhausted. She'd slept like the dead last night.

She sat down at her desk chair in the office and dialed 911. No messing around this time. Maybe they'd send someone other than P.B., but even if they didn't, she needed the cops. Someone was obviously looking for something and unless they'd gotten it out of one of those holes they would probably be back.

Naturally they sent P.B.

Roxanne could only shake her head as she saw his squad car pull up in front of the restaurant and his square blond head appear over the door.

He parked right in front, of course, with the lights on so as to draw as much attention to the scene as possible, it seemed.

She walked slowly to the front door and pulled it open.

She didn't know what she expected, but it wasn't the same old overly friendly P.B. he'd always been.

"Hey, Roxanne," he said with that trademark rise of one big square hand. "Hear you had another encounter with a squirrel."

He laughed at his own joke as his little partner— Officer Stuart?—got out of the passenger-side door.

She shook her head. "Unless this squirrel was the size of a gorilla, I don't think that's what we're dealing with."

"Well, we'll check it out for you."

He arrived at her side and gave her shoulder a squeeze with one hand. It was a companionable gesture, making her feel slightly guilty for all the awful thoughts she'd had about him since learning of the bet.

His next words, however, erased any pity she might have felt.

"I know you girls get all in a tizzy about your things getting messed up or not looking the way they should, so we'll just see if there was an actual intruder this time." He gestured toward his partner. "Stu, you wanna take the squad car around back? I'll meet you there. C'mon, Rox, let's take a look at what this giant squirrel did."

She rolled her eyes as she turned toward the door, resenting the feel of his meaty paw on the small of her back. How could she ever have accepted a date with this guy? Had he just hidden all this condescending crap?

Maybe so. And maybe he didn't feel like he had to hide it anymore . . .

That made her feel better, and she was happy to lead him down the basement steps to the destruction no wildlife creature could have wreaked.

"Holy shit," P.B. said, his tone reverential, as he stepped over the hole in the dirt. He strode into the room, bending to look at a cracked brick, then moved close to the wall to examine one of the patchwork holes.

He pulled a flashlight from his belt and shone it on the mud exposed behind the wall, looking all around the edges, and even prodding some of the bricks with a pen.

"This is bad. Any worse and I'd say you should get someone in here to look at this foundation."

She closed her eyes. *Damn.* "It's that bad? You think it's, it's been compromised?"

P.B. shrugged. "Nah. It's probably okay. But it sure as hell is a mess."

"What do you think they were looking for?" She caught herself wringing her hands in a very "tizzy-like" way and dropped them to her sides.

"Hey!" Officer Stuart yelled from the broken cellar door at the far end of the room. "I found an old padlock out here, maybe something from the door? And a sliver of metal, like maybe a broken tool or something."

"Bag it up, Stu," P.B. called, walking over to look into the hole by the trap door.

Roxanne started toward P.B. to see what he was looking at so intently, but at the sound of her movement he turned and held a hand out. "Hold it right there."

She jumped, her heart rate accelerating with another surge of adrenaline. It had been surging since she'd found the break-in.

"What? What is it?" She looked upward as if the

foundation had already started giving way and she was about to be crushed by three stories of eighteenth-century townhouse.

P.B. looked annoyed. "I don't want you kicking this stuff around. We gotta look at everything. Where it sits, how it fell, everything." He strode toward her, seemingly heedless of where he put his big bootheels.

Roxanne flushed and nearly made some churlish retort, when he said in a more hushed tone, "Let's go upstairs. I want to ask you something." He glanced over his shoulder, intimating he didn't want Officer Stuart to hear what he was going to say.

Roxanne turned and went up the stairs, P.B. right behind her. In fact, he was so close behind, she felt a little self-conscious about where her rear end was in relation to his eyes.

When they reached the kitchen, P.B. took her arm and pulled her away from the back door. Her back against the wall near the office, he stood very close. Too close for comfort.

"Do you know where Steve was last night?" His eyes were flat and intent, a cop's eyes.

Heat poured into her cheeks. "He was here. Until we closed, obviously." Then she remembered. "And just afterward. He came back when I was locking up because he forgot his backpack."

P.B.'s brows rose. "He came back," he repeated significantly.

She nodded. "Because he forgot his backpack."

P.B.'s head moved in the barest nod. "Uh-huh."

She frowned. "Why? What are you saying?"

"Did he know you were going to be here when he came back?"

"I don't know." Did P.B. think *Steve* had something to do with this? That was ridiculous. Surely he wasn't saying that. "It was late," she added, "but it wasn't that much later than I usually leave."

Though Steve had nearly jumped out of his skin when he'd seen her.

"You say he came back for the backpack?"

"Yes. I saw him get it." Her heart was beating fast, as if she herself were being accused of something.

"The one he keeps under the bar?"

"Yes."

"The one that's *always* under the bar?" he said again.

She narrowed her eyes. If she could have backed away from him, she would have, but he had her against the wall and was standing so close she would have had to push him away.

"What are you saying, P.B.?"

At this he crossed his arms over his chest and turned away, one hand stroking his chin as he thought, as if he fancied himself some kind of Sherlock Holmes.

She took the opportunity to draw a relieved breath.

"Tell me." He turned back to her. "Has Steve talked any more about his *research*? You know, all that stuff about Thomas Jefferson and the draft of the Declaration of Independence?"

She shook her head. "No. He hasn't said a word about that since that one night."

"He hasn't said a word," P.B. repeated slowly, as if that, too, were significant. "Not a word?"

"Well, no. But we don't talk history a lot."

P.B. raised one brow and she knew immediately what he was thinking. "No, I don't imagine you do much talking." He let that sit a beat, then added, "About history."

"Look, P.B., I'm not sure what you're insinuating, but you can't possibly think Steve had anything to do with this."

"Can't I?"

Roxanne's mouth dropped open.

"Look, Roxanne, he talks to me about it all the time. I'm telling you, Steve's obsessed. It's got to be him."

Roxanne stared at him in disbelief. "You can't be serious."

"Hey, I know it's a terrible thing to say." P.B.'s face took on a concerned expression. "But Steve hasn't been himself lately. He's been worried about the fact that he's not going anywhere, that he doesn't have a career, a future, you know. Same stuff you and I talked about the night I took you out. For a while there he even thought he might have to leave this job. You gotta know I hate to say it. But I think he might be getting desperate."

"So desperate he'd start digging in the basement walls for some mythical document?" She nearly laughed. "He'd have to be an idiot!"

"What do you mean?" P.B. demanded. "You heard him talk about that draft. There's *evidence*—history, theories, whatever. There's good reason to believe something's hidden in this house. Why wouldn't he try to find it? It's worth a shitload of money."

"Because it's ridiculous. If nobody's found it yet, after all the years this house has been lived in, worked in, remodeled—well, it's crazy."

"I think you'd better take another look at your basement."

She took a deep breath. "Besides, what about this: Steve doesn't *have* to break in to look around the basement. The last thing he'd have to do is take an axe to the cellar door, for God's sake. He's got keys. He can walk down there whenever he wants."

P.B. gave her what could only be called a pitying look. "But, honey," he said slowly, as if to an inquisitive first grader, "then it wouldn't look like a break-in. The man's not stupid. If it's an inside job, you make it look like an outside job."

Roxanne's cheeks burned. He was right, of course. You wouldn't start tearing up the basement and not make it look like a break-in.

"Was anything else missing?" he asked. "Even if he did know enough to make it look like an outside job, Steve's an amateur, he probably wouldn't think to swipe a thing or two to throw us cops off the scent."

"I—I haven't looked around," she said desperately, knowing in her heart that nothing else was missing. The kitchen had been immaculate this morning. Just the way it had been left the night before.

"Uh-huh." P.B. nodded, looking at her knowingly.

"P.B., I simply don't believe—"

"Hey." Steve pushed through the swinging doors to the kitchen and Roxanne jumped enough to bump her head against the wall behind her.

"Hey, big guy," P.B. said, too heartily, in Roxanne's opinion. "What's going on?"

Steve looked from P.B. to Roxanne. "That's just what I was going to ask."

"We were just about to call you. Where you been?" P.B. asked, still grinning like a used-car salesman and sounding like a radio announcer.

Again he looked from P.B. to Roxanne. "At the library. And you wouldn't believe what I found. It's just what I've been—"

"The *library*," P.B. repeated, looking at Roxanne.

Steve stopped. "What's going on here?"

Roxanne looked at Steve. "Steve, there's been another break-in. In the basement—"

P.B. put a hand out, his arm blocking Roxanne's chest as if she were about to step into a street teeming with traffic. "I'll handle this."

"*Handle* this?" Steve repeated.

"I'm the one who should explain," P.B. amended, puffing out his chest a little. "I've just finished examining the damage. She might even need to call in an engineer to check the foundation."

"The foundation!" Steve was obviously disconcerted. "What'd they do, detonate a bomb?"

To Roxanne, it was obvious Steve had no idea what was going on.

Or did she just *want* to think that?

She shook her head. P.B. was throwing out a theory. He didn't have any facts. That it was a theory that implicated a friend who had just betrayed him with a woman he'd wanted to date said it all.

"Come on," P.B. said to Steve, "I'll show you the damage. But you gotta be careful. Don't forget it's a crime scene. You can't be touching or moving anything."

"Come off it, P.B.," Steve said tiredly, stepping past Roxanne, with a quick glance at her. "Just show me what happened."

Before they got to the basement door, however, Officer Stuart knocked on the back door.

"You got a key for that?" P.B. said, directing an officious finger from Roxanne to the back door, even though she'd already started across the kitchen to unlock it.

She pulled the door open and let him in.

"I found this." Officer Stuart looked triumphant as he held one black glove aloft in his hand.

"No, that's mine," Steve said, shaking his head. "I've been looking for it. It must have dropped out of my pocket when I got out of the truck the other night."

He strode across the room toward the officer, hand out.

Behind his back, P.B. gave Roxanne a sad but meaningful look.

"'Fraid not, sir," Officer Stuart said, lowering the glove to his side. "Everything I find out here today is evidence."

13

Dessert Special of the Day
Apple Fig Turnover—<u>because turnabout's</u>
   <u>fair play</u>
Apples and figs sauteed in sweet butter
   with vanilla and cognac in puff pastry

Steve looked suspiciously from Officer Stuart to Roxanne to P.B.

"So you're saying I can't get my glove back until you figure out who broke in?" he asked.

P.B. scowled and glanced away. Then he jerked his head in the direction of the basement door and said, "C'mon. Let me show you this."

Steve's eyes met Roxanne's and she shrugged her brows. "I've got work to do," she said, turning away.

He watched her back, then followed P.B. down the basement steps.

The moment he and P.B. reached the cellar and

Steve's eyes adjusted to the light, P.B. turned to him and said, "You know I oughta punch you in the face, you dog. You could have at least told me you were going after Roxanne."

Steve stopped, glad P.B. had brought the matter up directly but distracted by the presence of a large hole at the base of the stairs. He knew why that hole was there, but who else would?

He tried to focus on P.B. "From the way you took that damn bet so seriously I figured you thought I was. Besides, it was something that just happened, kind of by accident. I wasn't trying to go behind your back."

P.B. shook his head. "Well, you could have told me you were *successful* anyway. Now what am I gonna do with these damn symphony tickets? Nobody I know's gonna wanna go listen to that shit."

Steve chuckled and after a second P.B. joined him.

Steve studied the hole, then cast his gaze around the basement. Chinks of wall were missing, which made no historical sense, but another hole at the bottom of the unused stairs to the outside trapdoor caught his eye. Those steps were too recent to be of interest to any historian, but the only logical reason to dig there was the historical one.

"This is some kind of mess, huh?" Steve said. "What do you think they were doing down here?"

P.B. shrugged. "Who knows? Maybe looking for drug money."

Steve had nothing to say to that. It didn't seem likely, but sounded like a typical cop suspicion.

He looked hard at P.B.

P.B. noticed the look. "What?"

Steve hesitated. "You shouldn't have told her about that bet, Peeb. She didn't deserve to have her feelings hurt like that."

P.B. shrugged and kicked a broken brick across the dirt floor. "I know. I feel a little bad about that. But still, she was stepping out on me. You know, in a way."

Which is why she told you she didn't want to go to the damn symphony, Steve thought, but he didn't say it. It was enough that P.B. admitted to feeling some guilt.

"So . . ." Steve moved back across the cellar toward P.B., holding out a hand. "Should we let bygones be bygones and all that?"

P.B. laughed and slap-grabbed Steve's hand. "Done. It'd take more than just some chick to undo our friendship, right? Hell, I've known you longer than I've known anybody, except my parents."

"And they *have* to keep in touch with you," Steve said with a grin.

It took P.B. a minute, then he punched Steve in the arm. "So tell me about what you found at the library. You seemed pretty stoked when you came in. Good news?"

Steve couldn't help smiling. It had to be a conscious decision but he let go of his anger toward P.B. Hanging onto it would have been a little like kicking a dog, then being mad at it for biting you. "The best."

In the interest of laying this rocky patch between them to rest, Steve told him about what amounted to his best day of research yet. Because today, he had found what he'd been looking for. A letter from Portner Jefferson Curtis to a Mr. Stanhope in May 1826, following up an apparent face-to-face meeting, further clarifying the terms of his will to include an object that "has been kept under lock and key," and would be kept "likewise sequestered until such time as the Notable Author, Mr. Jefferson, who is known to be ailing, has left this earthly plane, or I have done so."

Furthermore, he stated that this object "has been seen by none other than" himself for years, and that it was hidden, "quite cleverly", within his abode until such time as Mr. Stanhope had need of executing Portner's will.

This letter might have been enough to prove Steve's theory—or at least fuel it for the purposes of his book—but with the object in question undefined, Steve dug further. In a batch of letters he'd copied some months ago, Steve, remembering the name Stanhope, found a letter from June 1826 from one Mortimer Stanhope to Portner Jefferson Curtis of Alexandria, Virginia, declaring that Portner would be best advised to place what he suspected was "a document of significant historical merit" with the appropriate authorities at the Department of State. The Department of State was created by the Constitution and was supposed to keep "the custody and charge of all records, books and papers" of importance to the new Republic.

If that didn't strongly suggest that Portner's "object" could very well be Jefferson's "fair copy," Steve didn't know what would.

In addition, Stanhope wondered why Portner would want to keep something that could not "morally have been acquired, and therefore could not be honorably displayed nor employed for any profitable purpose."

Not only did this imply that the document in question had been stolen, but it also seemed to confirm that the draft was still in Portner's possession when he died less than a year after receipt of Mr. Stanhope's letter, and only three months after Jefferson himself had died.

It also confirmed that the draft had at one time been hidden somewhere within this very house. Meaning there was at least a chance that it was still here, in some form or other—most probably in a pile of decomposing parchment.

P.B. listened to this story in silence, feigning, Steve was certain, what little interest showed on his face. At the end of Steve's monologue, P.B. frowned, nodded, said, "Cool," then said he had to go.

Steve could only chuckle at himself. He was so excited about his find he'd had to tell *somebody*. That it was the last person on earth who would be interested served him right. He should choose his audiences more wisely.

The two of them left the basement and headed in their separate directions.

Roxanne was not in the kitchen when Steve passed through it again, though judging by her workspace she was obviously in the middle of something, and he wondered if she was avoiding him or P.B. Probably both, he thought, though she could hardly avoid him for long. He'd be back at work in a few short hours.

Climbing the three flights of stairs to his apartment, Steve thought about the hole at the bottom of the steps in the basement. Was it just coincidence that it was "under the first step" of both cellar staircases? He didn't see how it could be. But how many people knew about that will who didn't also know that the steps had already been investigated? Including, Steve believed, the cellar stairs, and not so very long ago either. Within the last fifty years, he was fairly certain.

Of course, there'd also been a hole at the bottom of the trapdoor stairs, which, as any decent historian knew, were built in the late 1800s, long after Portner's death, when the house had been owned by a grain merchant and the basement used for storage. So maybe the holes were for something else.

Steve reached the top of the staircase and turned left toward his apartment door, where he was greeted by the sight of a large cardboard box. On top of the box, written with a black marker in block letters was his name and address.

There was no return address. There was not even a postmark or any postage.

Steve fished his keys out of his pocket and slid one into the door lock, looking askance at the carton. When he got the door open, he pushed the box inside with one foot and put his backpack on the floor. He took off his coat, then dragged the box into the living room to examine it.

The cardboard had obviously been ripped open at some point and taped back up. But after a minute of trying to wriggle his fingers under the new packing tape, he still couldn't open it. He went to the kitchen to get a knife, wondering if he should call Homeland Security and report a suspicious package.

Could this have anything to do with the break-in? Some message the intruders left behind?

But that was ridiculous. For one thing, the box would have been here this morning, and he certainly wouldn't have missed it when he left for the library.

Or would he have? He'd been pretty distracted most of the day. Up until he'd found Portner's letter, in fact.

He stuck the knife under one flap and cut through the tape. First one side, then the other, then across the top. Then he pulled back the flaps.

With an *oof* as if he'd been punched in the stomach, he dropped the flaps and jerked away.

He stepped back so fast he tripped over his backpack and landed flat on his ass against the coffee table.

Heart pounding wildly in his chest, he took a deep breath.

They couldn't be real.

He sat on the floor, watching the box with wary eyes, waiting for one of them to poke its pointy head out the top and come slithering over the side. The rest of them would follow and before he knew it—

This was stupid. They couldn't possibly be real.

He stood up and shook off his fear as if an imaginary audience were watching. Then he reached out the hand containing the knife. His palms were wet and sweat prickled along his scalp. With the tip of the blade, he pulled the cardboard flap back again.

From as far a distance as possible, he peered into the box. Then he exhaled, sagging in relief, despite the imaginary audience.

They were fake.

It was a box full of fake snakes. Who in God's name would *do* this? How many people knew he hated snakes?

That was easy. Everyone, Steve thought. He wasn't shy about his phobia, figuring the more people who knew, the less likely it would be he'd end up in a situation with snakes.

He kicked the carton and they jiggled like they were alive. He felt a little sick to his stomach. There had to be hundreds of them. Big, small, fat, thick, black, green, brown and speckled. He kicked the box again and watched them quiver.

Then he noticed the envelope.

He hated to admit it even to himself, but with his adrenaline still pumping he didn't even like reaching into the box to retrieve the envelope, despite knowing they were fake.

What if some smart aleck had put one real one into the mix?

That's what he would have done, if he were trying to scare the shit out of someone.

He plucked out the envelope with two fingers and backed away to sit on the couch. With the knife, he sliced the top and pulled out the note.

It was one white sheet of paper, folded in half, upon which was written:

Don't mess with things you can't handle.

—R.

Roxanne?

Roxanne had done this?

A chuckle started low in his gut. Then it rose until it was an outright laugh.

He could kill her, he thought. She'd given him the scare of a decade. And yet he had to laugh. It was so perfect. He couldn't remember the last time his heart had pounded that fast from fright.

He shook his head in wonder. *Unpredictable.* And he thought he'd liked that. He chuckled again.

If he could handle a box full of snakes, he could certainly handle Roxanne Rayeaux, he thought with a smile.

He dropped the note to his lap and gazed at the carton of serpents. A fitting gift in so many ways . . . one that deserved an appropriate thank you.

So what, he speculated with a small evil smile, would scare her?

Roxanne barely got her prep work done on time, what with the confusion accompanying the break-in, but by the time the restaurant opened she was equipped to handle the crowd.

She couldn't say she felt particularly safe knowing the police—specifically, P.B.—were on the case, but she had at least come to the conclusion that whoever was doing this was intent on something other than money. For some reason that made it more bearable.

Rita pushed through the double doors. "Roxanne, Steve needs you at the bar."

It was early, so she hadn't any desserts going out yet. But this was the night the reservation book was full and she was anticipating another hectic evening.

"What does he want?"

"I don't know. Got something on his mind, though." She pushed back out the doors with a trayful of appetizers.

Roxanne could swear Rita was smirking.

Wiping her hands on her apron, Roxanne followed her through the swinging doors and stopped, caught by unexpected laughter at the sight of Steve behind the bar.

He wore a long, green rubber snake on his head like a turban, and another around his waist like a belt. He was talking to an older, white-haired man at the bar—a guy who was here a lot, she noticed—who seemed to be admiring the outfit, based on Steve's pirouette to show off the hat.

In the middle of his spin he saw Roxanne and stopped, spreading his hands wide.

"I see you received my gift." She leaned on the service bar, unable to quell her smile. "And decided to . . . wear it to work?"

"Hey, the ladies love me in rubber." He grinned.

Despite herself, she guffawed.

"And there's more where this came from." He took the turban off and put it under one arm like a helmet. "I took a bunch of these babies to the shoe repair guy down the street. Always wanted me a pair of snakeskin boots," he said, the last in a pretty good imitation of John Wayne.

"I'm glad you like them so much. I have to say, I wasn't sure how they'd be received."

He sauntered toward her, his eyes laughing and his lips quirked in a half smile she found decidedly seductive, and put the turban on one side of the bar. Then he leaned over and put his elbows on the service bar across from her. Leaning over as they both were, his face was close to hers. Her folded hands were near enough to touch his and a zip of desire coursed through her center at the thought of doing it.

The devil was still in his smile when he asked, "What *ever* inspired you to give me such a gift, darlin'?"

His voice was low with proximity, his eyes captivating. She could see the smile playing on his lips and wondered what he'd do if she inched forward and planted hers on them.

Actually, she knew exactly what he'd do, and she knew that it was something she would be foolish to invite again. Much as she liked to think about it.

She tilted her head and spoke in her best Southern drawl. "It was like this, sugar. I had a hundred dollars just burnin' a big ol' hole in my li'l ol' pocket. So when I saw these charmin' fellas in the shop window, I just knew I had to get 'em for you."

He laughed, a low, sexy laugh that she felt clear through her body.

"So I guess I got that hundred dollars back, after all," he said.

She let her gaze linger on his. "Guess you did."

"Miss Roxanne, might I have a word?" The nasal tone and precise diction could belong to no one other than Sir Nigel, who was suddenly standing just next to her right hip.

She hadn't even noticed him approach.

She straightened. "Certainly, Sir Nigel. What is it?"

The tall man cast a disdainful glance at Steve, who stood up with a look of exaggerated affront.

"Excuse me, I have many important duties to attend," Steve said, with a bow at Roxanne.

"I've just had word," Sir Nigel said with some urgency tingeing his voice, "from an associate of mine at the *Washington Post* that Chez Soi is being discussed for an imminent review."

"By the *Post*?" Roxanne asked, pulse thrumming. "When?"

"He couldn't tell me, precisely. I don't believe he knew, to be honest, but he wanted to give me the 'heads up.' " Sir Nigel used the phrase stiffly, making Roxanne smile.

"That's fantastic. But—God. That means we really have to be on our toes. We haven't even had time to work out all the new-business kinks yet. Have you told Monsieur Girmond?"

Sir Nigel drew himself up imperiously. "Of course not. My duty was to inform you before anyone else. I shall apprise him instantly if you so desire."

Roxanne knew full well that wasn't the only reason he hadn't told the chef. Sir Nigel and M. Girmond had no conflict that she could sense, but they circled each other with wary politeness whenever interaction was called for. It could be just the age-old front-of-the-house/back-of-the-house contention, but she wasn't sure.

"Don't worry about it. I'll tell him." Roxanne thought for a moment. "Sir Nigel, I know who the *Post*'s reviewer is, but not by sight. Is there any way we can find out what he looks like? It would be nice if we could know when he was here. Not that we'd cook any differently, of course, but we'd know to treat him with V.I.P. status."

"Of course," Sir Nigel agreed with a smug smile. "Which is why it's fortunate that I do indeed know what Mr. Richards looks like. I will be able to alert the crew the moment he steps through the door."

Roxanne beamed up at the man. He might be pompous and he might keep the waitstaff on their toes by being both annoying and frightening, but the man was a treasure.

He gave her a short bow.

"Oh, Sir Nigel, you are the *best*." She reached up and gave him a quick hug, finding his tall frame surprisingly bony underneath his three-piece suit. She could swear she saw him blush.

"It is part of my job, madam."

"And you are doing it excellently. Thank you."

He gave her another short bow when George blew by waving a check. "Got a soufflé order."

"Okay. Gotta go. I'll tell Monsieur Girmond," she said to Sir Nigel. With a quick glance over her shoulder at Steve, she pushed back through the swinging doors to the kitchen, fairly aglow with the knowledge that Steve had been looking at her, too.

The following Monday, Roxanne returned from the grocery store—lugging four plastic bags in two aching hands up the tall flight of stairs and vowing to look into elevator costs—to find two boxes next to her door.

She looked around as if someone might be watching her, then stopped trying to contain her smile. After placing her groceries on the floor, she opened the apartment door.

The cat greeted her with an attempt to get out, and as Roxanne pushed him back inside with a foot he yowled and wound around her feet.

"I know," she said, picking up the bags to bring them to the kitchen island. "I just got you some food, and darting out the door isn't going to get you any. You can just quit your bitchin'."

She quickly put away the frozen items, then opened a can of cat food and filled Cheeto's dish.

She went back to look at the boxes. They were plain brown cardboard with no writing and the flaps were folded together over-under, so they wouldn't spring open.

She nudged one, jerking slightly as it was much lighter than she'd anticipated. She dragged each of them into the apartment. Taped to one was an envelope with the letter R on it. Still smiling, she opened the note.

In a strong, slanted masculine hand was written:

I had to think: What is she afraid of . . . ?

Steve's writing, she thought, looking at the sharply crossed *t*'s and flourish-less loops. She should probably have it analyzed, figure out if this guy was all he seemed. And not all she feared.

Roxanne put the note down and eyed the boxes warily. Unless Steve was curled up inside one, she didn't think any of her greatest fears could be contained in a cardboard box, or even two.

Just as she was about to slit the tape on one with a fingernail, the phone rang. She hunted for the portable, finally finding it wedged between two cushions on the couch.

"Hello?" she said breathlessly, catching it on the last ring before the answering machine would pick up.

Skip laughed in her ear. "Oh my, I didn't interrupt anything good, did I?"

"I can't even imagine what you mean by that," she said primly.

He sighed. "I'm afraid that's probably true these days."

She put one hand on her hip. "What's that supposed to mean?"

"Only that a girl like you is not supposed to be burying herself in her work."

"Oh no, not that old rant. So what's a girl like me supposed to be doing, huh?" She walked back to the dining room and the boxes, giving one a little shake with one hand. It sounded like a bunch of wadded-up paper.

"If you have to ask . . ."

She laughed. "A lot you know, Skip. I am right now about to open a large, very curious gift from . . . hang onto your hat . . . a *man*."

Silence greeted this announcement.

"Skip?"

"Oh no." His voice was somber. "Tell me it's not from Martin. Please tell me he's not up to his old tricks. Or if he is, that you're not going to fall for it again."

"Oh, Skip." She laughed ruefully. "Did I really put you through so much, talking about him all the time?"

"*Me*? It's *you* I'm worried about. That guy's given you emotional whiplash more times than I like to count. Don't even open it, Rox. I mean it. Just write 'Return to Sender' on it and throw it right back in the mailbox."

"Relax. It's not from Martin." She smiled again. "And it's way too big to fit in the mailbox."

"Not from Martin?" He perked up instantly. "Who's it from?"

"Steve. Steve Serrano. You remember the guy—"

"Oh come off it, Rox. I remember the guy. Mr. Charming from dinner. Why's he buying you a gift? You getting some on the side and not telling me about it?"

Roxanne actually blushed. Good thing she was on the phone. "Mr. Charming, eh? I'll have to tell him you said so."

"You didn't answer the question." Skip's voice was increasingly intrigued.

"It's not really a gift. That is, I doubt it's . . . well . . . anyway, I bought *him* something last week because I was mad at him because . . ." She remembered the kiss he gave her that night in the restaurant. It had felt so . . . intimate. "Well, it's too long a story to get into here, but I gave him a bunch of rubber snakes and I think this is his, uh, revenge."

Skip paused. "You—what? You bought him rubber snakes?"

"He's afraid of snakes."

"Ah."

"And he says in his note to me on these boxes that he had to think about what *I* was afraid of."

"You guys are trying to scare each other?"

"Uh, kind of." Maybe they already *did* scare each other. Maybe this was just some kind of weird, elaborate foreplay. Could it be foreplay if they'd already had sex?

"So, what is it?" Skip's voice brought her back.

She bit her lip. "I don't know. I haven't opened the boxes yet." "Box*es*? There's more than one?"

"There're two."

"Well, open them! I want to know how good this guy

is. Let's see, what's Roxanne afraid of? Failure? Maybe it's a box full of bad restaurant reviews."

"Very funny. Don't you have a class or something?"

"It's lunchtime. Besides, I'm not missing this. Open them and tell me what's in them."

"Okay, I'm opening one."

She pulled on the flaps of the top one and, with a cardboard squeak, they unwove themselves. Spotting what was inside, she laughed out loud.

"What?" Skip demanded. "What's in it? Tell me!"

"Ch—ch—ch—" She couldn't stop laughing.

"Roxanne."

She pulled on the flaps of the other box and encountered more of the same.

"Cheetos!" she finally shrieked. "Oh my God. This is amazing. He got me a hundred dollars' worth of Cheetos!"

14

Dessert Special of the Day
Chocolate Decadence— <u>for people with</u>
  <u>no self-control</u>
Chocolate bombe filled with chocolate mousse,
  topped with chocolate hazelnut cream
  and surrounded by mini chocolate truffles

"So what's the shelf life on these things?" Skip asked, looking at the mound of Cheetos bags on her floor. There were thirty-eight of them. They'd counted.

Roxanne sat with her feet up on the table, an open bag in her lap and the fingers of her right hand completely orange.

She lifted the bag and looked. "The 'Best By' date is November of this year." She looked at the pile, nodding. "That oughta be about right."

Skip looked at her. "You are *not* going to eat all of

these." He picked up a bag. "Look at this—have you read the label? *Ten* grams of fat per ounce—"

"Skip, Skip, Skip," she said, shaking her head. "You don't understand, I'm not one of your wrestlers. I'm a pastry chef. I'm *supposed* to be fat. If I'm not fat, people will think my food's no good."

He gave her a deadpan look. "Rox, you never leave the kitchen as it is. Who's going to know you're not fat enough?"

She popped another Cheeto into her mouth.

"Your tongue is orange," Skip said, going into the kitchen. "Does beer go with Cheetos?"

"Everything goes with Cheetos. Bring me one, too, please."

He came back into the dining room with two open beers and a roll of paper towels. He ran off about four of them and handed the wad to Roxanne. "Here, you're going to need these. Or are you just planning to shower after your snack?"

She grinned. "Pull up a bag and sit down." At his wince she laughed. "Are my teeth orange too?"

"This is sick." Skip plucked a bag from the table and tore it open. "I've never seen you so happy."

She finished a big swig from the beer and ran her tongue over her teeth. "It's incredible. I've never felt so guiltless." She grimaced at him. "Better?"

He examined her teeth. "All clean. Once again, beer solves the problem."

She laughed. "I guess Steve got this wrong, huh?"

"What's that?"

"Well, he was hoping to *scare* me with something. Do

I look scared to you?" She placed a Cheeto between her teeth and closed her eyes, blissful.

Skip looked down at the bag in his hands. "He's scared *me* with them. And I'm becoming a little afraid of you." He looked at her sideways. "Are these things addictive? How many of these bags have you eaten?"

She waved a Cheeto in the air nonchalantly. "Five or six. So how do you think I should respond? Or should I respond at all? I mean, this is fun and all, but I don't want this guy getting any ideas."

Any more *ideas*, she amended silently.

Skip looked at her, his expression dry. "Trust me, after you eat all these, he won't be getting any ideas."

She laughed and popped another puff. "I'm serious. What should I do?"

He poked his nose in the bag and sniffed. "Send him your Jenny Craig bill."

She smacked her lips.

Gingerly, he pulled out a cheese puff and, after studying it, put it in his mouth.

"Oh," he said, closing his eyes. "Oh my God. I'm back in Joey Fannini's wood-paneled basement, listening to Cheap Trick." He opened his eyes. "This is amazing. I haven't had one of these since I was a kid. It's like time travel in a bag."

She nodded. "I know. Aren't they good? I don't think I've had more than one or two at a time for at least fifteen years."

A knocked sounded on the door.

Skip and Roxanne looked at each other.

"Mr. Charming?" Skip mouthed, eyes wide, grin maniacal.

Roxanne chuckled and got up to answer the door. With two relatively un-orange fingers she turned the knob and pulled it open.

Steve's face split immediately into a smile and he started laughing. "I see you got my gift."

She put the bag behind her back. "What makes you say that?"

He lifted a hand and brushed gently at her cheek. Roxanne's pulse jumped as if she'd been electrocuted.

"You've got an orange streak on your face," he said, pulling his hand back and shoving it into his pocket.

"Is that the devil at the door?" Skip came out from the dining room and held out his hand to Steve. "Hey, good to see you."

"Skip." Steve shook his hand, then looked down at the orange crumbs on his palm.

Skip brushed his hand on his jeans. "Sorry about that. I hope you know you're going to be personally responsible for the enormity of one formerly attractive pastry chef."

Steve's brows rose. "So I see."

"Apparently she's not afraid of Cheetos anymore. Not since she quit—"

"Skip!" Roxanne turned on him suddenly, knowing just where he was going with that statement. "Why don't you *go into the kitchen* . . ." She searched for a task.

"And get Steve a beer?" Skip provided. "Can you come in for a beer, Steve? I think we've got a few munchies lying around."

"No, I don't want to interrupt." Steve shook his head and backed up a step, one hand up. "I just wanted to be sure you got, the, uh . . ."—he gestured toward the bag in Roxanne's hand—". . . packages."

"It's no interruption," Roxanne said. "Come on in."

They heard the clink of glass against glass and then the thunk of a bottle landing on the counter.

"Besides," Skip called from the kitchen, "the beer's already open."

Steve gave her an ironic look. "Skip wins again. One of these days *you're* going to invite me over. I promise to decline, if that's what it'll take."

She crunched the bag closed in one fist and cocked her head at him. "Maybe Skip's are the only invitations you accept."

Steve strolled through the door, leaning close to her as he passed, saying, "Try me."

Their eyes met and Roxanne's body temperature sky-rocketed. Steve gave her a quick wink and continued on toward the kitchen, while Roxanne wiped the back of her hand across her forehead. Lord, she thought, was the guy on fire? Every time she stood near him she heated up like bread in a toaster.

She was drunk on Cheetos, that was it. It wasn't that she was unable to be within two feet of Steve Serrano without thinking about sex. She was just high on partially hydrogenated soybean oil.

She followed him into the kitchen, placing her bag of Cheetos carefully on the dining room table as she passed it.

"You didn't get yourself a bag," she said to Steve,

who sat on the stool by the kitchen island as casually as if he lived there. "I'm afraid you can't stay at this party without paying homage to the guest of honor." She inclined her head back toward the pile of Cheeto bags.

Steve laughed. "Not me. I don't touch that stuff. My body is a temple."

"Oh please," she said, "I saw you stuff that temple with a plate full of cheese fries not so very long ago."

They all laughed and settled in with their beers. Before long, talk turned to the break-in.

"It seems to me they're bent on destruction," Skip said. "Maybe it's somebody trying to scare you off, out of the business."

"Someone like you?" she asked. "You're the only one who's been completely against it from the start."

Skip's expression was hurt. "No I haven't. I've just wanted you to be happy. And we all know restaurateurs aren't happy. They're just crazy."

"Oh Skip, I know." She leaned across the couch—where they had migrated during the course of conversation—and squeezed his hand. "Of course I don't think it's you behind the break-ins. I'm thinking maybe it's somebody who lived here before and left something behind."

From the armchair, Steve gave her a dubious look. "Somebody who left something buried in the basement floor? Or behind a brick foundation that hasn't been disturbed for centuries?"

Roxanne turned to him. "Can you tell that? Can you tell the brick hasn't been disturbed?"

He shrugged one shoulder. "Most of the time, yes. If

the mortar's different, the pattern is broken, the bricks are not all the same age, you can tell someone's done some patchwork. But the wall where they were digging around . . ." He shook his head. "I don't know what's going on with that."

"Maybe they think there's some kind of buried treasure," Skip volunteered, with a kidlike grin.

"There is!" Roxanne said excitedly. "We thought of that, didn't we, Steve?" She looked over at Steve. "The Declaration of Independence, right?"

Skip scoffed. "The Declaration of Independence is in your basement?"

"Just a draft." At Steve's dark look she added, "Maybe. Steve, tell him the story."

Steve related the short version, finishing with, "But that would be ridiculous. Anybody who knew enough to be looking for that draft wouldn't just start digging around somebody else's basement. They're historians, academics. They'd have maps and documents and theories about where to search. They'd know the places that had *already* been searched. And they'd know to look for things like patterns in the brick."

"So you really don't think it has anything to do with that?" Roxanne asked, disappointed. She'd been hoping her intruder would turn out to be some nerdy guy in glasses with a history book in one hand and a shovel in the other. Not some drug-crazed former tenant as P.B. had suggested. Or Steve, as P.B. had ended up insisting.

The idea of Steve destroying her property in search of his theoretical draft was ludicrous, but like the circumstances of the bet between him and P.B., there was enough ambiguity in the facts to leave room for doubt.

And doubt about men was what Roxanne specialized in these days.

Still, would Steve be able to discuss this so casually now if he were the one looking around? Of course not.

Steve gave it another moment of thought. "It's doubtful. But if it's not that, I'll be damned if I know what they *are* looking for."

"It seems obvious they're looking for something, though," Roxanne mused, "doesn't it? Remember how in the first break-in one of the kitchen floorboards had been pried up?"

"I thought the squirrel did that," Skip said.

Steve laughed and Roxanne's eyes shot to his.

"You didn't believe that?" she asked.

"You *did*?" he countered.

She picked at the label of her beer with a fingernail. "It's obvious now, of course, that the first was an actual break-in. But I have to confess, for a long time I was really hoping it was just that squirrel."

"The one that hurled itself through the back window." Steve was smiling at her but it was a gentle smile, a teasing one.

"That never made sense to me either," Skip said.

"I chose to ignore that part of the equation," Roxanne admitted. "Besides, I figured if it was good enough for the police . . ."

Steve's expression darkened and Roxanne kicked herself for bringing up—even indirectly—P.B.

After a bit more discussion, Skip stood up. "All right,

kids. Tonight, I'm hitting the hay early. No more midnight Mondays for me."

They all stood up and Skip said his good-nights, then he trotted down the stairs.

Roxanne and Steve stood at the door, silent until Skip's footsteps stopped and the outside door slammed.

Roxanne was pretty sure Steve was going to leave too, but since he hadn't said anything she pushed the door shut and turned her back against it, looking up at him.

"I guess I should go, too," he said.

Roxanne nodded, one hand on the doorknob behind her without turning it. "Big day tomorrow?"

He laughed wryly and put his hands in his pockets. "Just the library. Again. That's how I usually spend my days."

"At the Library of Congress?" she asked.

He nodded.

"You're that into the history thing, huh? Are you taking a class or something?"

He shook his head. "No, I just like investigating things. I've been interested in Portner for some time now. He's kind of a fascinating character."

"So you're just doing it for fun?"

He shrugged. "Keeps the librarians busy and me off the streets."

"They should start paying you," she teased.

"I wish someone would." Then, at her look, he added, "For the library work, I mean, the research. You pay me just fine, boss."

He smiled and her stomach turned to jelly. *Boss*, she repeated to herself. *Remember that.*

"I knew what you meant." Slowly, she pushed herself away from the door and pulled it open.

She had to let him leave, she told herself. But, maybe it was the beers on nothing but a Cheeto-laden stomach, she couldn't quite remember just why this relationship was so wrong. So she owned the place—didn't most people meet the people they dated at work? So what if she was the boss? It wasn't like she would let the personal aspect get in the way of the professional.

Well, she thought, her reaction to news of that awful bet springing to mind, *not again, anyway.*

Remembering the bet only increased her resolve, however. She shouldn't trust him. If they got involved and later he did something that hurt her she would kick herself for not paying attention to the signs. And what bigger red flags could there be than that he might have made a bet about getting her in bed and there was a chance he was behind a series of break-ins at her restaurant?

And she was considering trusting him? Was she crazy?

Then again, if she just assumed she couldn't trust him and didn't let her heart become involved . . . what would be possible then?

Steve stepped through the door as she stared at the floor. It was silly but she was afraid that if she looked at him she might do something stupid. Like throw herself at him.

"Thanks for, uh, dinner," Steve said, amusement in his voice. "It wasn't quite as good as last time, but I guess that's because I provided this meal."

Roxanne laughed. "I'll cook you something better next time."

She looked at him quickly, nerves buzzing with implications she was both dying and afraid to make.

"That is," she added, "if Skip invites you over again anytime soon."

He was standing in the hall, looking as reluctant to leave as she was reluctant to let him. His hands were shoved in his jeans pockets and his eyes, though laughing at her joke, were uncertain.

Desire washed over her. He wanted to stay, she was sure she could see it. He wanted her again . . . as much as she wanted him again?

"Steve," she said, not sure what she intended to say next.

Their eyes met and she stopped breathing.

"Yes, Roxanne?" His voice was quiet and seemed to whisper along her nerves.

She stepped into the hall and put her fingers around one of his wrists, where his hand disappeared into his pocket. His hand came out and she took it in hers, looking at it.

They were strong hands, sculpted, somehow refined-looking. She imagined him at the Library of Congress, writing away as he researched whatever it was he researched.

His fingers curled around hers.

She looked up at him, stepping closer until their bodies almost touched.

She took a deep, tremulous breath, knowing she wasn't going to back away. Though her brain told her she was being stupid, self-indulgent, her body would not obey her commands to stop desiring this man.

"Do you think this is a mistake?" she asked him.

His eyes dropped to their clasped hands and his other came out of his pocket to snake around her waist. Pulling her gently but firmly into him, he brought his gaze to hers.

"I don't know," he said.

He looked so sincere. So serious and yet so uncertain, she wanted to take his face in her hands and tell him not to worry, it didn't matter.

But . . . she was the one who was worried, wasn't she?

"Are you afraid that it is?" she asked.

He shook his head slightly, a small laugh escaping. "If it is, it's the best damn mistake I've ever made."

That made her blush and she looked down briefly.

"How about you?" he asked softly. "Afraid?"

She shrugged one shoulder, then looked up at him. "Life is scary."

"Only if you live it," he said. With that he bent his head and kissed her.

Their lips met tenderly, experimentally. Soft kisses that followed one after the other. Roxanne's hands rose up his chest, and his clasped behind her back, keeping her close.

His embrace felt so warm, so fragile and sweet, she was almost taken off guard when his head tilted to drop kisses along her jawline and her breathing accelerated. His lips moved down to that spot below her ear and sucked lightly, sending shivers shooting through her body in all directions.

She gasped lightly, arching her neck, and that impulse, that overpowering thing within her, took over. It was a wave of longing, a physical demand that she knew she couldn't resist—didn't *want* to resist—an impelling force that turned her insides to lava and made her passion volcanic.

He moved against her, his desire hardening between them, and she pressed her hips against it. Her hands dropped to his waistband and she grasped two belt loops in her fingers to pull him closer, circling her hips into his just enough to massage that hardness.

He made a sound low in his throat. His hands held her buttocks and stilled her against him.

They stood a moment, breathing hard in the hallway, under the dim overhead bulb. Steve dropped his head to her shoulder, seeming to think about the next move.

Was he asking himself if it was a good idea to continue? she wondered. Had she read him completely wrong? Maybe he was regretting stopping by. Maybe he thought it would be wiser to stop it right here. Should she tell him she's sorry and let him go home?

He sighed. "Am I going to have to wait for Skip to invite me in again?"

Laughter bubbled up from inside her, relief cascading out of her lungs.

She took his hand again and turned, leading him back into her apartment. As she started down the hallway toward the bedroom he stopped her.

"Wait." He pulled her back toward the living room, turning out the light as he did, then turned her in his arms as if waltzing.

She smiled quizzically, thinking he wanted to dance.

But when he circled nearer the sofa, he lowered her as if in a dip, onto the cushions.

"I want you to think of me every time you sit on this couch." He lowered himself on top of her and kissed her, hard, his mouth devouring, his hands weaving through her hair to cradle her head.

Their hips met and circled together, their hands reached and sought each other's body, pulling up shirts and searching for skin amidst the fabric.

Steve's hands pushed her shirt aside, his long fingers finding the peaked nipple of one breast through the fabric of her bra. With a gentle pinch, he sent desire coursing through her.

Her hands fumbled for his jeans, undid his belt buckle, then popped open the button. She unzipped his fly and felt his hardness through the thin cotton of his boxers.

Steve's lips took the peak of one breast as his hands reached the top of her jeans.

Roxanne's hand found the opening in his boxers and Steve gasped as her fingers found flesh. She caressed the velvety softness of his skin and his hands stopped as if he were paralyzed above her.

"Just a second," he said, standing to pull off his jeans.

Roxanne sat up and watched him, saw him pull his own shirt over his head to reveal that defined, muscular chest, saw him push the boxers down to reveal the straining hard evidence of his desire.

Naked, he looked down on her like a warrior regarding his prize. His gray eyes were direct and glittery in the darkened apartment.

She pushed herself up to stand before him, then turned and moved toward the bedroom, unclasping her bra and slipping it off as she walked.

"Wait right there," she said in a husky voice.

Once in the bedroom, she opened up the bedside table drawer, pulled out a condom, then moved back to the living room, her eyes meeting his as she walked slowly across the room, unbuttoning her jeans.

She reached the floor lamp and turned the dimmer so that the barest candle of light shone. Then she pushed her jeans past her hips and stepped out of them.

"Oh my God," he breathed, then grinned at her. "Another thong."

She smiled her best slow smile and took one side of the thong, twisting it in her finger. Then she pulled it down, her eyes never leaving his. She could see him pulse with the effort of control, and his eyes burned into hers. She pulled off the thong and walked the rest of the way toward him, twirling it on one finger.

She dropped it on the floor by the coffee table and cupped his penis with her hands, then moved her fingers up and over it. Her eyes were still on his as she lowered herself to her knees, and took the long shaft into her mouth.

Steve shuddered and swore, his eyes closing as she took him in. His hands held her head, his fingers diving into her hair as she moved back and forth, holding his length in her mouth and moving her tongue to increase his pleasure.

He moaned and pushed his hips gently into her, his hands holding her head. "Oh God," he muttered. "Ah . . ."

He was nearly out of control, she could feel him
trembling with the effort, and she was the one pushing
him toward the brink. She controlled his every sensation, directed every reaction, anticipated every invol-
untary response he made. *She* did it.

She held him captive.

When he was on the verge of losing it, he pulled her
up and took her mouth with his, his tongue plunging
into her. She answered with a kiss just as hungry and
wound one leg around his hip. He grabbed it, pulled
her upward and she wrapped the other around him
too. Then he lowered himself onto the couch, sitting
with her on his lap.

Knees on the cushions, she rose and held his penis
gently as she unfurled the condom onto it. Then she
guided him toward her with one hand, lowering down,
then pulling up just long enough to look into his eyes.

"Say my name," she whispered.

He looked at her a long moment, his eyes intense
enough to see right through her.

"Roxanne," he said finally, in a voice as hot and
sweet as toasted honey.

She pushed him inside of her.

The sensation was brilliant.

He exhaled sharply, and his eyes seemed to look in-
ward a moment before boring back into hers.

She pushed herself onto the shaft again and her eyes
closed halfway with pleasure. He was so hard he filled
her and she rose slowly, not wanting it to end too
quickly.

His palm was hot as he took her breast and held it for
his mouth to find the nipple. Closing his lips around it,

he sucked, pulling hard, but she didn't care. She wanted it harder, wanted him to brand her with his lips. She lowered herself on him again, felt him deep within her, then rose. Her body clenched around him and he groaned.

Then he rose up, holding her impaled against him and lay her back on the couch.

"You've been in charge long enough." His eyes sparkled like the devil's own as he rose above her.

Then he thrust into her deep and she gasped with pleasure. He thrust again, then again, seeming to get deeper and harder with each plunge and chills raced up and down her spine. Her legs held his hips and she countered his every thrust as his penis coursed up and over her most sensitive spot again and again.

She cried out his name as she came. His eyes met hers and she could swear they held the light of more than just desire. Or maybe it was just her, bathed in the sensations of love as her body dissolved into starlight.

He pushed into her one final time, and with an uninhibited sound of release he came into her.

She held him as tight as she could then, with her arms, her legs, and her body, until they both melted into the cushions.

15

Dessert Special of the Day

Génoise, Crème au Beurre avec
　Langues de Chat—
<u>because you shouldn't put real Cheetos
　in a dessert</u>
Light butter cake with buttercream frosting
　and cats' tongues—pencil-shaped strips
　made of sugar, butter and vanilla

The restaurant was crazy. Just when Roxanne thought she'd surely seen the end of the boom of being the new kid on the block, another round of reservations would come in, filling up Friday and Saturday before they even opened on Wednesday.

A few things had gone wrong. The freezer had burned out (the one piece of equipment from Charters she'd counted on not having to replace) and they had to offer a world of unusual specials to use the food before she could get the new one in. On the plus side, business had been so good she had enough money to be able to get a new one, but it cleaned her out.

Then M. Girmond's sous-chef of twelve years had quit because of a sudden opportunity to head his own kitchen, and the replacement had yet to be found who would live up to Girmond's standards. In addition, she had to watch her normally buoyant and enthusiastic chef grow increasingly short-tempered without his right-hand man, which affected the entire kitchen staff and annoyed the hell out of the waitstaff.

For Roxanne, however, it was all a blur. She was cooking more, faster and better than she'd ever done in her life, while trying to manage accounts and keep the staff happy and productive. Before starting the restaurant, she had thought her biggest worry would be making ends meet despite slow business for the first few months. Now she thought running at capacity might kill them.

The synchronized waltz in the kitchen she had reveled in those first few heady nights had become more of a pinball game with the constant nightly pressure. The new sous-chef—Ralph, available on short notice—bumped into everyone, the dishwasher had been deported; her seafood purveyor had become unreliable—bringing grouper when she ordered sole, clams when she ordered mussels; and the bakery down the street was going out of business, meaning she now had to get up at the crack of dawn to make bread until another supplier of suitable quality could be found.

Nights, after leaving the crazy, hot atmosphere of the restaurant, she would crawl into bed exhausted. On Monday and Tuesday, when they were closed, she tried to catch up with her prep work and get ahead on the bread-making as much as she could.

A few times Steve had come down for dinner, and had stayed the night, at least until she got up before dawn to make the bread.

Those nights were crazy too, in their own way, but energizing. Their chemistry was incredible, but Roxanne wondered what was really going on between them. They talked, but never about themselves, about what was happening between them. And between being so tired and getting up so early, their time always seemed short. Too, too short.

Even aside from the doubts she had about her own judgment—she'd been crazy about Martin at first, too, though their chemistry hadn't been anywhere near as good—she worried about the fact that she and Steve worked together, and slept together, but rarely did anything else other than occasionally eat together.

Had she somehow signed up for a purely sexual relationship? Is this what she got for caving in completely to her desires before establishing some kind of friendship with Steve?

But then, she thought, they *were* friends, weren't they? Just friends who couldn't talk about the elephant that sat between them—the relationship.

They certainly had some fun at work, before the evenings became chaos. But when it came to seeing each other alone, they came together like shipwreck victims grasping at the lone life raft—and went off together like a flare, only to fade quickly after their moment of fire.

Maybe they were both just too damned tired for anything else, she thought, realizing that she was every bit as guilty as Steve was of dropping immediately off to sleep on the nights he was there.

"I don't know," she told Skip on the phone, after confessing what was going on. "It seems to be enough for him. And maybe it's all I can handle, too."

"That doesn't sound very romantic," Skip said.

"No, but . . . I just don't know."

"That's about the fiftieth time you've said that. What are you really worried about?"

For the umpteenth time she searched her heart, focusing on that feeling of dread deep in her chest. "I don't—" She stopped herself. "I guess I'm worried about being wrong. Being fooled. Like I was with Martin."

"I think you'd notice a wife and kids traipsing up those stairs," Skip had said, with an attempt at laughter.

Roxanne shook her head. "It's that bet. Or no, not the bet, really—I believe him about that. But it's like I was left with the feeling of mistrust after that—even though I *do* trust him now—and it won't go away. I mean, this is a guy whose best friend said to me he thought Steve could be guilty of a crime. A crime *against* me. Shouldn't I be taking that into consideration?"

"First of all, do you really think Steve wouldn't tell you if he found that draft he's been talking about? It's not like he's kept it a secret or anything," countered Skip.

"No, but if he's the one behind the break-ins, what

does that mean? Breaking and entering isn't exactly legal, even if he did plan to tell me what he found. But if he was planning to tell me about finding the draft, why wouldn't he tell me about looking for it? And why would he do *so* much damage? And if he wasn't going to tell me about finding the draft, then he was basically planning on stealing it from this house, and therefore from me."

"Hold on. Hold on. I'm getting confused." Skip inhaled loudly over the phone. "If the draft is found in your house, it would be yours?"

"I don't know, and frankly I don't really care. That's not the point." Roxanne put a hand to her forehead and squeezed. This whole situation was giving her a headache. "The point is, if Steve is digging around and making it look like a break-in, it means he's lying to me, probably because he's afraid the draft *might* be mine if he finds it on my property."

"Well, yeah, I guess that would be a pretty big breach of trust. But that just doesn't sound like Steve to me," Skip said.

"I know, but you and I barely know the guy. And if P.B. could think him capable of it . . ."

"P.B.?" Skip scoffed. "He was *bitter*, Rox, come on. I wouldn't believe a thing that guy said."

"But . . . it's the only theory about these break-ins that makes sense."

Skip laughed. "The only theory that makes sense is some guy looking for a draft of the Declaration of Independence in your basement? That's pretty pathetic. And I'm sorry, but a cop shouldn't be going around whispering suspicions about people without any real grounds for having them."

She sighed. "You're probably right but . . . maybe he *does* have grounds. Maybe he knows something about Steve that we don't. And maybe he was hoping I would say something to Steve so Steve would stop doing it and he wouldn't have to arrest his buddy."

"Or maybe he made it all up to get back at both of you."

"Maybe . . ." Roxanne felt the weight of the world descend on her shoulders. "Or maybe it doesn't matter who's doing what or lying about whom. Maybe I shouldn't be sleeping with a guy I could suspect of destroying my property."

And that, Roxanne thought, was the bottom line.

Even Skip had nothing to say to that.

It was a Thursday night and Roxanne was especially tired, wondering if maybe she was coming down with something, when halfway through the evening Sir Nigel edged uncomfortably into the kitchen, looking around like a kid who'd been summoned to the principal's office for the first time.

She looked up, surprised to see him. He almost never came through the swinging doors to the kitchen, as if pretending this part of the restaurant did not really exist was an essential part of his job.

"Sir Nigel," she said, scooping raspberry sauce out of a bowl and into a small pitcher with a spatula. "What can I do for you?"

"*He's here,*" Sir Nigel hissed.

She drew a blank. "I'm sorry?"

"He's *here*," he said again, big eyes directed toward the dining room. "Frederick Richards. Reviewer from the *Washington Post*."

Roxanne's heart leaped out of her chest directly into her throat. "Oh my God. Should we tell Monsieur Girmond? We should tell Monsieur Girmond." She wiped her hands on the towel at her waist and turned to look at Girmond. "Should we tell him?" She looked back at Sir Nigel.

"Of *course*." He made a motion as if pushing her. "Richards has just been seated by the fireplace, number twenty-four. I'll let you know what he orders."

"Make sure Rita waits on him," Roxanne directed, turning toward Girmond, then spinning back. "But don't tell her who he is."

Sir Nigel gave a curt nod and pushed back out the swinging doors, like a swimmer heading for the surface and air.

Roxanne moved swiftly toward M. Girmond. Just as she was about to reach him, the new sous-chef (who was admittedly annoying, simultaneously obsequious and arrogant) stepped on her foot and dropped a bowl of mussels.

"Watch it," he growled, before realizing who he was speaking to. "Oh, sorry, so sorry, Miss Rayeaux. My fault. Entirely. I should have been aware of you walking through my station."

She waved a hand and continued to M. Girmond as Ralph bent to the floor to pick up the mussels. She arrived at Girmond's elbow as he sliced a duck terrine with smooth, confident knife strokes.

"He's here," she said low, not wanting to alarm the

rest of the kitchen. "The reviewer from the *Post*. He's at twenty-four, Rita will be waiting on him."

M. Girmond nodded once, quickly. "Thank you for telling me, *ma biche*."

She smiled and squeezed his upper arm with one hand. "I know we'll do great."

He winked at her, then turned to Ralph, who still squatted on the floor, and said, "Where is the sauce, eh? The orange-ginger, for the terrine."

"I—yes, it's right here," he started to stand, then spotted another mussel and bent again. "If you had only let me know—"

"I called for it three minutes ago! Get up!" Girmond gestured with his knife. "You must pay attention, monsieur. It is all about attention."

Roxanne slipped back to her station. A minute later she heard the crash of a pan hitting the floor and turned in time to see Ralph dancing around as if he'd burned himself.

M. Girmond was yelling something, and Ralph was yelling something else, and for some reason two of the busboys were running in circles.

She raced over. "What in the world's going on?"

"I've just seen—Oh my God, what was it? A *rat*?" Ralph was near shrieking. "It had to be a *rat. Jesus Christ*, I've never seen one so huge!"

"*C'est de la merde.*"

Roxanne was shocked. She'd never heard M. Girmond swear before and she was pretty sure he'd just said the French equivalent of *bullshit*.

Girmond turned on Ralph fiercely. "There are no rats

in my kitchen. My kitchen is spotless. Get ahold of yourself."

"I'm telling you, it was right there." Ralph threw a hand toward the floor, where a sticky glaze now oozed underneath the overturned pan. "It made me drop the pan. All my sauce! *They* saw it!" He pointed to two busboys, prowling near the garde-manger station like hunters.

"Calm down, *salaud*," Girmond boomed, his voice so loud Roxanne was afraid the customers might hear him. She hoped none of them had heard his French, because M. Girmond had just called Ralph a bastard. "I don't care if it was a horse you saw, get me the sauce!"

"Monsieur Girmond!" she pleaded.

He swung to her, nearly decapitating a busboy with his elbow.

"*Il est un idiot! Un crétin!*" He threw out his hands in exasperation. "Look at him, he wears my sauce. This dish is getting *cold*!" He turned to his beautiful duck terrine.

"*There!*" Ralph screamed, hurling a finger outward and knocking over the bowl of mussels he'd just gathered from the floor.

"Number five, order up!" one of the line cooks said. Then, "*Shit!*"

Roxanne spun and saw a flash of orange, with a large piece of grouper in its mouth.

Her heart stopped as he leaped to the counter and headed toward the red-hot stove.

"Cheeto!" she yelled. "Not on the stove! Get him away from the stove!"

Rafe, the line cook, was nearest. Just as Cheeto was about to reach the burners, the cook swept an arm out and across, propelling the cat, along with several dishes and entrees in various states of assembly, sideways and onto the floor.

Roxanne exhaled and dashed toward the cat, but she slipped on the sauce that covered the floor and had to grab the sous-chef's workstation. Before going all the way down, she managed to steady herself.

Cheeto had made it to the pastry station and was trotting over its floured surface, eyes alert, tail high, the grouper still in his mouth.

Was it really him? She narrowed her eyes. There were black patches along his side that gave her pause. But what were the odds of another orange cat showing up in the kitchen?

From the pastry station, the cat leapt nimbly to the service counter and glanced at her. She lunged for him, ready to kill, and he took off for the swinging doors. But just as he reached them, Rita pushed through yelling, "I need the Paté de Campagne with the Canapés Micheline for the V.I.P. at twenty-four."

Cheeto screeched—a nearly human sound—as the door caught him broadside, and he dropped the grouper. He scooted toward the dishwashing station, Manuel in hot pursuit.

Rita stepped on the grouper and slipped, dropping her tray as she hit the floor with a curse.

Manuel, the busboy, threw himself at the cat but missed, colliding with Ralph's legs and making him drop a knife he'd picked up for God knew what reason.

Manuel screamed as the blade caught him across the fingers. Blood spurted instantly along his knuckles.

"Oh my God," Roxanne said, grabbing the cleanest towel within reach and heading for the busboy.

Cheeto leaped up onto the workstation of the only person in the place he recognized other than Roxanne, who was clearly going to punish him: M. Girmond.

Unfortunately, M. Girmond was plating a blanquette of veal, which went flying when Cheeto's front paws hit the edge of the plate.

"What is this animal doing here?" he bellowed.

"What the hell is going on in here?"

Roxanne turned, wild-eyed, to see Steve standing inside the swinging doors.

"People are starting to—holy shit," he said, taking in the mayhem around him.

Rita was rubbing her back and reading off orders to one of the line cooks. Manuel was dragging himself off the floor with Roxanne's help, clutching a bloody towel around his hand. And Ralph was scurrying around, bitching as loud as he could, wiping up sauce with one hand and picking up mussels from the floor like errant marbles with the other.

"There is *cat hair* in my consommé!" M. Girmond roared.

"Oh my God," Roxanne moaned again, her head on the table. "I am so, so sorry."

Around her were seated M. Girmond, Ralph and Rita. Sir Nigel and Steve stood on opposite sides of the table, Sir Nigel with his arms crossed, Steve leaning against the back of a chair.

The evening had been a disaster. They'd had to send George to the hospital with the bleeding Manuel, because he was the only one with a car who could be spared. Several dinners were ruined and had to be started over from scratch—causing a backup that they never recovered from—and cat hair had indeed been found in several dishes, one of which had gone out to a customer and had been returned, with a terse "No, I do not want it replaced."

M. Girmond was humiliated and furious.

Ralph couldn't stop excusing himself and explaining how none of it was his fault.

Rita kept rubbing her lower back, convincing Steve—and no doubt Roxanne—that a Worker's Comp claim was in the offing. And all he could do was watch Roxanne's misery in silence, unable to come up with one reassuring thing to say that he thought would mean anything. The night truly had been a disaster.

The review, it seemed fair to say, was probably going to be negative. Though they'd given him V.I.P. status, Frederick Richards had ordered several things they had to tell him were out, since the cat had ruined the base stock and the soup, and the sauce for one of the most popular items had waxed the kitchen floor. The reviewer had also had to wait an inordinate amount of time for his food, since the place was packed and both the kitchen and waitstaff had become short-handed.

"How did the cat even get *in* there?" Roxanne asked, raising her head enough to prop it up with her hands. "He was locked in my apartment." She straightened suddenly, a look of alarm on her face, and turned to Steve. "You don't think someone broke into my apartment, do you? And left the door open? How else would Cheeto have gotten out?"

Steve shook his head, having already had that same thought. "I already checked the place out, when I put the cat back. Besides, even if he'd been let out by burglars, he couldn't have gotten into the kitchen from the upstairs hall. He'd have had to go out one of the outside doors and come back in one of the restaurant doors."

"Then how did he *get* there?" She sounded angry at him, but Steve knew she was just upset. He also knew she considered this her fault, since it was her cat. But of course it wasn't her fault. It wasn't anybody's fault, though he would have loved to have been able to pin it on the irritating Ralph somehow. Steve just wasn't sure how to convey to her that it was an accident, pure and simple. Just saying it didn't seem like enough.

Steve exhaled. "Listen, Roxanne, this isn't such a tragedy. The place was still packed tonight, most people loved their food and the reservation book is still full for the weekend. So you get one bad review. Big deal. The fact that people are lining up to get in to this place ought to be more important."

"The people *did* love their food, didn't they?" M. Girmond echoed.

"And there, Mr. Serrano," intoned Sir Nigel, "is exposed the extent of your ignorance. Having the majority of your experience in what could only be termed a 'beer joint,' you obviously have no idea how the real culinary world works. A bad review from a reputable publication could be devastating for future receipts."

M. Girmond made a pained sound and took off his

glasses, pinching the bridge of his nose with two large fingers.

Steve gave Sir Nigel an exasperated look. "That's a big help, Nigel. I'm sure that makes us *all* feel better. Thanks for backing me up."

"I will not 'back up,' as you say, a false statement." Sir Nigel sniffed. "Reality must be faced."

"I'm with Steve on this one," Rita piped up. "We ran our asses off tonight. We did the best we could and most people were happy with the food, even if they did have to wait a little while for it. So what if some fancy-ass reviewer didn't like his paté?"

"He did not like the paté?" M. Girmond cried.

"I had nothing to do with the paté," Ralph said.

Rita glanced worriedly at M. Girmond and wound a finger around one of the long dangly earrings she wore. "I don't know if he didn't like it. He just didn't finish it. But maybe that's because the other appetizers arrived first and he was the last to get his. He didn't want to hold up the entrees."

Roxanne moaned and put her head back on the table. "Oh God. This is all my fault. I am so, so very sorry."

Steve wanted to shake her. She needed to take this as the mere pothole it was. They weren't going to go under because of one bad night, or even—Sir Nigel be damned—one bad review.

"Or maybe he just didn't want to fill up on the appetizer," Rita added, her expression increasingly anxious. "He had a little bit of everything, from soup to nuts. He had to save room."

"I didn't serve him any nuts," Ralph said. "Do we really serve nuts?"

"You know," Rita continued, spearing Sir Nigel with an irritated glance, "if I'd actually known who the hell the guy was, maybe I could have done something different. I don't know why you didn't tell me."

"That's my fault, too," Roxanne said. "I didn't want you to get nervous. And you, all of you, worked so hard. I just—just—"

"Look," Steve tried again, "this isn't the end of the world here. We did huge business tonight. Huge. So we had a problem with the cat. Maybe we could call the *Post* and explain to the guy—"

Sir Nigel's snort cut him off. "Oh yes. *Excellent* idea, Mr. Serrano. Let's call Mr. Richards and explain that there was an *animal* in the kitchen during dinner service. That will do us a world of good."

Steve shot him an angry look. "It was an accident, for Christ's sake. Half the evening was an accident. We've been favorably reviewed by every person who's come through those doors until tonight. And tonight was a fluke."

"An unfortunately timed fluke," Sir Nigel said dourly. "And you, Mr. Serrano, do not help things by sousing customers at the bar. Do you know how that looks to the diners waiting for tables?"

"What the hell are you talking about now?" Steve's back was ramrod straight as he turned again to Sir Nigel. Could the guy possibly think his dire pronouncements were helping? Steve was almost ready to crawl across the table and grab him by his prissy little vest lapels.

"That older gentleman you serve shots to every night until he can barely stand up." Sir Nigel's face was pinched with disapproval. "Do you really think we need a whiskey-swilling drunkard—"

"Ew, whiskey. I never drink whiskey," Ralph said.

"The white-haired guy?" Steve couldn't believe it. Nigel was really getting low now, to lay this at his feet. "Hey, he doesn't harm anybody. And he pays his tab. *And* he drinks thirty-year-old single-malt scotch. Do you know how much that costs? It's one of the most expensive drinks we have."

"So you're making very nice tips," Sir Nigel concluded. "And the fact that you have to pour him into a cab every evening doesn't concern you?"

"Actually, the fact that he's *here* every evening is what concerns me. And he frequently eats dinner at the bar. He's one of our best customers, if you want to know the truth. And I don't *pour* him into the cab. He's old. He doesn't drive after he's had a couple."

Sir Nigel's lips compressed into a disapproving line. "He *is* old. He should probably not be drinking at all. He could die at that bar and then where would we be?"

Steve laughed at the absurdity. "Now you're worried customers are actually going to *die* here? Don't you think that's going a little overboard?"

"Steve!" Roxanne's voice got his attention. "Sir Nigel. *Please.* This is ridiculous." She took a deep breath, put both palms on the table and pushed herself to her feet. "Steve's right," she said.

"Hah!" Steve shot a triumphant, if immature, look at Sir Nigel.

"But Sir Nigel's point is well taken." She sent Steve a quelling glance. "The bottom line is, we had a bad night. We were due for one, actually. We'd been lucky up to now. The fact that it was when the reviewer was here is unfortunate, but there's nothing we can do about that now." She looked at each of them. "You all did an outstanding job tonight, and I want you to know how lucky I feel to have each of you on the staff. Thank you. And George and Manuel, too. George called me from the hospital a little while ago. Manuel just needed a few stitches. He'll be back to work in a few days."

"I've never had stitches," Ralph said. "I've never even broken a bone."

"I've got George's tip money," Rita said, reaching into her apron pocket.

Roxanne shook her head. "You keep it, Rita. You worked nearly the entire room this evening and kept up better than anybody could ever have expected you to. I'll compensate George."

Rita started to beam, then realized the mood was still somber and simply said, "Thanks."

"Now I think we should all go to bed," she finished with a sigh. "I know I'm exhausted. You all must be, too. And once again, this was nobody's fault but mine. I'm very sorry all your hard work had to be compromised by this."

"It was not your fault, *mon ange*," M. Girmond said.

Murmurs of agreement rose from the rest of the group as they got up to leave.

Girmond stood and took her shoulders in his hands. "It was a terrible evening, but we will live to fight another day, *eh, ma biche*?"

He kissed her on the forehead, then turned to join

the rest of the crew in heading for the exits. All of them moved slowly as if weighted down by the events of the evening. All except Sir Nigel, that was, who appeared to feel his stature grow in the presence of a disaster that was entirely blamable on persons other than himself.

"See you all tomorrow," Roxanne called as they filed out of the dining room. "Thank you!"

Responses in kind drifted back.

Roxanne turned to Steve and their eyes met. She looked so sad and tired he wanted to gather her up in his arms and hold her. But there was something in her posture, a defensiveness, that stopped him.

"Shall I come up?" he asked quietly, with a quick glance at the departing employees.

She looked down at the floor and he had his answer. She wanted no comfort from him. He was more of a plaything, he surmised. Not someone who could offer her any kind of real solace.

"I think I just need to sleep," she said, looking back up at him. "I'm just so—"

"I understand," he said, more curtly than he'd intended. He didn't want to hear whatever excuses she felt she had to make for not wanting to be with him. It was clear that unless she was in a sensual mood there was no place for him in her life. "I've got a few things I should do here anyway, before tomorrow."

She lifted her brows, surprised. "Really? Anything I can help with?"

He shook his head. "No. You go on to bed. I can see you're exhausted."

She smiled wanly and, with a long last look, confirming their unspoken policy that they make no physical contact in the restaurant, she went toward the kitchen and the back door that would take her to her apartment.

Steve continued to stand in the dining room, feeling emptiness down to the core of his being. Had that really been the brush-off he'd felt it was? Had this been a turning point? A moment when they both realized the limitations of their relationship?

Because he had to admit, at least to himself, that if this really was just a sexual thing, he couldn't sustain it. He wanted more, he thought, his mind veering away from what that meant, exactly.

He simply wanted more.

16

Bar Special
Stinger—it sneaks up on you
White crème de menthe, cognac, over cracked ice

Steve couldn't sleep. He rolled onto his back and stared up at the ceiling, arms behind his head.

He should talk to her. Tell her—no, *ask* her how she felt. About him. Ask her if what they had was enough for her. Or if she thought something was . . . missing.

He grabbed the pillow from under his head and put it over his face. He had turned into Lia. Or Joanne. Or Corinne. Or any one of a dozen other women who used to ask him how *he* felt, when all he felt was a physical connection. He'd always thought that if you had to ask, you had to know the answer wasn't going to be good.

Was this some kind of cosmic payback? He'd finally met a woman he couldn't get enough of and she only wanted him for sex. It was a cruel irony, made worse by the fact that he had, in the beginning, actually tried to resist her. Hell, he'd even thought that she wasn't all that beautiful, what with how stuffy and prickly and high maintenance she was.

But none of that turned out to be true. She wasn't stuffy, she was shy. She may have been prickly at first, but it was defensive.

And she was about as low maintenance as they came. Ending up, as it happened, *too* low maintenance. She didn't need anything from him.

It was all so obvious now.

Steve threw off the covers and swung his legs over the side of the bed. He needed to do something, occupy his mind with something else. He got up, slipped on some jeans and a sweatshirt and pulled on his shoes.

He'd go down and investigate the kitchen. There was no way that cat had come through three doors to get into the kitchen—somehow getting out of the apartment, then outside, then inside the restaurant. He had to have come through the inside somehow. If nothing else, Steve could ensure that a disaster like tonight never happened again.

He crept down the stairs quietly, then let himself in the back door of the restaurant. Once in the kitchen he turned on the lights, squinting in the brightness and marveling at how clean and shiny everything looked, when just a few hours ago chaos had reigned.

His eyes scanned the walls and the ceiling above the stove, the workstations, around past the door to the dining room, over the office door, to the wall of refrigerators and the new freezer, to the back door again.

No obvious holes or gaps in the old tin ceiling. The walls looked solid enough.

The cat had been a mess when he'd grabbed him to take him back upstairs, squirming and fighting when Steve had first picked him up, desperate to get back to all that food that was now all over the floor. So Steve had ample time to notice that the animal was covered with dirt and flour and some kind of sticky sauce. It even had a flake of fish caught in one whisker. But it was the black streaks along the cat's sides that had him intrigued. It was soot, Steve was certain, but where had it come from?

He thought about his own apartment, how there was a mantel with no fireplace, just a hole for an old fashioned coal stove, probably used in the late 1800s to early 1900s. In his kitchen, too, he knew there was one of those holes behind the counter on the back wall, and at the roofline you could see the old chimney. No doubt a flue came all the way down to the first floor.

He looked at the new freezer in its alcove near the back door. It protruded into the kitchen a little farther than the old one had—it was a bigger and more efficient model—at about the same spot where his counter covered the stove hole upstairs.

Eyes raking down the stainless steel exterior, he smiled. There were wheels on this freezer, probably to make it easier to service. The last one had taken four burly guys to get out the back door, and even then it had cracked the back threshold.

Rolling up his sleeves, he grabbed hold of one side and rolled the thing out slowly from the wall.

Sure enough, behind the appliance was a stove hole partially covered by a round tin, the kind with spring-like metal pieces to hold it in place, just like in his apartment. Clearly, something had pushed the tin aside and Steve would bet anything it had been the cat.

He squeezed around the freezer and pulled the tin covering off, finding several cat hairs clinging to the side. He tried to peer in the hole but it was too dark. He thought about calling up through it, to see if Roxanne could hear him, but of course that would scare her to death. He smiled grimly at the thought that maybe he could practice a little subconscious conditioning.

Steve is the most handsome man you've ever seen. The smartest, wittiest, most . . . whatever, he couldn't even come up with anything that seemed remotely true.

Readjusting the wire clasps in back of the cover, he pushed it back into place, then thought he should do something more permanent than that. Maybe nail it shut, though he should nail the one in Roxanne's apartment first, so the cat didn't crawl in only to get stuck at the bottom. Or better yet, the whole thing could be covered over by a piece of plywood, unless whoever retrofitted the place had run plumbing up through the flue, as was common.

His eyes trailed around what was probably the original fireplace and what would therefore be brick but was now covered with plaster. The wall ran almost three feet beyond where the fireplace would have ended, to the back wall of the building. So if someone had run plumbing and/or electrical, they could have housed it in that three-foot space and not in the chimney.

He tapped the wall beside the fireplace. It sounded hollow. At floor level, there was a slight gap where the toe molding had been eaten away by some insect or small animal, and he wriggled two fingers under it.

The covering was boarded ribbing, as was typical for the late nineteenth century, that had been plastered over to match the chimney camouflage. He pulled gently and it gapped slightly. Curious, and knowing this area would never show, he pulled a little harder. A small shower of plaster rained down on his hand and a crack ran up the wall.

He stopped, reluctant to cause any more damage than necessary.

Still, his curiosity was piqued. He should ask Roxanne if she'd mind if he looked in here. Aside from being a possible escape route for her curiously exploratory cat, it could contain interesting historical details.

He pulled on the panel again and tried to look in. Too dark. He needed a flashlight.

His right hand holding the plaster-covered wood, he tried to slide his left hand through the crack to see what he could feel, anticipating all manner of spiders or maybe even a dead mouse or two.

Webs, for sure. He flicked what was probably a dead roach aside, then felt . . . nothing. About three inches back there was a space where the floor ended. He ran his fingers over the edge of the floor. It was smooth and rounded.

He pushed his hand farther into the space and felt nothing. No pipes, no wires, just the edge of the floor. He pushed his hand in up to his wrist and let his fingers drop. The tips barely brushed another piece of wood about eight inches below floor level.

Steve caught his breath, as his fingers backed up and found what could be a riser, just below the lip of the floor. His pulse accelerated as he considered that this cavity could possibly have contained an old staircase, one that went *down*. He pictured the basement and knew there was no staircase on this end. If there were, it would have blocked the outside cellar entrance, the one that had been broken into and was now boarded up.

When had that entrance been installed? Late 1800s? He tried to remember the exact year, and thought it had been something like 1868 or 1870, fairly soon after the end of the Civil War. So if there had been a staircase here, they would have had to take it out to make room for the trap door entrance.

Under the first step . . . he remembered, blood thrumming through his veins.

Steve could picture the words written in Portner's spidery scrawl.

Includes the contents under the first step as described to my Executor . . .

Steve's lungs felt near to bursting and he exhaled, realizing as he did that he'd stopped breathing. This could be the spot, he thought. No wonder all those earlier excavations had found nothing in the old staircases. There was a *back* stair. One that nobody had considered or knew existed for probably a hundred and fifty years.

Elation flooded his veins like oxygen and he tried to temper it. He could be wrong. It could be anything. An old pantry or dumbwaiter. Maybe even an early-twentieth-century trash chute. If there had been a back staircase, surely someone would have known about it, or at least suspected.

Then again, this place had always been privately owned . . . And the theories about the fair copy—

known mostly in academic circles—had never truly been believed.

Steve examined the plaster covering the old fireplace and the wall beside it. He picked at a piece with one fingernail near where it had cracked. A couple coats of paint were obvious, as was an old layer of wallpaper.

This space had been covered over a long time, there was no doubt about it.

This could, he thought, fighting heart palpitations, be *it*.

Roxanne tiptoed down the stairs. Steve hadn't answered her knock on his door. He was probably as exhausted as she was, only without the neurotic inability to fall asleep that she had.

Lying in bed telling herself she needed to deal with her troubles alone had not, after a couple hours, made any sense to her. She knew she would feel better with Steve beside her, just holding her and assuring her that she was not alone, that her fear that she would lose her business was not justified. It *was* just one review, after all. She had to be jumping to the worst conclusions.

That Steve could make her feel better was something she was sure of. She had just been so sure she was going to dissolve into tears the moment she left the restaurant that she felt she had to turn him away earlier. She was too afraid to let him see her that way.

Thinking about it, though, as she lay alone in her bed, she knew in her heart of hearts that he would understand. In fact, of all the people in the world he would probably understand the best. After all, he was nearly as involved in this restaurant as she was.

How silly she'd been to think they had nothing in common, she reflected. They lived in the same building, worked in the same restaurant, dealt with the same people day in and day out—the plain truth was, she had more in common with Steve than she'd ever had in common with Martin.

All this time she had thought she wanted someone cultured and urbane, but she understood now how completely superficial that was. Steve seemed to understand her, and he certainly seemed to care. He made her laugh and, best of all, they had *fun* together.

What did it matter that he wasn't a patron of the arts or a season ticket holder at the Kennedy Center? Who cared that he probably hadn't worn a tuxedo since his high-school prom? If he could hold her in the middle of the night and allay her fears, he was a man she knew she could fall in love with.

But right now it was too late. He was asleep and she had to lie in her bed alone, with nothing to do but go over and over all that had gone wrong that night.

She reached the landing for her apartment and her eye caught on a patch of light outside the window. She leaned toward the glass.

In the back alley, just outside the kitchen, two patches of light from the window and door illuminated the asphalt and glanced off the hood of Steve's truck.

Someone was in the kitchen.

Her pulse jumped and the hair all over her head prickled with dread.

Someone was here. The intruders had come back. And they were looking for whatever it was they sought, in the kitchen, again.

She had to call the cops, and quickly. Maybe they could catch them red-handed. She ran down the hall to her door, adrenaline pumping as she went for the phone, but with her hand on the doorknob she stopped.

Steve hadn't answered her knock.

Do you know where Steve was last night?

P.B.'s voice from after the last break-in echoed in her head.

There's good reason to believe something's hidden in this house. Why wouldn't *he try to find it?* P.B. had insisted.

Roxanne closed her eyes. It couldn't be. She knew what she was doing; she was fearing the worst because she'd just had the scary idea that she could fall in love with this man. Now she was trying to sabotage him in her head.

And yet . . . suppose it *was* Steve? No matter what she told herself, no matter what she felt for him, there *was* the chance that he was behind the break-ins. Would she be stupid not to admit that? And if he was behind them, if it was him in the kitchen right now . . . did she really want the cops to find him? *P.B.?* Did she really want Steve *arrested*?

She swallowed over a sudden lump in her throat and moved slowly back to the stairs. *Just call the police*, part of her said. *You've got to trust someone sometime, so trust now that it's not Steve.*

But she didn't. As much as she wanted to, she couldn't. It just made too much sense that the odd damage that had occurred at each break-in had been done by someone searching for something. Something that had been hidden pretty thoroughly, and a long time ago, if digging behind a brick foundation was any indication.

With quiet stealth, she slipped down the stairwell and opened the door to the back alley. Propping the door open with a rock she kept nearby for bracing it when she had groceries, she inched toward the back door to the restaurant and peered through the windowpanes.

The first thing that met her eye was the freezer, rolled toward the center of the room at an angle so that it didn't have to be unplugged.

Her stomach did a little jump. Then her hands rose and gripped each other at her mouth, as if holding in a scream. Wanting to cross the doorway, she ducked down below the door window and scrabbled left, then leaned against the wall on the opposite side. From this angle, she could see behind the freezer.

There, on the floor, with his hands tugging at a portion of the wall, was Steve.

She spun away from the door window, pressing her back against the outside brick wall, and squeezed her eyes shut. Disappointment and grief fell into her chest as hard as a piano from an upstairs window, followed quickly by a familiar sense of failure.

Stupid, she thought. How had she been so stupid? She *knew* she shouldn't have trusted him. She'd been duped again. Where was her judgment? Why couldn't she tell a good guy from a louse? How could she end up here again—used by another man who only wanted her for one thing? And it wasn't love.

Shit, she nearly said out loud, anger taking over. Had he slept with her so that she would overlook something like this? Or had that just been a perk?

P.B. had been right about Steve. She could hardly believe it.

She tipped her head back so it rested on the brick wall. She told herself she should be glad it was just Steve looking for his stupid document and not some hardened criminal with a weapon. But she wasn't glad. She couldn't be. This meant that Steve had lied to her more times than she could count. He'd pretended he knew nothing about the break-ins and he obviously had no intention of telling her if and when he found what he was looking for.

Whether or not she would be the rightful owner of that draft if he found it didn't matter. What mattered was that Steve decided it was better to lie and keep his actions a secret—allowing her to live in fear of being robbed—than to trust her and ask for her help.

She pressed the heels of her hands to her eyes and tried to stop tears from squeezing through her lids.

Great. She'd screwed up her restaurant and discovered she was involved with another liar, all in the same evening. Total personal and professional devastation.

She squatted down beside the door, then slid onto her butt, for some reason unable to move from the spot. She dropped her hands to the ground beside her, feeling the pebbly asphalt beneath her, the bits of broken glass and old tar and God knew what else.

If she sat here long enough, she thought, maybe it would turn out not to be true. Maybe when she opened her eyes and stood up she'd see nobody in the kitchen. Maybe she was so exhausted that she was sleepwalking and had hallucinated the whole thing.

But when she opened her eyes the patches of light were still on the ground, and the noise from inside the kitchen was soft but still there.

Unbidden, memories of the first break-in flooded back to her. That was the night she'd brought the bottle of wine to Steve's apartment. The night he'd been leaving for some engagement—with some kind of tool stuffed in his duffle bag.

She sat up straighter. *That's right*, she thought. She'd even commented on the handle, saying it looked like some kind of gardening equipment. Then he'd arrived home late, after she'd thought she'd heard glass breaking.

She covered her face with her hands. Why hadn't she remembered that before?

Because, she thought with sudden and cynical certainty, she hadn't wanted to know, hadn't wanted to see what Steve really was. Good old Roxanne, deluding herself again from the very beginning.

Chances were, if she sat here long enough, Steve would come out and find her.

What would he say? How would he explain? And more important, how would she react? Would she buy his excuses like she had with Martin all those years?

She had to think. She knew she would come to work tomorrow and find evidence of a new break-in, so she had to figure out how to respond.

Slowly she stood up and crept back to her apartment, suddenly more tired than she could bear. She'd figure this all out tomorrow. She'd deal with the new break-in tomorrow.

She'd decide what the hell to do about Steve *tomorrow*.

"I'm *going* to talk to her, Dana," Steve said into his cell phone, standing on the steps of the Library of Congress. It was a relatively mild day for winter and the sunshine felt good. "I'm just going to wait until after the weekend."

"Why?" she countered in her characteristically blunt way. "You're only going to agonize and work out speeches and water it all down until you say nothing at all."

She had part of it right, he had to admit. He had been agonizing and working out speeches.

"You don't understand," he said, watching three suited men in black overcoats get out of a black sedan and walk toward the Supreme Court building. "The restaurant's booked. We're just coming off of a hellish night. And Roxanne's still getting up before dawn to bake all the damn bread. I don't think springing the idea that I'd like to take apart a corner of her kitchen would go over very well right now. Especially considering there's probably nothing there anyway."

"Oh, for Pete's sake," Dana said. She was obviously in the van with her kids. Her language was way too clean to believe she was alone. "I'm not talking about your darn historical discovery or theory or whatever it is. I'm talking about your *feelings*, Steve. When are you going to talk to her about your feelings, you repressed clod?"

Steve sat down on the top step and leaned his backpack on the step below. "I was thinking I'd do it at the same time," he said, his head in one hand. "In my own cloddish way."

"What do you mean?" she demanded.

A car horn sounded in the background and Steve wondered if in her vehemence she was driving erratically.

"Should we get off the phone until you get where you're going?" he asked.

"They weren't honking at me. Tell me what you mean by doing it at the same time. You want to put your feelings in a historical context? Tell her your heart's been hidden all these years and you found it behind the freezer in her kitchen?"

"Hey, that's good. I should be taking notes."

"I'm serious, Steve," she said. "I don't want you opening up that bag of candy. That's for Daddy. You had yours in the store, remember?"

Steve lifted his head, squinting in the sunlight. "What?"

"Sorry, Steve, hang on a second."

Below him, he could hear water cascading over Neptune's statue in the fountain at the front of the building. A family of tourists stopped to look at it and the young boy raised a hand and said, "Ooh, look at the snake, Daddy!"

Steve thought about the box of rubber snakes and smiled. Dana had claimed that proved Roxanne had feelings for him. Nobody was that creative or went that far out of her way to prank someone unless they cared about him.

On the phone, Dana's voice achieved a tone Steve was glad she wasn't using on him, so reminiscent was it of their mother's. "Do you want me to stop this car, Justin? Because I will stop this car and take that away from you. Put it back in the grocery bag. *Now.*"

Steve pictured his nephew's mischievous face and smiled. The kid had spunk. He was the only one in the whole family who wasn't scared to death of Dana when she got mad.

"What I'm saying is," Dana said—and Steve waited to see who this was relevant to, him or Justin—"You've never talked this way about a woman before and I don't want you talking yourself out of what you're feeling for her. You're much better off just striking while the iron is hot."

"Are you talking to me or Justin?"

"Justin is much more emotionally mature. He knows to say 'I love you' when he feels it, don't you, sweetie?"

In the background Steve heard Justin singing, "I love you, Mommy! I love you, Mommy!"

"Great," Dana said, laughing, "now look what you've started."

"I didn't bring up the L word."

"See?" she exclaimed. "That's just what I'm talking about. Can you not even *say* it?"

"Dana, I'm going to talk to her. I've already said this a dozen times. My plan was to tell her about my discovery, then couch it in a kind of teamwork way."

"Teamwork?"

"Yeah, you know, if I find this valuable thing, of course it will be yours. I just want to use it in my book and then it will create success for both of us, or something like that. Stressing the 'both of us' part."

"Oh Steve," Dana said, her voice deadly serious and somewhat pitying. "That's just awful."

"Well it's not so easy, Dana. If I tell her about the hidden staircase, then tell her how I feel about her, she'll think I'm buttering her up so I can dig in her basement. Same problem if I tell her about my feelings, then tell her about the hidden staircase. The way I figure it, it has to be at the same time."

"That makes it seem like you think they're equally important."

"No, no, I had it better than that. It's written down in my notes someplace."

"Oh yes, be sure to bring your notes."

Steve put his head back in his hand as a chilly breeze kicked up. "Dana, if we talk about this any more I'm going to have your voice in my head when I talk to her and I won't be able to say anything."

"No, that's good. I'll *tell* you what to say."

He laughed.

"I'm serious. It's very simple. Just say . . ." She paused. "Did I tell you you could open those Pop-Tarts?"

Steve shook his head. "Well, that's good, but that's not really the point I'm going for."

"Don't be stupid," she said.

In the background Justin sang, "Mommy said 'stupid'! Mommy said 'stupid'!"

"Quiet, honey." To Steve she said, "You just say, 'Roxanne, I'm in love with you.' Simple as that."

"Yeah, right." He scoffed. "I thought I'd say something more like 'I'd like to see more of you' and 'Maybe we could go out on an actual date sometime.'"

Dana sighed elaborately. "Jeez, Steve, don't go overboard or anything."

"Dana, if I go in there and say 'Roxanne, I'm in love with you,' she'll laugh at me."

"No she won't."

"Yes she will."

"Then why are you in love with a woman who would do such a thing?"

Steve thought about that. Because she *wouldn't* do such a thing. She wasn't mean. And she did care for him, he was fairly certain. So why was he so afraid of what she'd do?

He cleared his throat. "Look, she could have any guy she wants. She's gorgeous. And—"

"And she wants *you*. It's obvious. The woman has, what, two discretionary hours a week and she chooses to spend them with you? Come on."

"I'm convenient."

Dana clucked her tongue. "See, there again, I have to ask. If you believe that, why do you feel so strongly about her?"

"I don't know." He grabbed his backpack and stood up. "And I'm getting more confused by the minute. But right now I really have to go. If I don't get this research done today, I'll have to wait until Monday."

"No word from that editor you wrote to?"

"Nothing." He fought back the now-familiar despair. It had been weeks since he'd sent that letter.

"All right," she said. "I'll let you go. But here are my last thoughts to you. First, you need to figure out what's more important to you, the girl or the evidence for your book. If it's the girl, all you need to do is tell her you love her. That's what she wants to hear. Trust me."

"Whatever you say."

They hung up. Steve stood on the steps and looked up at the Library of Congress. He'd been working on this book for three years. It was the key to his future plans—he couldn't give that up for a girl he just met a couple months ago, could he? That would be idiotic.

But could he really put the book ahead of Roxanne? Ahead of the most amazing woman he'd ever met—who, inexplicably, seemed interested in him?

Was this really an either/or question?

No, he thought, but Dana was still right. This wasn't just a case of knowing what Roxanne wanted to hear. He needed to make a decision. What did he want to say?

Did he want to tell her he loved her?

He closed his eyes a brief moment, seeing Roxanne's sad, tired face from the night before, and answered the question with unexpected ease.

Yes, God help him, he did.

He arrived back home with just enough time to change and get down to the bar. Apprehension fueled his energy and he couldn't help worrying that his impression last night about a turning point, when she hadn't wanted comfort from him after the dinner fiasco, would prove correct. After all, what else could that mean, if not that she was pulling away from him? He was nothing to her but a convenience is what he thought it meant, but he hoped he was wrong.

He let himself in to the bar and saw Sir Nigel in the dining room fussing with tablecloths and moving silverware around. Rita came through the doors from the kitchen, tying her apron around her waist.

"Hey, Stevie," she said, impish smile breaking across her face upon seeing him.

"What's up, Rita?" He tried to sound lively as he

made his way around the bar to the service end, but he felt like a kid on the day his oral report was due. He was so sure something bad was going to happen, he couldn't act naturally.

"Nothin'." She approached the bar. "Don't you love this place now? It's so pretty here. And I love that there's no more smoke."

He smiled at her. "You love it here, huh? Well, who would have thought?"

She laughed. "I know, it's weird. But I do. By the way, I took a message for you earlier. Some chick called on the house phone. I wrote it down on a napkin."

Rita was about to sit on a bar stool when Sir Nigel spoke.

"Miss Rita, could I have a word?" He crooked a finger at her.

Rita turned to Steve and rolled her eyes. "The prime minister calls," she said in a lousy British accent.

Steve laughed and punched the cash button on the register to make sure there was money in the drawer. Yep. He pushed it closed and turned to shelve the rack of clean glasses sitting on the cold chest.

She was here, he was sure. She was always the first one here. He thought about going back to the kitchen for something, maybe he was in need of lemons or some other kind of garnish. But he was well stocked, another thing he'd accomplished last night in his insomnia.

Things were pretty calm as the crew set up, everyone moving quietly in the wake of last night's trauma. Just before five thirty, when the doors opened, Roxanne came out of the kitchen to the service bar.

He turned and smiled at her, taken aback again, as he

sometimes was, by how beautiful she was. But she did not return it.

"I need a pitcher of ice water," she said softly, looking toward the dining room.

"Sure," Steve replied in a voice too jovial to be real. If she knew him at all, she'd recognize that voice as rampant uncertainty.

"I remember!" Rita called from the dining room. "It was some woman who said she was an editor—Susan something. I put it on the liquor shelf next to the register."

Steve glanced at Rita, then back at the liquor shelf, where a cocktail napkin lay with Rita's big loopy writing on it. *An editor? As in, a book editor?*

"Thanks, Rita."

He grabbed a pitcher and looked at Roxanne, who was looking into the dining room.

"Anything else I can get you?" he asked. "Coffee? Tea?" The end of the joke—*Me?*—died on his lips as she settled her dark eyes on him.

"No," she said firmly.

Something was definitely up, he thought. Dread curled in his stomach and the cocktail napkin was forgotten.

He filled the pitcher with ice and used the soda gun to fire water into it. "Is everything all right?" he asked.

"Fine."

Oh God. He knew that 'fine.' There wasn't a woman alive who hadn't perfected the nuance of that.

"Roxanne," he said low, bringing her the pitcher, "what's wrong?"

She looked away again. "Nothing." She took the water, then added, "I'll talk to you later."

There was nothing reassuring in that statement, and Steve was tormented by it the entire evening. Though he tried to forget about it, write it off as part of her terrible mood from the night before, he knew it wasn't that. He knew, somehow, that whatever shit was about to hit the fan was coming straight for him.

The night was busy again, but he felt as if he dealt with it efficiently. He was getting used to this crowd and their brand of drinking. The white-haired gentleman was back, as he always was—the man Steve privately referred to as Red Top because he always had to call him a Red Top Cab—and Steve took particular pleasure in serving him this evening, knowing Sir Nigel was annoyed every time he poured the man another drink.

About halfway through the evening, Steve realized that in his distraction he'd forgotten to tell Roxanne how the cat had gotten into the kitchen. He'd secured the downstairs hole as much as possible last night, but she still needed to block the upstairs one. If she came out again he would tell her.

But she didn't come out. Despite the fact that he found himself stealing glances at the kitchen doors more and more often, he knew Roxanne would never emerge from them. No, she'd made it a point to try not to come into the front room when customers were present. He'd called her on it once, telling her she should come out *more* often, rather than less. That if people knew the place had such a young and beautiful owner it would get even more popular. But she'd slapped that idea down quickly enough. She seemed annoyed when anybody mentioned her looks, asserting that she would *never* use her appearance to try to increase business.

By the end of the night, he was exhausted and wired, as usual, but it was all tinged with apprehension. So when Roxanne emerged after the waitstaff had left and it was just the busboys mopping up the kitchen floor, he knew the other shoe was about to drop.

"Hey." He stopped wiping down the bar and came toward her, the towel still in his hands. "You look tired. Is everything okay?"

She stood stiffly at the end of the service bar, not meeting his eyes. "I am tired. I'm always tired."

"I know. It's been crazy. But I thought tonight went pretty well."

She nodded. "Comparatively."

"Listen, Roxanne, we don't have to talk here, or even at all tonight if you're too tired," he said, thinking for a moment that maybe, just maybe, this wasn't about him. "Or I can come up later, if you want, and you can unload your troubles on me. I'll even rub your back." He tried a smile.

Her eyes flashed up to his and he knew he'd made a mistake.

"Look, Steve," she said, and then paused for so long he had time to think he should leave, now, before she said whatever it was she was about to say.

Because it wasn't going to be good. He could see from the look on her face that it was not going to be good.

But he was too late to save himself.

"You and I both know," she began, taking a deep, seemingly fortifying breath, "that it's a bad idea to mix business with pleasure. I've been worried about this for a while now, and I've decided it's just not working."

For Steve, all the air left the room, as if he were in an airplane and a bomb had gone off.

"What do you mean?" he asked.

He knew what she meant. He knew exactly what she was getting at. She was done with him. Through. Finished. But what he wanted to know was why. What had happened that made her change her mind about him?

"I mean, we've had a nice fling." She swallowed. "And it's over now."

"A nice fling," he repeated. All he could do was stare at her, the bar towel now balled up in his hands.

"That's right." Her gaze turned steady, and her face was hard. Resolved, like a general demoting him to a private. "We got what we wanted from each other and now we're done."

"We're done," he repeated. Then, "We're done," in a more conversational tone, anger, disappointment and disbelief warring within him. "Well, that's good to know."

She didn't move. "I think you knew that it would happen sometime."

He shook his head, holding his hands up in exaggerated innocence. "I didn't. Really. So thanks for the update."

He should ask her why, he knew. He should sit her down, drag it out of her, see what this was all about. But he couldn't bear to hear her tell him that she just didn't feel anything for him. Couldn't bear to hear the words he'd said to so many others coming back at him.

Instead, he reacted with anger. Sheer, petulant, frightened-of-his-own-feelings anger. "Anything else, boss? Want me to clear out so you don't have to look at your mistake anymore or what?"

"You don't have to go," she said quietly. "Unless you want to."

He didn't hear the question in her voice. Just the suggestion.

"Oh I *want* to." He threw the towel onto the floor. Then he laughed. Throwing in the towel, as literally as possible. "I want to be as far away from here, and you, as possible."

He rounded the bar and let the service door slam down behind him.

She gave him a penetrating look. "Do you really?"

He stood as close as he dared and stared her down. "You bet I do."

Her eyes didn't waver, but she didn't say anything. She just continued giving him that stony look.

He didn't know what else he'd expected. It wasn't as if he'd ever talked about his feelings or treated their affair as anything other than a fling himself.

It was just . . . he'd just . . . he'd *felt* something, dammit. For her.

And she had felt nothing.

He had no right to be angry. He had no right to think ill of her. But he couldn't be around her, not for another minute.

Not without something in his chest breaking into a thousand pieces.

He took a last deep breath and said quietly, "Good-bye, Roxanne. And good luck."

He walked out the front door, wishing, as he did, that she had made it easier on them both and just killed him.

17

Dessert Special of the Day
Deep Freeze—cool and collected,
  until the room heats up
Champagne sherbet with lemon and orange syrup
  folded into Italian meringue

Roxanne wasn't sure why there had been no evidence of a break-in that morning, but it didn't matter. She knew what she'd seen and she knew what she'd had to do.

So why did she feel so awful about it?

Two days after she'd done it, she got a terse note from Steve saying that he was moving out at the end of the month. It wasn't exactly a surprise, but the feeling of despair it gave her was. How could she be sorry he was moving when he'd been, for all intents and purposes, vandalizing her property?

The following Friday night, Rita was the first to arrive at work—usually she was the last. Roxanne was in the kitchen pulling a *genoise* cake from the oven when the waitress came in.

Roxanne was startled to see her and her stomach flipped at the thought that Rita might have shown up early because she wanted to talk about Steve.

Roxanne knew they were good friends, and she knew everyone was unhappy he was no longer working there, but she had no desire to tell anyone about Steve's illicit search of her building. Not just because it was humiliating to her, but because she felt that if he was willing to move out and give up his search, she was willing to let the incidents go. He was just a man blinded by greed, who obviously felt he had to lie to get what he wanted. And what he wanted was that draft of the Declaration of Independence.

Not her.

With Steve gone, George had covered the bar the next evening—making it obvious how skilled Steve was. George could not come close to keeping up, and after that, Roxanne had hired a guy from the Italian restaurant down the street. She'd had to offer him a substantial raise in order to get him fast, which had not endeared her to his former employer, but it was that or let chaos reign.

"Hey, Roxanne," Rita said.

Roxanne turned the cake out onto a wire rack. It had to cool before she could fill it with butter cream, then layer it, glaze it all with apricot and ice it with *glacé royale*.

"Hi, Rita. You're early today." She wiped her hands on a towel, hoping against hope this had something to do with restaurant business.

"I know. I wanted to be sure to remember to give you this. I found it this morning." Rita reached into the large leather purse that was looped over her shoulder and pulled out a newspaper. "I couldn't believe it when I saw it."

She unrolled the tabloid, and Roxanne saw that it was *D.C. Scene,* a small entertainment paper that concentrated on the younger, more night-life-oriented type of subscriber.

"Read this," Rita said, pointing to a column that was headed WHO NEWS?

Roxanne took the paper from her and looked where she pointed. "In culinary news, Senator Robert Rush was seen canoodling with a very young, very blond, very pretty aide at the hot new restaurant in Alexandria, Chez Soi. In those intimate environs, cheating seems to be the rule, not the exception, as film director Francois LaBoroque was also seen there with a pretty starlet not too long ago."

Roxanne's face flushed and her palms went damp. "Is this true?" She looked up at Rita.

Rita shrugged, looking slightly surprised. "I know about that senator guy, I waited on him. And he was playing some serious footsie, if you know what I mean. I don't know about that French guy. But . . . don't you think this is good?"

"Good?" The word came out like a missile.

Rita looked taken aback. "Well, yeah. Uh, I mean, it's publicity, right? People like their restaurants to be cozy and romantic."

"But they don't like to be followed there by the paparazzi." Roxanne stepped closer and lowered her voice, since a couple of the busboys had just shown up. "Rita, you didn't talk to this paper, did you?"

"Me? No!" Rita held a fist to her chest and looked so spooked Roxanne wasn't sure if she was being honest or was just reacting to the look on Roxanne's face.

"No, of course you wouldn't," Roxanne said, collecting herself. Rita was not the type to go talking to a newspaper. "I'm sorry for even asking. I'm just . . ." She opened the paper again and looked at the column, digesting what this meant. It made the whole place sound like some sort of dirty, clandestine restaurant of ill repute. "I'm surprised, is all. And bothered, I guess."

"Bothered? I thought you'd be glad. It calls us the 'hot new restaurant in Alexandria,'" Rita protested, pointing to a spot in the column. "I think that's good. And you know how people love to see celebrities. I bet *more* people come here because of this."

Roxanne put a hand to her forehead. Maybe Rita was right. Maybe she was just primed for disaster because of that awful night when the reviewer was here.

And the awful moment when she realized Steve was the one behind the break-ins.

"Do you think so?" she asked doubtfully.

"Absolutely! I think we owe whoever wrote this a thank you. Especially if that reviewer decides to trash us."

Roxanne closed her eyes against the words and suppressed a shudder. *If that reviewer decides to trash us . . .* She didn't know what would have to happen for that reviewer *not* to trash them, but she still dreaded the occurrence.

"Are you okay?" Rita asked. "I shouldn't have shown this to you. I just, I really thought it was good."

"No, no. I'm fine." Roxanne turned back to her cake and touched it with a light finger. It sprang back perfectly. She looked at Rita. "And I'm glad you told me. Thank you. I just . . . well, I guess I have to think about it."

"Okay." Rita turned toward the linen closet and opened the door. She grabbed an apron, wound the strings behind her back and turned toward the swinging doors to the restaurant. Just before she pushed through she said, "Don't forget, Roxanne. There's no such thing as bad publicity."

Roxanne nodded and mustered a smile, one that died on her lips the moment Rita went through the doors. She looked at the door through which Rita had passed, the wheels in her head spinning wildly. Hadn't Rita said something the other night about an *editor* calling? Roxanne hadn't given it a thought at the time, but now she remembered the comment clearly.

In her mind's eye she pictured Steve's apartment. It was sparsely furnished and usually quite neat, except for one corner . . . that paper-strewn corner where his computer sat. What did he write? she wondered suddenly. She never even thought to question it before, just thought it was part of that hypothetical 'research' Steve was always talking about. But now she had to wonder. What on earth did Steve have on all those printed pages?

What would Steve be doing with an editor if he *wasn't* writing for a newspaper?

And if he *was* writing for a newspaper, if he were responsible for something like that gossip column, wouldn't he send his buddy Rita to see how Roxanne took it? Wouldn't he tell her to put a positive spin on it?

Was he doing it to get back in her good graces? Was he that desperate to stay and continue his search of her property?

But that was stupid. He'd made his search look like break-ins before; so why wouldn't he just break in again to search if he wanted to? He didn't need to work here for that. Didn't even need to live here. And he certainly didn't need to be sleeping with her.

Maybe he was doing it to get back at her. Make her restaurant look bad.

She put a hand to her head. She should have talked to Steve. Should have told him what she knew, that she'd seen him, and asked what he had to say about it.

She *would* do that, she decided, realizing she had to get down to work or the evening's desserts would not be ready. She would call him up, arrange a meeting, and clear the air.

Or maybe, just maybe, she would go have a look at what was on those pages . . .

Roxanne looked out her kitchen window the next morning and cursed under her breath. Steve's truck was still there. Fine time for him to start hanging around, she thought. The one day she'd like to get up there for a quick little look. Just a peek at those pages to see exactly what she was dealing with.

If he really was writing the column, would she take that as a good sign or a bad one? Would it mean he was trying to help her, or hurt her?

She couldn't stand the thought of him working

against her. Couldn't stand the idea that he might be so angry that he would deliberately try to sabotage her.

On the other hand, if he was trying to help her what would that mean? Would she forgive him for the break-ins? *Could* she?

She wasn't sure. All she knew was, she had to get in there and see for herself.

Two hours later, Steve was gone. She spent another twenty minutes watching the back alley to be sure he hadn't forgotten something and come right back, then she went up the stairs to his apartment.

She took the key out of her pocket and inserted it into the lock. But she didn't turn it.

She knew she hadn't a right to go in. She knew that what she was doing was illegal. Snooping. Spying. Breaking into his house to read his private documents.

She took the key out of the lock and stared at the door.

But how private were those documents if they contained gossip about her restaurant for the press?

She put her hand on the knob.

Don't be ridiculous, part of her scolded. *You have absolutely no evidence that he was behind that. None. Not one shred.*

She dropped her hand.

Except for that "editor" message.

She put her hand back on the knob.

And then, of course, there were the break-ins. Searching his apartment would just be tit for tat.

The break-ins. If he was capable of that, he was capable of any kind of duplicity. It was perfectly conceivable that he was behind the gossip column.

She took her hand from the knob and lay it on the

door, then put her head against it. She wasn't going to go in. She couldn't do it. It was an invasion of his privacy, no matter how she looked at it. Even though part of her hated herself for not being able to do what it took to investigate the matter, she could not let herself in.

After a second she pushed off the door and headed back down the steps, her footsteps heavy on the treads.

She needed to talk to him, that was all. She just hoped she didn't end up falling for any weak argument he offered because she missed him so much. After all she'd been through, surely she was stronger than that.

On Sunday, the review came out.

"It's not so bad," Skip said, sitting at her dining-room table with the magazine section in his hands the following Monday. "He says right here, 'I might give this restaurant another try after it's been around long enough to improve its service . . . ' " He trailed off.

She turned a wry look to him as she emptied a pot full of water and put it back on the counter. "And the next sentence . . . ?"

"*If* it's around long enough," Skip read dourly.

Roxanne looked up at the dripping ceiling and adjusted the pot under it.

Skip continued reading.

"He said he loved the scallops of foie gras," he offered, "and the turbot gallettes with black butter sauce would have been 'divine' if they hadn't been cold. So really," Skip concluded, closing the magazine, "he didn't say anything bad about the food, except that it was cold and you didn't have a lot of what was on the menu."

Roxanne turned back to him, leaning on the counter.

"If you had read that review about any other restaurant, you would never plan to go there. You probably wouldn't even have noticed it said anything nice about the food. Just cold, late and not available. Not to mention the place was packed and everyone had to wait for their food."

Skip held out his hands, imploringly. "Hey, if the place was packed it says to me it's popular."

She smiled at her friend. "Thank you, Skip. But let's be realistic. The first line says it all."

She had memorized it. Or rather, it had emblazoned itself on her mind the first time she read it. *Going to a restaurant owned by a former* Sports Illustrated *swimsuit model should have been my first clue that the food would be scarce.*

"Yeah, he kind of blew your cover there, didn't he?" Skip acknowledged. "But you had to know it would come out sooner or later."

"I guess. I just didn't anticipate that when it did, it would be so public, or used so meanly." She sighed. "There goes my credibility."

"Roxanne, don't be ridiculous. If anything, that will help you. Look, you know the food is good, and if people want to come because of the celebrity factor, let them come. They'll find out what a great restaurant it is and come back for that. Whatever works."

"I know. That's not . . . well, okay." She hadn't meant her credibility with the public; she was thinking of Steve. Steve, to whom she had actually lied about being a model.

Well, she thought resignedly, maybe that made them even. He'd lied about vandalizing her building.

She felt a drop on the back of her hand and turned, looking up. Was the water coming from yet another crack? She leaned across the counter and flipped on the overhead light, but the bulb blew immediately.

"Dammit," she muttered, bending over to get another pot out from under the stove.

"What's going on over there?" Skip got up from the table and joined her in the kitchen.

She shook her head, positioning the new pot. "It's a leak. I don't know what to do about it. I guess I'm going to have to go up there and fix the stupid thing. It's probably the trap. The same problem I had with mine when I first moved in."

Though part of her was glad she now had a legitimate reason to let herself into Steve's apartment, another part, the moral part, didn't trust herself to do it without doing something she might later regret—like snooping around.

Skip looked at the water oozing through the overhead sheetrock. Then he looked at her. "When does he move out?"

Roxanne shrugged and didn't look at him. If she did, the sympathy on his face would make her cry, she was sure. "Two weeks or so."

"Have you seen him?"

She shook her head. "He's been pretty careful about going up and down the stairs, I think. I haven't even heard him except once. And that night . . ." She had to take a deep breath to keep the emotion from showing in her voice. "It was so late, he wasn't likely to run into me."

Where had he been? she wondered anew. Back with

that girl he'd been seeing before her? Out with someone new? Had he gotten another job? Maybe there was some other woman at some new bar with whom he hit it off. She had no doubt, in fact, that would be the case. Steve hit it off with everybody.

"Look at you," Skip said, with such kindness Roxanne felt the tears well in her eyes. "You're devastated by this. Have you even asked him about that night?"

Roxanne pushed off the counter and wiped a couple tears away impatiently. "I'm not 'devastated,' Skip. My God, he's just a man. One I've only known a few months. I feel hurt, sure, but I'll get over it. I've gotten over worse."

But had she? She'd asked herself this a lot over the past week, as she struggled to get out of bed and wrestled with herself to be productive. She even had to talk herself out of going upstairs and trying to start things up again—thefts be damned—because she just missed him so much.

But what kind of idiot would she have to be to go out with a guy she *knew* was dishonest?

In some ways this was different from the pain she'd felt after Martin, because this time she'd hoped she'd finally found a guy with some character. Not just someone to love, but someone who really *deserved* to be loved, someone who would never let her down. This was worse.

With Martin, she'd always thought he needed love for his character to blossom. He had so much weakness to be babied, so many mistakes to be excused.

Steve, however . . . she swallowed over the lump in her throat. Steve had been strong and sexy, and his con-

fidence had been infectious. *How could he be a liar, too?*
she wondered for the millionth time.

But she was kidding herself. Excusing his flaws just
as she'd tried to excuse Martin's, time and again. Martin was a cheater, Steve was a liar . . . What was the difference?

"No, I haven't talked to him about that night," Roxanne added then, in a stronger voice. "I don't need to
be talked into believing another con artist's excuses.
You know that better than anyone."

Skip shrugged his shoulders, nodding. He couldn't
argue with that, she could tell; he knew how she was.
And besides, she'd shown him the area where Steve
had been looking. He'd seen the damage to the plaster.
So it hadn't been Roxanne's imagination.

"Thanks for coming by, Skip, but you don't have to
worry about me. I'm upset, but I'll get through it. That's
one thing the last couple of years has taught me."

"All right. You call me if you need anything." He
patted her on the back and they walked toward the
front door. "So what are you doing with the rest of your
day off?"

She pulled a hairband from her pocket and finger-
combed her hair into a ponytail. "Day off? What's that?
I've already been up, baking bread, for your information. And now, since Steve's not home, I guess I've got
to go upstairs and see what's leaking."

"You don't have to let him know you're coming?
What if he's up there with—" Skip cut himself off.

But not before his words speared Roxanne's heart
again. Not that she hadn't already thought of that. "In

an emergency situation, which a leak qualifies as, I can go in without notice. But more important, I know he's not here because his truck's gone, as it has been every day since he quit."

"I'm sorry, Rox. I didn't mean to bring up—"

"It's nothing I didn't think of myself." She forced a smile. "You go on now and grade your papers. Thanks for offering to help, but I can handle it. I can handle it all."

Truer words were spoken every day, by everyone, Roxanne thought, as she let herself quietly into Steve's apartment. She didn't feel like she was handling anything, certainly not well. Mostly she felt as if she were bumping along in a rough current, just waiting to hit the next rock in the stream.

Though she'd knocked, long and loud, to be sure he wasn't there, she still felt strange opening the door to his private world. She knew she had a perfectly valid reason for being here today, but she felt like the snoop she'd almost been the day before anyway.

She went straight to the kitchen and set her toolbox down on the floor, willing herself not to look at the computer in the corner.

Glancing around the kitchen, she wondered if he had read the paper that morning and seen the review. Would he care that they'd been slammed? Would he say anything to her about the modeling thing? Maybe, now that they weren't seeing each other, it didn't matter to him what she may or may not have said about that in the past.

A few plates were in the sink, in which a few inches of water was still sitting. Apparently Steve had intended to let the dishes soak, but the water had instead run down the drain and leaked out of the trap. The top dish was covered with crumbs and despite her resolve not to poke around, she ran her finger through them, thinking of Steve up here alone, making himself some toast or a sandwich, and working at his computer.

Despite her resolve, she glanced toward the corner where all his papers lay. The question would plague her, she knew, until she found out for sure. Besides, what would it really hurt, just looking at a couple of pages? She wouldn't dig, she promised herself. And if it was anything personal she'd stop immediately.

Before she could change her mind, she strode over to the corner and picked up the top sheet of paper.

> *Portner's main concern at this juncture seemed to be in securing a home for his collections. Though no one was quite sure where he had acquired all that he sold, he was known in town as being a "purveyor of all things unique."*

She picked up a stack of papers and read a page in the middle.

> *In August of 1784, just after Jefferson arrived in Paris . . .*

She looked in a stack on the opposite end of the table.

> *Note: Portner's letter to Letitia, 1825.*

It was all history. Research. Notes about Portner Jefferson Curtis and those around him. She breathed a huge sigh of relief. There wasn't a gossip column in sight. In fact everything she laid eyes on was so academic in nature she found herself wondering if he was writing a book.

Could that be why it was so important that he find that draft?

Would that matter to her if it was?

She straightened the pages she had rifled through and stood back to look at the desk, making sure it looked the way she'd found it.

Then she turned back to the kitchen to get to work, wondering how on earth her heart could continue to ache over someone who had done her so wrong.

Steve stared at the first line of the restaurant review.

"You didn't tell me she was a model," his sister said, scooping another helping of scrambled eggs from a cast-iron frying pan. "No wonder she's a bitch."

The kids were upstairs and her husband had had to work today, so when Steve called that morning looking for someone to help him drop his truck off for service, he'd been invited for Sunday brunch.

"I didn't know," he said, wincing at the expletive his sister chose to describe Roxanne. "Turns out I didn't know anything about her."

He did, however, quite clearly remember Roxanne telling him countless times that she would never make a living off her looks, and that she didn't want to use her appearance to bolster business. He'd even mentioned once that she could be a model and she hadn't owned up to anything. In fact, as he recalled, she'd thrown it back at him as if he'd been a jerk for even bringing it up.

"Hmm, well," Dana said, refilling his orange-juice glass, "I guess that's understandable, in a way."

He looked at her. "It is?"

"Sure. Like the reviewer said, who would trust some rail-thin supermodel to have a decent restaurant?" She shoveled a forkful of eggs into her mouth.

"I guess you wouldn't publicize it, but that's no reason to keep it from people you're, you know, close to."

"Oh Steve," she said, in a tone so pitying he felt annoyed. "She didn't deserve you, you know that, don't you?"

"Thanks," he grunted.

He continued reading the review, feeling the pit of his stomach drop lower with every paragraph. "This is going to kill her," he muttered.

Dana looked up at him over her eggs, eyes alert. "So what?"

He dropped the magazine and met his sister's eyes. "I don't hate her, Dana. It'd be easier if I could, but I don't."

The two sat silently for a while before Dana said, "So tell me more about this editor who called. She's interested in the book?"

Steve nodded. "Yeah. She wants to see the whole thing when it's done. Which I told her would be in the next couple of weeks."

"So you're going to ask Roxanne about the basement before that? See if those steps are the ones?"

He rubbed a hand on the side of his face and shook his head. "I didn't tell the editor about that. I just told her about the mystery, the conflicting reports, that kind of thing, but that nothing had ever been found. The unsolved mystery aspect of it seemed to intrigue her."

"But if you found the thing," Dana insisted, "the book would be even better, wouldn't it? A shoo-in for publication, don't you think? I mean, jeez, something that's been hidden for two hundred years—something as famous as the Declaration of Independence. The whole country would be interested in that. That's the kind of thing you hear about on the news. I bet the *Post* would even excerpt the book. So why don't you just ask Miss Fancy-Pants, huh? What could it hurt?"

"I guess we'd find out, wouldn't we?"

"So you're going to do it?"

"I don't know." He shook his head. "I really don't know."

He didn't want to. He didn't want to ask Roxanne for anything. He had the answer to his question of whether she came first or the book did, he guessed. If he didn't want to ask her about excavating the basement now, apparently even *avoiding* her came first.

They sat in silence a few minutes more.

"Listen, why don't I get my neighbor to watch the kids, and I'll come over after we drop off the truck and help you pack some stuff up today."

Steve glanced at her, a half smile on his lips. "And why would you do that?"

"Because I'm a nice sister, that's why."

"Uh-huh. And?"

"And," Dana chewed a piece of toast, studying him. "We can get out that metal detector Mom gave you and see what's in that basement."

Steve shook his head, smiling ruefully. "I gave Roxanne back the keys to the restaurant. Besides, a metal detector wouldn't be much help looking for parchment."

Dana sighed. "Still. So there's no getting down there without her permission."

"That's right. But that would have been true anyway," he said with a firm look.

"All right, all right. I'll come help you pack anyway." At his expression she added, "Because I don't want to see you become one of those guys pining over the one that got away."

He was silent a long moment, wondering if that was what he was doing. Pining. If this hole in his gut and the vacuum in his brain was sorrow. If his inability to hold on to his anger was—he debated admitting this even to himself—love.

He took a deep breath. "Okay. Thanks. I could use an extra pair of hands."

They finished brunch and Dana unloaded the kids on her neighbor. Steve led the way to the mechanic and Dana followed in her car. After leaving the keys in the drop box, they got in her car and drove to his place.

"Jeez, no wonder you're in such good shape," Dana said as they tackled the last flight of stairs to his apartment. "I'll help you pack, but I'll be damned if I'll help you move. How'd you get everything up here, anyway?"

Steve laughed. "A little at a time."

They reached the top landing and Steve put his key

in the lock. Turning it left, however, he didn't feel the resistance of the deadbolt. Had he forgotten to lock it this morning?

He pushed the door open and was greeted by a *clink* of metal and a curse muttered in a female voice.

Dana behind him, he walked swiftly into the kitchen.

Shimmying out from under the sink, in a scene painfully reminiscent of the first time he met her, was Roxanne.

He narrowed his eyes as she pulled herself out from the cabinet, rubbing her forehead with one hand.

"Shouldn't you be wearing a swim suit for that?" he asked, trying to make his tone light but not quite succeeding. "No wait, that was your *last* job."

"Hello, Steve," she said, her eyes catching on Dana, behind him. She dropped her hand and there was a slight red mark where she'd obviously bumped her head. Her eyes moved back to his. "I guess you read the review."

He nodded, feeling a twinge of pity despite all efforts not to. "It wasn't so bad."

She looked up at him then with such appreciation in her eyes for that small comment that he could feel his resolution to stay angry begin to crack.

Her gaze dropped and her cheeks reddened. "I, uh, I know I misled you about—"

"Don't worry about it." There was no point discussing it. No point in hearing about how he didn't merit that bit of honesty in their relationship, if you could call what they'd had a relationship.

She glanced quickly back up at him. "Yes. I suppose

it doesn't matter now." She looked at the contents of Steve's cabinet strewn around her on the floor. "I'm sorry about this. Water was leaking into my apartment. Turns out it was the trap. I'm just finishing up."

It had been barely more than a week since he'd seen her, but his eyes drank her in like a nectar he hadn't tasted in years.

"The trap?" he said. "I've barely been home today to run the water. How would it be leaking?"

It sounded more like an accusation than he'd meant it to, and an injured look crossed Roxanne's face. He reminded himself to harden his heart. She had dumped him like an unwanted bag at Goodwill with barely a thought to his feelings. Why should he worry about hers?

"You left the sink filled with water." She gestured above her head to the counter, which was covered with the dirty dishes he now remembered leaving in the sink. "I guess the drain stop was leaking, too."

He didn't know what to say. They stared at each other a long moment before Roxanne's eyes shifted once again to Dana.

With a quick glance at Steve, Dana moved toward her. "Hi, I'm Dana."

She leaned down to shake Roxanne's hand, which Roxanne extended, but they both noticed the grease on it first.

"Oh, sorry." Roxanne laughed nervously and rubbed the hand on her jeans, then looked at it again and shrugged at Dana. "Nice to meet you."

Dana nodded, studying her. "You, too."

He could read the thoughts on Roxanne's face, the

question about who this woman was, the assumption that she was somebody she wasn't. It was funny, Steve never considered how his sister looked as a woman, exactly, but seeing her through Roxanne's eyes he realized how pretty she was, with her wavy shoulder-length hair and big blue eyes. He decided not to enlighten Roxanne about her.

"I can finish that," he said, for lack of anything else to break the silence. He gestured toward the pipes.

Roxanne shook her head. "That's okay. I think I'm done. Just, if you wouldn't mind, check it to make sure it's not still leaking in a little while."

He nodded. "Sure."

She started to put the bottles that had been under the sink back in the cabinet.

"I'll do that," Steve said. *You just go* was the subtext, and they all heard it.

Dana looked at him assessingly.

Roxanne stopped immediately and stood up. "Okay. Sorry to have interrupted." She put some tools back in her toolbox and turned back, her eyes seeking Steve's. With a quick glance at Dana she said again, "Sorry. Bye."

"Nice to have met you," Dana said as Roxanne passed on her way to the door.

"You, too," Roxanne said, not turning back.

"By the way, I'm Steve's sister," Dana called.

Steve gave her an exasperated look.

Roxanne stopped dead in her tracks, then turned swiftly. "You're his sister?"

The relief on her face was so obvious to Steve, he couldn't help wondering what the hell was going on.

Why should she care if Dana was his sister, when she was the one who had pronounced their 'fling' over?

"Oh, by the way, I didn't get a chance to tell you," Steve said, *because you dumped me quicker than lightning*, "but I figured out how Cheeto got into the kitchen that night. You might want to check the stove hole in the old chimney in your kitchen. He came through the one in the restaurant, behind the freezer. I found his fur on it."

Roxanne looked like she'd been struck. "Behind the freezer?"

He nodded. "Yeah. Sorry I didn't let you know earlier. Hope he hasn't disappeared again."

She shook her head, staring at him as if he'd just told her he'd discovered a ghost. "Behind the freezer," she repeated.

"Yeah, I did what I could to secure it down there, but you should block your end off."

"I will," she said vaguely.

They stood there another moment so awkwardly that Steve added, "That's all."

She blinked as if awakening. "Okay. Thanks." Her voice was dazed, then she shook herself out of it. "Oh, and Dana, it was nice to meet you. I didn't even know Steve had a sister." She gave them both a strained smile, then turned and let herself out the door.

Steve and Dana stood in silence.

"Wow," Dana said finally.

Steve sighed. "I know. She's a looker, that's for sure."

Dana turned amazed eyes to him. "No," she said. "Well, *yeah*. But that's not what I meant. Are you sure you understood her when she called things off?"

He crossed his arms over his chest to still the flash of

emotion he still felt, the desire he couldn't quell. She'd looked so vulnerable. How could that be when she'd so coldly rejected him a week ago?

He turned to his sister. "There was no *mis*understanding it, Dana. She could not have been clearer."

Dana looked at the closed door, shaking her head.

Steve frowned. "Why?"

"Because that girl is in love with you, Steve. I'd bet my life on it."

18

Bar Special
Scarlett O'Hara—<u>after all,</u>
   <u>tomorrow is another day</u>
Southern Comfort, cranberry juice, lime juice

Roxanne walked down the stairs in a trance.

What had just happened? Had he figured out what she must have seen and concocted a story for it?

She let herself into her apartment and dropped the toolbox, heading straight for the kitchen. She knew just where the old stove hole was. Behind a little useless cabinet that had been installed to camouflage it. For a while, the door to that cabinet had been falling open on a regular basis. It wasn't until this week, when she was desperate to keep herself busy during daylight hours so she wouldn't think about Steve, that she'd finally gotten a new latch for it.

Had that been Cheeto? Opening the cabinet and going for the hole? Could he possibly be that clever?

She went straight to that door now and unlatched it. She flipped on the overhead light, then realized she had yet to replace the bulb. Standing back so the window light would illuminate the space, she saw that the stove hole cover had indeed slipped off and lay on the floor. Soot dusted the old chimney face.

Something had been going in and out of the hole, that was for sure. She brushed her fingers against the brick, then rubbed their blackened tips together. Maybe the cat had been chasing a mouse.

She remembered how filthy Cheeto was the night he'd gotten into the restaurant kitchen. He'd been covered in food and dirt and dust, but some of it had been black. Some of it was soot.

She sat on the floor and put her head in one hand, looking at the sooty fingers of her other.

Steve hadn't been looking for that damn document that night, she thought. He'd been doing something *for her*. That's why there hadn't been any sign of a break-in.

She felt like crying. She wanted to run to him, tell him, apologize, to go right upstairs and plead with him to forgive her. But he was up there with Dana—his *sister*, thank God.

Besides, even though Roxanne might have been wrong about Steve, how could he forgive her for thinking the absolute worst of him? For accusing and convicting him, even if just to herself, of being a common criminal? What kind of person was she to have no faith in someone she cared about?

She'd blown it. She'd taken something that had been wonderful and had thrown it away.

She had ruined everything with her worries and her fears.

Or had she?

Several hours later, after the sun had gone down, Roxanne was standing on a chair in the front hall, reaching for the lightbulbs she kept on the top shelf of the closet to replace the one that went out in the kitchen, when she heard Steve and Dana talking as they came down the stairs.

It was nothing personal. Steve seemed to be thanking her for something and apologizing for getting her home so late.

Steve must be driving her home, Roxanne thought, and her nerves started to tremble at the knowledge that now was the time. She had to act. Quickly.

Her heart hammered as she grabbed the carton of bulbs, jumped down, and dragged the chair back to the dining-room table. Then she put the lightbulbs on the counter in the kitchen and glanced out the window to the alley below.

Steve's truck was already gone.

The coast was clear.

She wasn't sure how much time she had, so she rushed to the bedroom, carefully applied some makeup, took off her clothes, put on her black Chinese silk robe and headed for the door.

Roxanne hadn't been in Steve's apartment five minutes when she heard the front door open. She was sitting on Steve's bed, debating whether or not this was the most mortifying thing she'd ever done or the bravest, when the option of backing out of it was taken from her hands.

He was here.

Should she take the robe off? What did one do when one was hoping to seduce someone? Be subtle or blatant? Naked first? Clothed and apologizing later?

Then again, how subtle was it to be in his bedroom, robed or unrobed? She should have sat on the couch. Or maybe she should have waited until he came home and just knocked on his front door. She could have let the robe fall from her shoulders at the door, and she would have been closer to making a clean getaway if he didn't seem amenable.

Heart fluttering and hands trembling like autumn leaves in a stiff breeze, she leaned back on his pillows and tried to arrange her hair artfully around her. She had brought a candle so he would see it was her, but the room was still pretty dim. She wasn't sure he would notice it from the living room. She could be sitting here for hours while he worked on his computer or made dinner or something.

Come to think of it, she realized she didn't see any light coming *from* the living room either. Yet someone had definitely come through the front door. Why hadn't they turned on the light?

As quietly as she could, she pushed herself off the bed and tiptoed to the door.

Someone was rustling around in the living room, but from here it looked perfectly dark. She crept down the hallway, inching her head slightly forward around the corner until one eye could see the room.

In the corner stood a tall man with a flashlight, and he was going through Steve's papers.

Roxanne's heart leaped to her throat and she backed into the hallway. It wasn't Steve, standing there with a flashlight looking over his own papers. This man was bigger, bulkier . . . this man was shaped more like— Roxanne caught her breath.

It all made sense. He would know all the details, he'd been fascinated by the story, he was the one who had implicated Steve to her . . .

Roxanne's blood began to boil, and before she gave it a second thought, she flipped on the hall light and stepped out into the living room.

P.B. spun on his heels and issued a heartfelt "*Shit!*" the moment he set eyes on her.

Roxanne stood there with her arms across her chest and adrenaline pumping in overdrive. "Hello, P.B."

"Roxanne! I—hi—uh, where's . . ." He craned his head to look past her, as if expecting to see Steve emerge from the hallway behind her. When he didn't, P.B. frowned at her and said, "What are you doing here?"

"I was just about to ask you the same question."

P.B.'s face relaxed then, and he turned off the flashlight, putting it into his back pocket. "I was just picking up some stuff for Steve."

She looked at him in disbelief. A half laugh shot from her throat and she said, "*What?*"

His head swaggered a little as he cooked up his story—no doubt bolstered by her failure to deny that Steve wasn't here—and he put one hand arrogantly on his hip. "Yeah. Uh, Steve's at my place and he wanted some of his notes. So I, uh, volunteered to come pick them up. On my way back from the store."

It was then that Roxanne noticed the plastic grocery bag P.B. held, in which several pieces of paper had already been stuffed.

"So Steve's at your place, and you came here to get stuff for him."

"That's right." P.B.'s face was cocky. His eyes raked her from head to toe, no doubt taking in her obviously naked state beneath the robe.

Roxanne crossed her arms over her chest and pulled the neck of the robe closed with one hand. "Forgive me, P.B., if I tell you that I think you're full of crap. I think you're here ripping Steve off, just like you tried to rip me off."

P.B. chuckled, but a malicious gleam appeared in his eye. Roxanne suddenly wondered if she might be in some danger. P.B. was a cop. He had ways of making crimes disappear. His own crimes, that was.

"I don't know what you're talking about," he said lightly. "And you haven't answered *my* question. I thought you and Steve broke up. What are *you* doing here?"

At that moment, the front door opened and the lights in the living room came on. Steve halted in the foyer as he caught sight of the two of them.

"What's going on here?" His eyes swept from Roxanne, dressed as she was, to P.B., holding his grocery bag full of papers, and back again.

Roxanne and P.B. gaped at him.

Steve's expression went from shocked to confused to angry. "Someone want to answer me?" He let his gaze settle on Roxanne and his expression seemed to soften slightly. Then he turned to P.B. "P.B.? Why don't you go first?"

Roxanne breathed a sigh of relief. He couldn't have come back at a more opportune time.

"Yes, P.B.," she said, stepping farther out into the living room, arms around her middle to keep her stomach from leaping straight out of her body. "Why don't you tell Steve the reason you just told me for why you're here?"

P.B. looked from one to the other of them and tried to muster a chuckle. "It's funny, really." His eyes appealed to Steve. "You'll laugh, Steve-arino."

Steve pushed his hands into his pockets and walked slowly toward him. "I don't know why, but I doubt that, P.B. So let's dispense with the niceties until we get to the bottom of this, okay?"

He reached P.B. and took the bag from his hand, then looked inside. One by one he pulled the papers out, nodding as he read them as if it was all just what he expected to see.

"I, uh," P.B. began. "See, I was just, there was this, this thing, see. And after listening to you, um . . ."

Steve looked at him almost pityingly. "I'll tell you what, Peeb. I'll save you the trouble. I already know what you were doing here. And I have to congratulate you, you put your hands on a lot of the right stuff." He held up the pages.

"*She* was here first," P.B. blurted, gesturing toward Roxanne. "She was going through this stuff, I just took it from her. It's evidence, that's what it is."

"That's not true!" Roxanne gasped.

Steve turned and looked at her, his expression unreadable as his eyes searched her. Her cheeks reddened.

"She doesn't really look dressed for a robbery, do you think, Peeb?" He glanced back at his friend. Then he added, "But I'll deal with her," he turned back to her, pausing—and she wasn't sure, but she could swear she saw a slight smile—before adding "later."

Roxanne's entire body heated up at the prospect.

He faced P.B. again, then walked slowly around him to place the pilfered papers back on the desk.

"But you," Steve continued. "I finally figured out it was you behind the break-ins. After that last one. The one when you dug the holes under the steps."

"Me? Behind the—? What the—?" P.B. blustered, scoffing and rolling his eyes from Steve to Roxanne as if they were all in on the joke. "That's crazy. I didn't break in here. That was, that was . . ."

"Cut it out, P.B." Roxanne had never heard Steve's voice so cold. "I know I told you about the will, about how Portner had hidden something under a set of stairs in the house. I just didn't think you were that interested. So I kept thinking, who knew anything about history, about this obscure cousin and his possible theft, yet would bother to dig under stairs that any reputable historian knew were built after the Civil War? Then it struck me. I realized that I hadn't told you about that. Nor had I told you that the staircases had all already been investigated. You were the only person who might have known just one piece of that puzzle, and who would have been motivated enough and had access to go looking for this thing right now."

"Oh, come on. Lots of people would want to find a draft of the Declaration of Independence," P.B. protested.

"Sure, but nobody else believes it was really here. And why now? The issue has been dead for years in historical circles. *You* were the only person I told about those letters I found, the ones confirming the hidden document was one of Jefferson's. The *only* one, P.B. So it had to be either you or me. And I knew it wasn't me."

Roxanne swallowed. *She* hadn't. She had believed P.B. The obviously lying, sleazy, reprobate P.B. What was the matter with her?

"I was trying to help you, man," P.B. said, finally settling on a plan of defense. He slapped Steve's shoulder with a broad palm and gave a laugh of bravado. "Come on, I knew you were afraid to do it, 'cause of her. That's right." He nodded at Roxanne. "He wanted to look around, but he didn't want to piss you off, Miss High-and-Mighty. Thought you'd be an unreasonable bitch and not let him—"

"Shut *up*, P.B." Steve grabbed him by the shirt front, and even though P.B. was the bigger of the two men Roxanne saw uneasiness in P.B.'s eyes. "Who do you think you are? And who the *fuck* do you think you're talking to? You can't just make up anything you want and have us all believe it."

Roxanne cleared her throat. Both men looked over at her. "Is that why you told me you thought Steve was behind the break-ins, P.B.? Because you were trying to *help* him?"

Steve's eyes glittered as he turned back to his former

friend. "You said *I* was behind them? You told her *I* was the one digging up her basement? Is that . . . ?" He turned back to Roxanne, his face fierce. "Is that why . . . ?"

Roxanne looked down, too ashamed of believing P.B. over him to look him in the eye.

Steve looked back at P.B., then shoved him, hard, letting go of his shirt as P.B. stumbled back into the desk chair. He caught himself between the printer and the wall.

"Hey, you were the one doing all the investigating, looking for that copy of the Declaration of Independence," P.B. said belligerently, poking a finger through the air at him.

"For *the book*, P.B. Remember the book I'm writing? You knew why I was looking for that information, and it wasn't to start digging."

"Oh come on. You know you wanted to look. Besides, if you hadn't kept talking about it, telling everyone, making it into such a big damn story, I wouldn't have been interested in it at all. Nobody would have. Seems to me it could be *anybody* looking for that thing now. You made it sound so valuable and all."

"No, it couldn't have been anybody," Steve said, his voice low and barely controlled. "It could only have been somebody stupid enough to think they could break in and dig around and never have anyone be the wiser. It had to be a cop, *the* cop called to the scene so the report would never be filed. It had to be someone whose friend was inadvertently telling him where to look. Jesus!" Steve spun away from him, one hand raking through his hair as he tried to cool off. "How could I have been so stupid?" He turned back. "I *knew* that squirrel thing was bogus. What'd you do, scrape it off the road?"

P.B. looked away, not answering.

Steve glanced over at Roxanne, who straightened when his eyes fell upon her. "And you believed him?" he asked, his voice quieter but the emotion no less powerful. The disbelief in his eyes was painful. "You thought I was trying to rob you?"

She shook her head. "No." She cleared her throat. "No, Steve." She paused. "Not at first."

Steve exhaled heavily and gazed at her, the hurt clear in his eyes.

She spoke quickly, glancing at P.B. "At first I thought he was just jealous. Bitter, you know, about . . . about us. But then . . . then I saw you, the other night, after Cheeto got into the kitchen. I went downstairs and I saw you looking behind the freezer, pulling on some of the plaster wall, looking behind it. And I just . . ." She shook her head again. "It was just too easy to believe I'd made another mistake, that I'd trusted the wrong guy. Again. I'm *so sorry*, Steve. You can't imagine how sorry I am."

His expression did not change during this speech, but his eyes never left hers. She could see his breath moving his chest up and down, betraying his agitation, and wished she could go to him and hold him, tell him in every way she knew how, that she would be sorry for the rest of her days for not believing in him.

Several long moments of silence later, Steve turned back to P.B. with a sigh. "Listen, P.B., I don't know what to do about you. You've broken in to my apartment, you've betrayed me, you've lied, you would have stolen, if you hadn't been so inept. Tell me, would I be wrong to turn you in to your department? What would you do?"

P.B. sighed and looked at his feet. After a minute he looked up, his face contorted. "Hey, man, I answered your question for you. You don't have to look down there now. And I would've told you if I found something."

Steve shook his head. "I don't believe that for a second."

P.B. didn't look at him. "Okay, okay. I'm getting out of here. I can't deal with this right now."

He started toward the door, then turned as he reached it, realizing that nobody was going to stop him. "For what it's worth, Stevie, I'm sorry."

Steve just looked at him.

P.B. turned the knob and left.

Several minutes ticked by before Steve turned to Roxanne. She flushed from head to foot as he let his gaze take in her attire, then her position near the hall that led to the bedroom.

"I didn't know you were writing a book," she said softly. "I should have. I should have asked what all that research was for."

"You did. I just didn't tell you." He tilted his head. "And I didn't know you spent ten years as a model in major magazines. That makes me the more oblivious one, don't you think?"

She shook her head. "I made it sound like I'd never do that. I didn't want you to know."

He gave a short laugh. "I guess neither one of us knew much of anything about the other."

She looked at the floor. "I guess we just didn't know each other very well."

"Or trust each other very much."

She made a pained face. "I'm so sorry, Steve. I don't know what to say. I just didn't know who to trust. Not because of you, but because of me." She laughed once, shortly. "Talk about baggage."

She looked up at him. His face was impassive, contemplative. A long silence stretched between them.

"And what," he said finally, "did you hope to accomplish here tonight?"

Roxanne was relieved to hear a gentle tone in his voice. At least she thought she'd heard it.

"Well," she began, "I wanted to apologize. *Really* apologize. So I, uh, I thought if I came up here—"

She stopped as she heard his footsteps on the floor, looked up to see him walking slowly toward her.

"If you came up here . . . ?" he prompted.

Her hands knotted in front of her. "Yes, ah, you see, I thought I'd need to get your attention first, make sure you would listen and not just slam the door in my face." She let go of her hands and brought two fingers to play with the lapel of her robe. "Which is why I . . . wore this. Because we always seemed to, or rather we never had trouble with . . . you know. And I so wanted you to hear my apology—"

He reached her, then, and before she could finish the sentence he swept her up and off her feet, into his arms. Her hands went automatically around his neck.

"I don't want any damn apology, Roxanne," he said low, his face close to hers as he held her against his chest. "I want to know how you *feel*."

"How I feel?" she repeated, breathless. She couldn't take her eyes from his.

"About me," he added quietly.

Her eyes were swimming in his, their gazes locked as if they were each other's lifeline.

"Oh Steve," she said, her voice husky with emotion. "I'm in love with you. Totally. Completely. Head over heels."

A slow smile curved his lips and lit his eyes. "Head over heels, huh?"

She smiled back, tentatively at first, then more broadly. "That's right."

"That's all I need to know."

With that, he carried her down the hall and into the bedroom.

"And just so you know," he added, before he kicked the door shut behind them, "I'm in love with you, too."

"Head over heels?" she asked.

He laughed. "Over and over."

"Then that's all *I* need to know." She put her hands to his face and kissed him.

Epilogue

Six months later

Bar Special
Old-Fashioned—<u>the way it should be</u>
Bourbon, sugar syrup, angostura bitters, water

Dessert Special of the Day
Wedding Cake and Champagne—
   <u>made for each other</u>
White cake with raspberry cream filling,
   vanilla fondant, candied flowers,
   and the best bubbly $100 can buy

The knock on Roxanne's door came at 7 p.m. exactly. Roxanne glanced at the kitchen clock and smiled. He was right on time.

   She checked her face in the hall mirror, brushed a finger beneath each mascara'd eye and pinched her cheeks. Then, smoothing the fabric of her sleek black cocktail dress one last time, she opened the door.

What she saw took her breath away.

Steve, in a tuxedo.

"When you said dress up, you meant dress up," she said, her eyes raking him hungrily from head to toe. He looked . . . classic. Like he belonged in a 1940s movie right next to Cary Grant. He'd even had his hair trimmed.

He stood casually, his hands in his pockets, and appreciated the sight of her with a low, "Mm, mm, mm." He tilted his head, and his eyes—she could swear they were actually twinkling—met hers. "You look incredible."

She smiled, unable to contain it. "Thank you."

He held out an arm. "Shall we?"

With a light laugh, she took his arm, closing the door behind her. "This is awfully fancy for a trip to our own restaurant."

"You're thinking about this the wrong way. We're not going to our own restaurant. We are going to have the Chez Soi *experience*. Just like any other patron. Though I suspect we'll be given something of the V.I.P. treatment."

She looked him up and down again. "I'll say. I can't wait for Rita to see you in that tux."

Sir Nigel opened the door for them with the broadest smile Roxanne had ever seen on his face. "Good evening, mademoiselle, monsieur. Your table is almost ready. Would you mind waiting at the bar a moment?"

It was a Wednesday night, but there was a fair number of people in the restaurant anyway. Two seats at the near end of the bar were open and they made their way to them, saying hello to some of the regulars as they passed.

Steve had just pulled out a bar stool for her when the white-haired gentleman who was always at the bar—the one Steve had said only ordered thirty-year-old single-malt Scotch—rose from his seat and came toward them.

"Hello," he said, his face creased and kindly. He was shorter than both Steve and Roxanne, so she sat to even them up a little.

"Mr. Shumaker," Steve said, taking his outstretched hand. "How are you tonight?"

"I'm fine, fine," he said, looking the two of them up and down. "You all look fit for a coronation. What's the occasion?"

"Just checking out the restaurant from the other side of the kitchen doors," Roxanne said with a smile. "Can we buy you a drink, Mr. Shumaker?"

"Well, that'd be lovely." His eyes crinkled when he smiled and he took the seat Steve offered him as Roxanne ordered their drinks. "Though I fear I have to take you to task, Miss Rayeaux, for depriving me of my favorite bartender."

Roxanne glanced up at Steve, who stood next to her, his arm circling her on the back of her chair. "Now don't go pinning that on me. Steve's the one who got his book published. Besides, he'll be back, part-time."

"No kidding. You got your book published?" Mr. Shumaker looked at him with delighted eyes. "The one about Jefferson's cousin?"

Roxanne laughed again. "Is there anyone you *didn't* tell that story to?"

Steve glanced around the bar. "Nobody here."

"And when is this book coming out, young man?" He looked expectantly at Steve.

"Next spring." Steve's smile was beyond gratified. The culmination of all his hard work had been better than his wildest dreams. The advance he had received had been much larger than he'd expected, and the publisher had decided to devote quite a bit to publicity, since there was already so much to be built on.

"They're even sending me on a book tour," Steve added. "Ten cities, can you believe it?"

"Wonderful, wonderful," Mr. Shumaker said. "I think I heard something about the discovery you made here. Do you mind if I ask a little bit about it?"

"Sure, fire away," Steve said.

To Roxanne's surprise, Mr. Shumaker pulled a pair of glasses and a small, spiral-bound pad of paper from his breast pocket.

"Tell me what led you to that spot in the cellar. In fact, tell me everything. Start at the beginning." He grinned and donned the glasses.

Happily, Steve launched into the story of how he'd followed the theories, studied the house's history, then found the letters and discovered the missing staircase.

Roxanne sipped her drink, watching Mr. Shumaker take notes while Steve talked. He continued to ask questions and Steve answered, warming to his topic like a mother going on about her newborn.

"So if it wasn't for the cat," Mr. Shumaker concluded at the end of the tale, "and that night that resulted in the first review of this place, the bad one, this 'fair copy' of the Declaration of Independence might never have been found."

"Maybe not," Steve said, "though I like to think I might have found it without Cheeto's help."

Roxanne corrected him. "Don't forget, we're calling him Sherlock now."

"That's right." Steve chuckled. "Mr. Holmes."

"So you dug at the base of where that hidden staircase would have been," Mr. Shumaker reviewed, "and found the . . . jar, was it?"

"Yes, an old pickling jar. One of the larger types, with the document folded once and rolled up inside." Steve leaned forward. "And it's interesting. Because Portner had sealed it with a combination of mutton tallow, beeswax and camphor, the parchment was protected from humidity. And being in a basement, which is a pretty constant fifty-five degrees, it was protected from heat. Finally, being buried, it was not exposed to sunlight. So despite being folded and neglected for nearly two hundred years, it held up incredibly well, better than the final copy we're all familiar with."

Mr. Shumaker shook his head as he finished writing. "That's just fascinating. So where is the document now?"

"It's on indefinite loan," Roxanne said, looking warmly at Steve, "to the Library of Congress."

Mr. Shumaker sat back in his chair. "Well, that's mighty generous."

"We haven't decided what we're going to do with it yet," Roxanne said, "but it didn't feel right to auction it off."

Elaine Fox

Mr. Shumaker tapped his pencil eraser on the table and looked at them both shrewdly. "I heard you also included a one-hundred-dollar donation. What was that about?"

Steve laughed. "Where'd you hear that?"

He smiled. "I have my sources."

Steve shook his head. "Restaurants. The last place you want to be if you have a secret."

Roxanne's hand found Steve's as she said, "I guess you could say that hundred dollars had been burning a hole in our pockets for quite some time, so we decided to give it away."

"At least for the moment," Steve murmured.

Roxanne glanced at him.

"Last question," Mr. Shumaker said, taking off his glasses and setting them carefully on the bar. "What ever happened to that big friend of yours, Steve? The policeman? I heard he was somehow involved in this. Unfavorably involved, I should say."

Steve and Roxanne both gaped at him.

"My God," Steve said. "How do you know all this?"

Mr. Shumaker smiled and looked down at his lap. "I'll be honest with you, Steve, because I like you. You too, Miss Rayeaux." He leaned toward them, his voice dropping conspiratorially. "I work for *D.C. Scene*. I have, you might say, a nose for news." He tapped the side of his nose with a gnarled finger.

Roxanne gasped as the penny dropped in her mind. "You're the gossip columnist."

Mr. Shumaker wiggled his eyebrows and grinned like an Irish leprechaun. "I hear things, I write them down." He patted his breast pocket. "But don't worry, I won't print anything you don't want me to. The only reason I printed that other stuff was because I was here that night the *Post*'s reviewer came . . . and well, I just wanted to be sure my favorite restaurant was going to be around for a while despite what he might write."

"You've got to be kidding," Steve said. "That was *you*? You *saved* us."

Mr. Shumaker chuckled. "Everybody loves a scandal. That's one constant about living in D.C. Not to mention everyone loves to dine with the rich and powerful."

"I don't know," Roxanne said slowly, unsure what to make of this turn of events. She still didn't like the idea of showing up in a gossip column. "I think it was Richards's second review that really saved us."

The old man's eyes twinkled as he looked at the two of them. "Richards owed me a favor. After I found out a little gossip about him."

Roxanne's eyes widened. "You *blackmailed* him to review us again?"

Mr. Shumaker laughed. "He was happy enough after he ate here again. Said he would have raved whether I had anything on him or not."

"Well . . . I just don't know what to make of that." Roxanne continued to look at the man curiously. He *had* saved them—that second review had brought the crowds rolling in—but had it been . . . ethical?

"Now don't give me that pretty look, missy," Mr. Shumaker said with a wag of one bony finger. "I'm not divulging what I had on him. That was part of the deal." He smiled impishly. "And you wouldn't feel sorry for the man, either, if you knew what I know about him."

Roxanne couldn't help it, she laughed.

"So what happened to the cop?" Mr. Shumaker asked again, looking at Steve.

Steve hesitated. "Oh, I don't know. I'd rather you didn't publicize P.B.'s part in this."

"No, no," Mr. Shumaker waved a hand. "Off the record. I'm just curious. Only thing I'm going to write about tonight is your book. With your permission of course."

It was all Steve needed to hear. He explained that after they'd discovered P.B. was behind the break-ins, they decided that they had to inform P.B.'s bosses. Even though they thought this was just a one-time thing, if he was so unscrupulous as to use his position to cover up something like that, they reasoned, they couldn't in good conscience let him continue to have the power of a police officer.

Lucky for P.B., his captain let him simply quit, telling him that a bad evaluation would be placed in his file so he could never work on a police force again, but that since Steve and Roxanne were not going to press charges, he could not be prosecuted.

"I never liked that guy," Mr. Shumaker said. "He was loud and disruptive. Not nearly as funny as he thought he was. A good way to ruin a nice Scotch on a winter's evening."

Steve laughed a little and looked down at his plate. "He's not so bad."

"Well, I'll leave you two to your drinks." Mr. Shumaker put his palms on the bar and stood up. "I hope you enjoy your dinner. I know I'll enjoy mine."

"Thank you," Roxanne said.

"Oh, one last question?" he asked, turning back to them with his impish smile.

"On the record or off?" Steve asked.

"Up to you."

Steve chuckled. "Depends on the question."

Mr. Shumaker raised a shrewd brow in his direction. "I'm just wondering about you two. What's next for Alexandria's hottest couple?"

"We're just enjoying the success of the restaurant," Steve said, leaning on the back of Roxanne's chair with a contented smile at her. "On the record."

"And the success of Steve's book," Roxanne added. "On the record."

Mr. Shumaker nodded. "Good to know. Best of luck to you both. And remember, if anything else develops I'll be right here to report on it if you want. Or rather." He looked toward his seat down the bar. "Right over there. Third stool from the right."

The three of them laughed and Mr. Shumaker moved back to his seat.

Sir Nigel appeared before them and with a short bow said, "If you'll follow me. Your table is ready."

Steve winked at Roxanne and they followed Sir Nigel across the room to the coziest table in the place.

Steve pulled out her chair and she sat.

"I could get used to this treatment," she said. "Not to mention the sight of you in a tuxedo."

Steve sat in the chair across from hers.

At that moment, Rita pushed through the kitchen doors with two glasses and an ice bucket containing a bottle of champagne. Without a word, she set the bucket next to Steve, placed the glasses on the table, then opened the champagne like the seasoned waitress she was.

Roxanne watched her in surprise. "What's this?" She moved her gaze to Steve, who shrugged innocently.

Rita smiled what could only be described as a shit-eating grin and said, "On the house."

Roxanne laughed. "How generous."

Steve was silent until the waitress left. Then he turned his eyes back to Roxanne, a smile playing on his lips.

Taking her hand, he spread the fingers out over his palm. "You know," he said with a smile, "I was tempted to give Mr. Shumaker a different answer when he asked what was next for us."

"Were you?"

Their eyes met, Steve's uncertain and Roxanne's curious.

"What did you want to say?" she asked. Something about the look on Steve's face made her heart rate accelerate. She curled her fingers around his.

"I wanted to tell him," he continued quietly, "that we might be getting married."

Roxanne's breath left her body. "*What?*" The word was a mere whisper.

Steve leaned back and pulled a small velvet ring box from his pocket. Placing it on the table between them, he added, "But I needed to get your answer first."

Roxanne gazed in shock from Steve's face to the box on the table. With trembling hands she reached out and opened it. Inside was a diamond ring, simple, elegant, and obviously expensive.

"Oh my God." She looked back up at him.

"So what do you say?" he asked, his expression growing nervous.

She laughed, so giddy her head was spinning. "I say yes. Of course!"

Steve exhaled as if he'd been holding his breath for an hour. "Oh thank God."

She laughed again and reached out to grab him. He kissed her then and they laughed together, until he pulled back and took the ring from its box.

"Here, let me," he said. He held her left hand and slid the ring on her finger.

"Steve, it's *gorgeous*." She gazed up at him, happier than she'd ever been in her life. "I love it."

"Good." He grinned. "Because I spent about a hundred bucks on it."

Author's Note

The missing draft of the Declaration of Independence I used in creating the subplot in this story was not entirely a figment of my imagination. Though it hasn't been proven, there is reason to believe a "fair copy" of the declaration did exist but was for some reason not preserved.

According to the U.S. National Archives & Records Administration (NARA), in 1823 Thomas Jefferson wrote that before submitting his Declaration of Independence to the Committee of Five (the group appointed by Congress to produce a document that would make the case for the colonies' independence to the world), he sent a draft to Benjamin Franklin and John Adams, "requesting their corrections . . . I then wrote a fair copy, reported it to the committee, and from them, unaltered to the Congress."

According to NARA, however, that "fair copy" of the draft, incorporating the changes made by Franklin and Adams, if it existed, has not survived to this day.

Unless of course you believe in my fictional Jefferson cousin, Portner Jefferson Curtis, and his faithful biographer, Steve Serrano, both of whom *were* figments of my imagination.

Fill your Spring with blossoming romance brought to you by these new releases coming in April from Avon Books . . .

As an Earl Desires by Lorraine Heath

An Avon Romantic Treasure

Camilla, countess, sponsor, benefactress, has reached a staggering level of social power and has used it to the full throughout her life. Only one man has managed to distract her attention from high society—and he has kept it with a passion he cannot hide. Now she who guards herself so carefully must learn to give the thing she protects most: her very heart.

She Woke Up Married by Suzanne Macpherson

An Avon Contemporary Romance

Paris went to Vegas to party away the sting of turning thirty all alone. But when she wakes up the next morning she's not alone anymore—she's married! To an Elvis impersonator! It seems like the end of the world as she knows it. But with a little hunk of Young Elvis's burnin' love, Paris is starting to think that getting married to a stranger is the best crazy thing she ever did . . .

A Woman's Innocence by Gayle Callen

An Avon Romance

Now that he finally has the infamous traitor, Julia Reed, in jail for treason, Sam Sherryngton hopes justice will be served. But suddenly facts aren't adding up. The more he learns, the more Sam doubts her guilt—and the less he doubts the attraction for Julia he's been fighting against for so many years . . .

Alas, My Love by Edith Layton

An Avon Romance

Granted no favor by his low birth, Amyas St. Ives managed through sheer will and courage to make his fortune. Now he thinks he's met a kindred spirit in the beautiful Amber, but when he discovers her true identity the constraints of social standing seem unconquerable. Yet with a passion like theirs, is there anything that love cannot overcome?

REL 0305